Billionaire Mogu[illegible]ys

Scarlett Avery

Edited by John Hudspith

Proofread by Jamie Betts, Melody Fuhrman, Chrissy Becker, Janet Mowdy, Doris Hires Collins, and Jacks Larson

ISBN 978-1-77498-123-8

No part of this book used automated software or AI in its creation. The content was written by a human (Scarlett Avery, the author). The cover was professionally designed and the interior was professionally formatted.

Dedication

For my readers who are unapologetic about their addiction to smut, but also need all the feels.

Get the BILLIONAIRE MOGUL—RHYS Secret Chapter

Join my mailing list and grab the Exclusive Secret Chapter or Storyboard for this romance.

Great extra goodies. Hot deals. Zero spam.
www.MyRomanceAddiction.com

Chapter 1

Rhys

Even though it feels like my balls are melting, I'm too starved to bother with a shower before filling my stomach.

What a day.

The maître d'hôtel recognizes me when I enter the hotel's restaurant and offers a slight head bow.

"Mr. Hartford," he says.

"Good evening."

"Let me show you to your table."

Dinner service ends at ten p.m. Unfortunately for me, by the time I got back to the hotel it was eleven p.m. This is my third hellish day in a row in Ho Chi Minh City. Thank God for the top-notch service at my usual stomping ground. One phone call, and I was set. No wonder the thirty-nine-story Reverie Saigon Hotel in Vietnam is synonymous with excellence.

I follow the maître d' through a bustling and animated crowd. Even at this late time, the luxurious restaurant is packed. As we pass a table, two gorgeous blondes rake their eyes up and down the length of my body, eyeing me like I'm a juicy steak.

"Nice," the one with the blue eyes mouths, touching her bare neck.

"Oh yeah," the other mouths, squinting her brown eyes at me, almost as if she's committing every part of me to memory.

I respond with a polite smile and keep walking.

You're losing your touch, Hartford.

The blatant desire shining bright in their eyes, is a reminder that I've been a little too serious about adulting lately. If my day hadn't whipped my ass—scratch that—if this week hadn't been a complete mind fuck, I'd invite them to my table. A red-hot night of raunchiness isn't on the cards for me. Not when I have more shit to shovel bright and early tomorrow morning.

"Since you pre-ordered your meal, a waiter should be out shortly," the maître d' says when we arrive at my table. "Can I get you a drink in the meantime?"

I need at least five drinks just to mellow out after the day I've had, but let's start with one. "I'll have a local beer, please—"

My phone rings.

I look at my screen and smile wide.

The maître d'hôtel excuses himself with a head nod. I respond in kind before answering.

"Noah!"

"Hey Rhys!" my best friend says. "Trolling bars for a victim?"

"Don't ever quit your day job," I say. "And for your information, I don't have to go very far. I already have *takers*."

"Plural?"

"Plural."

"Mr. Player," he says. "It's good to be you."

"Well, we can't all be Rhys Hartford."

I slide my weary body onto one of the seats and lean back, biting down a groan.

The blondes are still staring, throwing flirtatious glances my way.

Sorry, ladies. I'm jetlagged, bone-tired, and my head is so crammed with stuff, it's about to explode.

It's pretty pathetic when your bed is calling you more than two willing pussies.

I catch sight of a waiter approaching, balancing a tall glass of beer on a tray, and I let out a silent prayer.

Hey, sexy thing. Come to Daddy.

I thank the waiter before bringing the glass to my lips, guzzling down a quarter of my drink.

"Seriously, am I calling at a bad time?" Noah asks. "I know your trip has nothing to do with pleasure."

"Nope. I'm in Ho Chi Minh City to put out fires." I drop my glass on the table. "My day started at six a.m. and I'm just having dinner now."

"Ouch," Noah says.

"I'm brain-dead."

"Being the COO of one of the leading audio bass headphone companies in the world isn't all it's cracked up to be," he says with a laugh.

"Tell me about it," I say. "I swear to God, I got gypped."

"In what sense?"

"I should've set my sights on the CEO title of SCORE MAX Audio Bass instead of being the chief operating officer. That's the cushy job—"

"One your business partner holds. You want to dethrone Beckett Christensen?"

"I'm thinking of it."

"Vietnam isn't treating your kindly."

"So far, the days have been interminable and punishing. And it's hotter than Hades down here—ball-melting scalding-hot is a more accurate description of the heat level. While I struggle to breathe in this oppressive humidity, pretty boy Beckett is in LA party-hopping and hogging the attention of the press."

"What's new about pretty boy Beckett getting the attention of the media? Isn't that an everyday occurrence?"

"Yeah, but he's making headlines for another reason these days."

"Trouble in paradise? I thought Beckett and you have the perfect partnership?"

"We do," I say. "That said, I sure as hell can't wait to get back to LA. The only plus side to this trip—other than dealing with this production crisis that blindsided us—is that we get to hang out for a few days. When are you flying in?"

"About that..."

"You can't make it?"

"I can't."

"What happened?"

"I thought I'd be able to steal four days while production is shooting another scene without special effects, but I have to stay put in Doubtful Sound. The freak storm in New Zealand delayed production, and now we're playing catch-up."

"Another time, then." I try to hide my disappointment.

"I'm really sorry. We haven't seen each other since I left LA, and I was looking forward to it, but this is my big break. I can't screw it up—"

"I know how much this opportunity means to you. This TV series will change your life. You do what you have to do. We'll connect eventually."

"Thanks for understanding," Noah says.

"If things weren't as hectic on my end, I'd try to make it to New Zealand, but after Vietnam, I'm heading to South Korea."

"The timing is off for both of us," he says.

"That's what happens when your best friend is the special effects supervisor on the most watched fantasy drama series set in a medieval fictional world. I hope UTV.com knows you're their secret weapon."

"Says the guy sitting on a multibillion-dollar company."

We both laugh.

"Listen, Rhys, I have a favor to ask."

"Shoot."

"Keira called me—"

"How's your baby sister's trip to Thailand?"

"So far, bumpy."

"What happened?"

"On the second day after she arrived in Bangkok, a little girl pretending to need help approached her and her friend. Turns out, the girl was a decoy for a group of thieves. Keira's bag, containing her iPhone, was stolen."

"Shit."

"Yeah."

"Did they steal her wallet?"

"They did," Noah says.

"Fuck."

"The thieves didn't get much. They made out with coins."

"What happened to her money?"

"Keira carries her ID and money under her clothing—a habit she acquired from living with the nuns."

"Sneaky."

"Yeah, my kid sister can be pretty smart," he says. "About that favor..."

"Does it have to do with Keira?"

"As a matter of fact, it does!"

"Do you need me to send her money for a new iPhone?"

"Nah. She bought a replacement flip phone that's functional. She can send and receive text messages. She says it'll do for now."

"Okay. How can I help?"

"It's a big favor."

Why is he beating around the bush?

"Noah, you're my best friend and you've been there for me more times than I can count. Unless this has to do with ordering a hit on someone, you can ask me anything."

"Keira decided to travel for another two weeks since she has a travel companion. She's going to Laos next."

"Good for her."

"She's ready to come out of hiding, Rhys." The weight of his words hangs heavy in his extended silence.

"This day was bound to come." I play it down, but this is huge.

"She doesn't want to go back to London—"

"With good reason," I say.

"No one can blame her for not wanting to set foot in that city ever again after everything she's had to endure," Noah says. The anger in his voice has somewhat faded. Still, a tinge of it remains. Not that I can blame him. His little sister has been to hell and back. "Keira visited me here right after leaving London, but New Zealand isn't her home." He pauses. "She's ready to go back Stateside..."

I remain silent.

"She insists she's doing better—and I'm sure she is... that was the whole point of her isolation—but I don't want her living alone in a house or an apartment. She's not ready yet." He lets out a loud sigh. "I know I'm asking a lot and I also know this favor might put a serious wrinkle in your pussy time." He laughs at his own joke. I don't.

"What's the favor?" I think I know what's coming.

"Can she stay with you?"

There it is.

"In between running your empire, attending fancy galas and holding onto your rank as one of the most eligible bachelor playboys in LA, I'm also asking for you to big-brother her... like you did when she was growing up." I rake a hand through my hair. "She looks up to you."

I haven't been on her list of favorite people in a while.

"I wouldn't ask if it wasn't important," Noah says. "It's not like she has anyone else. LA can be a big bad city. She just needs a little time to get back on her feet."

Myriad emotions conflict inside me.

"I don't want to have to worry about her when I'm on the other side of the planet." Noah soldiers on. "With you, I'll have the peace of mind she's safe because you'll watch over her."

I pinch the bridge of my nose before scrubbing a hand over my face in frustration.

I know I told him he could ask me anything. This wasn't on the list.

"I'll send you money to cover her expenses—"

"Shut up about that, Weatherly!"

Chapter 2

Keira

I smile wide at my travel partner.

"I'm so happy you talked me into doing this, Mikki," I say. "I get to cross Thailand and Laos off my list! Yay!"

"This little jaunt was the best way to ease back into our urban jungles," Michaela says. "Imagine the shock of going from near isolation to living in a hyped-up mega metropolitan city like LA again, or in my case, going back to the City That Never Sleeps."

That's the understatement of the century.

"I can't believe we're a few hours away from leaving the sanctuary and the safety of being anonymous," I say. "These past two and a half weeks were a great transition, but I predict returning to LA will be a jolt to all of my senses." I take a long sip of my refreshing mango juice.

I'm dreading and looking forward to going back. Dreading, mostly.

"When you say jolt, are you talking about the frantic pace of the city or the frantic pace of your heart when you're near your new roommate?" She narrows her green eyes at me.

"Rhys is just doing Noah a favor," I say.

"I get that your big brother's best friend would open his door to you, but can you handle it?" she asks, genuine concern in her voice.

"It's no different from crashing with a family member," I say, trying hard to convince myself it's nothing more.

Michaela twirls a forkful of noodles, poking through an equal portion of chicken and shrimp, before bringing the perfect bite to her mouth. "But he's *not* family." She shoves the food in her mouth and chews, her eyes still glued to me.

"In many ways, he's the only family I have in the US right now."

"But he's *not* family."

"Fine. He's not family." She wins. "I lost everything when I left London. What other choice do I have? It's not like I have any money left to live on my own in a city like LA. Heck, I don't even have enough to rent a pantry in someone's kitchen for three months." I push around my food on my plate. "Nearly every wealthy neighborhood in LA has a guesthouse. I'm sure Rhys has one. He'll shack me up there and forget all about me. That way, I won't invade his space."

"What if he doesn't have a guesthouse?"

"He *has* a guesthouse," I say. *Please God, he surely has one.*

"Guesthouse or not, you'll be living really close to him," Mikki says.

"No big deal." *I hope.*

She stares at me like I'm blowing smoke through my ears.

Okay, maybe I am.

"Keira, you showed me photos. Rhys Hartford's gorgeousness is on a planetary scale. How are you going to live with—or near—that man without either tripping all over yourself or fanning yourself all day long? And, I'm not talking about fanning your face."

She's wrong.

Rhys isn't gorgeous.

He's DEFCON 2 degree of hotness.

When he walks into a room, I'm certain panties drop.

Mine have a few thousand times.

I cross my legs to stifle the pressure building. My body is keenly aware I no longer have to adhere to my vows of chastity.

No, no, no, Keira. Just no!

Hot embarrassment floods through me because once again Rhys is taking up every bit of space in my brain.

Despite the A/C in the restaurant, my whole body is flushing.

Will I survive living that close to a DEFCON 2 state of emergency? How am I going to manage to avoid melting into a pool of heat when I'm around him?

I've asked myself those questions a million times since Noah announced Rhys was more than happy to welcome me into his home. Since I can remember, those two have been as tight as brothers. I've often felt left out—and a little bit jealous—of their bromance. The age difference between my brother and me has never played in my favor.

You can do this, girl.

You're not that silly teen and teenager who drooled all over your older brother's best friend like a loser.

So what if Rhys Hartford is insanely successful, wildly talented, and a self-made, badass mogul?

He's just a man.

I flash back to that kiss I stole from my long-time crush—the kiss I'd longed for.

One kiss.

One dear-God-make-me-yours-because-no-way-can-it-get-better-than-this-with-any-other-man-on-Earth-or-any-other-galaxy kiss.

One passionate, sensual kiss that's been haunting my lips for years.

One kiss that didn't go further... no matter how much I begged.

One kiss that left me so undesired.

One kiss that crushed me.

"Keira?" Mikki's voice snaps me out of my trance.

"Sorry. What were you saying?" I ask, meeting her gaze.

"Are you still with me or are you already in LA?" she says.

"Smartass!"

"You know you're kidding yourself about Rhys?"

"I'll manage."

"Right," she says.

"I will."

I grab my drink and hide behind it, that way she can't see I'm lying.

"Okay, let's play your game," she says.

I don't like the sound of that.

"If you're that detached, you should use this perfect living arrangement with the sexy blue-eyed COO to your advantage."

"In what way?" I ask.

"Rhys can devirginize you!" I nearly choke on my drink. "You'd get your wish. You've been pining over him for years. Men love knowing they're the first to mark you. It's primal—centuries of alpha coding and all."

"But I'm not a virgin."

She ignores my protest. "Gifting a man with your *born-again virginity* is better than the first time you punched your V card. No pain. No fuss. No mess."

She's put a lot of thought into this.

My gaze lowers to her glass. "Did the waiter lace your mango juice with vodka or rum, or both?"

"Like you haven't thought about it!" Her response comes out faster than a whip crack.

"Rhys is my older brother's best friend, and he's made it abundantly clear he sees me like a kid sister—"

"That was then. This is now," she says. "You're twenty-three and you're all woman—"

"Mikki—"

"Guys get freaked out when their best friends are in the picture. Noah lives far, far away. What a perfect time to push the envelope!"

Perhaps I confessed too much to her.

She grabs her glass, wraps her lips around her straw, and sucks on her mango juice, her smiling green eyes locked onto mine.

She's so smug.

"Thank you, Dr. Knight, for your insightful assessment," I say.

"I might not hold a PhD, but I'm a great listener... and you've had a lot to say about sexy Rhys in the two months we've known each other." She grins around her straw.

I definitely told her too much.

"Rhys must have a girlfriend or a fiancée." It's really not something I want to think of, but I have to face reality.

"Your brother would've told you," she says. "Not to mention, when the press labels you Luva Boy Rhys, chances are, variety is your middle name."

I'm sure he has them lined up.

The parade of women hanging from Rhys's arm in photos on the internet is dizzying.

"Even if your idea wasn't preposterous—which it is, just so we're clear—Rhys would still reject me. I'm not subjecting myself to that again. His loyalty to Noah is unwavering, almost etched in his skin, tattooed in blood. The way I trip his best friend's kid sister meter has been the bane of my existence." I huff in frustration.

Mirth dances in Mikki's eyes. "Perhaps you need ammunition."

"I'm afraid to ask."

"You might want to buy a bottle of *'Eau de Vage'* at the airport and spray it on from head to toe to drive the message home that you're ready and willing. Think about it, perfume that smells like a narcissistic celebrity's private parts will help you seal the deal. What red-blooded man doesn't want that?"

She dissolves into giggles.

I can't help but do the same.

Our joyous outburst elicits suspicious glares from patrons trying to enjoy their meals.

I pray most of them don't speak English because our conversation is over the top and inappropriate.

It takes both of us a while to find our composure.

"Heck, I might have to take a page from that celebrity's book," I say. "After all, she sold out in a matter of hours. Since I have nothing to fall on when I land in LA, bottling my feminine scent and selling it to the masses might be my second wind."

"I can see it now," Mikki says with an exaggerated hand gesture. "Think bigger! Think a whole line of products—shower and bath gels, soaps, body creams... and even candles."

I play along. "Now you're talking."

Mikki taps her chin with her finger, her eyes lifted to the ceiling. "I wonder if you'll have to stamp a 'use by' date on your products? I'm sure over time, that shit smells nasty."

Her comment makes us lose it again.

More and more patrons glare at us.

It's a struggle to stop laughing.

"Seriously, Keira," Mikki says when she's able to talk again.

"I'm jealous. I have to endure my stepmother while you get to play house with a dangerously hot artist-turned-billionaire."

She makes it sound like a fairytale.

It's anything but.

I haven't told her the whole story.

No amount of '*Eau de Vage*' will help Rhys warm up to me. Not after what I did.

It's complicated between us.

Alas, beggars can't be choosers, so now I'm stuck living with a guy I'm sure hates my guts.

Chapter 3

Rhys

No matter the time or the day, LAX is a zoo.

I'm stationed in front of the exit, awaiting Keira's arrival. I'm sure she'll be beat when she gets here. I've been keeping an eye on her arrival time all evening, so I knew she was delayed. The trip back home was rough sailing. She texted in Hong Kong, freaked out. Her flight departed late, causing her to miss her connecting flight. I cut to the chase by demanding she pass me to the airline attendant so I could buy her a new ticket. She was supposed to arrive at one o'clock this afternoon. It's ten at night. Poor thing.

The doors open and another wave of people pours out.

I still don't see her.

Hopefully she'll come out soon. She texted me when she landed on LA soil. That was an hour ago. Since she's been out of the country for a while, I'm sure immigration must be a bitch.

"Oh, Rhys!" A loud voice pierces through the high decibels of the crowd.

My attention shifts to a tall salon-blonde wearing an inch thick of makeup, rushing towards me.

Philomena Tartersault.

She waves an animated hand over her head, while pulling a large suitcase behind her. She nearly knocks a few people over in her determination.

I do a double take.

What the fuck?

The tech vlogger is wearing a ribbed white tank top and from the way her nipples are greeting me, it's clear she forgot to wear a bra. Her skin-tight jeans reveal a camel toe I don't care to see. She's a beautiful woman, but in my opinion, her uncanny knowledge and the way she brings down tech-talk to an understandable level are sufficient. The artifice is unnecessary.

"Philly," I say as she approaches me. Without heels on, she's a couple inches shorter to my six-foot-two.

"Rhys!!!" She grins wide.

I cringe.

My name comes out sounding like Reeeeeeeese.

She leans forwards to do that Euro air kiss thing on both cheeks.

I'm awkward at it, but I oblige.

Considering she's from Oklahoma and she's never set foot in Europe, it comes off as fake.

I distance myself from her.

"Did you come to pick me up?" she asks, swatting my chest. Her gaze rakes my body from head to toe. She was born with brown eyes, but thanks to contact lenses, today they're green. The last time I saw her, they were blue.

"I'm afraid not."

"Are you sure?"

"I'm sure."

"Tsk." She frowns. "Too bad."

"C'est la vie."

"Ooohhh, you're speaking French. I'm rubbing off you, aren't I?"

She doesn't speak French. She just likes to pepper her commentaries with *voilà, y'all!*

"So, what's new at SCORE?" she asks. "Any scoops?"

"I'm just getting back into the swing of things."

She frowns again. "What do you mean?"

"I got back three days ago from an extended business trip in Southeast Asia. Beckett was holding the fort while I was away."

"I just came back from a trip as well. New York," she says.

"Hence why you're at the arrival gate."

"You're so funny," she says with a giggle. "My little tech vlog caught the attention of celebrity superstar and lifestyle maven Gail Voopowski."

"Who?"

"She's a big actress. She even won an Academy Award, a Golden Globe Award, and a Primetime Emmy Award. She's sooooo stunning and such a super smart businesswoman... a real boss lady... just like *moi*."

"Got it." I nod. "Congratulations on catching her eye. Is Gail venturing into the tech business?"

"No. On top of being the CEO of an incredible lifestyle-magazine-type website—voop.com—she's venturing to greater heights. She has a new perfume that sold out in like a nanosecond, and she needs top vloggers to spread the good word as she rolls out a new shipment. Thanks to my four-point-six—and counting—million subscribers, I was on the list. They're looking for massive exposure and they're willing to fork out the money."

Philly pulls out a small bottle from her handbag and sprays her body.

The strong scent assaults my nostrils.

I choke.

Fuck, that stinks.

"Oops," Philly says. "I might've sprayed a little too much on."

"I'll survive." *I hope.*

"What do you think?" Philly asks. "Do you like the scent?"

Philomena is one of the leading tech and gadget vloggers. Her YouTube channel has several billion views. A shout out from Philly and you're golden. And since Beckett and I are on her list of favorites, I weigh my words.

"It's hmmm... unusual. It's hard to put into words."

Smooth. Well played, Hartford.

She shoots me a sultry glance.

"It's a scent a player like you knows *very, very* well."

She cocks an eyebrow.

I frown my confusion.

"I don't follow," I say.

"I'm pretty sure you've had that particular scent... and taste on your lips more times than you can count."

Perhaps she had too much to drink on the plane.

"We could be at this all night long. Why don't you spell it out, Philly?"

"It's called *'Eau de Vage'*." She closes the gap between us. "It translates to, pussy juices."

Not what I expected.

"That's quite the marketing hook."

"Trust me. It's more than a hook... it's a promise," she says. "The scent is supposed to awaken a man's primal feral nature."

You mean the primal need to run away? "I see."

"Is it working?" She puckers her lips into something I'm sure she thinks looks sexy. Too bad for her it has zero effect on me.

I tread carefully. "There are so many scents competing for attention at an airport."

"You're right." She shoots me a come-hither look. "Let's go out tomorrow night and let's make sure the night ends at my place. It'll give us a chance to put the theory to test. You, me, and a lot of *'Eau de Vage'*."

The blatant suggestion nearly knocks me up the side of the head.

I ponder on a suitable answer.

One that won't offend her.

She keeps talking. "I've been hinting at it for a while, Rhys... I hope the message is loud and clear this time around."

"Philly—"

My eyes move over the eager vlogger's shoulder. A pair of tone, tanned legs approaching, catches my attention.

Nice.

My gaze travels up the woman's body, taking in her sexy frayed jeans shorts and form-fitted black sleeveless tank top. Her face is devoid of any trace of makeup, and yet, she's absolutely gorgeous—

Whoa!

The flecks of gold and green twinkling from her hazel-green eyes give her away.

Keira?

"Rhys?" Although she's still standing right in front of me, Philly's voice comes from a distance.

Keira waves, flashing me a brilliant smile.

My heart jackknifes in my throat. I wave back.

I take Keira in as she approaches, a huge grin stretching my lips.

"Do you know her?" I'm aware Philly is annoyed, but I can't find it in me to care.

"If you'll excuse me, my new roommate just arrived."

"You live with a woman?" Philly's tone goes up several octaves.

"I do now," I tell her.

"Why did you lead me on?" Philly's face is red with anger.

My eyebrows hit my forehead. "Come again?"

"I thought we were going out tomorrow night and ending the evening at my place to test *'Eau de Vage'* and have sex. A lot of dirty sex." She's actually upset. How delusional.

Don't piss off the vlogger.

Don't piss off the vlogger.

Don't piss off the vlogger.

"I never misled you," I say. "You proposed dinner. I never agreed."

"Come on, Rhys, I'm offering you a chance to enjoy my *vage*."

God, I hate that word.

"I don't offer that to every guy... but you're special... I really like you," she says in a raspy voice, batting her eyelashes at me. She even sticks out her chest as if to sweeten the pot.

"My Saturday night is already booked. I'm spending it with her." I jerk my chin to a smiling Keira. "Have a great weekend, Philly."

"But I can show you a good time," she says.

She doesn't know when to quit.

"Let's keep it professional."

Sorry doll, it's a hard no for me.

Philly's eyes move to Keira.

"You can't be serious. She looks like a little girl."

I glare at her. "I wasn't asking for your permission."

I walk away without giving Philly a chance to respond.

With eager steps, I stride to my best friend's little sister.

"Hey," I say.

"Hey." She drops her bag to the floor, then she removes her baseball cap.

My bewildered eyes travel up and down her petite form, unable to believe how different she looks from the last time I saw the five feet two inches fresh-faced girl standing in front of me.

"You look... your body... your hair... your..." *tits. That was some eloquent prose.* I pause, searching for my next words because so far, I've done a shit job at stringing a cohesive sentence together. I manage to pull my eyes from her chest long enough to say, "Holy...Wow."

Spoken like a man who co-owns a multibillion-dollar company, Hartford.

She's so tanned. And she's changed. A lot.

Keira lets out a small laugh before putting the baseball cap back on.

She shoves her hands into her pockets, anchoring her jeans shorts lower on her hips, revealing a bit of her taut stomach.

Goddammit.

The succulent sight makes my mouth water.

Is she doing that on purpose?

I pull my eyes up to hers. "You should've at least texted me a photo to warn me."

"Surprise!" Her hazel-green eyes dance with mischief.

"I'm going to have to tell your brother off."

Her expression turns serious. "I requested Noah not to tip you off."

I wonder why?

"What happened?" I ask. "You look so different."

She licks her lips slowly, as if looking for her words.

I commit the tempting view to memory.

She averts her gaze. "There's so much to tell." She hesitates.

"We can talk about it, but not here... someone might recognize me."

Guilt hits me.

"Sorry, I didn't mean to push."

"It's okay, Rhys."

There's a novel's worth of words to share, but we simply smile at each other for a long beat.

I was worried about this encounter. I'm glad to see it was all in my head. Her parting words were a slap in the face and since then, we haven't talked much. After the tragedy that ripped her world apart, I reached out via text. Her responses were succinct.

"Welcome home!" I break the silence.

"It was time."

"You weren't ready until now."

She answers with a slow nod.

"We're acting like strangers," I say. "Come here and give me a big hug, Cocoa Puffs."

Her lips purse into this—admittedly adorable—little unimpressed pout.

"What?" I feign ignorance.

"I'm not a kid anymore, Rhys."

There's no mistake she's all grown up. My body has known that for years. My brain is still fighting with reality.

"I go by Keira these days."

"Stop arguing with me, *Keira*," I say. "Come here." I don't give her a choice. I pull her body to mine.

She's tentative at first. She doesn't embrace me the way I would've hoped, so I tease her, like I used to. "I'm not going to break. Hug me like you mean it."

She laughs.

Her body softens like melted butter against the hard angles

of mine. I don't hear her sigh. I feel the rise and fall of her chest, and her breath exhaling.

Thank God her cross-body bag acts as a buffer between my chest and her breasts.

I sigh in relief.

I lay my cheek against the top of her head, enfold her tiny body in my arms and inhale deeply.

"You smell like fruity watermelon candy," I say.

"You can still smell it?" Her voice comes muffled against my chest.

"I can."

"Michaela and I thought it would be fun to try a new scent of shampoo. It's really popular in Bangkok. I'm not so sure I like it. It's a little too strong for my taste."

At least you don't smell like 'Eau de Vage'.

This was supposed to be a quick hug, but I can't let go.

She does nothing to break our embrace.

Holding her like this fills my veins with the warm hum of familiarity I missed.

"It's good to see you again, Keira."

"Ditto, Rhys. Thanks for taking in a stray kitten," she says with a little laugh.

"I wouldn't have it any other way, Cocoa Puffs."

I squeeze her tighter.

I close my eyes, relishing the moment.

"Where's my welcome home hug?" a man asks.

Surprised, my heart slams against my chest and my eyes fly open.

A familiar face stares at me, blue eyes squinting into slivers of curiosity.

"Shane, you can't creep up on people like that," I say.

"I didn't creep up on you. If your eyes were open, you would've seen me approaching..." I'm not sure I wanted Keira to know that. Shane's gaze shifts to the woman I'm still embracing. "You two are so wrapped up in each other, you're oblivious to everything around you."

Leave it to Shane Dennison to tell it like it is.

I let go of Keira like her body is on fire.

"Where's my hug, man?" Amusement is painted all over Shane's face.

"Fuck off!"

"Your rejection cuts deep."

"We haven't seen each other in a very long time." My finger waves between Keira and me.

"In your defense, she's a hell of a lot prettier than I am. I'd hug her too," Shane says.

I shake my head.

Keira blushes.

"Keira, I'd like to introduce you to Shane Dennison—good friend, Food Network celebrity chef, top notch personal trainer, co-owner of Fit Thonix Sport Challenge Equipment, newly minted billionaire tycoon, and last, but not least, sharp-dresser. And, as you might have already noticed, he also has a smart mouth."

She laughs.

"Shane, this is Keira Weatherly."

Shane's eyes widen as he takes in an unrecognizable Keira. He blinks a few times, his silent question on the tip of his tongue.

I give him a tight nod in response.

He cocks an eyebrow as if to say, *Holy shit.*

That's exactly how I feel since seeing her.

I became friends with Shane through Beckett. I like him. He's a good guy with a solid head on his shoulders. I've relied many times on his advice. I might've had a few too many when I confided in him about Keira after tragedy shook her world. Still, he doesn't know everything.

"Keira is back in LA and she's staying with me," I say.

"That's good," he says. He moves his attention away from me. "You couldn't ask for a better housemate," he tells Keira.

"I'm sure I'll be in the way," she says.

"Nonsense!" Shane says.

"I agree," I say. "And I'm proud her brother would ask me to watch over her since he can't."

Shane's brow puckers before a slow smile spreads across his face as if to say, *Watching over her, my ass.*

I ignore him.

"Where are you coming from?" I ask him.

"I was in Cuba and then Miami. I just finished shooting a special for Food Network comparing Cuban food from the homeland versus Miami Cuban-American cuisine. It's a great segment to end my contract with Food Network."

Thanks to a ridiculously profitable business venture he embarked on with his younger brother and two other partners that made all of them billionaires, Shane hasn't been shooting nearly as many shows for Food Network in the last couple of years. However, the consummate professional in him wouldn't end his contract early.

"That sounds delicious!" Keira says.

"I just need time to settle in. Give me a few weeks and I'll have a cookout at my place," Shane says. "I learned so much in Cuba. I can't wait to put it into practice. I'll send you an invite via Rhys," he tells Keira.

"Thank you! I'd love that!" she says.

"Do I also get an invitation?" I ask.

"We'll see," he says.

I chuckle.

"Do you need a ride?" I ask him.

His phone chimes before he can answer me.

He glances at the screen. "Thanks. The chauffeured car is here."

"Anytime," I tell him.

His gaze bounces from mine to Keira's.

"You two don't need a back seat passenger, anyway," he says with a grin. "All right, I'm off. Keira, welcome back to LA and I can't wait to see you at my place."

"Thank you, Shane. I can't wait!"

"Rhys. I'll see you around." He pats me on the shoulder.

"Absolutely!"

With that, he's gone.

"You must be tired," I tell Keira. "Let's grab—"

I stop midsentence, my eyes searching around her.

"What are you looking for?" she asks, mimicking me.

"Where's the rest of your luggage?" I point to the backpack at her feet.

"Oh, Michaela and I left our luggage at the concierge desk of our budget-friendly hotel to grab a quick meal before leaving. When we got back, our luggage was nowhere to be found."

"What?"

"Yeah. Leaving Bangkok was a freaking nightmare."

My protectiveness flares at her admission.

"Your luggage just disappeared?"

"It's not clear if our stuff was stolen or misplaced, but we didn't want to miss our flights. After a frustrating half-hour of useless explanation from the hotel manager, we made the decision to leave the little belongings we had behind."

"You poor thing."

"I know, right? When it rains, it pours."

I pick up her backpack before circling her shoulders with one arm. "Don't worry, Cocoa Puffs, I'll take care of you," I say, pulling her closer to me.

She looks up and rolls her eyes... but that doesn't stop her smile.

~

One look is all it took to flame my attraction for her.

As if the distance tampered it to begin with.

Hugging her jacked up my desire to unreasonable levels.

Which is why I find myself in this predicament.

Trailing behind Keira is an ungodly test of the unshakable bound of my friendship with Noah. I can't help but zero in on her legs.

Damn.

To add to my torture, with each step, she gives me an uninterrupted view of her ass, swishing in those jean shorts that mold to her twin globes. I get that her luggage was stolen and she might not have anything else to wear, but come on, I'm only a man. She might've lost a bit of her curves, but that ass is still mouthwatering. And as God is my witness, I just want to bite it.

No, no, no.

This is ludicrous.

I have way more self-control than that. It's not like I'm Beckett Christensen.

Determined to lessen my mounting desire, I white-knuckle my grip around the straps of her backpack, hoping to contain my twitching cock.

It's in vain.

I give myself a good talking to, scolding myself.

Alas, my cock has a mind of its own tonight.

I even adjust myself, so I can keep walking without tripping.

It's a lost cause.

Biting Keira's ass is the last thing I should be thinking of. I know full well I'm being a dirty fucker right now, but not having sex in a long time will do that to a man.

Adulting comes at a steep price.

This living arrangement is going to be the bane of my existence. I already know it.

Cocoa Puffs is like a kid sister to you.

I repeat the warning over and over in my head as a reminder.

It's like my cock is mocking me.

"My car is over there," I tell Keira.

She turns around and looks in the direction of my pointed finger.

She freezes and her jaw drops.

"That's your car?!"

"It is."

She does a double take.

"Holy speeding bullet! Rhys Hartford, you're living it large." The genuineness in her words is touching.

"For a one-hit wonder no one remembered until five years ago, I'm doing okay for myself." I wink at her.

"You're totally pulling my leg." Her delicious unpainted, full lips curve into a big smile.

"It's been a great ride," I say. "I've learned from my previous mistakes. This time around, I keep my ego in check. I'm just grateful and humbled I get a second stab at making a name for myself. I don't take it for granted."

"You wear success well," she tells me. "I've been keeping a close eye on your climb to the top—"

"You've been stalking me?" I ask, amused.

I'm as guilty as she is. I've made it my mission to track every aspect of her career—even the heart-wrenching ones.

"I've been keeping *tabs* on you."

"I thought you'd forgotten all about me," I say in a low voice.

An awkward silence stretches between us as we keep walking.

"Your car must've cost a hundred thousand dollars." She veers the conversation as she closes in on my vehicle.

The base model is two hundred thousand dollars, but no need to bog her down with numbers.

"It's a luxury vehicle," I say.

"What model of Benz is it?"

I disable the alarm. "It's a Mercedes-Maybach," I answer, before opening the door to let her in.

"I'm proud of you, Rhys," she says, slipping into the passenger seat. I place her bag in the back seat behind her.

"Right back at ya there, kid."

"Please," she says. "I ran away from my career because I couldn't handle it."

"You're being too hard on yourself."

She shrugs.

I close the door and circle the metallic black car. After removing my suit jacket and placing it neatly on the backseat, I slide behind the wheel. As I place a hand on the stick shift, I catch sight of those toned, tanned legs.

Goddammit.

I want to feel how soft those legs are or even see how they would look wrapped around—

Put a lid on it.

With herculean effort, I rein in my inappropriate thoughts. Desperate to regulate my body's heat, I play with the A/C, turning it way up. Chivalry demands I make sure she's okay with the temperature, but I need to cool the hell down.

As cold air blows into the car, my eyes are drawn back to her legs like a goddamn magnet.

You're supposed to watch over her. Not lust after her.

Listening to the voice of reason, I drag my gaze away from the embodiment of temptation and rev up the engine.

I curse the hour drive back to Manhattan Beach.

Those legs are going to fuck with my head every other mile.

I already know the memory of her ass encased in her jean shorts will haunt me all damn night and feature prominently in my dirty dreams. The same goes for her gorgeous legs.

Chapter 4

Keira

And the Oscar for the best hug ever goes to Rhys Hartford!

Thank God he cranked up the A/C.

I desperately need to cool down.

My body is still humming like an electric generator after that bear hug. I could've stayed wrapped up in his arms forever.

My eyes drop, and the manly hand clutching the stick shift becomes an obsession.

I loved the feel of them on my bare shoulders.

I'm sure I'd love the feel of them on my legs—

Don't go there.

As his speeding bullet emerges from the parking lot, I focus on the City of Angels. The city is buzzing with energy. Everywhere I look, people are all decked out in their Friday night best as they head to their favorite drinking hole to kick off the weekend.

"London is something else at night, but nothing compares to LA. Not even New York."

"I agree," Rhys says.

I spoke the words out loud?

I turn to him and smile.

He smiles back before changing gear.

On their own volition, my eyes drop to his hand.

I have to stop doing that.

"My arrival must be cutting into your Friday night entertainment," I say.

"Hardly," he says. "After being away for three weeks, I decided to stay late at the office to play catch-up. Once I called it a day, I headed to a private gentlemen's club to hang out and shoot the breeze before driving to pick you up."

"Hence the suit?"

"Hence the suit."

"The suit suits you."

"Eloquent!" He smiles before returning his focus to the road.

"I know, right? After what seems like a thirty-hour flight, I can still come up with a clever play on words."

He laughs.

Even though my brain is yelling at me to look in front, my eyes are glued to the navy pants that fit him perfectly. The crisp white shirt and the tie with a cool pattern complete the sleek look.

There's something about a man in a white shirt.

And then there are the kickass silver cufflinks...

So. Freaking. Hot.

I've been stalking him online to keep track of his milestones, so this isn't the first time I've seen him looking like a bona fide businessman. In person, the suit porn effect is overwhelming. I was unprepared. I'm practically blinded by his hotness. Everything about him emanates power.

I squirm against the seat, seeking relief. When that doesn't work, I cross my legs and squeeze them tight.

I catch Rhys staring for a brief moment before his gaze shifts to the road ahead.

What a man.

I still remember the teenage boy who used to solemnly promise one day he'd be successful enough to own a serious collection of top-of-the-line athletic shoes. The polished man sitting next to me can afford anything he wants.

Rhys combs a hand through his thick silky brown hair.

The years have been good to him.

His angular jaw is so decisively masculine. The 5 o'clock shadow is outrageously sexy. I like it on him. The long eyelashes framing his glacier-blue eyes still make me weak in the knees.

Some things never change.

"I guess the suit is just part of the veneer of being a successful businessman," I say.

"At first, wearing a suit every day wasn't a natural thing for me like it was for Beckett. That said, when you're on top, the clothes make the man. It's all about playing the part."

And what a man you've become...

"The first years we started SCORE, I felt like I was playing dress-up. I was trying to hide my insecurities behind expensive bespoke suits. In my head, I was still a has-been rapper, desperate for significance. Beckett confessed he was in the same boat, unsure we'd be able to pull it off. He was as concerned as I was about falling flat on his face."

"But you didn't. You thrived."

"We surprised everyone... even ourselves," he says with a smile.

"From musicians to moguls!"

"More like artists to moguls," he says.

"Yeah, but you lose that cool play of words." I grin.

He laughs.

"Speaking of playing the part... your hair... it used to be so long and full. What happened? Was it a requirement?" he asks.

My curtain of hair was my pride and joy.

Our eyes lock, and the words tumble out. "The purpose of living in a Nepalese monastery for a long period of time is to atone for sins. For others, it's time to ponder and reflect. We're required to respect a certain way of life." I advert my gaze. "Nuns shave their heads. The rest of us aren't held to those standards. That said, a month into my journey, I decided to rid myself of all traces of my former life." I pause. "I cried so much when they shaved my hair off, even though I requested it. It was so scary."

I glance at Rhys.

He glances back.

"That was a bold move," he says.

"Michaela swears I gave her the courage to follow in my footsteps. Her hair is even shorter than mine. Her stepmother is going to have a shit fit when she sees her."

"What's that all about?" Rhys asks.

"It's too long to explain, suffice to say, it involves a lot of drama," I tell him.

"Got it." He nods. "It seems Michaela and you were looking for the same thing. Sometimes, you need a blank slate to spring forward."

"One of the nuns kept telling me that. Even though I stopped shaving my head three months ago, it's still really short," I say, running my fingers through my hair. "Some days I'm okay with the length, others I struggle. Some days I recognize the girl in the mirror, some days I don't. It's amazing how attached I was to my hair and how it was linked to my identity. Crazy, right?"

Rhys shoots me a side gaze. "Short or long hair... you're fucking perfect to me."

I close my eyes, feeling the words vibrate through me like a meteorite just smashed into the ground.

"On the plus side, the short hair showcases your beautiful features a lot more."

Something pinches in my chest.

"Did you just call me beautiful?"

"Like you don't know what you look like?"

The warmth of his compliment runs through me. I blush as a smile creeps up on my lips.

"Another bonus, you can't hide your dimples anymore, Cocoa Puffs."

"Will you always call me by that nickname?"

There's a twinkle in his eyes and his lips twitch.

The memory of that day slams into me and I'm three years old again, pulling a stool to the pantry and grabbing hold of the giant family-size box. I sat on the floor, naked, and ate Cocoa Puffs straight out of the box. Grandma was horrified when she found me. She said I was bouncing off walls for an hour until I got really sick and puked all over the place.

I cross my arms over my chest.

"The nickname bothers you?" Rhys asks.

"A little. It's like you still see me as a kid."

"You think I haven't noticed you're all grown-up?" Something about the way he says that...

My eyes lock with his.

Under the dark interior of the car, I can't make out what I read reflecting in them, but God, am I ever hot under the collar.

I don't trust myself to say a word.

A moment of long, heavy silence stretches between us.

"I've noticed, Keira." His gaze rakes my legs, moving up my thighs, over my breasts before landing on my face. It's like his eyes are caressing me. I swallow hard. The air-conditioning blasting through the interior of the Benz is inadequate as my body heats up like I'm about to combust. "Believe me, I've noticed."

My breath escapes in a shaky gasp. "Okay," is all I can manage.

Chapter 5

Rhys

We get to my place not a minute too soon.

I can't stand this torture any longer.

If I wanted to test my ability to drive with a hard-on, mission accomplished.

I let Keira get out first.

I need a minute.

I lean over the steering wheel and I close my eyes for a beat, trying to control my raging cock. As it is, the fucker is getting harder than steel, and there's no way I can let her see me like this.

Down, boy.

I don't want to freak her out and I don't want her to think I'm a pervert.

God, please give me strength.

"Are you okay, Rhys?"

I drag my hand through my hair and take a deep breath before I look up.

Her eyes shine with genuine concern.

"I'm okay. I'm still jetlagged. I've only been back a week." *Partial lie.*

"Jetlag is a bitch. I already know she'll be whipping my ass for the next week."

Her earnest laugh elicits mine.

I get out of the car, grab my jacket, and her backpack from the backseat before joining her at the front of the vehicle.

"Let's go inside and I'll give you a tour," I say.

"From the eye-popping glimpse I caught as you rolled into your three-door garage, I hope said tour involves a golf cart because touring your big ass mansion sounds like exercise."

"Are you criticizing my pad, Cocoa Puffs?"

"No, bigshot, I'm impressed. I know I've said before, but I'm so proud of you, Rhys."

"You haven't even seen the interior yet."

"Lead the way, Mr. Mogul!"

"Please." I give her an indignant look. "My mama raised me right. Ladies first."

She giggles. "How's your mom?" she asks over her shoulder.

"She's doing really good. She can't wait to talk to you."

"Same here."

I let Keira inside the foyer of the side entrance, drop her bag on the floor, and place my jacket on the console. Without thinking, I take her by the hand. The contact is electrifying. She looks up, her eyes wide with bewilderment. A voice in my head yells at me to let go of her hand, but that would be awkward.

I lead her through the house.

Keira is all oohs, aahs, and *oh, my God, I can't believe this house*, throughout the tour.

I can't help but chuckle at her appreciative exclamations and comments.

"Let me show you the best feature of the house," I say when we return to the kitchen.

"I knew you had LA bowing at your feet, but this is already too much. I don't think I can handle more."

"You make me sound like an emperor or the King of England."

"News flash! With your wealth... you're as powerful."

I sometimes get a little self-conscious about my success. In some instances, I struggle with it. It's been a hard road for me. For a while, I thought 'failure' was my middle name.

"Trust me, you're going to want to see this," I say.

"All right." She says that like I'm twisting her arm. Her huge grin suggests otherwise.

I lead her to the expansive backyard and she clamps her hands over her mouth.

"Holy shit!" That comes out muffled. "Are you kidding me right now?" she asks, her eyes as wide as dinner plates.

"I know, right?"

She gasps at me, her jaw dropped.

"I end my day here," I tell her. "This is my favorite spot—"

"And soon to be mine."

I chuckle.

"Did the house come with this incredible pool when you bought it?"

I shake my head. "No. I rented an apartment while the house underwent extensive renovations. The previous owner had a massive, curved resort style pool with a stone bridge and a waterfall. It was a bit much for my taste–cumbersome and a pain to clean. A lap pool for exercise and a separate lounging pool fit my lifestyle much better. I stole the idea of a shallow pool surrounding a cozy sitting area on all sides from an A-list celebrity. The addition of the fire pit in the center is perfect for cooler nights."

"It's such an oasis, I often have dinner out here and then kick back and look up at the stars."

"This is living it large," she says with a calculated nod.

"You get to enjoy it too, dimples." I tap the tip of her nose.

Amusement shines bright in her eyes. "Is that my new nickname?"

"You were complaining about Cocoa Puffs."

"I guess it's an upgrade," she says.

"It is."

"As for your invitation, trust me, I intend to make good use of your lounging pool. I just need to buy a bathing suit."

Unbidden, my mind is assaulted by a series of saucy images of her parading in a rainbow of different sexy-as-all-fuck bikinis.

Dammit.

I was doing so well, but now, my mind goes into the gutter again.

~

The tour ended when Keira's stomach started to growl. She insisted on a shower first. Since she arrived without luggage, she ended up wearing one of the souvenir t-shirts she bought for me. I gave her a pair of my boxer briefs since my shorts were huge on her. I ditched the suit for more casual clothes, then I made my way back down to the kitchen.

While she was freshening up, I was getting everything ready. Thank God for skilled chefs. I planned on eating in the dining area, but she didn't want me to fuss. We enjoyed a succulent late dinner at the granite kitchen island. Keira practically inhaled her food.

"More Perrier?" I ask.

"Yes, please!"

I top her glass and mine.

After such a long flight, she was worried wine would knock her out.

"Thanks again for the iPhone," she says for the tenth time since I handed it to her.

"It's nothing."

After hanging up with Noah, I texted my executive assistant. Keira's new phone was waiting for me when I got back to LA.

"Don't kid yourself. I may have been hiding in a monastery for seven months, but I know how much a new iPhone costs. I also know this is the latest model."

"Anything you need, just ask. Don't hesitate. Like I said, *mi casa es su casa*." I wink.

"You're the best." Her shy smile blossoms into a full-on grin. Her hazel-green eyes dotted with sparks of gold lock onto mine. "I can't thank you enough, Rhys."

She reaches for my hand but changes her mind.

A shiver races down my spine at the near touch.

Before she left LA, she hated me.

The tide has turned.

"I like *su casa* and I love *su chef*!" She looks down at her empty plate. "That meal was out of this world—such a decadent departure from the frugal vegetarian meals we ate at the monastery."

Ah. That explains the weight loss.

"I'm glad you liked it," I say.

"I've been here a New York minute and already I feel so pampered." She smiles at me.

"I never thought I'd have all of this." I extend my hands out. "Or that I could hire the services of a bona fide Michelin-star chef to stock my fridge and freezer with incredible meals."

"How does one find a Michelin-star chef?" she asks.

"Beckett's older brother hired him."

"It makes sense Holt would need help given he's a single dad and a busy music mogul."

I nod. "The chef rotates between my place, Beckett's and a bunch of other friends' kitchens in Manhattan Beach."

"You really are living the good life."

"I'm doing my best." I wink.

"How is Holt? He came out to some of our concerts when he was still living in London."

"He's giving the music industry a run for its money. The guy is on fire. His recording label is skyrocketing, and he keeps turning out chart-topper after chart-topper. When you're settled in, you should get in touch with him. When I told him you were coming back, he said he was eager to talk to you—"

She shakes her head. "It's okay." Her hazel-green eyes are clouded with a veil of sadness.

I don't push.

"I can't believe I get to call this place home for the next little while." She changes the subject. "I'll fall from grace when the time comes for me to move out and find a crappy, but affordable, apartment of my own. God, given my shaky financial situation, I might have to find a roommate."

Her statement bothers me to no end.

"You already have a roommate. Me."

"Rhys, I'm not paying my way," she says. "It's like I'm mooching off you."

"You're not," I tell her. "You're my guest. You can stay here for as long as you need. There's no rush for you to leave."

"I'm sure your girlfriend will think otherwise."

My eyebrows lift to my forehead. "Girlfriend?"

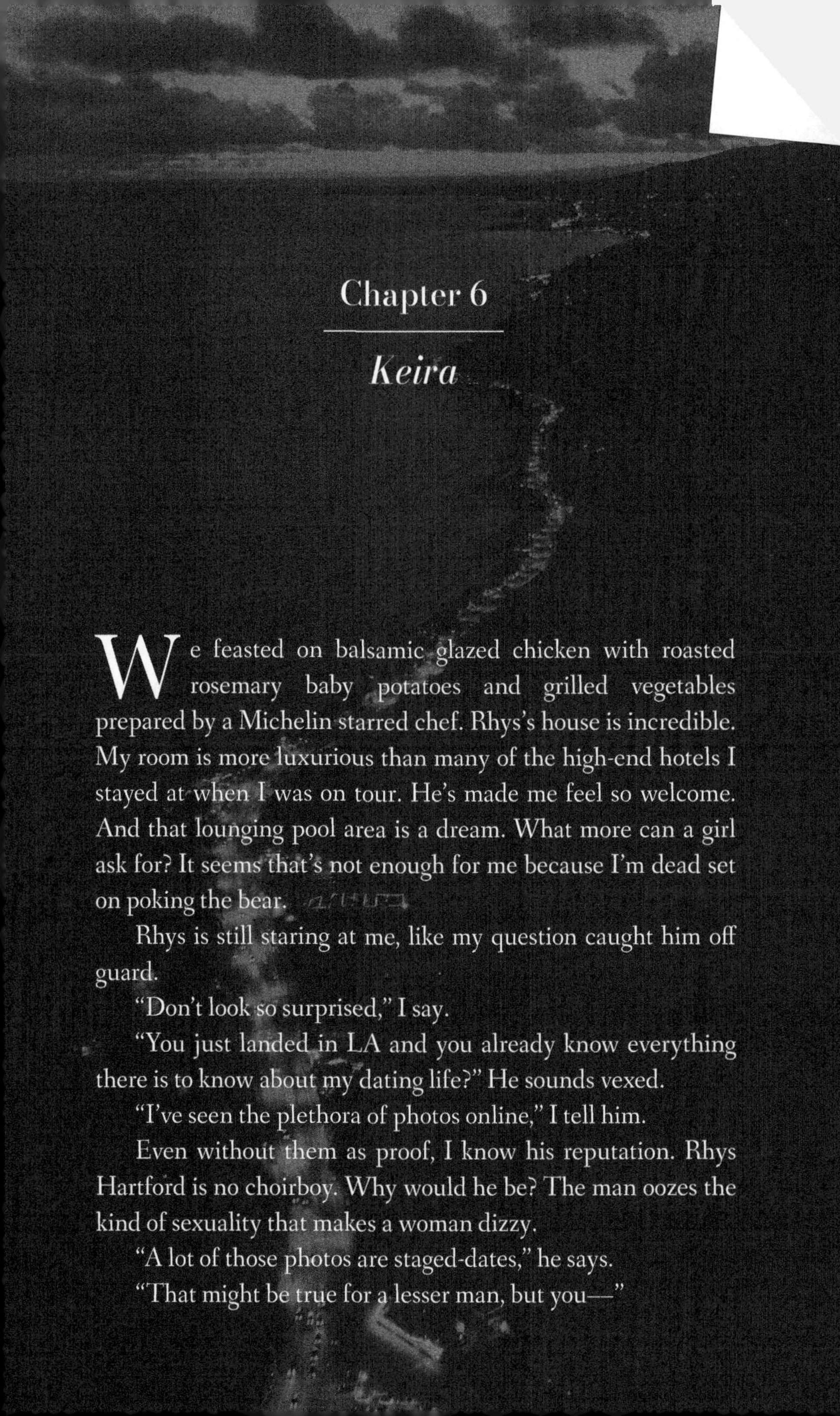

Chapter 6

Keira

We feasted on balsamic glazed chicken with roasted rosemary baby potatoes and grilled vegetables prepared by a Michelin starred chef. Rhys's house is incredible. My room is more luxurious than many of the high-end hotels I stayed at when I was on tour. He's made me feel so welcome. And that lounging pool area is a dream. What more can a girl ask for? It seems that's not enough for me because I'm dead set on poking the bear.

Rhys is still staring at me, like my question caught him off guard.

"Don't look so surprised," I say.

"You just landed in LA and you already know everything there is to know about my dating life?" He sounds vexed.

"I've seen the plethora of photos online," I tell him.

Even without them as proof, I know his reputation. Rhys Hartford is no choirboy. Why would he be? The man oozes the kind of sexuality that makes a woman dizzy.

"A lot of those photos are staged-dates," he says.

"That might be true for a lesser man, but you—"

"It doesn't mean I'm seeing those women off the red carpet."

There's a part of me that's yelling at me to quit while I'm ahead, but another part of me soldiers on.

"You talk about your chef working on rotation. That's also your MO since I can remember. You've always had a predilection for rotating more than one woman at a time." To my chagrin, I've witnessed it with my own two eyes. "I've overheard Noah refer to your dates by the day of the week... Saturday Sally, Monday Gisele, Double Tuesday with Tracy and Tamara—"

"Stop!" He drops his glass on the table with a thud, causing Perrier water to spill. His blue eyes fix on me, a stern expression on his face. "You haven't seen me in three years. What do you know about my fuck schedule?"

"Like your weekly hookup calendar isn't bursting at the seams?" I roll my eyes.

He looks at me like I've suddenly grown horns.

Maybe I have because right now, the devil in me is doing all the talking.

"You're assuming a lot, Keira." There's a warning in his voice.

Old, unresolved emotions prompt me to run my mouth.

"I don't want one of *your girls* to lose her shit when she finds out I'm crashing at your place. It's best for me to be prepared."

His blue eyes turn dark indigo.

Ah-ha!

I hit the nail on the head.

Rhys was always a catch, but now even more so. The last thing I want is for some psycho bitch to come after me, clawing my eyes out.

"If we're going to live together, we should be honest with each other," I say. "I have a right to know."

He furrows his brows as if surprised by my demand.

He studies me long and hard.

I wince a bit under his inspection, but I hold his gaze, lifting my chin in defiance. He might be the most handsome man on the planet and nearly impossible to resist, but I, Keira Weatherly, can handle him.

I'm not backing down.

The air between us is so thick, I could slice it with dental floss.

I break the silence. "You're a player, Rhys. I get it." I can't stop the verbal onslaught. "What's the nickname the press has for you again?" I snap my fingers, feigning to search my memory. "Luva Boy Rhys!"

"I hate that nickname!" he says.

"Because it's justified?"

He purses his lips into a thin line of discontentment.

I continue, my thoughts spinning out of control. "All that to say, no need to sugarcoat it for me. Just make sure you give me a heads-up. I'll return the favor if I decide to bring a guy back to your place."

That's an empty threat since men have been the furthest thing from my mind for a long time... present company excluded.

His eyes narrow to such tiny slivers, I can barely see his striking blue irises.

I challenge his stare.

His expression is ice cold when he speaks. "Over my dead body you'll bring a guy to my house to fuck."

His words are like a slap across the face.

He lets out a sarcastic laugh. "I knew we had unfinished

business. I just didn't know you harbored this much resentment towards me."

There's a flash of hurt in his eyes, and it breaks a part of me.

Rhys stands up and pushes his stool back so quickly, it falls to the floor with a loud clatter.

I jump in my seat.

Shit.

"Rhys—"

"You must be tired." His tone is clipped. "Don't worry about the dishes. You know where you're sleeping and you know where everything is. You also have my number in case—"

"Where are you going?"

"It's clear my presence turns your stomach." His words are as heavy as lead.

"No, it doesn't—"

"I'm going for a drive. Don't wait up for me." My plea falls on deaf ears.

"I'm sorry."

He cocks an eyebrow, his sharp gaze filleting me open. "It's a little late for that, don't you think?" Arctic air emanates from his body.

"I'm jetlagged."

God, that sounds lame.

His incredulous stare makes me wish I could dig a hole and crawl into it.

"Well before leaving LA you were hot-cold, hot-cold," he says. "Pick a temperature, but please stop with the bitchiness. Since you have concerns about coming nose-to-nose with the women I fuck, I'll make arrangements to find you a hotel or some other place for you to stay. I'll get on it first thing tomorrow. I might not be able to find an accommodation until Monday, but this is a big house, we should be able to ignore each other until then."

His gorgeous features morph into such disdain.

"Rhys—"

I reach out for his arm.

He steps back, putting a galaxy between us.

Fuck.

"Good night, Keira."

With that, he's gone, his receding back fading with every angry step.

A minute passes.

Another.

And another.

After five minutes, realization sets in like a storm.

I just sit there cursing my stupid mouth.

My head is all sorts of fucked up, my heart pounding into my ears.

Where did all this come from?

I guess it's true what they say. There's a fine line between love and hate.

This isn't the first time I've allowed my feelings for him to make me act like a complete bitch.

This time, I might have gone too far.

Chapter 7

Rhys

I prop my elbows on the bar, motioning with my glass to catch the bartender's attention.

"I'll have three more fingers."

The bartender nods and obliges.

I thank him and polish off the amber liquid in one gulp.

Before he can walk away from me, I ask for three more fingers.

He cocks an eyebrow, but I maintain my position.

"I'll have another round," I tell him.

He hesitates for a beat.

"What? You have my credit card and I'm running a tab. What more do you need?"

"Very well, Mr. Hartford," he says in a calm tone that betrays the worry veiling his eyes.

The rational part of me understands where he's coming from. This is my fourth drink in a short window, but I need to smooth the edges before I lose my goddamn mind.

"Thanks," I say when he finally pours the amber liquid in my glass.

Salvation.

I gulp down half my drink.

She infuriates me.

Who the fuck does she think she is, judging me?

She thinks she has me pegged.

She knows nothing.

The mountain of conflicting feelings that coursed through me as Keira barraged me for no good reason was too much to handle. I needed to get the hell out of there—and I needed to get out fast—before I did something I lived to regret. I wanted to drag her over my lap and spank her until she found a new attitude as much as I wanted to silence her lips with a heated kiss.

After driving around in circles, I decided to attack my problem head-on. While I was waiting around to pick up Keira, I killed some time at my stomping ground.

I'm back at the Quintus Hotel.

I bypassed the gentleman's club and headed straight for the whiskey bar. This is my warm-up before I head to Dark Compulsion—the private adult club hiding behind the hotel. It's a little past one o'clock in the morning, so things should be hot and heavy by now.

And of course, my thoughts veer to Keira.

Fuuuuck!

My sour mood kicks up a notch—or ten.

It's my own damn fault for putting my cock's needs in the backseat while I raised to the challenges and demands of running a company.

I should learn to channel Beckett.

Taking SCORE to new heights has never slowed him—or his cock—down. I pull tail just fine, but compared to him, I'm a novice. Then again, I have a lot more discerning taste. Although, the pretty boy has changed his ways recently.

Time to swing the pendulum to the other side.

Only two things will do tonight—expensive whiskey and a willing pussy.

"Drinking alone, Mr. Hartford?"

I lift my head and catch sight of the tall, impeccably dressed man I saw a few hours ago.

Larkin Gallagher.

The two stout men that double as his shadow stand guard at the door.

"Larkin!" I greet the owner of the Quintus Hotel by lifting my glass.

"Can I join you?" He doesn't give me a chance to answer. He pulls up a stool, unbuttons his suit jacket, and sits at the bar next to me.

"You own the place." I gesture around the bar with my glass in hand.

My curt tone doesn't faze him. "You're in a cheerful mood tonight."

"A big fucking ray of sunshine."

"I'll have what he's having," he tells the bartender.

I shoot him a side gaze. "You don't even know what I'm drinking."

"Mr. Hartford, how long have you known me?"

I let out a small laugh.

"Of course you know." Sarcasm is thick in my tone.

Larkin knows everything.

I swear, the man has eyes in the back of his head.

The bartender serves Larkin his drink.

"Thank you, Miguel," he tells him. "Cheers!" he says to me.

I offer a small nod in response.

"This is outstanding," he says, lifting the glass to eye level to appreciate the liquor.

I give him another small nod in agreement.

"Twice in one evening." Larkin cuts to the chase. His eyes, the same amber color as the liquid swirling in his glass, study me. "I assume the refined whiskey isn't the reason for your return."

"You'd be surprised," I say, polishing off my drink. I lift my glass, ready for another drink.

Larkin places a hand on my arm.

He shakes his head at the waiter who scurries off.

"I'll have to demand you hand over your keys," he says.

I shake my head at him. "I'm in control."

"Friends don't let friends get behind the wheel when their head isn't in the game. It's stupid, reckless, dangerous, and potentially lethal."

"I'm in control."

He lets out a heavy sigh. "Miguel texted me. Only a few select patrons ever get my personal attention. Everyone else deals with a bodyguard. You're not driving your car back to your place. I'm not budging."

It's my turn to sigh. "I came here to clear my head, not get babied or lectured."

"In my experience, it's easier to deal with thorny situations when you're sober."

I let out a sarcastic laugh, my eyes dropping to my empty glass.

"It's ironic coming from me considering alcohol is damn profitable for many of my businesses," he tells me. "Like I said, friends have each other's back. If you give me your keys, it'll put my mind at ease."

I oblige with the same enthusiasm as a five year old agreeing to go to his room for time out.

I fish for my keys in the pocket of my jeans and hand them to him.

Larkin slides them on the bar. Miguel grabs them and puts them out of reach.

Great.

I'm grounded.

"I'm a good listener, Mr. Hartford."

I consider his invitation.

"Women are fucking complicated," I say.

"The entire gender at large or one in particular?"

I choose not to answer his question. "That's what I like about Dark Compulsion. Uncomplicated."

I don't allow women into my head, but a tiny spitfire seems to be doing a good job messing me up.

"Why aren't you there now?" Larkin's tone is challenging. "There's still a bevy of women eager to find a match for the evening. Panties will drop the second a pretty boy like you walks into the room."

Keira's words ring loud in my ears, her indecipherable expression, still haunting me.

Was it disappointment?

Jealousy?

That time of the month?

I shake my head.

Damn you, Keira.

"I was just having a few drinks before heading there," I say.

"Well, you're done drinking for the night." That challenging tone again.

I hold his warning gaze.

"The best way to forget a woman is to top another, Mr. Hartford," Larkin says. "Two women, if you have a lot to exorcise... three, if you need to fuck yourself into a sex coma."

I can't help my laugh.

A message flashes across my phone screen, forcing my gaze down to the bar.

I shouldn't care, but I vowed to take care of her. I'd never let Noah down.

"If you'll excuse me," I tell Larkin.

"Of course." He nods and turns his attention to his drink.

I snatch up my phone.

Three words.

Keira: I'm so sorry.

I drop my phone on the bar with a growl.

Larkin shoots another measured glance in my direction. "Everything okay?"

"It was until a few hours ago."

"Weren't you picking up your best friend's little sister from the airport?" he asks.

"Mission accomplished. The package was safely delivered to my home." *And now peace of mind is a thing of the past.*

Larkin nods a few times before speaking.

"You're kidding yourself and you're wasting your time, you know that?" he says.

I knit my eyebrows in confusion. "What are you talking about?"

"If a woman has you by the balls, expensive whiskey and casual fucks won't do shit."

Thanks, Keira, for cock blocking me.

Chapter 8

Keira

And the Oscar for the biggest idiot and most ungrateful person on the planet goes to Keira Weatherly.

My tired eyes are wide open, my gaze fixed on the ceiling as I ponder on the many ways I royally fucked up.

There are a number of things I regret in life.

Insulting Rhys after his warm welcome just topped the list.

Contrary to our last major blowout three years ago, I had the decency to avoid dragging a sensitive and personal issue into the matter. Sex is just sex for Rhys.

Propping my face in my hands, I groan.

There I go again.

I pull my short hair in frustration.

It's easier to believe my mouth ran away from me last night, but if I'm honest with myself, I wanted him to feel the sting. His bewildered expression suggested I might've hit the jugular with my words.

Now, I hate myself.

I really, really hate myself.

Even after a restless night, guilt lingers like a bad hangover.

I extended an olive branch, but Rhys didn't respond to my text message.

I don't blame him.

Too little. Too late.

I tried to wait up for him, but my jetlagged body gave in to exhaustion.

What time is it?

I look at the clock on the bedside table.

Seven a.m.

I sigh, fling the covers off my body and sit up.

I try to find my bearings as I allow my gaze to travel around the large bedroom decorated with so much flair.

I can't help but shake my head at my own idiocy.

I get up and walk to the large windows.

Dawn is long gone. The sun is already shining in the sky.

LA is awake.

I let my sensitive eyes adjust to the light. The brightness is both a gift and a curse, as it enhances the throb in my head from the lack of sufficient sleep. As I soak in the warm rays, in the hopes of jolting my body into action, a thought pops into my head.

He can't be mad at me if I cook him breakfast!

He used to love my pancakes.

Before his stormy exit last night, Rhys told me not to bother with the dishes, but I couldn't help it. After stuffing the dishwasher and cleaning an already spic and span kitchen, I know where everything is.

With a new mission to focus on, I step into my day.

I exit the bedroom and glance at his door, which is located across from mine. Our living arrangement is too close for comfort, but beggars can't be choosers. Ironic, considering my bad behaviour. Rhys's door is closed, so I can't tell if he's up or not.

At least I won't bump into him.

I tiptoe as quiet as a mouse to the spa-like bathroom, hoping the wood floor doesn't creek under my steps. Once I'm behind the closed door, I exhale in relief. I pull the t-shirt Rhys gave me to make up for not having any pjs over my head and drop it to the floor. I look at it and shake my head, pushing away the thought that my naked body was touching something that touched his.

Sigh.

I brush my teeth and take care of business first. Once I'm done, I enter the massive white tile shower. I allow the water to wash away my sins. Five minutes later, the soothing streams from the rainfall showerhead have perked me up. Wrapped in a fluffy white towel, I head to the door. I open it, and peek right then left.

The coast is clear.

I emerge from the bathroom and rush to my bedroom undetected.

So far, so good.

Since the hotel lost my luggage, I only have one set of underwear. I washed it last night, but it's still damp. I jump into the clothes I wore last night, commando.

Sigh.

The advantage of having short hair is I have nothing to fuss over. I walk to the mirror and comb my fingers through my strands.

Done!

I tiptoe down the stairs. When I reach the kitchen, I freeze.

Sweet baby Jesus.

I experience a full-body clench at the sight of a shirtless and sweaty Rhys. His back is to me with his headphones around his ears. His body moves to the beat of a song I can't hear while his hips swing from left to right in a deliberate sway.

I approve.

I'm quite partial to the little dance move and rejoice when he does it again.

Yes! Yes! Yes!

He picks up the tempo when he does this cool hip hop move.

That's what I'm talking about!

I join in by gyrating my hips, circling a hand over my head, pretending I'm riding Ginuwine's pony.

'Magic Mike' will never die, and from the looks of it, Rhys is auditioning for a part.

You're hired!

For the finale, he grips the counter with both hands and pumps his hips back and forth, undulating them really slow as if he's fucking someone.

I nearly lose my shit.

I'd gladly mount this man like he's a stallion and ride the everloving daylights out of him.

Another brisk hip pump as he raps a song I don't recognize.

I've always been enraptured by his rich voice.

Oblivious to the way I'm checking him out, I continue to devour him with my eyes.

Lord have mercy.

I've had many fantasies of Rhys's body. Seeing him in the flesh again blows all those lustful memories to pieces. The mouthwatering man standing before me is breathtaking, and I'm lapping it up like a woman who hasn't had a tall glass of water in a month. Stalking him online made it easy for me to ignite my wet dreams.

Rhys cracks open a bottle of water, tips his head back, and

guzzles some of its contents. His tattooed arms are on full display.

A picture is worth a thousand words.

Whoever said that has never cast their eyes on Rhys Hartford's body art. In his case, a picture is worth a *billion* words. The billion-dollar man is a sight for sore eyes. Since the last time I saw him shirtless, he's added quite a few tattoos to his collection. They're all so colorful and intricate. A few of them are homage to his late father. The rest is just badass.

Is it wrong to want to lick the sweat dripping down his back with my tongue?

Yes, it's wrong.

God, wrong feels so right.

If I had a superpower, I'd want to be able to move objects with my mind. Case in point. I'd love nothing more than to will those running shorts to drop to the floor. I doubt men run commando—I don't think the family jewels like to dangle in the wind—so I'd also have to take the boxer briefs into consideration in my devious plan.

My eyes travel to his firm and biteable ass.

Watching Rhys from behind as he walks is a thing of beauty. It rarely happens because the gentleman in him demands I walk in front of him.

This is such a treat.

My gaze brushes down his tanned, muscular legs and defined calves before settling on that yummy ass again.

God was good to you, Rhys Hartford.

I'm so busy drooling, I jerk when he turns around.

"Jesus!" The bottle he's holding drops to the floor, splashing water all over the place. "Keira?!" He yanks the headphones off his head and lets them drop around his neck. "What the hell are you doing standing there?"

Drooling over you?! "I just entered the kitchen. You didn't hear me walk in... headphones and all."

"You can't sneak up on me like that."

"I'm sorry." *Not sorry.*

"I'm not used to having someone living in my house."

Based on what played out between us last night, I might not be here for long.

I bite back the snarky remark.

I coax the gentler Keira to come out. "It won't happen again, I promise."

He picks up the bottle, throws it into the trash bin, and wipes the floor with some paper towels. After washing his hands, he's standing in front of me again.

I get to admire him from the front—all six-feet-two inches of him.

Under the morning light, Rhys's stunning glacier-blue eyes are translucid under his dark brows and damp brown hair. Last night's five o'clock shadow is now a scruffy beard. The dark stubble dusting his square jaw only adds to the appeal.

I take the rest of him in with one languorous eye-sweep—his broad shoulders, the lines of muscle wrapping his arms, accentuated by the tattoos, and his six-pack. His running shorts hang low enough for me to salivate over the carved lines of his V-muscle. I also get a glimpse of the happy trail of brown hair disappearing under the shorts.

Heavenly Father.

"Are you checking me out?" His grin is playful, bad-boyish. Lethal.

Uh, uh-huh.

"I didn't mean to objectify you—I mean stare..."

He rewards my sass with a pantie-melting smile.

"I couldn't help but notice the new ink. They were hiding

underneath the long-sleeves of the shirt you were wearing last night."

"I keep getting new ink whenever the mood strikes," he says.

"They look good on you." *Amazing, really.*

"Thanks."

He stalks towards me.

I take a step back.

I can handle that much hotness at a distance. Close up? Hell, no.

"Just a little housekeeping," he says. "If we're going to live together, you can't look at me like that when I'm shirtless."

"Like what?"

"Like you've never seen a sexy man before."

"You're full of yourself." I roll my eyes.

"Gotcha."

We both laugh.

"You're not mad at me anymore?" I ask.

"You want to know if I'm going to kick you out?"

I nod. "I can understand if you don't want me here."

"You pissed me off last night, Keira." I wince. "I was fuming."

"I'm so sorry, Rhys. I shouldn't have said those awful things to you. You didn't deserve it... not after the hospitality you showed me."

"Damn right you shouldn't have," he says. "While we're on the subject, I don't bring women back to my house. Ever. So, you don't have to worry about a parade of fucks while you're living with me."

The words sting, but I asked for it.

"I don't have a merry-go-round of women coming in and out of my home. If I was seeing someone, I'd have enough respect for you—and her—to tell you."

My heart skips a beat at those last words.

It's like a sliver of hope.

"Okay."

"I understand you're all grown-up..." His eyes brush down the length of my body—pausing a little too long at my breasts—before meeting my gaze again. "And you have needs, but I stand firm. I don't want any assholes running around in my house. I don't need to know—"

"I was just talking shit. I'd never disrespect you like that."

"Good." He considers me for a long beat. "You're going to need new clothes."

I look down at my body. "You don't like my fashion selection?"

"You're too pretty to wear baggy, unflattering clothes."

I blush.

"Let me go for a swim, then we'll have breakfast and I'll hire a chauffeured car so I can pick up my car."

"What happened to your car?"

"It's parked at one of my favorite hangouts. I had a few too many to drink while I was processing last night's blowout, so I couldn't drive home." Another wave of guilt washes over me. "I could use one of my other cars, but I don't want to leave the Benz there all day."

"My bitchy outburst was uncalled for." I hang my head low. "I'm such an idiot. Thank you for not throwing me out on my ass."

He places two fingers underneath my chin, forcing my gaze to his.

"I won't renege on my word to your brother."

"Thank you."

"This roommate arrangement is as new for you as it is for me, Keira. We're going to have to learn to live together."

"I understand."

"Don't insult me like that ever again."

"I won't. Never again."

"We've never had the kind of relationship where you'd know anything intimate about me. Don't make assumptions. You want to know something? Ask."

A flood of questions flies across my brain, but only the most urgent one burns the tip of my tongue.

Could you ever want me nearly as much as I want you?

Chapter 9

Rhys

Keira barefoot, hair still damp, in my boxer briefs with tanned legs—I wanted to wrap around my neck—on full display first thing this morning is a sight I'll never forget for the rest of my life.

What a wake-up call.

No matter how much I tried to keep my eyes levelled with hers, it was impossible not to let them drift. I already knew she wasn't wearing a bra. I saw it hanging to dry in the bathroom last night. Even though the t-shirt she was wearing was three sizes too big, I was still able to see the outline of her nipples. The desire to get her out of that damn t-shirt so I could suck and lick my way from the valley of her breasts, down her taut stomach, all the way to her pussy, was overwhelming.

I had to swim a few extra laps just to cleanse my impure thoughts.

Damn her.

I was hoping the jetlag would keep her in bed much longer. I didn't expect she'd be standing in my kitchen, staring at me like she wanted to eat me. There were so many emotions veiling her eyes. Each one of them tugging at my balls.

Was that lust?

Last night's harshness and edge were replaced with fragility and vulnerability. I can handle that much better.

Keira insisted on preparing a breakfast of champions. Like I'm going to refuse pancakes and bacon. After picking up my car, we're on the road. While I was doing my laps, I suggested she figure out the items she needs the most and pinpoint a few shops. We're headed to the first address.

"You used the products I bought you," I say.

The scent of the lavender permeates throughout the car. I remembered it's her favorite scent, so I made sure to buy her a basket of bath products. I got her the expensive ones imported from Verona, Italy.

"Did I use too much?"

"Not at all. You smell... really nice."

She flashes me a wide grin.

"That was great foresight on your part, Mr. Hartford." The corners of her mouth hint at the slightest smile.

"It would be a shame for you to smell like me."

"That could be misconstrued as a double entendre," she says.

X-rated thoughts dance through my head.

Indeed, it could.

I hold her gaze a little longer than I should as I change gear.

I return my focus to the road.

"On a serious note, after rudimentary accommodations, a string of dingy bathrooms, and toilets that are nothing more than a hole in the ground, I feel as pampered as a queen at your place."

"Holes in the ground?" I ask, horrified.

"Yup."

"Even for women?"

"Yup. In Nepal, you don't always get separate bathrooms for men and women, and since men can't aim for shit, let's just say I learned to hold it whenever I could."

I laugh my head off.

The GPS announces we're approaching the first address on her list, so I start looking for parking. It doesn't take long for me to find a spot. We get out of the car and stroll side-by-side, glancing at the shops along the way. I'm not sure I've ever been in this neighborhood. It's like playing tourist for the day.

"French Appliqué!" Keira points an eager finger. "We're here!"

"What the hell?" I mutter under my breath when we arrive in front of a chic boutique.

When she said she needed underwear, I figured I was going to end up in an awkward situation, but I thought I could handle it.

I'm ill-prepared for this.

If the salacious underwear on the mannequins in the window is any indication, I'm in real trouble.

You're testing my resolve, God.

"At the monastery, we were expected to wear modest clothing and underwear, aka, boring, basic cotton. I'm so looking forward to buying super sexy combos."

I'm not going to survive this.

Unaware of my mental anguish, she saunters into the shop.

I'm rooted in place.

I'm taking my best friend's little sister lingerie shopping for *super sexy combos.*

I must have a death wish.

Noah is built like a tank. He's going to strangle me and then kill me.

Keira pokes her head out. "Are you coming in?"

"Right behind you," I say.

Since I don't date, and I can't remember the last time I had a girlfriend, I never set foot in a lingerie shop. Walking into French Appliqué is like entering paradise. Every corner of the store jacks up my senses.

This is torture.

"Hello, I'm Nadya, may I help you find something to your liking?" A tall blonde with an Eastern European accent asks. Her eyes are riveted on me.

"Hi, Nadya, it's not for me. It's for her."

We all laugh.

"A man who takes his woman lingerie shopping? Is there anything sexier?" Nadya says.

My eyes grow wide at her comment.

I ready myself to correct her, but Keira precedes me.

"I know, right?" She giggles. "I'm such a lucky girl," she says in a coquettish voice. She even has the audacity to lace her arm with mine.

What the hell is she doing?

She looks up at me, her ridiculously long eyelashes fluttering a mile a minute. "Thank you for spoiling me, baby."

Baby...

The words travel straight to my cock.

"What did you have in mind?" Nadya asks Keira.

"What would you like to see me in, baby?"

I shoot her a warning look.

Her grin only widens.

"Let me rephrase," Nadya says, pulling our attention to her. "What scale are we looking at here? Baby-making combo? Role-playing? Virginal? Romantic? Naughty? Something that will bring him down to his knees?"

That last one is an option?

"At French Appliqué, the saucy possibilities are endless," Nadya says with a shoulder shrug.

Like an old-fashioned slide presentation, images of Keira in each tempting combo flash in front of my eyes, the clicking sound of the carousel thumping in rhythm with my pulsating cock.

My mouth is dry.

My eyes bounce from the blonde to the pint-sized brunette.

Keira's eyebrows arch in the form of a question.

Nadya awaits my answer.

I clear my throat. "I'll wait outside."

With a decisive step, I head to the door.

One more minute in this store and I'll embarrass myself.

"But baby, if you're outside how am I going to pay for the collection of lingerie sure to bring you down to your knees?" Keira throws that question over my shoulder.

That stops me dead in my tracks.

My mind goes straight to the gutter.

What kind of game is she playing?

I thought she spent seven months in a monastery, not acting school.

I turn around to face her.

"Shoot me a text when you're ready," I say in a controlled voice. "Whatever you need, just"—I wave a frantic finger around the store—"buy it."

"Awww." Nadya places both hands against her heart. "You two are adorable."

Yeah, a fucking barrel of fun.

I squint my eyes at Keira, warning her.

She responds by grabbing a random item from the rack.

"Before you go. What do you think of these, baby?"

My eyes drop to the panties she's holding.

Jesus. The woman is determined to kill me.

"Oh, our crotchless panties are very popular," Nadya says. "Very naughty... if you know what I mean."

I don't bother to answer.

I turn on my heel and bolt out of there while I'm still able to hold on to a shred of my sanity.

When I'm outside, instead of distancing myself from the landmine, I stand in front of the window and peer inside like a lost puppy.

Keira is aware my eyes are on her.

She looks at me from over her shoulder a few times and winks.

Devious woman.

I stare down at the stupid bulge between my legs and shake my head.

You are so fucked, buddy.

~

An hour and two very tall lattes later, I'm sitting at a coffee shop, chomping at the bit to put an end to this suffering.

My eyes close on a frustrated sigh.

I wasn't willing to accept defeat last night. Just to prove Keira wasn't fucking with my head, I went to Dark Compulsion, determined to lose myself balls-deep in a warm pussy.

It was in vain.

Half an hour after walking into the club, I was sitting in the back of a chauffeured car, heading back to my house.

It wasn't for the lack of drop-dead gorgeous candidates.

My cock simply refused to rise to the occasion.

Funny how *he* didn't have a problem reacting to Keira holding a pair of crotchless panties.

God knows I prepared myself for this day.

After a marathon-like run and swimming enough laps to

qualify for the Olympic team, I took matters into my own hand. Literally. A cold shower and jerking off twice this morning did nothing. I'm as horny as a beast and aching with longing for a woman I have no business lusting after.

Stupid crotchless panties.

Only a lobotomy could put an end to the loop of salacious images running through my mind since I fled the lingerie shop.

I wonder if those crotchless panties come in different colors—

STOP!

The more distance I put between myself and the devil's den, the better. Willpower isn't enough when confronting a ballbreaker enemy like French Appliqué. I pull out my phone and shoot Keira a text.

Rhys: Are you done?

Keira: I just tried the last combo! Talk about doing a one-eighty from the basic undies I arrived with.

Rhys: So, you're set?

Keira: There are so many gorgeous options, my mind is dizzy.

So is mine.

Keira: The bras are amazing. The. Best. Fit. Ever. I didn't try on the panties—of course—but I'm pretty sure they'll fit beautifully. I even feel confident enough to buy one of the crotchless pairs. Two, actually.

I groan and pinch the bridge of my nose.

Keira: I'll just grab a couple combos. I'll go to a discount store next week to buy cheaper lingerie.

Rhys: Nonsense. Why would you run around town when you can get everything you need at one shop? Whatever fits, buy it.

Keira: I don't want to abuse your generosity.

Rhys: You're not abusing. I'm offering.

I've always considered myself an alpha, but maybe I was wrong. Perhaps there's a masochist dormant inside me. Why else would I be pushing?

Keira: Are you sure?

Rhys: I'm sure.

Keira: There are quite a few I like.

Rhys: Just get them. Get them all.

Goddammit, my water bill is going to go way up while she's living with me. Looks like I'll be taking cold showers every morning and night. Multiple times on the weekends.

Keira: You're not just saying that?

Rhys: I'm a straight-shooter.

Three little dots bounce up and down.

They bounce again.

And again.

Still no message.

Rhys: Everything okay?

Keira: Sorry, I couldn't type there for a minute. I was laughing my head off.

Huh?

I frown as I reread my last reply.

Rhys: What's so funny?

Keira: You talking about being a straight-shooter while I'm wearing the baby-making see-through bra, crotchless panties and garter belt in red with the five-inch strappy heels Nadya insisted I wear strapped to my feet is kind of hilarious.

I'm not laughing.

Her reply kicks me dead in the dick.

Rhys: You can't buy the baby-making combo.

Keira: Why not? I thought you said I could buy anything that fits.

I narrow my eyes at the screen.

She's pushing my buttons.

Rhys: Not. That. One.

Keira: All right, grumpy roomie.

Rhys: It's grumpy **landlord** to you, young lady.

Keira: LOL! You're hilarious.

Rhys: I'm serious.

Keira: I got the message loud and clear, Mr. Hardball. No baby-making combo. No biggie. I'm not ready for kids yet, and it's not like I'm seeing anyone.

Jesus Christ.

Rhys: So, you're done?

Keira: Yup! All done. I'm just about to strip out of the baby-making combo and put on my sensible underwear and **your** t-shirt.

Another visual I didn't need. She's wearing her shorts, but borrowed another t-shirt.

Rhys: I'll be there in ten.

Fuck my life.

~

"You're back!" Nadya says when I walk into the shop.

"Yup." Just like earlier, my body is on edge. "She's done?"

"She should be. Why don't you go and see for yourself?" Nadya winks at me.

Nope. That's not a good idea.

"It's okay, I'll wait—"

I freeze midsentence when I catch a glimpse of the most enticing vision I've ever seen in my life.

Keira?!

My legs move on their own volition, drawn to her like a magnetic force. I stand behind her and I can't believe my eyes.

What.

The actual.

Fuck?

Her gaze catches mine in the mirror.

Our eyes lock, and I swear, you could toast marshmallows from the fire emanating from our heated stare.

I swallow hard.

The sight of her is so salacious, it almost knocks me to my ass.

It's as if all the air has been sucked out of the shop as I gasp in admiration.

Keira in my baggy clothes is a vision, but seeing her now is enough to cause heart failure. She's wearing a sexy-as-all-fuck silk and lace robe and whatever goes underneath it in a seductive shade—pale green silk with soft pink lace on the edge. The combination only intensifies her hazel-green eyes. It doesn't go unnoticed how the luxurious fabric caresses her soft, supple skin. The short length accentuates her tanned legs.

Is there such a thing as lingerie lust?

If so, I'm there.

I'm mesmerized by her beauty.

I drink her in.

My stomach tightens and I push the confusing feelings down, reminding myself who she is.

Noah's baby sister.

Still, the mental beatdown is no match for the mouthwatering vision standing before me.

She smiles, and small dimples pierce her cheeks.

"Nadya suggested I try on this kimono set for fun," she says.

I just stare, words escaping me as I commit every perfect inch of her body to memory.

Her lips part, and her tongue peeks out to wet them.

"It's pretty, though," she says. "I've never owned anything in silk before. But I don't need it. Who would I wear it for?"

Me.

She doesn't avert her gaze when she says that.

My eyes don't leave hers.

My pulse races as fast as a speeding train.

She continues when I remain speechless. "It makes me feel feminine... especially, the chemise."

Is that what you call it?

"It's from France."

Bless the French.

"Even the name of the brand sounds chic—*Marjolaine. Ooh Lala!*" She giggles.

I don't crack a smile.

"I've felt like a tomboy since shaving my head. And since I've been walking around in your clothes, I've looked like one. This is such a departure." She fusses with her short hair.

I find my voice. "I told you yesterday, Keira, you're perfect."

Her lips part in a warm smile.

"Maybe I just need a proper haircut and some makeup."

"Maybe you don't need a damn thing."

"Rhys Hartford, always the supportive big brother figure." Her tone is almost challenging.

My jaw tightens as my eyes slide over her body. Her chest heaves up and down. With a tinge of satisfaction, I catch the shaky breath she exhales.

"Your breasts..."

The words drop from my lips without my consent.

She lets out a little laugh.

"You noticed my breasts, Rhys?"

"I was never blind."

"I can tell you more about it later, if that's okay."

I nod. "Of course."

Silence ticks between us and awareness trickles in.

I'm still staring at her without shame.

I give her another onceover.

"Buy the kimono set and everything else that fits." It isn't a suggestion. It's an order.

She shrugs. "If you say so. You're paying after all." Her answer is flippant, dripping with effrontery and impertinence.

Keira always knew how to poke the bear in me.

I'm up for the challenge.

"Yes, I am." I hold her gaze. "And I'm used to getting what I want."

She blushes from ear to ear.

Chapter 10

Keira

"I'*m used to getting what I want.*"

Myriad stores later, and his words still ring in my ear.

When a guy tells you that while his heated gaze roams over your body, what does it mean?

I wish I could confide in someone.

I miss not being able to talk to Mikki every day.

"You didn't buy enough clothes." Rhys's voice pulls me from my thoughts.

My gaze snaps to his. "You're crazy. I got plenty of stuff."

"You got casual outfits to hang out at my place with," he says. "What about outfits for a dressy or formal evening?"

After half a day of shopping, we're driving back to Manhattan Beach.

"No one knows I'm in LA. I doubt I'll be getting invitations to chi-chi parties anytime soon."

"What if I need someone to accompany me to an event?"

A snarky remark is on the tip of my tongue, but I suppress it. Instead, I channel softer, gentler Keira.

"I'm sure there're no shortages of women who would die to hang from your arm."

"What if I want *you* on my arm?" he says.

I'm not sure how to read into his admission.

"You can't stay locked up in my house forever, Keira. You'll have to show your pretty face at some point." His words are a reminder I'm back in paparazzi land.

"You're sure you want to be seen with me?"

"I'd be honored to be seen with you."

"Does this have to do with your brotherly duties?" I don't give him a chance to respond. "Don't worry, I'll make sure to tell Noah you're taking good care of me."

"This has nothing to do with your big brother."

I shiver under his onceover.

"Wouldn't you want to be seen with someone whose star is rising? After freefalling out of space, my lackluster star is kind of floating sideways. I'm a has-been. It's over for me. I committed the cardinal sin. I broke my recording contract."

Rhys shoots me an unimpressed side-gaze.

"If anyone knows anything about a comeback, it's me," he says. "After Dad's death, I did a piss poor job of picking up the pieces of my shattered life. Falling on your knees isn't the problem, Keira. Not getting up is. When the underdog triumphs, everyone stands up and cheers."

"Oh, wise one. When did you become a Buddhist monk?"

He laughs.

Rhys Hartford.

Cruelly bullied in school well into his teenage years.

Former rap star one-hit wonder.

More famous for his many rehab visits than his musical career.

He now owns the town that used to ridicule him.

He knows a thing or two about making a comeback.

"I'm not sure I'm ready yet," I say.

"I much prefer that honest answer."

I just nod.

"You can't flounder forever. An idle mind is a dangerous mind… for a bratty woman like you."

I narrow my gaze at him.

"More sage wisdom, spiritual guru?"

His glacier-blue eyes fix on me.

"Something like that," he says with a grin.

"At least you didn't call me a girl." I roll my eyes.

"You made it perfectly clear today you were anything but." His voice is as rough as gravel when he says that.

Did the temperature go way up in the Benz?

I fan myself to cool down.

I wish I could do the same for the heat mounting between my legs, but that would be unladylike.

"You have a clean slate, dimples."

Not that I'd tell him, but I kind of like my new nickname.

"You can go in any which direction you want. Have you put any thought to what you want the next stage of your life to look like?"

"Not really," I say. "One thing is certain, I'm not going back to being a stupid popstar."

"This is LA. Any dream is within your reach."

I consider him.

"You're incognito until people clue in to who you are," he says. "Take advantage of it."

I nod.

My worries dissipated when no one recognized me during my shopping extravaganza. Even without my baseball cap on.

"Promise you'll think about it?" he says.

"I promise."

"That's my girl."

That's all I've always wanted to be.

Sigh.

"Can I ask a question?" From the trajectory of Rhys's gaze, I already guess what it is.

"My breasts?"

"Yes." He looks pained.

I laugh.

"Men and boobs!" I shake my head.

"Pardon me for being a man, but I'm curious. You don't look anything like you did before."

"My boobs were stupid heavy, and I couldn't wear cute tops without a bra that looked like a contraction. I wore a sports bra over a regular bra to try to hide my size, but I was just kidding myself. And there was the constant pain. Getting a breast reduction was the best decision I ever made."

"This is news to me—the surgery and the chronic pain."

"It's not like I was going to talk about my boob problems with you."

"Fair enough."

"As for the surgery, we weren't on talking terms at the time."

He nods. "I see."

"I got the operation done in a hush-hush private clinic in London in between tours."

"Did Noah know?" he asks.

"Not at first, but I did tell him when we started talking to each other again. He was ecstatic—"

"Because he wouldn't have to go around decking assholes to protect your honor?"

Rhys isn't entirely wrong. To Noah's discontent, my breasts got me a lot of unwanted attention.

"One less thing for him to worry about," I say. "In any case, when I told him, I asked him not to tell you."

"That would explain why I was in the dark." Rhys's lips purse.

Right before leaving LA, I cut off all communications with my older brother.

My ruthless ambition also caused a rift between Rhys and me.

I can't take back that day.

I can't take back the words.

I can't take back the hurt shining in his eyes.

"Men put large breasts on a pedestal, but it doesn't work for everyone." I keep talking. "My frame is far too small for large breasts." 40 DD works in Porn Valley, but I cursed mine. I'm much happier with my perky B cup.

"Not all men are obsessed with size," he says.

"Perhaps, but my experience with big boob lovers was never pleasant."

"Got it."

"And then there's the lack of practicality of carrying watermelons on your chest in my former profession. Even before leaving for London, I knew my oversized boobs would be a liability. I was right. Singing isn't enough anymore in the music industry. Record companies expect you to put on a show. Vertiginous dance moves and double D's don't go hand-in-hand."

"I can just imagine."

"After the surgery, to avoid public scrutiny, I wore a padded bra stuffed with socks right up to the point I left London. The record company insisted on it."

"Really?"

"Keeping the brand pristine was their only concern," I say in a formal corporate tone.

"Wow."

"It was a small price to pay," I say. "I couldn't handle all the jumping up and down required in choreographies. Not to mention, I was tired of men being oblivious to the color of my eyes. Big boobs lead to erroneous assumptions when your breasts precede you when you walk into a room."

Rhys explodes in laughter.

"I can't tell you how much I missed your sense of humor, dimples."

I can't tell you how much I missed you.

"I have another question," he says.

"Inquiring minds want to know..."

He winks, and my stomach flutters.

"I expected the jetlag to mellow you out, but I was wrong. You're as sharp as a whip."

"One of my many qualities," I say. "So, what's on your mind?"

"What was that about in the lingerie shop?"

"What do you mean?" I feign ignorance.

He changes gear.

My eyes drop to his large hand.

When I look up, he's staring at me.

"I'm talking about your little act."

"Chill out," I tell him. "I was just having some fun."

"It was misleading."

"Where's the crazy and unpredictable Rhys? The rapper who could bring down the house with his edgy rhymes. The daredevil who never backs away from a challenge?"

"The daredevil is still alive and kicking. For the rest, Rhys grew up and he no longer raps. He's wheeling and dealing." He flashes me his trademark pearly-white smile.

Thank God I bought a new pair of designer shades or else I'd be blinded right now.

"You're too stuffy," I tell him. "You need to loosen up."

"That's your assessment after not seeing me for three years?

You haven't been in LA twenty-four hours and already you want to ransack my life," he says with a laugh.

I don't answer.

I study his gorgeous profile and his chiselled features. He didn't shave this morning. I'm more than okay with that. In my opinion, men's eyelashes are underappreciated. Same for earlobes. His are prime examples of that. He left the COO porn suit home today. He has the California hunk vibe on point in his fitted black jeans and black t-shirt.

What a man.

I comb my fingers through my way-too-short hair, wishing I could run my fingers through his. Rhys has the best hair—dark brown, thick with a slight wave. He's sporting a kickass layered and feather cut—close shaven on the side with the longer layers on top styled with gel. The haircut drips with boldness and masculinity.

My eyes drop to his mouth and those lips I've only been able to taste once. I'd give up a vital organ in a heartbeat for a second kiss.

"Earth to Keira!"

I snap out of it.

"You said it yourself last night at dinner, you work too much. My role as your new roommate is to shake things up for you," I say.

"Oh, yeah?" He cocks an eyebrow.

"Oh, yeah." I stand my ground.

"And when did you decide that?"

My eyes shift left to right. "Just now. I made an executive decision!"

"If you think I need to inject more fun in my life, I cease to understand how your fake girlfriend act at French Appliqué fits. It made me uncomfortable."

"What made you uncomfortable, my harmless shenanigans... or imagining me in sexy lingerie?"

Whoa!

I have no idea where that came from, but since this is the first time in my life I see playboy Rhys Hartford blush, I'm pretty proud of myself.

"You're playing with fire," he says. His voice is gruff.

I consider him for a few beats.

"I'm okay with that." I don't recognize my raspy voice.

He shoots me a measured glance.

His gaze slides back to the road, but his reaction doesn't go unnoticed. He tightens his jaw and white knuckles the wheel.

Keira, one. Rhys, zero!

For the rest of my natural life, I'll never forget the hunger in his gaze when he was drinking me up in that kimono. His dreamy blue eyes were dark, hooded and something flashed behind them that caused my whole body to shiver. For as long as I can remember, I've been dying for him to look at me that way and I went about it in all the wrong ways... until today.

Thank you, French Appliqué!

Chapter 11

Rhys

I place the glass of vodka on the rocks I just polished off on the table and get up to start dinner.

If I keep my head occupied, my mind won't slide into the gutter.

After a torturous day, I needed a stiff drink to tame my stiff cock. I'm still in the same fucking predicament. At least Keira is nowhere near to witness my struggle.

The second we got back to the house, she declared she needed to wash off the day's grime. She felt a little dirty from trying on clothes all day.

I didn't argue.

I needed time to get my head screwed back on straight.

I head to the fridge, scour its contents and quickly decide we're keeping it simple tonight. I pull a few things out and place them on the counter. I turn to the pantry to grab potatoes, but my step falters.

Keira is singing.

I love her voice.

She walks into the kitchen and it's as if the rug is pulled from underneath me.

Every muscle in my body tightens.

Why is she doing this to me?

"Hey, what's for dinner?" she asks.

"I was thinking barbecue. Steaks. Sausages," I say as my eyes rake her body.

"That sounds delicious! I'll help."

"I thought you were taking a shower."

"I was." She points to the towel wrapped around her chest. "As I was stepping into the shower—and for the record, I may never be able to leave because of your spa-like bathrooms—"

"I told you, you're welcome here for as long as you want."

"Good to know."

The vodka on ice softened the edge, but her coquettish smile and batting eyelashes set me back to square one.

Great.

"As I was saying, just before jumping into the shower, it dawned on me to check my phone to make sure my battery wasn't dead."

She walks over to one of the stools at the kitchen island where she left her crossbody bag, and rummages through it. My eyes are transfixed by her butt wiggling underneath the towel.

"Bummer. My phone is dead." She waves her phone in the air. "I'm going to plug it in. I want it to be charged just in case Noah or Michaela call, since I left them messages this morning and I haven't heard back from them."

"Okay," is all I manage.

Her proximity is so overwhelming, I don't dare to breathe.

Keira frowns.

"What?" I ask.

She strides towards me, barefoot.

"Remember what I said earlier in the car about this new

uptight Rhys I barely recognize?" She pokes my chest a few times with her phone.

Each thump reverberates to my cock.

Without thinking, I grab her wrist and pull her close. Our bodies aren't touching, but there can't be more than an inch or two between us.

She gasps, her eyes wide as she takes me in.

"I was going to say you're as stiff as a mannequin, but that ninja move proves me wrong."

She giggles.

I stare at her, my nostrils flaring as I desperately try to regulate my heartbeat.

Once again, thoughts of spanking her ass come to mind.

"Why are you so tense?" she asks.

Because my cock is as stiff as steel.

"You caught me by surprise," I tell her. "I'm not used to having a woman walk around my place in nothing but a towel."

She gives me a one shoulder-shrug. "We'll have to learn how to live together..."

I consider her.

She's playing me.

"Let's make sure we buy you a robe the next time we're out shopping," I tell her.

Her smile is dangerous.

"*We* already bought a robe, remember?" she says. "Would you prefer if I walked around in the kimono instead?" The challenging way her hazel-green eyes hold my stare is as much of a trap as her loaded question. And I just walked straight into it.

I close my eyes on a prayer.

Please, God, help me out here.

I let go of her wrist and point to where she came from. "Get out of here!"

"Yes, sir!"

With a little smile stretching her lips, she saunters out of the kitchen. She gives me one last look over her shoulder, and she's gone.

Now I can't stop thinking of what she's hiding underneath that stupid towel.

So much for not thinking of her in a sexual way.

I didn't expect she'd keep provoking me like this. I sympathize with Adam in the Garden of Eden when he succumbed to Eve's temptation. Lucky for me, I'm still standing. And goddammit it's not easy. There's only so much I can take before I snap like a fucking twig.

I will not bite into the forbidden fruit, I repeat over and over in my head.

I focus on my hit list.

Marinate the meat.

Another drink.

Then, an ice-cold shower.

Absolutely no jerking thinking of her.

You got this!

I return to the meal preparation.

My phone rings.

I wipe my hands and snatch it from the counter.

Of course, it's Noah.

Fuck.

"Hey, buddy!"

"Hey," he says. "Is Keira okay?"

"Yes, she is. She's here."

He lets out a loud exhale. "Thank God. I was worried. I've been trying to call her, but there's no answer."

"Her phone battery is dead," I tell him. "She just plugged it in."

"Got it," he says. "I know I keep repeating myself, but

thanks again for doing this. And thanks for buying her a new iPhone."

"Stop saying that. It's not a big deal."

"It is a big deal. My sister is a handful. We both know it."

Yes, she is.

"And the mouth on that girl," he says.

Don't remind me.

"She never shies away from speaking her mind," I tell him.

"No, she doesn't. The woman can drive any rational man insane."

I'm teetering on the edge of insanity as we speak.

"You know as well as I do, when she wants something, there's no stopping her," he says.

"Been there, done that."

"Exactly! She's as stubborn as a mule."

"I won't argue with you."

"And opinionated."

"Very true."

"Even though I'm eternally grateful, I can't help but feel guilty," he tells me.

"What are you talking about, Noah?"

"I want to make sure you guys aren't locking horns."

I frown at the phone. "Why would you say that?"

"When I texted Keira last night to make sure she arrived safely, I inquired about you."

She never mentioned it.

"She told me you were out clearing your mind. I've had to walk away from her a few times myself in the middle of heated debates, aka her trying to get her way. What did she do or say to piss you off?"

"We're still learning how to live together."

"I speak from experience... not an easy task, which is why I can't thank you enough for being willing to put up with her."

He chuckles. I laugh. "She texted me earlier to let me know you were taking her underwear shopping?! What the hell, man?"

"She arrived with nothing more than a backpack and the clothes on her back."

"What the fuck are you talking about?"

"There was a screw up at the hotel. It's unclear if her luggage was stolen or lost."

"I didn't know about the luggage."

"I suspect she didn't want you to worry," I say. "It was a rough trip back to the US for her."

"Sounds like it. You also took her clothes shopping?"

"I did."

"I'll wire you money to cover those purchases—"

"Absolutely not!"

"Stop being a stubborn ass, Hartford," he says. "The deal was for you to give her a place to crash. Not buy her a new wardrobe and God knows what else."

The crotchless panties flash in front of my eyes.

"This goes above and beyond your big brother duties. She's *my* little sister and *my* responsibility."

I get where he's coming from. His mom did a good number on him growing up. Still, a wave of possessiveness takes over me.

"She's in my house, under my roof, so she's *my* responsibility. We made an oath a long time ago. When you can't step in, I do."

Noah laughs on the other end.

"What's so funny?" I ask.

"There are no bounds to your fierce loyalty," he tells me.

Loyalty runs both ways.

"None," I say. "After all, you saved my ass more times than I can count."

"Yes, I did," he says. "While we're on the subject of

assholes, don't let any fuckers around her. And if a moron thinks he has a chance with her, I can count on you to make sure the body disappears without a trace. You have enough money to hire the best hitmen."

"First, those scenarios only happen in Hollywood. Second, Keira is twenty-three. It's not like I can ground her."

"Why the hell not?"

We both laugh.

"I'm a lucky bastard to have you as my best friend," he says.

I groan under my breath.

He'd crush me with his bare hands if he knew I was harboring impure thoughts towards his sister. Built like a gladiator, his nickname, the Hulk, is justified.

"Of course you are, idiot," I say.

"Asshole!"

I chuckle.

Noah lets out an insufferable sigh. "I'm trying hard not to get into her business, but I can't help it. It's wired in me to protect her." He's has done a better job of taking care of his little sister than their mom ever did. "Now that she's talking to me again, I don't want to screw things up by being in her face."

"I get it."

His need to watch over his sister is as strong as mine. Hence, why she shut us out of her life for three years when we expressed our reservations and concerns. She wanted fame at any cost. Showbusiness is a cutthroat business. I should know. Keira being Keira, she thought she knew better and didn't need our advice. The rift that ensued put a mountain of stress—and sorrow—on Noah. I didn't fare much better.

"I'm being overbearing," Noah says. "You have everything under control. She's in good hands. Nothing will happen to her under your watch."

I think of how many times my *good hands* have jerked off to thoughts of biting her peachy ass. Thank God Noah can't see my guilty face.

"Rhys?" Noah says.

"She's in good hands," I tell him, hoping to convince myself.

"That's all I need to hear. All right, I'm off. We got hit by another bad storm, so everyone is spending a lot more time indoors—"

"That sucks."

"As long as it doesn't get worse and affect production again, I can live with it. We already lost a day of shooting earlier this week. In any case, I'm heading next door to my neighbor's. He has a bunch of friends coming over and we're going to watch a *footie* game. He's still trying to convince me their football is better than ours."

"As if," I say.

"Thank you!" Noah says.

We chuckle.

"What time is it over there?" I ask.

"Four-thirty in the afternoon."

"Got it. Have fun."

"Tell my sis I called. Ask her to shoot me a text when her phone is charged."

"Will do."

I hang up and stare at my phone for a long while.

You need to shut out all thoughts she's a sexy woman. She's Cocoa Puffs, not damn dimples!

Since the house is too big for me to shout, I head upstairs to deliver Noah's message. I stride to the bathroom I designated for her. The door is ajar. A light cloud of humidity still floats in the air, but there's no sign of Keira. I trail to her bedroom. The door is closed.

I knock.

No answer.

I knock again.

I press my ear to the door, but it's quiet.

"Keira."

Still no answer.

I turn the knob and when I open the door my whole world unravels.

A sleeping beauty is curled up on her side completely naked and passed out to the world.

My eyes narrow, my pulse thunders, and my cock aches at the glorious sight.

Shit.

My jaw tightens.

Any tighter and my teeth will crack.

God, she's beautiful.

When she's sleeping like this, she isn't Keira the ball-breaking smart mouth. She's Keira, the sweet and vulnerable little lamb.

Stop staring, you fool.

Allowing my eyes to linger on my best friend's little sister's naked body is a speedy way to shorten my life.

My head gets it.

The rest of me?

Not so much.

If I stand here one more second, I'll come in my jeans.

Step away from the landmine.

I'm just about to close the door behind me when I notice her precarious position at the foot of the bed.

If she falls, that's gonna hurt.

I approach her and reach for the white towel she's sleeping on to cover her nakedness.

Damn, it's damp.

Maybe if I can just scoop her in my arms gently enough, I

can ease her further onto the bed and make her safe. I drop to my haunches, gently touch one hand to her shoulder.

Bad idea.

There's no escaping the softness of her skin against my fingers or the faint rumbling of her breath catching sharply in her chest.

God, I'd revel in the softness of her perfect skin.

Unable to help myself, I inhale deeply.

Notes from her lavender products tickle my nostrils.

My eyes fall to her perky, soft tits, capped with mouthwatering pink nipples. They're begging to be sucked. And by God, I want to be the one to suck them.

I can't help my gaze from traveling south.

A full bush.

It's not something you see often in LA. I like it on her.

I can just imagine sliding my tongue—

She's Noah's sister!

Not a conquest!

Get your head in the game!

Snapping out of it, I resume my mission.

I carefully slide one hand under her bunched-up shoulder, and...

I freeze when she lets out a moan.

"That's good," she says, "that's real good..."

She's dreaming.

Be still my pounding heart.

I'm about to try to move her when she suddenly stretches and I'm frozen once again.

"Yummy," she says and curls up again.

I wonder what she's dreaming about—cock or cake?

Get on with it, man!

Right. Focus. A little shove.

But no.

The sleeping beauty turns towards me, her breasts coming into view, so close, so beautiful.

So damn...

"Do that again." She wraps her arms around my neck.

Then she snores. Nuzzles her nose right in the crook of my neck and snores.

Jesus Christ!

If she wakes up now, I'm sure she'll scream the place down.

Crap.

Let go, dimples.

"No," she says and lets out a sexy-as-fuck moan.

Her plea travels straight to my balls, a reminder I've gone without for too long.

I need to get out of here. Now!

I give it another go, try to edge her back a little.

The outcome is the last thing I needed.

Keira's lips stroke my cheek, her soft, warm breath caressing my face.

Fuuuuck!

She moans again, sending tingles dancing through my balls and my cock swelling.

My pulse is racing, my breath ragged.

Wild thoughts cloud my judgment.

The beast inside of me roars for release between her soft legs, and I'm seconds away from giving in to the forbidden temptation when by a miracle of God, sanity hits me upside the head.

What the fuck are you doing?

If I don't escape this perilous situation, I'm doomed.

I ever so carefully untangle Keira's arms from around my neck.

She grumbles her displeasure, but thankfully, she's still lost to dreamland. When she rolls over and snuggles the pillow, I do a mental victory lap.

Mission accomplished.

My eyes land on a word tattoo I noticed when she was walking in front of me when I picked her up at the airport. I'm pretty sure I know what prompted her to etch her skin in ink, but we haven't talked about it yet. With everything that's happened today, it slipped my mind.

I grab the top sheet and cover her with it, but not before soaking in her blinding beauty one last time.

It's a dick move, but I can't help it.

I back away, my jaw tight and my cock hard as my eyes still linger on that peachy ass.

Once I'm outside her bedroom, I practically kick open the door to my own bedroom. Once I'm inside, I powerwalk to the bathroom, turn on the light with my elbow and close the door in a well-coordinated move.

I lean against the door, close my eyes, and hang my head low.

I'm a thirty-one-year-old successful executive, but you'd never know by the way I'm pining after my best friend's little sister like an awkward teenage boy.

I don't want to fuck Keira.

I don't want to fuck Keira.

Fuuuuck. I want to fuck Keira.

I've been crushing on her for years, but always managed to keep my desire in check. Noah's presence was the constant reminder she was the last woman on earth I should be lusting after. Now that we're living under the same roof—and Noah is nowhere in sight—I don't know what to do with myself.

I huff with frustration.

My cock is hard enough to cut diamonds.

I'm in agony, desperate for release.

I push off the door and strip on my way to the shower.

"Jesus." I groan as I pull my jeans and boxer briefs down my legs, freeing my eager cock.

I turn on the water and step under the rainfall showerhead.

Fuck, it's cold. Too cold.

I adjust the temperature to something more bearable.

I want to tame my dirty mind, not freeze my nuts off.

Warm water rolls off me as my eyes fix on my cock that's as hard as titanium steel.

I need salvation.

I slide my hand down the firm ridges of my stomach until my fist closes around my cock. I squeeze the head and groan.

My need is pressing.

My balls aching.

It won't take much for me to shoot my load because the sight of Keira's naked body is the most sinful thing I've seen in a long while. The image is permanently seared into my mind and safely tucked away into my spank bank.

I stroke myself, my hand pumping my fat cock at a frantic pace. I grunt every time my hand slides back up over my tip. With each stroke, the fucker seems to thicken and lengthen. This isn't the first time I've jacked off with Keira as the object of my desire—I've done it too many times to count—but this is the first time I've been within shouting distance of her while taking my pleasure.

I want her.

Bad.

I want her in my bed, her lips swollen from my ravishing kisses, her eyes hooded from having her pussy fucked, her body mellowed out from multiple orgasms. I want her on her knees with her pleading hazel-green eyes up to mine as she takes care of my cock between her luscious lips.

Scratch that.

After years of longing, I'd have no other choice but to fuck her sweet mouth until I explode in the back of her throat. She'd struggle to swallow every single drop of me.

One hand against the tiles, my fist tightens around my cock and I pump hard, twisting my palm at the head the way that always does it for me.

I stroke faster, eliciting a series of curses.

I'm no longer in control.

The buildup brewing at the pit of my stomach is intoxicating, causing my balls to pulse.

I stroke with more desperate determination.

"Shit," I say through gritted teeth.

My pulse races as I flash back to the carnal images of Keira from earlier—her in my boxer briefs, her in that sexy-as-fuck kimono and chemise, her with a towel wrapped around her chest, and her naked and vulnerable. My God, those pink nipples.

My hand slides up and down every thick inch of my cock. Each stroke is pleasure and pain.

I groan as I pick up speed.

So damn close.

So damn fucking close.

My balls tighten, heavy and ready to explode.

One firm stroke.

Two.

Three.

God.

"Oh, fuck, fuck, fuck."

I don't even recognize my own voice.

It belongs to another man.

One nearing the deep end.

One consumed by lust.

One who doesn't give a damn if his inappropriate thoughts fan desires he has no business having.

Goddammit.

The world blurs around me. There's only my desire for her and my throbbing cock ready to explode.

My hand moves faster, and I groan as my balls tighten.

My abs contract as a wave of pleasure washes over me. Growling like an animal, I explode, my release blasting from my swollen head. My body jerks, one leg trembling as every nerve ending comes to life in a furious rush.

"Christ!"

I brace myself against the wall to avoid falling to my knees.

Hot cum jets out onto the tiles in a translucent splattering gush as I suck in a long shuddering breath.

My head hangs down as the water pelts my back, my mind spinning as I struggle to regulate my heartbeat.

Then, reality slaps me across the face.

I'm still hard.

My much-needed release didn't even put a dent into the perverse thoughts still bouncing around in my head.

I doubt anything will until I have her.

If I have her.

"I'm fucked," I mutter.

I need to get my head out of my ass.

Noah asked me to watch over his little sister, not fuck her into oblivion.

Chapter 12

Keira

After what seems like twenty-four hours of blissful and uninterrupted sleep, I'm a new woman. I usually drink coffee to perk up, but this morning, I'm bouncing off the walls.

"Want another muffin?" Rhys asks.

"Yes, please! I'll have another almond poppy seed one."

"More coffee?"

"Absolutely!"

He gets up and heads to the counter.

I'm famished. I can't believe my jetlagged body wasn't even able to stay awake for dinner. Poor Rhys. After playing chauffeur all day, I ditched him for a pillow and the most comfortable bed I've ever slept in. And the dreams. Oh boy! I dreamed I was being kissed all over by some unseen hunk of hotness. I swear I woke up wet.

Rhys is back in no time with a tray.

He drops a latte bowl in front of me.

"Thank you!" I say, impressed. "This is so very French."

"I prefer my first coffee of the day to swim in a pool of

steamed milk, topped with a mound of froth," Rhys says. "A cup just won't do, hence the latte bowl. Not to mention, those French are pretty smart." He winks.

I swear that's the sexiest wink *ever*.

He sits down across from me at the kitchen table and grabs a bowl of coffee and a plate containing two muffins. He's already had a blender of healthy peach and spinach flavored smoothie. Then again, we had a rigorous workout this morning. That was exhausting.

I sat by the pool timing his laps while he did the actual workout. I did clap and cheer when he beat his previous record. That required just about as much energy as not ogling him in his sexy swim trunks. I admire the man's dedication. He was at it like a champ.

While he took a shower, I took care of breakfast. Thanks to his housekeeper and personal chef who keep his fridge and freezer full, it was a matter of warming up homemade muffins, pulling out fruits, and a couple jars of overnight oats.

Voilà!

It's good to be rich.

"Do you remember how to ride?" Rhys asks.

"I assume you're not talking about a bicycle?"

"Of course not." He rolls his eyes.

Rhys worships motorcycles. It's nothing unusual for someone living in California, but he takes it to another level.

"You can ride one of my bikes, and we can drive up to Malibu," he says.

I frown. "I haven't been on a bike in a while. Not to mention, I don't have any gear, and you always frowned upon riding without being suited up."

"You remember," he says, rewarding me with a huge smile.

"I remember everything my *amazing* teacher taught me."

Growing up, I had to do everything my brother and his best friend did. For my sixteenth birthday, Rhys got me lessons to learn how to ride a motorcycle. The lessons were great, but I much preferred when he was my teacher. Still, that present was a defining moment. I felt so grown up.

"Good girl. Noah's bike is in remote storage. He didn't want to leave his car or bike while he was renting the house. That said, he left his gear and yours in my garage."

Shock and surprise hit me at once. "He kept my gear?"

"He didn't want to get rid of it."

"Now I'm riddled with guilt." I wince.

When I turned eighteen, Rhys and Noah bought me my own bike and gear. A year later, I sold the bike to move to London with my best friend. I still remember the crushing look of disappointment on my brother's face. I suffered from tunnel vision at the time, so I didn't have the luxury to care.

Rhys reaches for my hand across the table.

I close my eyes, relishing the contact.

"Stop beating yourself up. You were going after your dream."

"And look where it landed me," I say.

He holds my gaze.

"Hey, I said stop beating yourself up. You want to go for that ride or not?"

I answer with a one-shoulder shrug. "Okay."

"That's it? That's all I get?"

I'm confused by his reaction.

"What am I missing?"

"Yesterday, you were on my ass to do something fun." A highly inappropriate visual flashes in front of my eyes. "Show me a little enthusiasm, woman!"

"Jeez, you're a tough audience, Hartford." I roll my eyes.

"Riding up the coast of Malibu straddling the finest piece of machinery money can buy is living the dream. It doesn't get any more *fun* than that, Cocoa Puffs!"

"Dimples. Call me, dimples," I say with my best James Bond impression.

"You kill me," he says with a laugh. "So, we're doing this?"

"Ride, baby ride!" I punch my fist in the air.

"That's more like it. If you're uncomfortable riding on your own, you'll ride behind me."

"Deal!"

He looks out the window. "Since the sun isn't beating down, threatening to melt the asphalt, this should make for a comfortable ride."

It's a rare gray Sunday, but I'm sure the sky will clear up in no time. This is Los Angeles after all.

"Let's make a day of it," he says.

"Yep, let's do it!"

As if I'll say no to riding behind Rhys with my arms wrapped around his body, absorbing his warmth with my chest pressed against his back.

~

"God, this view... even under the blanket of gray sky, it's unbelievable." I place a hand on my forehead and get on my tiptoes to soak in the beauty Mother Nature bestowed upon us Californians.

"It never gets old," Rhys says.

"No, it doesn't."

We're standing on the top of the world.

Okay, I'm exaggerating a little bit.

The ride from Manhattan Beach was stop and go. After an hour straddling a bike, Rhys needed a break to stretch his long legs. I was dying to use the bathroom. We stopped by King of the Sea for lunch. Fish and chip shops are a dime a dozen in London, but none of those eateries come close to this place. It's a quiet, quaint restaurant perched in a small alcove in the hills with a view to kill.

After a lip-smacking lunch, we stopped by O'Dwyer's Fine Ice Creams for dessert. Armed with a small cooler bag filled with ice packs and pints of ice cream, we decided to stop at one of the many rest stops along the Pacific Coast Highway to Malibu to enjoy our sugary treats.

I turn to face Rhys. "I can't believe I was able to live without this for three long years."

Say what you may about this state or this city, but good luck finding anything as breathtaking as this million-dollar view stretching as far as the eye can see anywhere else in the country.

"It's good to be back?"

"It's fucking good to be back," I tell him.

"Good." He offers a warm smile. "I'm ready for dessert. Let's go sit on the blanket."

There are people hanging out, but they're far enough away to give us some semblance of privacy.

"You've thought of everything," I say. I remove my armored motorcycle jacket and lower myself until I'm sitting on my knees. He takes a seat next to me. "Do you come here often with..."—I hesitate, pulling my lower lip between my teeth—"your girlfriends." I swallow the lump in my throat and avert my gaze.

"You have the balls to ask the question, but not enough bravado to look me in the eyes when you do?"

I'm sure my face is as red as a tomato when I muster up the courage to meet his gaze.

"Do you?" I croak.

He arches an eyebrow. "What's up with this new fascination with my love-life, Cocoa Puffs?"

"You're right. Ice cream first!" I say with a grin.

"You can be such a brat, Keira." He shakes his head.

"You still love me, though," I tell him.

He holds my gaze, and I shiver.

I can't read his expression.

I've teased him like this a million times in the past, but for some reason this feels different.

"You're lucky I've known you since you were in diapers," he says.

Not quite the answer I was hoping for.

He unzips the cooler bag and pulls out three pints and two plastic spoons. I got the Euro Praline Kick. It's the perfect blend of roasted hazelnut ice cream, Gianduja chocolate sprinkles, and French Valrhona Caramelia Pearls. Rhys opted for the Malted Crunch—dark Belgian chocolate sprinkles and crunchy malted milk balls. We also got a must have—Nothing Boring About It, dubbed the best vanilla ice cream ever.

I dig into my ice cream and shove a heaping spoonful into my mouth.

I close my eyes on a moan.

"This is insane!" I say. "Here, you absolutely have to taste this."

Without thinking, I scoop up a spoonful, lean over and force-feed Rhys.

His blues eyes are staring right at me as he wraps his mouth around the spoon. The sight is so sensual, my pussy throbs.

Dear God.

He unlatches his lips from the spoon, swallows the ice cream down and licks his lips. "Want some of mine?" His offer comes out in a low voice.

I simply nod because anything that might come out of my mouth would betray me.

He feeds me a spoonful of his rich chocolate ice cream. I swear to God, it's the most sensuous thing in the whole world.

The connection between us is so strong. Electrifying, even.

"To answer your earlier question, I don't really have girlfriends," he says out of the blue.

Aaaand... the moment is gone.

Shit.

"The next thing you're going to tell me is you're as celibate as a monk," I say.

"I never said I was celibate. *I said*, I don't have girlfriends."

I force down my jealousy long enough to ask, "Why not?"

"When I was in high school, most girls wouldn't give me the time of day. I was under Noah's protection, aka the football star's dumb sidekick who struggled to read because of his dyslexia. I'm not complaining because it allowed me to focus on what was important—becoming the best rapper on the planet. Once I signed a contract with a bona fide record company and I had a big fat advance lining my pocket, Dana came back into the picture—"

"Dana Mickelson?" I frown. "According to Noah, the pretty blonde every guy wanted in high school mocked your learning disability like so many idiots did, but he couldn't punch her in the face because she was a girl and my brother doesn't raise a hand to women."

"Yeah, that Dana."

His blue eyes turn stormy.

What did the cunt do?

"When I tumbled and my career was dropping faster than an elephant out of the sky, Dana was gone. She was done with me because I couldn't buy her things anymore."

"So, she latched onto you like a leech until you were no longer her personal ATM machine?"

"Pretty much."

I shake my head. "So much for stand by your man."

"After her, I was in and out of rehab, so a relationship was the last thing on my mind." He shrugs. "That's why." He moves his attention to his ice cream.

I do the same, weighing my words. "That was long ago. Now you're this big success story. Women must be tripping all over you. How else would you have earned your player nickname?"

"You really have been stalking me," he says.

"Just a tiny bit." I pinch my thumb and finger together and squint an eye.

He doesn't hide his amusement.

"In the past, I've struggled with challenges and life's setbacks in the worst possible way because I didn't know how to cope. I'd get fucked up real good on drugs so I didn't have to deal with reality. That's how I handled things when my career was being flushed down the toilet and the overwhelming feeling of only being capable of failing. I refused to accept my dad's death, so I showed up at his funeral strung out on a cocktail of drugs. I disappointed my mom and disrespected his memory. I knew it. I just didn't know how else I was going to be able to stand over Dad's casket as they lowered it into the ground. Building SCORE..." his words trail as his pained eyes meet mine.

"You don't have to continue," I tell him.

"No. I want to answer your question."

"Okay."

I hate bringing up bad memories, but I'm dying to know.

"Building a successful business felt like climbing Mount Everest *backwards*. That first year was brutal. It was extraordinarily stressful and overwhelming. Because I was clean, I was aware enough to understand it wasn't only about me anymore. It was about making my mom proud, keeping my word to the business partner who believed in me, and not letting all the staff we employed down. I couldn't get away from the day-to-day pressures or challenges by snorting cocaine, popping ecstasy, or uppers and downers to escape. When shit got too heavy, I'd hop on my Harley in the middle of the day and ride up the coast to breathe and clear my head. This rest stop is one of my favorites... the view and all."

"Oh, wow."

"After Dana, I promised myself I'd never let a woman make me feel like shit ever again. The circumstances in my life made it easy to avoid relationships."

"Just because she didn't stand by you when you most needed it doesn't mean all women are flighty."

"True, but Dana is one of many. Over the years, I've been used by a number of women who wanted to further their careers. They'd get close, then suddenly they're singing in the shower, slipping a USB stick in the pockets of my jeans or pants, emailing and texting demos, or bombarding me with links to their videos. In their mind, one night is sufficient to shoot their fame, fortune, and social status through the stratosphere. With SCORE, we're still on the fringes of the music industry, so there's no escaping the type."

"I'd like to say I'm surprised, but I'm not. I know the type. Those overnight-stardom-seekers pollute industry events. A guy who looks like you, with your reputation and your colossal success, would attract them like bees to a honeypot."

"Exactly. It gets old really fast. Thanks to Beckett, I've found ways to keep things *uncomplicated.*"

I arch an eyebrow. *Well, that couldn't be more convoluted.* "Care to elaborate?"

"It's not the kind of thing I can talk to you about."

"Why not?"

"Because."

"You can talk to me about anything."

"Not this."

I'm itching to push him to confess, but last night's blowup is still fresh in my mind. We're in a good place again, I don't want to open my big mouth and screw things up.

"Okay," I say.

A few tense seconds tick by.

"I've never invited any other woman into my sanctuary. You're the first."

"I'm honored." *And flattered. And giddy.*

I guess that gives me a leg up over whomever he partakes in *uncomplicated* with.

Take that, bitches!

"You should be." He play-punches my arm.

We laugh.

For a few long minutes, we enjoy our ice cream.

I look up to the sky.

"It's still really gray. It doesn't look like it's going to get any better today."

"No, it doesn't. If it starts raining, we'll head back."

I nod.

This has been a great day so far. It wasn't over-the-top crazy, but it was fun. And I get to spend it with him.

"I have a question," he says.

My eyes lift from my pint to meet his.

"I'm all ears."

"Why Nepal?"

"A few reasons. I'm not sure if you ever get used to the scrutiny of being in the spotlight. Just because you're a public figure, people think they're entitled to a piece of you. As if downloading one of your songs or buying one of your albums gives them that right." I shake my head. "It doesn't." I sigh. "Add to that the grim reality of being an artist these days—everyone is a photo away from becoming paparazzi fodder. It was suffocating, but I kept reminding myself it was all part of the fame-game. After the tragedy, I felt trapped living in London—"

"Fucking paparazzi," Rhys says.

"Yeah, that's the other reason I fled. A bunch of them became my shadows in the hopes I'd divulge how I was coping with the tragedy by hounding me. Bunch of leeches."

"Fucking paparazzi," he says again.

After many failed attempts here in the US, my best friend Chelle (Michelle) Camden and I left LA, determined to secure a spot on Superstardom's UK show. The number one singing competition television show at the time was turning nobodies into somebodies. Chelle and I desperately wanted that. We both made it to the top ten finalists on the other side of the pond, but watched heart-broken as the number one spot went to another singer. We figured it was over.

When the judge declared the top nine finalists were going to audition for a new girl group, we never thought the two of us would make the cut. Trinity Hughes and Henley Douglas were the other two girls in our group. Chelle and Henley, died in a car accident while they were trying to get away from pestering paparazzi chasing after them a few days after a scandal involving Chelle went viral. The news was devastating.

"The record label allowed very little time to mourn," I say. "They wanted me to get right back on the horse—"

"But you lost two members of your group, for God's sake."

"They felt two weeks was enough. They were ready to turn a girl band of four into a duet."

Rhys's jaw drops.

"I couldn't do it. They kept pushing, reminding me of the contract I signed, but my heart was weeping. I couldn't sing, let alone perform. Harry Bullard, one of the producers, offered to help me get over *the hump* by allowing me to seek comfort all over his dick—"

"Fucking asshole," Rhys says, shaking his head.

"That was my breaking point. I had to get the hell out of London. Coming back home wouldn't stop the paparazzi. As I was desperately trying to find a way out, I remembered you telling me about Jace's story."

"You took a page from Beckett's cousin's book?"

I nod. "I wasn't dealing with the reality of leaving rehab on the heel of a successful career as a rock star like Jace was. I needed to disappear, so I followed in his footsteps. Many connecting flights later to trick the press, I ended up in the same monastery he stayed at—the last place on earth anyone would ever think of finding me."

"That was brave."

"In hindsight, it was, since I didn't know anyone there."

"Did you get the tattoo on your back in London or in Nepal?" he asks.

Of course he saw it.

"In London. A couple weeks after the funerals."

He nods.

"It's a great homage," he says. "Tattooing the word *unique* is powerful."

"I think so."

"I really like how it runs vertically down your spine." The praise from him means a lot.

"Thanks."

"What's the flower?"

"A lotus sits like a crown on top of the U. It symbolizes self-regeneration and rebirth."

"Very fitting," he says. "Did it hurt?"

"Like a fucking bitch!"

He laughs.

"The artist started with the letters as a warm-up. U made me cry. N and I, I bit my lower lip and grimaced the whole time, praying to God it would be over soon. I could barely tolerate the last three letters, but I was determined, so I didn't back down."

"Good for you."

"I have no idea how you find the courage to have that many tattoos." I point at his arms.

"You get used to it."

"I'll take your word for it. I'm not doing it ever again."

"Never say never." He winks.

Sure.

I stare at him for a long beat, unsure if I should ask the question that's been burning my tongue for over a year.

"What is it?" he asks.

"Did you sleep with Chelle?" I whisper my question.

Rhys squints. "Wh—what?"

"Did you have sex with my best friend?"

His jaw literally drops open.

He tries to speak, but nothing comes out.

He's dumbfounded.

"Did you?" I ask again.

"Why the fuck would you ask me that?" He practically yells his question.

I jump.

I debate just how far to push this.

"Chelle said you had sex. Multiple times. And..."

"Spit it out!"

"And you were the first guy who..."

"Who what?"

I wince.

"Chelle bragged about how you were the first one to take her to the dark side."

It doesn't register.

"Anal sex." I spell it out.

"Whoa!" His eyes are enormous. "No! Hell no! Fuck no! That's outright bullshit!" he says. "Maybe there's a punishment when you correct the lies of a person who's passed away, but I'm not going to let this slide. I can't. I'm not sure of the context of that conversation, but I never had sex with Chelle. NEVER!"

I flinch, but soldier on.

"You wouldn't lie to me?"

He gives me a pointed look before tossing the pint of ice cream on the blanket, the spoon smearing chocolate all over the place. Anger rolls off him.

"She swore you did." I add the explanation in a rush.

He draws his eyebrows together. "When the hell did she tell you this?"

"A couple months before her death. Our friendship was strained, and we barely spoke to each other unless it was related to the group. On that particular day, she was in one of her prima donna moods, and decided to turn me into her whipping girl."

"Before you left... before the blowup—"

"Rhys..." I shake my head, remorse eating at me. "It was all my fault. I lost my shit and insulted you for being a friend."

"I warned you. Showbusiness and fame change you. Some people believe they'll remain unaffected when they make it big, but they're fooling themselves. When you become a star, you see the world differently. The world sees you differently. Chelle was an extreme case. All the baggage she was carrying didn't help when you couple that with instant international fame."

"No, it didn't," I say. "She was unrecognizable and unbearable in the end."

"Just so we're clear, I never slept with her," he says. "I had zero interest in her. She was your best friend, and that was the extent of my relationship with her."

"I guess she spat those hurtful lies in my face because I was trying to convince her this douchebag she was seeing was using her. She told me I was jealous and proceeded to rear-end me with her words. She even rambled on about knowing of the placement of many of your tattoos—"

"There are photos of me all over the internet. Not to mention she's saw me in swim trunks when I had parties at my place before my career went up in flames."

"Fair enough," I say.

Rhys places two fingers under my chin and locks eyes with me. "Chelle's story was fabricated," he says. "Do you believe me when I say I never had sex with her?" The sincerity shining bright in his eyes is unwavering.

I nod. "I do. Hearing it from you makes all the difference."

A familiar conflict surges in my chest when I think of Chelle, her sudden death, and how she betrayed our long-standing friendship. I mourn the girl I left LA with. I have issues with the spiteful, and frankly, bitchy woman she became in London. Chelle was well aware of my true feelings for Rhys even though I pushed him away and told him to stay away. After all, she was my best friend and confidant. She was devious enough to plant the seeds of doubt in my head.

"Good," he says.

He stares at me, his eyes shifting from mine to my lips.

His gaze is so intense, it ignites something inside me.

The seconds ticking away feel like years.

For a few suffocating beats, I pray he'll kiss me.

A loud bang jolts us and lightning forks across the sky.

"Oh shit." Rhys scrambles to his feet as raindrops start to fall. "Let's hit the road." He packs everything in a flash.

I stand up on unsteady legs, my mind still reeling, and my body still humming.

Thanks for nothing, Mother Nature.

Chapter 13

Rhys

It's bumper-to-bumper, as a swarm of vehicles crawl to their destination. The ride up to my little sanctuary was relaxing. The return home is a bitch.

The storm hit hard.

It's like the sky ripped open. A rarity for SoCal. We seek shelter, huddled with a few other people under the roof of the bathroom stalls. Not the best place to be. Half an hour after the rain subsided, I made an executive decision. Riding a motorcycle when the roads are wet isn't ideal. I don't plan on going fast, so we should be okay. The fact today is Sunday, plays in our favor. I'm a safe driver, but since Keira is the pillion rider, I'm extra careful. Thank God, I'm not dealing with an anxious novice. She shifts her weight, mirroring me on turns in perfect synchronization. It's as if we're one.

All my senses are on alert. My eyes are fixed on the road, watching out for potential threats. It's bound to happen since Angelenos can't drive for shit when the roads are slippery.

Keira is wrapped around me, her head pressed against my

back, her arms circling my waist, holding me tight as we travel at a safe speed.

Just as I'm thanking my lucky stars we'll make it back to my place in one piece, thunder roars and it's pouring again.

Fuck.

From the mirror, I spot the nose of a cargo truck gunning down the highway. Those motherfuckers are an annoyance on a sunny day. Worse on a day like today.

I curse.

I grip the handle of my custom Fat Bob tighter and steady it.

Even though the Harley-Davidson is a sturdy bike, I've never missed my SUV or one of my many cars more than I do now.

Time to get off the highway. Fast.

I move one lane.

Then another.

A row of bumper-to-bumper vehicles prevents me from moving one more lane.

Shit.

To my left, another cargo truck inches forward.

A bigger one this time.

The fucker zooms by us like a speeding bullet. In doing so, the 18-wheeler's tires hit a puddle, splashing enough water to fill a swimming pool straight at me. I mentally prepare myself, white knuckling the bike's handles, praying to God I keep my eyes open. My breath hitches from the impact against my visor.

Jesus.

My heart pounds and adrenaline shoots through my veins as I struggle to regain control of the seven-hundred-pound beast roaring between my legs.

If I let the bike fishtail, we're dead. Cars around me honk their horns, only adding to my stress. It's a tug-of-war for a few frightening seconds, but years of riding kicks my instincts into gear.

Keira's arms close around my chest like a vice.

At least, I haven't lost her.

The cargo truck is long gone and oblivious to its destructive wake.

Fucker.

When I see an opening, I change lanes.

I don't have far to go to reach the exit.

Thank God.

I rev up the engine and leave the jungle behind.

I spot a gas station and set course towards it.

Once I get there, I turn off the ignition and lift my visor.

Dirty water drips everywhere.

I look up to the sky and exhale on a prayer.

My father must've been watching over us because that was a harrowing experience. One I'm not looking forward to repeating anytime soon.

Fuck, I'm soaking wet.

I caress Keira's thigh, soothing her.

"Hey, you okay?"

She nods against my back.

"Get off," I tell her.

She does.

I do the same.

I remove my helmet and hook it on the bike's handle.

Then, I remove hers.

"You okay?" I ask again, inspecting her from head to toe.

She doesn't answer.

She's as wet as a kitten after a bath.

As freaked out, too.

Her eyes are as wide as plates.

Dammit.

I grab her shoulders.

She's shaking.

Shit, shit, shit.

"I'm so sorry about that," I say. "I guess we should've waited a little longer. That was a bad call on my part."

She blinks up at me.

She must be in shock.

"Keira!" I shake her hard.

She laughs.

Unrestrained, full, belly laughter.

I furrow my brows together. "What am I missing?" I ask.

"Holy shit!" she says. "That was scary. And freaky. And bloodcurdling. Even though I saw my life flash in front of my eyes, it was a hell of a rush. I'm still high. It was as exhilarating as stepping on stage for the first time."

She cracks up again.

Her laughter is the most beautiful sound in the world... after her voice.

Relief bursts through me that she's laughing and not crying.

"You promised me fun, and you delivered in spades, Rhys!"

Her girlish attitude is a throwback. And just like that, I'm fourteen and she's the excited six-year-old standing in front of me, grinning from ear to ear after completing her first round on roller skates without assistance. She's wearing the same wondrous expression. Noah and I used to drag her along to the matinee circuits at our favorite roller-skating rink when he'd wake up to find his mother's latest boyfriend in her bed.

"I have many talents, but that fun-filled adventure was courtesy of Mother Nature," I say. "Seriously, are you okay?"

"I might have to scrub my body for a solid twenty minutes because I swear dirty water is running down my back, but I'm okay."

"Nothing hurts?"

She wiggles like a ragdoll.

I can't help my laugh.

"Nope. I'm in tiptop shape."

"Let's get you home."

It's a long ride back to Manhattan Beach, but we make it safe and sound.

We hop off the bike and make our way to the house, leaving behind us a trail of wet footprints.

"I can't get over your eye-popping toys," Keira says as we pass my collection. "You have several millions sitting here."

"Crazy, huh?" I say. "It's unfathomable that six years ago I hit rock bottom and now I have a dozen-and-a-half luxury cars and a handful of pricey custom bikes lined up in my expansive garage."

Other than one bike I would've died for, I lost everything before entering rehab. Money, mansion, cars, friends, status, and dignity. All gone. My parents, Noah and Keira were the only ones who didn't turn their backs on me.

"Are you going to get your bike serviced?" she asks as we enter the house.

"Absolutely," I say. "No doubt top-of-the-line Harley Davidson bikes are built to weather whatever, but I don't want to take a chance. That was a lot of water."

"Yeah." She looks down her body. "And I'm still drenched in most of it."

I chuckle.

"I'm soaked down to my socks and boxer briefs."

"Same here, minus the boxer briefs," she says. She wipes the back of her hand across her forehead, smearing mud there.

When she looks down at her hand, she rolls her eyes. "It's all over my face?"

"Yup."

"I'm pretty sure I smell like mud, so why not have it all over, right?"

"I'm not faring much better. We're in this together, dimples," I tell her. "I'm sure I stink."

"At least we don't smell like *Eau de Vage*." My eyes hit my forehead. "Then we'd really stink."

I explode in laughter.

"You know what I'm talking about?" she asks, surprised.

"Sadly, I do," I say before laughing again.

"Is it the signature perfume of one of your *uncomplicated* hookups?" she asks with air quotes.

"That would've sent me running the other way." I laugh again.

Keira joins me.

"That awful synthetic scent is enough to convince any guy to become celibate for life," I say. "That's just wrong. It's a slap across God's face. You can't ever—and shouldn't try—to imitate a woman's natural, glorious scent—"

I groan internally when the words come flying out of my mouth.

Her eyes bulge out of her skull.

"Sorry. That was way too much information," I say.

What was I thinking?

That's the problem. I wasn't. She's so easy to be around, and so easy to talk to.

"Come on, let's get out of this wet and dirty clothing," I say.

"Good idea."

I walk to a basket tucked out of sight.

I unzip my leather jacket and peel it off my shoulders before dropping it in the basket.

My drenched t-shirt sticks to my torso like a second skin.

Unpleasant notes of my body odor tickle my nose, and I grimace.

Someone needs a shower.

"Leave your jacket in the basket," I tell Keira over my shoulder. "Since it's still early, we'll stop by a dry cleaner after we take a shower. If this stuff dries without proper care, it'll be useless."

"Sounds good," she says from behind me.

"We'll also take our leather pants. We'll make a pit stop to the cobbler for the motorcycle boots. Bring yours down when you've stripped out of them."

"Okay," Keira says.

I proceed to remove my boots and soaked socks.

Her presence looms behind me.

When I turn around, I bring my hand to my chest, fearing I'm having a heart attack.

Holy fucking hell.

"Wh—what are you doing?" I ask.

My eyes travel the length of her heavenly body.

Blood roars in my ears as my cock swells.

"I'm doing what you told me." She smiles sweetly.

"Huh?"

"You said to dump everything in the basket." She throws my words back in my face. Words I regret ever saying because the sight of her standing a little too close in nothing more than a wet t-shirt and a pair of pink bikini panties. Her white t-shirt does shit to hide her protruding nipples peering through her sheer bra.

The sight is making my cock drunk.

I just want to reach out, pluck them and twist them between my fingers until she moans in ecstasy.

"What's the point of going upstairs in wet clothes and

coming back downstairs with them?" she says. "By stripping now, I save your expensive wood floors." She leans in like she's plotting a conspiracy. "You're welcome."

"I would've cleaned the floors," I say in a gruff voice. "You didn't have to get undressed down here."

She waves a finger at her body. "You've seen me in a bathing suit plenty of times. In fact, I was in one this morning as you were doing your laps. What's the big deal?"

Yesterday's shopping trip was nearly the end of me. Underwear shopping and bikini shopping on the same day? A man can only take so much. And now, I'm paying the price.

Keira doesn't wait for my answer. That's a good thing, because my brain can't string a sentence together. She walks around me to the basket.

My eyes follow her.

She bends over, flashing me a majestic view of her ass.

My blood turns to fire.

She has the audacity to look over her shoulder, a sly grin stretching her lips.

Little cock-tease.

But fuck if I don't want to bite that ass. And then I'd let her ride my dick until her legs gave out—

Stop it!

It's official.

All rational thought has left the building.

Gone.

Done for.

Ladies and gentlemen, you're witnessing a guy unraveling faster than a knitter's yarn.

I really need to get laid so she doesn't affect me like this.

She straightens and stares at me, daring me.

As God tests my will, I stare back.

Our eyes lock, and the heat slowly reaches combustive levels between us.

A slow cocky grin stretches her lips.

I should register it's a precursor to no good, but I don't. I'm too consumed.

"Where do I leave the t-shirt and my underwear? I'll remove them now—"

"No!" I extend a hand to stop her.

"Relax," she says. "I'm pulling your leg. No need to get your boxer briefs in a bunch."

And if her gaze doesn't drop to the evidence of how my body reacts to her taunting.

Fuck.

My phone rings, putting an end to my torture.

I fish for it in the back pocket of my leather pants.

"I have to take this. It's Mom," I tell her.

"No problem," she says with a one-shoulder shrug. "Tell her I say hi."

"I will."

"I'm going upstairs to take a quick shower, and then I'm going to soak in your luxurious bath." There's amusement in her voice. "I love being your roommate. I kind of like us getting to know each other better."

And... she's off.

Little devil.

She saunters out of the transition area, humming a song, and wiggling her butt. I stand there ogling like a fool.

Forget about a cold shower.

I'm going to fill a bucket with ice and dip my aching cock and swollen balls for relief.

Chapter 14

Keira

That was a hotter-than-hell standoff.

The energy between us was sizzling.

It may have been my delusional and desperate mind in the past conjuring stories, but what just played out between us wasn't in my head.

It was real.

His bulge was very real.

It was impossible to ignore.

My heart is pulsating as hard as the throbbing between my legs. Heat pools between my thighs, leaving me tangled up in a knot of desire. I'm so wet, it's practically dripping down my thighs.

I push off the bathroom door, peel off the t-shirt and remove my underwear, chuckling at Rhys's freaked out expression.

Poor guy. I thought he was going to have an aneurysm.

I step into the shower and adjust the temperature of the water until the bathroom fogs up with steam. I duck under the rainfall showerhead and gasp.

It's scolding.

I play around with the temperature so I don't end up looking like a lobster. I shampoo, rinse, and condition in a snap. I then grab the mesh shower pouf we bought yesterday, pour a copious amount of peony scented body wash and scrub off the grime from the storm. Closing my eyes, I inhale the beautiful floral scent.

This is living.

The water streams down my body like a gentle caress.

My skin tingles.

Scratch that.

Every inch of me tingles.

Even though the water is warm, my nipples pucker to the point of pain. I press my legs together in the hopes of containing my mounting arousal, but it's in vain. I slide a hand down my body, caressing over my belly as I travel lower.

I pause, catching myself.

I can't do this under his roof.

That would be wrong. And a little perverted.

As I weigh the war raging inside me, his loaded words from earlier ring in my ears.

"You can't ever—and shouldn't try—to imitate a woman's natural, glorious scent."

The ache between my legs intensifies.

I squeeze my thighs together, moaning.

The recurring fantasy of Rhys bringing me to orgasm with his mouth is within reach. The realization is overwhelming. We've never talked about anything sexual before—other than him echoing my protective big brother's advice to remain a virgin until I was thirty.

We crossed a line today.

I need release.

The idea of solo-play under Rhys's roof is a little taboo. Unthinkable, even.

Fuck it.

My hand slides between my legs. When my fingers tease my pussy lips, I tilt my head back with a long exhale. Impatient, I stroke my engorged clit, moaning out my pleasure before applying more pressure.

Bless leather pants.

That was quite an eyeful. I was ready to drop to my knees and beg him to reveal what I suspect is a huge, thick, pulsing cock.

Damn.

I trace circles around my swollen, throbbing clit, relishing each revolution. I switch it up with rapid side-to-side movements before slapping my pussy, crying out with bliss.

A forbidden thrill courses through me.

I wish he were here with me under the spray of the water.

I'd wash his dirty parts... he'd wash mine.

I'd much prefer his hands against my clit, bringing me to orgasm. I'd return the favor with my hand pumping his cock. Unless he prefers me to use my mouth. I'm okay either way. The idea is so intoxicating, I place a hand flat against the tiles to steady myself.

I need more.

My fingers skate faster over my clit as I moan. I ease two fingers inside my pussy, sinking them all the way in, filling me. I let out a strangled cry at the intrusion as my muscles contract. I curl my fingers up and pump in and out in a slow, sinful rhythm.

This is so intense.

I've pleasured myself hundreds of times thinking of him, but he's never been this close.

I pick up speed.

I'm there. I'm so fucking there.

Dear God—

A knock at the door—just as I'm about to dive off the cliff—interrupts my naughty solo session.

"Keira!" Rhys's voice booms from the other side of the door. I almost shriek. "Mom invited us over for dinner tonight. Hurry!"

There's nothing like the mention of your fantasy's mother to kill a perfectly good orgasm.

Chapter 15

Rhys

A series of knocks breaks my concentration.

I lift my eyes to the ajar door.

Arianne pokes her head in my office. "You wanted to see me?"

"I did." I stand up. "Come in. Let's take a seat over there." I extend a hand.

"Okay."

She takes a seat on the couch in the comfortable sitting area located in the corner of my office. I sit across from her in one of the large leather chairs. She places her phone next to her before smoothing the fabric of her elegant light-blue dress before crossing her legs at the ankles. Her brown eyes fix on me expectantly.

"You look great, by the way," I say.

"Thank you." The beautiful blonde who has my business partner Beckett by the balls smiles wide.

I still can't believe it.

I leave the country for a little over three weeks, and forever bachelor Beckett Christensen is suddenly attached. I swear to

God, I thought Hell had frozen over. It just proves a leopard can change its spots.

"Thanks for carving out some time to meet with me," I say to kick start our conversation.

"Is this about the production side of SCORE Yours?" Arianne asks, suddenly nervous.

"No. It's not."

"But you still like the idea?"

"Two days later and I still love the idea!" I say. "It's a game changer for us and will help us kick it up ten notches."

"I'm glad you're still on board. I was worried that after sleeping on it, you might have second thoughts."

Arianne has a solid head on her shoulders and a great business mind. I knew she was an ace from day one. I never expected her to come up with a ground-breaking idea so quickly.

"I think the slogan will resonate really well with our audience," I tell her.

"That's my favorite part," she says.

"It's an attractive selling proposition—one our competitors can't make. Who wants to be like everyone else? Sameness is a crime."

"Exactly!" she says. "I just came out of a brainstorming session with Beckett and the marketing team. Everyone feels strongly that we need to milk this differentiating factor for all it's worth."

"Beckett texted me as you were making your way to my office. I agree."

The idea behind SCORE Yours is to take our kickass headphones and turn them into must-have gadgets—out-of-the-box top quality sleek painted headphones customized to our customers' taste. We're going to crush the competition. Simply obliterate them.

"Good!" She claps. "If this isn't about the new concept, how can I help you?"

"I have a female situation I need help with."

She knits her eyebrows in confusion. "You need my advice about a woman you're interested in?"

"No." I shake my head. "We're not talking about that kind of situation. We're talking about my best friend's baby sister—"

"That's more like it," she says. "You had me worried there for a minute."

"Why is that?" I chuckle.

"As if Luva Boy Rhys needs my advice about women. That'll be the day."

I lean forward. "Can I make a confession?"

She mimics my move. "It won't leave this room." She zips her lips shut with a hand gesture.

"I hate that nickname with a passion."

Her back stiffens. "Oh, I'm so sorry, Rhys." She places a hand against her chest and lifts the other one in the air. "I'll never say it again. Promise."

"Thanks." I wink. "Now, back to my problem."

"I'm all ears."

"Have you ever heard of a girl group by the name of Lucky Break?"

She stares at me, batting her eyelashes furiously. I can't read her expression.

"Maybe you've never heard of them. They were really big in the UK—"

"I lived in London for two years, remember?" she says.

"Of course."

"I was there when Lucky Break was topping the charts. Those girls were on fire. They were unstoppable. At twenty-nine, I'm a little older than most of their fans, but I'm guilty—and proud—to call myself a fan girl!"

"This makes this conversation even easier!" I say. "My best friend Noah's little sister, Keira—"

"Oh my God, are you talking about Keira Weatherly?"

"Yes, I am."

"The same Keira Weatherly who disappeared without a trace after the tragic accident?"

"Yes, that Keira."

Arianne is dumbfounded.

"Like I said, she's my best friend's little sister."

"Oh my God," Arianne repeats. "I can't believe this." She shakes her head. "The press was on a mission to hunt her down after she fled London, but she vanished into thin air. Was she in hiding in LA the whole time?"

"No. She wasn't. She arrived on Friday night. Today marks her third day back. She's staying with me."

"Your new roommate is a big singing sensation. Wow. Just wow."

I cock an eyebrow.

"Sorry," she says. "You're also a big singing sensation, and so is Beckett, but to be fair, I didn't know your music until you hired me. I know every single one of Lucky Break's songs by heart."

"You're forgiven."

She wipes the back of her hand against her forehead. "Thank God."

I cut to the chase. "Could I twist your arm to spend next Saturday with Keira?"

Arianne's face drops.

"If it's too much to ask—"

"Holdup!" She lifts a hand. "You want me to spend the day with Keira Weatherly? From Lucky Break?"

"Yes. I'd really appreciate it."

I tell Arianne about Keira losing her luggage and Saturday's shopping trip. I omit the part about how much it was a torturous experience for me.

"She got a few pieces, but there's so much more she needs. I'm not the best shopping companion. Keira's mom is dead—"

"Oh, I didn't know that," Arianne says. "In interviews, she's never really talked about her mother."

"It's a sore subject," I say.

"Got it."

"I'm the only one she has in LA. Her best friend Chelle—"

"The paparazzi can be such vultures," she says.

"They're not all assholes, but the ones who were after Chelle and Henley for a scoop are nasty parasites."

"I agree."

"Going back to what I was saying, I'm sure Keira will have a lot more fun if she goes shopping with a woman to buy whatever else she needs."

"I would be honored," Arianne says. "Can my best friend Phoebe Pedersen tag along?"

"Why not? It would be great for Keira to hang out with new friends."

"I know what it's like to land in a new city and not know a soul. It happened to me when I moved to Silicon Valley, again when I moved to London, and more recently, when I landed in Los Angeles. In terms of shopping, I had to start a wardrobe from scratch because my London-friendly clothing was a liability under this heat. I'm the perfect candidate for the job! Phoebe referred me to the best personal shopper in the city. She's great!" She waves a finger down the length of her body. "Case in point!"

"So, Keira is in good hands," I say.

"She's in *really* good hands."

"I can't thank you enough, Arianne."

"Don't thank me yet. Wait until Phoebe and I are done with her."

"I look forward to it." I smile wide. "I'll get Keira a credit card under my account so I'm not a bottleneck during your shopping excursion."

"Lucky girl," Arianne says.

"I promised her brother I'd take care of her."

"And it seems you're doing a damn good job of it," she says. "So many shops... so little time... so much money to spend..." She grins from ear to ear. "Is there a limit to your generosity?"

"Within reason," I say.

"That's entirely subjective, Mr. Hartford. I suspect your bank account is very different from mine."

I laugh.

"Fair enough. I'll let Keira know she needs to call me when she passes the ten-thousand-dollar mark."

"Whoa!" Arianne says. "That's not generosity. That's every girl's wet dream come true."

My eyebrows hit my forehead.

Arianne blushes.

"That came out wrong," she says. "I mean, a ten-thousand-dollar limit is an eye-popping amount. Well, for us mere mortals, it is. For you billionaires, I'm sure it's a drop in the bucket," she says with a laugh.

"Keira arrived with nothing."

"What about her things in London? She was always photographed in amazing fashion."

"She left everything behind. She doesn't want anything to do with that life anymore."

"I understand." She gives me a firm nod. "If she arrived without anything, that means she needs the basics like makeup, beauty products, and feminine protection."

I groan.

"Oh, sorry about that. I forgot that's a touchy subject for most men. To this day, my father freaks out when Mom asks him to buy feminine protection."

I offer an uncomfortable smile. "You'd know more than I would."

"Gotcha! We're starting from scratch!" Arianne grabs her phone.

"What are you doing?" I ask.

"Evernotes. It's a godsend," she says. "I'm a bit of an obsessive planner. I'll have Keira's shopping expedition mapped out to the minute. I'll share the master plan with Phoebe so she can add her insight."

"Whoa! This isn't like mapping out SCORE Yours," I say.

"Are you kidding me? I get to have a role in Keira Weatherly's new look. This is serious business."

"You're supposed to have fun," I remind her.

"Organization *is* fun."

I lift my hands in surrender. "Your call."

"Is it okay if we squeeze in a few hours of pampering?" Arianne's eyes bounce up to mine. "A new wardrobe requires a mani and pedi– Oh my God. She doesn't even have nail polish!"

I flash back to Keira's unpolished dainty toes.

I push away the tempting visual.

"Keira mentioned she might need a haircut—"

"I know the perfect hairdresser!" She runs a hand over her shoulder-length hair.

"I'm convinced," I say.

"But my hair is nothing like Keira's. She used to wear a lot of colorful wigs on stage, but she has the most beautiful hair—ridiculously long, full, and thick."

Not anymore.

I stand up, circle my desk, and snatch my phone.

"About Keira's hair..." I take a seat next to Arianne.

I swipe a few times until I find the photos we took on Saturday.

Keira wanted selfies of us to send to Noah.

I hand Arianne my phone.

Her eyes practically bulge out of her head.

"That's Keira Weatherly?!"

"That's her. She's the same gorgeous girl, but a lot has happened since she ran away from London."

"No shit," the words drop out of Arianne's gaping mouth.

Chapter 16

Keira

I let out a long, suffering sigh.

"I'm bored!" I say to no one in particular. I'm all by myself, kicking back in the seating area of Rhys's lounging pool.

I'm staying at one of the most luxurious mansions in Los Angeles, and I'm utterly bored.

I look around the stunning garden.

There's nothing to do!

"Booze it is!"

I stand up, climb up on the ledge, and pick up the tray.

My tropical fiesta is going well.

Piña colada number two really hit the mark!

I make my way back to the house, balancing the tray I'm holding with both hands. Rhys's shallow lounging pool has become my oasis. I usually wait for the sun to move west before taking up residence there for a few hours as I soak up vitamin D.

I enter the kitchen, singing a song and shaking my hips. I drop the tray on the granite kitchen island and stride towards the refrigerator, still dancing to the beat in my head.

My phone rings.

"Oh my God, someone cares I'm alive!" I say out loud.

Between the time difference and my brother's exhausting schedule, speaking to Noah has turned into a cat and mouse game. I hope it's him.

I rush to the tray where I left my phone. A smile stretches my face as I answer the video call.

"Hey, you!"

"Right back at ya!" Michaela grins wide.

"It's so good to see your beautiful face again!"

"Ditto!"

"Text messages are okay, but after living with you for two months, I miss the face-to-face," I say.

"Sorry. Getting back to New York has been a big fucking adjustment. I miss Nepal. I miss my freedom. I miss you."

Sadness veils her pretty green eyes.

"Is everything okay with your dad?"

She gives me a one-shoulder shrug. "He's still allowing my stepmother to walk all over him. I hate it when he does that. I hate her."

"I'm sorry, Michaela."

"Don't be. It's not your fault," she says. "On top of that, she's been barraging me about my hair. And she's nasty about it."

"Don't tell me, she's unable to appreciate your trend-setting and edgy haircut?" I say, running my hand over my short hair that desperately needs a proper cut.

"Pretty much. She's also fed up with the supposedly unbearable attitude I collected somewhere between Nepal and Thailand," Michaela says. "Dear Step-mommy wants to drag me to a shop to buy a wig."

"What?"

"Well, don't you know, short hair is a travesty on a pretty girl." The sarcasm in her voice doesn't go unnoticed.

"Err... I don't even know what to say to that."

"It's ridiculous! I'm twenty-three years old. She doesn't have a say on my haircut." Michaela's gaze moves away from the screen. She glances at the distance before locking eyes again. "As usual, she's talking out of her ass."

I laugh.

She joins me.

"Enough about my unpleasant stepmother. I want to hear all about your living arrangement with one of the hottest men in the country. How is it to shack up with Luva Boy Rhys?"

"Where should I start?" I tap my chin, pretending to think hard. "Should I start with the way I insulted him a few hours after landing in LA, and how he was so pissed off, he stormed out and left me alone in his house."

"What?"

"Or should I tell you all about stripping down to my sheer underwear and wet white t-shirt on Sunday after a hair-raising brush with death in my crusade to show Rhys I'm more than his best friend's little sister?"

"Holy shit!"

"Or should we start with my new reality of being nothing more than a Stepford wife, trapped in a big ass mansion with nothing to do, waiting for my husband to come home with the bacon."

Her face drops.

"You've been holding back on me," Michaela says. "Your text messages suggested it was a rocky start between you two."

She's right. I've been circumspect, unwilling to reveal too much. Partly because I'm still embarrassed by my attitude on the night I arrived.

"What you just described is what bad reality TV shows are made of."

Fact!

"Do you want to start from the beginning and fill me in?"

I spill my guts to my new friend.

She listens her eyes wide with amazement, firing a thousand questions my way.

"So, what's the plan for the rest of the afternoon?" Michaela asks when I finish my story.

"I took a cab to the grocery store and liquor store this morning to stock up. I was about to prepare piña colada number three, fill a bowl with more chips, and another with homemade salsa and guacamole to continue my tropical fiesta for one when you called."

"That really doesn't sound like much fun."

"It's not. I miss our structured life in Nepal." I let out a long sigh.

The nuns and priests at the monastery assigned tasks to everyone living under their roof. Even though we were there for introspection, the manual work was a welcome distraction. Along with a few other long-term guests, Michaela and I were in charge of tending to the organic garden.

"There has to be something you can do around the house," Michaela says.

"Rhys has a housekeeper who cleans from top to bottom, so it's not like I can contribute. He has a top-notch chef who comes in to fill his fridge and freezer, so it's a waste of time for me to use YouTube to learn how to cook '*A delish meal in 30 minutes or less*'. The groundkeeper and his crew keep the greenery well-manicured. The pool girl doesn't need my help. Not to mention, I'm pretty sure she hates my guts."

"What do you mean?"

"She gave me the evil eye when she saw me this morning

stretched out on the lounge chair, reading in the shade. I most certainly didn't appreciate her line of questioning as she tried to figure out who I was."

"Who the hell does she think she is?"

"Thank you!"

"She gets paid to clean the pool, not double as an investigator."

We may not have been friends for long, but Michaela always has my back.

"Tough luck, bitch. I live here. You don't."

We laugh.

"All that to say, every aspect of Rhys's life is well taken care off," I say. "There's only so much tanning I can take before I start feeling like a grape turning into a raisin. I rearranged my few belongings in the wardrobe half a dozen times already. If I don't find something to do, I'm going to scream."

"It's no surprise you're alone during the day, but what about evenings? Don't you spend them with Rhys?"

I shake my head.

"He's been working late for the past three days."

"But he comes home eventually."

"It's almost as if he has a sixth sense."

"What do you mean?" Michaela asks.

"I guess I was a little naïve and didn't fully understand Rhys's COO position. His schedule is as busy as the President's."

"But even the first in command goes home at some point," Michaela says.

"He comes back really late. I wait for him on the couch, but always fall asleep."

"What about the morning before he leaves for work? That might be a good time for you guys to connect."

"I swear to God, the man moves around like a ninja. Either

that or he leaves for the office before the roosters wake up. I usually wake up to an empty house."

"Text him and tell him you're eager to spend the evening with him."

"I already did that."

"What did he say?"

"He gave me an airtight excuse for his absence."

"Which is?"

"*We're gunning forwards with this new revolutionary project. It's eating more time than I expected, so I have to play catch-up at the end of the day.*" I pretty much memorized the message.

She furrows her eyebrows.

"What?"

"It sounds like he's avoiding you."

"I refused to admit it to myself, but you're right," I say. "After the bike ride, his mom invited us over for dinner. After getting ready, I met him downstairs in the kitchen and already, I could tell, something had shifted. His walls were up. I was so dead set on provoking him. Now I regret flashing him."

"Oh shit." My best friend's eyes are so apologetic.

"It's like I can't help it. I always find a way to screw things up with Rhys." I let out a sigh. "Maybe I misread him?"

"From what you described, it seems unlikely," Michaela says. "Women can fake it. Men can't."

"Now, I'm wondering if it's not an after-effect of our near-death experience. Maybe it was all the adrenaline rushing through his veins and bulging his manhood. Maybe it had nothing to do with wanting me. Argh!" I pull at my hair. "He says I'm hot-cold, hot-cold, but he's not much better."

"*Maybe* you should stop tap dancing—"

"I've done that. Many times. He always dismisses me. I don't even know why I bother keeping hope alive."

This is maddening.

Unrequited lust-slash-love sucks big time.

"Isn't it a good thing if he dismissed you considering you were a teenager when you first threw yourself at him? Only predators cross that line."

Okay, I might've been blinded by desire and I might've missed that important point.

She waves a finger at the screen. "Now that you have an extensive luxury collection of them, pull on your big girl *crotch-less* panties and—"

I burst out laughing. "Oh my God, that's hilarious."

"I'm just using your story, girlfriend," she says, grinning from ear to ear. "Like I was saying, tell him how you feel in no uncertain terms." She pauses. "If he still proclaims you two aren't meant to be, don't you think it's time for your heart to let go?"

Chapter 17

Rhys

Thank God it's Friday!

For the next two and a half days, I'll be able to think with my head... the one on my shoulders.

After dropping Keira off at Arianne's place in Marina del Rey, I drove straight to Golden Finger—the award-winning whiskey bar at the Quintus Hotel.

I'm a free man!

When I enlisted Arianne's help, I was hoping to catch a break from Keira's ever-present sexiness. I didn't expect it would turn into a weekend affair. Arianne wasn't joking when she said she was mapping things out. On Thursday morning, she declared after a long conversation with her best friend, it would be best if the shopping expedition started on Friday night since there's a lot to do.

I didn't argue.

Neither did Keira.

In fact, she was jumping up and down with excitement.

Throughout the week, she alluded to being lonely, longing for me to come home earlier at night.

Distance was my only salvation.

I take another swig of my drink, already feeling the tension of the week roll off my shoulders.

And what a week it's been.

Five days of unbearable hard-ons.

Five days of blue balls.

Five days of cold showers.

Five days of jerking off like an insatiable teenager.

In other words, five days of pure fucking hell.

Guilt nags at me for using work as a buffer between my eager cock and the object of my desire, but I'll do whatever it takes to avoid succumbing to temptation. At least I know she'll have fun this weekend.

"You're lost in thought, buddy." I lift my eyes to see a familiar face.

"Shane! What are you doing here?"

His gaze drops to my tumbler. "I'm about to follow in your footsteps."

"The only way to ring in the weekend!" I lift my tumbler.

He looks around before meeting my gaze. "Are you drinking alone or is Keira in the ladies' room?"

"I'm here alone."

"You left the pretty girl at home?" His bright blue eyes sparkle with curiosity.

"No, I found the pretty girl some girlfriends to hang out with."

He furrows his eyebrows.

"Have a drink with me. I'll tell you everything."

He takes a seat and motions for the waiter to bring him what I'm drinking.

The waiter wastes no time pouring three fingers of exquisite whiskey before sliding the glass in front of my friend.

"Here's to you spilling your guts," Shane says, lifting his glass.

"Here's to you being my sounding board!" I clink my glass with his.

"That sounds heavy."

I nod. "You have no idea."

We both take a long swig of our drinks.

"What's weighing on your mind?" Shane asks.

"I'm fucked." There's no point in sugar coating it.

"Keira?"

"Keira."

He laughs. "I could've told you that at the airport."

My head jerks back from his admission.

"What are you talking about?"

"The expression on your face as you were hugging her suggested there was a lot going on between you," he says. "Is there?" Leave it to Shane to cut to the chase.

"It's—"

"Don't say it's complicated. It's a given. You wouldn't be sitting here mulling things over if it wasn't."

"Fair enough. I won't bullshit you."

"I appreciate it," he says. "Before we dive right into it, I have to ask. What happened to Keira? She looks dramatically different."

I tell him what I told Arianne.

"That explains it," he says. "You have the hots for your best friend's baby sister."

My eyebrows lift to my forehead.

"It was a wild guess. I didn't expect to hit the nail on the head."

I run my fingers through my hair. "Well, you did."

"If that's the case, what's the problem?"

"Noah."

"Isn't Keira an adult?"

"She is."

"Is it unrequited?"

I shake my head. "It's not. She's made it clear in the past she was interested. Since she was only sixteen at the time, I dismissed it as a teenage crush. I was already a grown man. No way was I going to lead her on or even consider looking at her that way. But Keira is persistent. She became a hell of a lot wittier at finding ways to catch my attention as the years rolled by. My blinders were safely on, so I was somewhat oblivious to her advances... well, that's what I told myself." I pause. "Frustrated, she stole a kiss to drive her point. Sure, she was eighteen at the time, but she was still Noah's little sister. On top of that, the age difference was still a factor, I was just getting my life back on track after rehab, and Beckett and I were just starting SCORE. I was juggling a lot of balls. That was simply too much baggage for such a young woman—"

"Did you tell her?"

"I did. After the kiss, I pushed her away and told her it could never happen again. She gave me the silent treatment for six long months. When Noah told me she was leaving for London to pursue a music career, I thought I'd give her some advice to prepare her for the reality of a business that can be unkind and cruel. Let's just say, she wasn't receptive."

"You have history together," Shane says.

"A lot of history. Which is why I was uncertain about her living with me. After three years of tension and distance, I wasn't sure how it would play out between us."

"Are things tense?"

"The first night they were. So much so, I had to get the hell out of my own house. I needed space."

"Is that why you're here now?"

I shake my head.

I tell him about Keira spending the weekend with Arianne and Phoebe.

"I see. You have the weekend to yourself."

"Yes. I can think freely."

"Think about what?" he asks.

"How to navigate this thorny situation. She's going to be living at my place for a while."

He nods a few times, but doesn't offer a response.

I polish off the rest of my drink.

He does the same.

"Do you want her?" Shane asks.

His frankness doesn't surprise me.

I ponder his question for a beat.

My wet dreams kept me company all week long. After sliding into bed, I'd imagine her...

Under me.

Beneath me.

On top of me.

Surrendering to me.

I shake my head.

"I'd be overstepping my boundaries," I say.

"That's a roundabout way of answering my question," Shane says.

I'm being evasive for a reason. It's one thing to admit how I feel about Keira to myself, it's another to admit it to someone else.

"There's still the age difference," I tell him.

Shane chuckles.

"What's so funny?"

"In a town like LA, eight years is hardly an age difference," he says.

"She's still Noah's little sister," I say. "There's something called the bro code amongst guys. Breaking it is sacrilege."

"It's clear your best friend is protective—"

"Very. He doesn't want his baby sister to end up in the same toxic merry-go-round of bad relationships like their mother."

"I totally understand where Noah is coming from. If I had witnessed the things he had, I wouldn't want my sister involved with an asshole or a douchebag who takes advantage of her and treats her like shit."

"Exactly."

"You're neither an asshole nor a douchebag," he says. "From the sounds of it, you treat Keira with a lot of respect... and care. You're a solid guy. Someone Noah trusts—"

"Hence the problem."

He shakes his head. "No, that's not a problem. You're using that as an excuse—as a false barrier. Same for the age difference and whatever else that's been incubating in your overactive mind as obstacles." He allows for a pregnant pause. "You want her? Go after her. Plain and simple."

Chapter 18

Keira

"Truth or dare?" Arianne's mischievous brown eyes hold her best friend's gaze.

"Truth!" Phoebe answers before drinking a gulp of her cocktail.

"How was your first time?" Arianne asks.

"Awful!" Phoebe says before brushing her shoulder-length dark-brown hair behind her ears. "He was my age, and he had no idea what he was doing. He fumbled a bit with my lady parts and then rammed into me like a missile. It hurt so much, I cried. Two minutes later, he was calling out God's name, and I was praying for it to be over. Not that I could guide him, but even I knew, I had been shortchanged."

"Ditto," I say before taking a sip of my drink.

"Mine didn't fumble his way around because he was older... but now I know, he knew shit about sex!" Arianne says, disgust painted all over her pretty face.

"Hello!" Phoebe lifts a hand over her head.

They high-five each other.

Clearly, there's something I'm missing. That said, I'm a little too buzzed to bother asking.

We've long lost count of how many drinks we've had, but since we're partying at Phoebe's house after a long day of shopping, it's all good. It's just us girls. Her boyfriend didn't want to be in the way, so he's crashing at his brother's house.

Last night, over pizza, Arianne and Phoebe drilled me with questions about my former career. I answered all their questions. They were total fan girls. They oohed and aahed, wide-eyed and amazed. Secretly, it was adorable.

Tonight was barbecue night. With our bellies full, we've moved on to the entertainment part of the evening—the mortifying embarrassment of playing truth or dare. We're sitting on the floor, circling the oversized coffee table weighed down with unfinished drinks and too many desserts for three people. We've already exhausted the list of fun and safe questions. As the evening progressed—and Phoebe kept the cocktails flowing—the questions became a lot more interesting.

"Your turn, Ari," Phoebe says. "Keira, you ask the question." She hands me the iPad.

I scroll through the list of questions until I find a more risqué one.

"Ready?" I ask Arianne.

"I'm an open book. Just flip the pages till you get to the good parts," she says, giggling.

We laugh.

We're a bunch of happy drunks.

"Truth or dare, Arianne?"

"Truth!" she says. "I didn't like the last dare."

"Have you ever watched another couple have sex?" I ask. "Porn doesn't count." I just threw that last part in there to add a little spice to the evening.

"Oh, that's an explosive one." Phoebe's eyes widen.

"No," Arianne says. "But..." She leans in and motions for us to mimic her. "This doesn't leave this room." He circles her finger between us.

"My lips are sealed," I say, even though I have no idea what's about to come out of her mouth.

"I'll go to my grave with your secret," Phoebe says.

Arianne looks left, then right.

Maybe she's a little too tipsy to remember no one else is in the house.

"Beckett says there's a room dedicated to exactly that at Dark Compulsion. You can watch couples get down and dirty all night long." She straightens and waits for our reaction.

"What's Dark Compulsion?" I ask.

"An exclusive high-end adult club hidden behind the Quintus Hotel, where the crème de la crème goes to play," Arianne says. "Beckett is a member... so are all the guys in his entourage."

Whoa!

"Ooohhh!" Phoebe's brown eyes are huge. "Kinky! I like it!"

My cheeks flush as my mind conjures some pretty X-rated scenarios involving a strapping, tall roommate with gorgeous blue eyes and sexy body art.

"Is Rhys a member?"

Shit.

I blame the alcohol for that lapse in judgment.

Talk about outing yourself.

Arianne cocks an eyebrow. "Are you two...?"

"Yeah, I've been wondering about that as well since yesterday. Are you banging the one-hit wonder turned COO?" Phoebe asks.

"Phoebe!" Arianne looks horrified.

"What?" Phoebe says. "Just because I have the courage to ask the question you're too chicken to ask, doesn't mean you should reprimand me."

"I did it with a lot more tact," Arianne says.

"My question is legit," Phoebe says. "Why else would Rhys finance Keira's shopping trip?"

"That's none of your business, Phoebe Pedersen." Arianne frowns her discontentment.

They're talking as if I'm not in the room.

"He's like a big brother," I tell them. "And remember, I landed in LA without much."

Phoebe shoots me a suspicious side gaze. "I can assure you, my brothers would never finance a shopping spree to the dollar store, let alone high-end designer shops. Had I landed somewhere in the world with nothing more than a backpack and the clothes on my back, my brothers would've recommended I hit thrift stores."

I can't help my laugh.

Phoebe is hilarious, and she has zero filters.

"You just don't know when to quit, Phoebe," Arianne says. She moves her attention to me. "To answer the question that started this inappropriate line of questioning..." She glares at Phoebe.

Her best friend shrugs.

"I didn't ask Beckett if Rhys was a member or not. I assumed he was since all the guys hang out together."

That's where he finds his *uncomplicated* hookups. Noted.

"I was just curious." I shrug, doing my best not to look affected.

"If I'm not allowed to ask about her relationship status with the billionaire mogul, can I at least ask about something intriguing I read online about him?" Phoebe asks Arianne.

"As long as it's not a personal question," Arianne says.

"Thank you, Mom."

Phoebe's mocking tone and facial expression crack me up.

She shifts her focus to me. "Is it true Rhys started rapping, and I quote, *As a personal challenge to prove I was more than my dyslexia. It was a middle finger to the condition that robbed me of my confidence*?"

"Oh yeah, I read about that as well," Arianne says, a glint of curiosity shining in her eyes.

"Rap music was Rhys's metaphorical *fuck you* to his neurodivergent disorder," I say. "He struggled with words. Rap music is a flurry of words coming at you in rapid succession. Mastering rap was his way of taking control."

"Interesting perspective," Arianne says.

"Unlike a book, he could memorize words of a rap song," I say. "He's still dyslexic—he'll always be. It's not a disorder he can ever change or get rid of, unlike his stuttering—"

"He used to stutter?" Arianne asks.

"My earliest memories of Rhys don't include his stuttering, but according to my brother, it was pretty bad," I say. "That's how they became friends. Noah came to his rescue when two bullies were using Rhys's face as a punching bag. Noah fought them off and then swore he'd look after a scrawny Rhys. Thanks to his mom's crusade, Rhys gained control over the stuttering, but dyslexia is something he'll have to deal with for life. Reading was always a challenge for him, something he hated because it reminded him he wasn't like everyone else. To cope, he became really good at memorizing what he heard—from other people, the television, the radio, or music. When he discovered rap, it was like a whole new world opened up to him. He'd listen to the lyrics over and over and over again. When he discovered he shined at it, he started seeing himself in a new light. Noah said rap music changed him from an awkward shy guy to a bold, cocksure, and confident man. Even his stage name—Hijinks—reflected that cocky side of him that was hidden behind his insecurities."

"What a story!" Phoebe says.

"Is Noah the same age as Rhys?" Arianne asks.

"Yes, they're both thirty-one. They were ten years old when Noah became Rhys's defender."

"Ten?!" Arianne asks. "Isn't that young to have the ability to fight off two bullies?"

"Noah was the Hulk-in-the-making from the womb. My big brother is six-seven."

"Whoa!" Arianne's eyes bulge out of her skull.

"That's a venti cup of goodness," Phoebe says.

"Rhys's stuttering and dyslexia made him an easy target. Noah taught him how to fight and defend himself for the times he wouldn't be around. Thanks to my brother, he was able to go from a weak defenseless kid to a fearless warrior"

"That's true friendship," Arianne says. "Is your brother in the music industry as well?"

I shake my head. "Along with being my big brother, Noah became my guardian at a young age—"

"What?" Arianne stares at me, incredulous.

"When our mom died, our maternal grandmother became next of kin. When she died, Noah was forced to give up his NFL dreams. He had everything to make it pro, but I was a kid when we lost our last living relative."

"What about your dad?"

"Our mom was a single mom." I give her a sanitized version of the truth.

Phoebe nods. "Got it."

"Had Noah not being of age, we would've ended up in foster care. He wasn't even old enough to buy liquor, but he became a parent. My big brother hung his cleats and took on odd jobs to put food on the table and keep a roof over our heads. I was only thirteen, so I couldn't contribute. Not that he would've let me if I could. He wanted me to focus on school."

"He carried a lot on his shoulders," Arianne says.

I nod. "I liked to tease him and say that God gave him broad shoulders for a reason."

Arianne and Phoebe offer a warm smile.

"What kind of work did he have to do to get by?" Phoebe asks. "He didn't have much experience at the time. It must've been grunt work."

"My big brother worked in the movie and TV industry because the hours were flexible. Since he was below the line, aka he was part of the crew of people that moved stuff around on a set, the work didn't require overtime. Over the years, he collected a bunch of online degrees and worked his way up the food chain. Now, he's a special effects supervisor for UTV.com."

"Both Noah and Rhys are resilient," Phoebe says.

"Yes, they are."

"Your brother will never know what kind of football career he could've had, but in terms of second career, he landed in a pretty good spot. Same for Rhys."

"You're right, Arianne. When Rhys lost his fame status, he thought it was over for him. Nothing would ever measure up to that defining one-hit. The massive success of SCORE proved him wrong." I try hard not to gush.

"Hence, why he can now afford a membership at an exclusive sex club!"

Arianne and I explode in laughter.

Leave it to Phoebe to come to that conclusion.

"I guess so," I say.

"Speaking of kinky hangouts, I'm totally adding Dark Compulsion to my bucket list!" Phoebe says, clapping.

"Sorry to burst your bubble, but you'll need a black American Express card to pay for the membership," Arianne tells her.

"We can always use hers?" Phoebe points at me.

My head whips in her direction. "Hell no. Rhys would kill me."

When Rhys handed me the card on Friday, I nearly passed out.

"I'm okay with him killing you as long as I get the membership," Phoebe says.

I play-punch her arm. "Hey, I thought we were friends?"

"We are, but I'm dying to know what happens at that club," she says. "If you have to be a casualty, so be it."

I roll my eyes.

"Let's keep the game going," I say.

"Well, it so happens your head is on the chopping block next," Phoebe says, grinning from ear to ear.

I hand her the iPad.

She scrolls through the list of questions from a quirky article she found on the internet. "Truth or dare?" she asks me.

"Hold on, I need liquid courage for this." I take a quick sip of my drink. It's a lot more fun to drink piña coladas amongst friends. I drop my glass on the table and ready myself. "Okay, hit me!"

"I already asked you a question," Phoebe says.

"Oh yeah. Truth!"

"What's the sexiest thing someone has ever said to you?" Phoebe asks.

You're fucking perfect to me.

I don't have to give it a second thought, but I never get to voice it because my phone rings.

If it isn't the sweet talker…

"It's Rhys," I tell Phoebe and Arianne. "I'll take it. After all, I should thank him for allowing me to spend all his money."

They laugh.

"While you're at it, can you talk to him about *my* membership at Dark Compulsion?" Phoebe points an animated finger over her head.

"You're crazy," I tell her.

"No, just persistent."

"That, too," I say. I answer Rhys's call. "Hey."

"Hey," he says.

I get up and gesture to my new friends I'll be outside.

They nod.

"Am I calling at a bad time?" he asks.

"No." I step in the backyard and close the side door behind me. "This is good."

I got a text from him last night, but this is the first time we've talked since yesterday afternoon. When he suggested a sleepover at Phoebe's, I jumped at the chance—anything to avoid the uncomfortable vibe that's settled between us.

"How was day two of shopping?" he asks.

"You mean, my ten-hour whirlwind cash-spending extravaganza?"

"That answer scares the shit out of me."

I laugh. "Don't worry. If I reach the limit on your American Express Black, I'll be forced to stop."

"There is no limit."

"Oops!"

He groans.

"Kidding!"

"You had me worried there."

"Just keeping you on your toes," I say.

He chuckles.

"No one pestered you?" he asks.

That was my big concern.

"No. No one recognized me. I went incognito today. I used a baseball cap to hide my face, and I asked Phoebe and Arianne to call me by my middle name, Eve, instead of Keira. Small things that make a big difference."

"Good," he says.

"Funny, there was a time, that's all I wanted—to be recognized—now, I want the complete opposite."

"You just need time to ease back into it."

"I'll be skittish for a while."

"There's no rush," he tells me. "You're back at Phoebe's?" he asks, changing the subject.

"Yup!"

"What are you girls up to?"

"We were going to go out to a salsa club, but we're pooped from running around," I say. "We decided to stay in. We've been drinking and playing truth or dare."

"God save us all."

I ponder for a fraction of a second before diving right in... liquid courage and all.

"Have you been avoiding me all week, Rhys?"

Silence.

I answer for him. "You have been avoiding me."

"Let's get on a video call."

My stomach twists in a knot at his suggestion.

Shit.

I should've kept my big mouth shut.

"Okay," I say.

A second later, his handsome face fills the screen.

"Your hair hasn't changed."

"Tomorrow is spa and hair day."

"Got it."

We stare at each other for a beat.

"Aren't you going to answer my question?"

His lips twist. "I was avoiding you."

I hang my head in defeat.

"You did nothing wrong. It's all on me," he says. "There's something between us."

He's going to let me down gently.

"Okay," I say.

"Okay?" he looks offended.

"What do you expect me to say? I don't know where this conversation is going."

"Fair enough. I'm the one who called." He pauses. "Last Sunday, after the bike ride—"

"I shouldn't have flashed you. I'm sorry."

I hide my face in my hand.

I mentally prepared myself and thought I would be able to handle another rejection, but my heart is already breaking.

"I'm not sorry."

I lift my eyes up to the screen.

"You're not?"

"I'm not," he says. "My only regret is not manning up."

"Huh?"

"I'm not going to rehash the past, because we're in the here and now."

That was German to me.

"I was thinking we should go out for dinner tomorrow night."

Dinner?

That's not what I expected.

The flicker of hope dies, and my heart sinks again.

"That sounds good," I say, incapable of mustering an ounce of enthusiasm.

"Since we live together, it's easy to do things backwards..."

I frown my confusion. "I don't follow."

"I want to take you out on a proper date before we explore what's been playing out between us since you arrived."

I'm pretty sure I misheard him.

"A date?"

"A date."

"As in a date-date?"

"Yes. As in a man taking out a woman he's unreasonably attracted to for a nice meal at a fancy restaurant."

My heart climbs into my throat.

"Are you shitting me right now?"

"Okay, that's not the reaction I was expecting," he says. "Perhaps I was reading into things—"

"Don't you dare back out, Rhys Hartford. You know exactly how I feel about you." I pause to catch my breath. My heart is beating so fast. "But this is— I mean— Holy shit— Just, wow."

He bursts out laughing.

"I've been thinking—"

"Obviously! And for the record, I like how you think."

His glacier-blue eyes meet mine, and I swear my pussy flutters.

"What am I going to do with you, dimples?"

Keep me?!

"I can keep avoiding you or we can dive in with both feet."

"I vote for the latter."

I'm so elated, I could fly.

His grin is epic. "We're on the same page."

I worry my bottom lip, debating if I should ask the question burning my tongue. I have a tendency to put my foot in my mouth when it comes to this man, and I don't want to ruin this perfect moment.

He narrows his gaze.

"What is it?" he asks.

"What about Noah? He's still my big brother, and that's always been a deterrent for you."

"Not anymore."

"It's not?!"

"This isn't about Noah and me... this is about *us*." The lust radiating from his eyes is so searing hot, it could set my body ablaze. "If you want to go out on a date with me, that's all that matters—"

"I *definitely* want to go out on a date with you," I tell him. "I've been waiting practically my entire life to go out on a date with you. I'm fucking excited to go out on a date with you!"

He laughs his head off.

"Seriously though, should we tell Noah?" I ask.

"We'll cross that bridge when we get there."

"Okay."

I can finally put years of repressed emotion behind me.

He flashes me an arresting smile.

"What?" I ask.

"You've always had this strange effect on me, Keira. On one hand, I want to fuck you senseless. On the other, I want to protect you from guys... even me. I no longer have to be torn or feel guilty for having inappropriate fantasies about you."

I'm temporarily paralyzed in a stupor.

"You fantasize about me?" I croak when my brain kicks into gear again.

He nods.

Holy. Fucking. Shit.

A hot flush of heat crawls up my neck and my cheeks burst into flames. My pulse hammers in my neck and I squeeze my thighs together, trying hard to suppress the sweet ache growing between my legs.

"There's nothing stopping me now. I finally gave myself permission to have what I want... and that's you, dimples."

His confession is so enormous it wrings the air from my lungs. I simply stare at him wordlessly as my lips part in an O.

I'll never forget this defining moment for as long as I live.

Rhys and Keira... finally!

Chapter 19

Rhys

Where the hell is she?

I'm at our meeting spot. Waiting. Worrying. Eager.

For our first date at the upscale steak house at the Quintus Hotel.

I run my hand through my hair, cursing under my breath.

I should've picked her up.

Keira has been texting me every five minutes. She's close, but that does little to ease my worry. She's already forty minutes late for our date. If I didn't know better, I'd think she stood me up. I wanted to pick her up at Phoebe's so she could stuff her purchases in my trunk, but she insisted on meeting me at the restaurant. Something about wanting to surprise me. I didn't push, but now I regret it.

After an afternoon of pampering, Arianna, Phoebe, and Keira were caught in a never-ending gridlock caused by a catastrophic accident that closed a major artery. Since Keira had to return to Phoebe's house to grab her stuff before coming to meet me, it only made matters worse.

I'm just about to shoot her a text to get an update, when I spot a gorgeous woman striding to my table.

I do a double take.

Keira?

Holy transformation!

Since she arrived in LA, Keira has been hanging out in a bikini, unless she's sporting her trademark short-shorts, t-shirts, and flip-flops. The stunning woman smiling at me takes my breath away.

I stand up to greet her and take her in.

From the arresting design of her dress, to her silver strappy high heels, to her dainty toes painted in the same hot pink shade as her dress, to her barely there makeup that enhances her beauty, and the diamond studs that pierce her ears. Keira looks like the woman of my dreams.

"You made it safe and sound," I say.

"I'm so sorry for being this late, Rhys. This is so embarrassing." A remorseful expression morphs her beautiful features.

"You're here now and that's all that matters."

"God has a funny sense of humor."

"What do you mean?"

"After waiting years—and I mean, years—to grant my wish, *He* orchestrates a freaking nightmare of an accident that causes me to be forty-five minutes late for my first date. Sheesh. You'd think God would show me a little compassion. But *noooo*, *He* decides not to cooperate. Tardiness isn't sexy." She lifts her eyes to the ceiling. "Not cool, God. Not cool."

She's talking super fast, and it makes me grin.

I tap the tip of her nose.

"I wasn't going anywhere, dimples. I would've waited all night long, if I had to."

She giggles like a schoolgirl.

I lean in and whisper in her ear. "You look absolutely ravishing and if I didn't think we'd draw too much attention, I'd kiss the hell out of you."

I pull away and take pleasure at the blush creeping across her cheeks.

"It's the new me... courtesy of you," she says. "Two and a half days of shopping? A girl can't ask for much more. I'll never be able to thank you enough." Her sincerity is touching. "And thanks for the compliment." She smiles. "You look pretty hot yourself." She eats me up with her eyes. "You wear a suit so well you should be forced to walk around with a license."

I laugh.

"Thanks, but I'm not the one causing heads to turn. You are," I tell her. "I love everything about the new look."

"You do?"

"I do."

"Check this out! Pockets!" she says, sliding her phone out. From the way her hand shakes, I'm guessing she's a little nervous. "If tuxedos have pockets, cocktail dresses should receive the same treatment."

"You're hilarious, as usual."

"There's nothing usual about tonight."

"You're right, dimples," I say. "The new hair color suits you."

"Thanks. That took a lot of convincing."

"Why the reticence?"

"In a city like LA, being a blonde is a foregone conclusion. It's something that never appealed to me. According to Phoebe's hairdresser, blonde is the only way to go with my short hair. He was adamant. Both Arianne and Phoebe had to lobby pretty hard."

Her shapeless cut has been replaced with a cover model

hairstyle—short and tapered in the back with longer layers on the top of her head.

Unable to resist, I comb my fingers through her silky soft strands. "I love the hair."

"I love it, too."

"The blonde brings out the gold in your hazel-green eyes," I say. "And the purple and gold shades of your eye shadow make your eyes pop like crazy."

"I agree," she says in a small voice.

"Are you turning shy on me?"

"Maybe a little."

"Come on, you've known me forever."

"I have a thousand butterflies fluttering in my belly. I'm that nervous," she says. "I still can't believe this is happening."

Tracing her chin with my fingertip, I say, "It's happening, dimples."

She places a hand over mine, and smiles.

"This dress on you..." I let my words trail as my gaze travels down the length of her body, appreciating every delicious inch of her.

Keira is clad in a hot pink dress with thin spaghetti straps and a seductive neckline that showcases the swell of her breasts. The bodice fits her slender body to perfection. The lower part of the dress flares out. Everything she's wearing is on point.

"It's such a departure from the super skimpy outfits I used to wear on stage or in our videos," she says. "I was told this is a midi length because the hem hits me mid-calf. I feel feminine in this dress."

I lean into her. "You look smoking hot in it." I murmur in her ear. "I can't wait to find out which of the French Appliqué lingerie you're hiding underneath it."

"That's quite the conversation starter," she says, fanning her face.

"Let's sit down."

"Okay."

I pull a chair for her and watch as she lowers herself to the seat in an elegant movement.

I round the table and sit across from her.

"I already ordered champagne—rosé, your favorite. It's already on ice."

"Yes, please!"

I motion to the waiter, and he approaches, balancing two flutes on a tray. After thanking him, he hurries off.

I lift my glass.

She mimics me.

"Here's to me finally getting my head out of my ass!" I say.

She laughs.

"I mean, here's to me getting down and dirty with my fantasy girl!"

She laughs harder.

"I got it wrong again," I say. "Clearly, I don't date much or else I'd be more eloquent."

Her expression turns serious.

"It's most likely *not* going to be *uncomplicated* between us."

"I want to get *complicated* with you," she says.

"Since I might be a little rusty in the dating game, do you promise to take it easy on me?" I say with a wink.

"Only if you promise to return the favor."

"Deal." We exchange a warm smile. "Here's to us, dimples!"

"Here's to us!"

We clink our glasses and drink in celebration.

Dinner was outstanding. No surprise there. Larkin wouldn't have it any other way. Since it was Keira's first time at Charcoal, she was blown away by the experience. The advantage of dating someone you already know and care for is bypassing the tedious small talk.

We drive back to my house in a comfortable silence, stealing furtive side glances every so often. The energy between us is hot enough to light up firecrackers.

"Your place or mine?" she asks as we approach the house. Her tone is playful—Keira-like.

I play along. "You choose. I'm easy."

"If we go to your place, do you promise to drive me back to mine in the morning?"

She kills me.

"Promise," I say.

"Thank God. I'd hate to do the walk of shame to the bus stop in the morning."

"I won't let that happen."

"Glad I'm dealing with a gentleman."

"Fair warning, once I get you behind closed doors, I might not be such a gentleman."

"Duly noted," she says.

Just like when I picked her up from LAX, I have to focus on driving with a hard-on. The mental countdown to losing myself between her legs started the second she arrived at the restaurant looking like a fucking goddess.

When we arrive at my place, I park the car, get out, and circle the front of the vehicle to help her out. I wrap my hand around her shoulders and guide her to the house, doing my best to tame the beast inside.

"Full disclosure, I'm a little—a lot—nervous," she says when I close the door behind us.

I cup her beautiful face in my hands. "I won't rush you."

I want her so much it hurts, but I'm willing to take it slow.

"Okay," she says.

"Are you a virgin?"

She shakes her head.

She's no longer saving herself for me.

"No, but compared to your *uncomplicated* hookups—"

"Don't," I say. "This night is about you."

She responds with a shy nod.

"Can I ask how many guys you've been with?"

She averts her gaze.

"I asked you a question, Keira."

"Can I ask you the same question?" she says, meeting my gaze.

"I've been with a number of women, but I've always used protection and I get tested regularly." There's no point in lying to her. "That said, I haven't been with anyone in a long time."

"Really?" her eyes grow as wide as quarters.

"Really. I wasn't joking when I told you to take it easy on me."

She giggles.

"To answer your question, I've only been with one guy," she says. "He was a neighbor I trusted. He was my age and neither of us wanted to turn twenty and still be a virgin."

My eyebrows hit my forehead.

"You're surprised?" She picks up on my reaction.

You bet I am. Shocked, even.

The music industry after parties are notorious for debauched sex, easily accessible drugs, and free-flowing booze. The fact she was able to weather those vices says a lot about the woman she is. God knows she's a hell of a lot stronger than I ever was.

Then, it hits me.

"That was four years ago. No one since?"

She shakes her head. "I've been on dates, but I never let it go far. It's a turn off for most guys, but I don't care." She pauses. "I always promised myself I'd never be like my mom and sleep around with men to fill a void. It's the same desperate and destructive cycle I witnessed Chelle fall prey to in her quest to be accepted by guys who didn't deserve her..." She sighs. "That's why I kept my legs closed."

I nod in understanding.

Keira's mom died in a car accident when Noah was sixteen. Keira was eight. Their mom's then-guy-of-the-week was at the wheel, drunk. Since her mom was living at Keira's grandmother's place, Noah and Keira weren't uprooted. Their grandmother became their guardian. Before she died, she told them the truth—Noah was conceived in a boy's locker room when their mom was fifteen by one of the football team's star athletes, and Keira is the result of a bathroom bang in a bar Eva worked at. The guy was in LA for business. Eva never saw him again. Noah's dad never wanted anything to do with him.

Until the shocking revelation, they didn't know they were half siblings. They just thought Noah took after their dad. Keira's unwillingness to fuck around is justified.

"I hope I won't disappoint you—"

I press two fingers to her lips to silence her. "That'll never happen, Keira."

My gaze bores into hers for a short beat.

Unable to resist, I lean in for a kiss. It's soft at first, but it's enough to send a buzz to my balls. I kiss her again, a little more forceful this time, then swipe my tongue across her upper lip and groan. "You taste as fucking good as the first time your lips touched mine."

"Don't stop kissing me," she says, grabbing hold of my jacket.

She had the upper hand when she stole a kiss years ago because she caught me by surprise. That's not the case tonight.

"Say the magic word, dimples," I tell her.

"Please," she says.

"You can do better than that."

"Please, Rhys, don't stop kissing me."

I smash my lips to hers, allowing my tongue to slip into her mouth.

She moans.

I kiss her like I'm going to war and this is the last time I'll have the privilege of tasting her lips.

I kiss her like breathing is optional.

I kiss her to make up for all the wasted years I didn't have my mouth on her.

"I doubt I'll be able to stop kissing you tonight," I say, pulling back from her.

"You don't have to ever stop," she says before pressing her mouth to mine again.

I'm not like Beckett or some of my buddies. I kiss some of my hookups, but I've never kissed a woman the way I'm kissing Keira—with passionate abandonment.

I wasn't sure how this night would play out.

I mentally coaxed myself not to push too hard, but now, I want everything all at once with her. I want her in every position, and I want us to christen every wall in my house.

Fuck.

Our lips are frantic and hungry for one another.

My hands travel down her back until I grope her ass and squeeze hard.

"Jesus," she gasps into my mouth.

I grind, pressing my length against her stomach.

"You're so hard," she says.

There's no denying my desire for her. "Because I want you so damn much, dimples."

She practically purrs as I drop open-mouthed kisses along her neck.

"Oh, God, Rhys." She places her hands against my chest, pushing away from me.

"What?" I ask, confused.

"This is too much," she says.

"You wanna stop?"

Putting the brakes on isn't part of the program tonight, but I'm a gentleman. It's her call.

"Hell, no. If you continue rubbing against me like this, I'll come without you having to do much more. It's so intense I feel like I'm about to combust."

"We're in the same boat."

I grab her neck and pull her into me, sliding my tongue over her mouth before plunging between her plump lips. I grind against her with more urgency. She responds beautifully, grips my shoulders, and the kiss turns incendiary.

Jesus, she's a hot little thing.

"How far can I take this?" I ask her between kisses.

"I'm all yours."

Thank the fuck God.

"I can push your boundaries?"

"I'm up for anything with you, Rhys. I trust you implicitly."

Her admission fans the alpha in me.

Raging desire threatens to tear me apart at her willingness to submit to me. Everything about this woman calls to my deepest primal instincts to make her mine.

I lift her in my arms, and she wraps her legs around my waist, my mouth coming down hard on hers. I traverse the house and climb up the stairs in a rush. My feet eat the floor underneath me as I stride down the hallway to my bedroom. When I get inside, I turn on the light with my elbow, drop her to her feet, and slam the door behind me.

I grab Keira by the shoulders and shove her up against the door and kiss her roughly. The mix of her intoxicating scent and the adrenaline coursing through my veins makes me ravenous. Our tongues dance and lips smack as our hands explore each other in a mad rush.

"God, I want you," she says.

"Not nearly as much as I want you."

I fumble with her zipper, inching it lower before pulling down the spaghetti straps of her dress.

"Fuck," I gasp at the hedonistic sight of her sexy thin lace bra and the pink circles of her areolas crowned by her hardened mouthwatering nipples. "I bought that?"

"Newsflash, you bought everything I own..."—she pulls her lower lip between her teeth—"including the crotchless panties I'm wearing." Her teasing tone is an outright provocation.

With impatient hands, I unhook her bra and slide the straps down her arms. I toss it to the side and give her incredible tits all the attention they deserve. I don't spare her. I cup, grope, knead and massage, relishing the size of her tits in my hands.

"Oh, God," Keira says, digging her fingers into my forearms.

I lick and suck on the tight points of her nipples like a goddamn savage. Needing more, I flick and twist them between my fingers, inflicting pain and pleasure.

Keira whines in response. A beautiful sound of agony and bliss.

I capture her lips in mine and kiss the everloving shit out of her, all the while dry humping her against the door.

She circles her hands behind my waist, pulling me closer, demanding more.

I give it to her.

I grind my impossibly hard cock against her in a slow, languorous movement.

Goddammit.

Her desperate moans are driving me out of my mind. I'm so fucking turned on, it wouldn't take much for me to come in my pants.

What a waste of cum.

"Are you wet enough for me?" I don't give her a chance to answer. I slide a hand under her dress. "Fuck! You *are* wearing crotchless panties."

"Told you," she says on a breath.

"Damn." I slide a finger inside her and pump in and out while I massage her clit with my palm.

"Fuck," she pants.

"I hope you bought those damn panties in every color of the rainbow," I say.

"I only got a few. I didn't want to abuse your generosity."

"Woman, those are so damn sexy. Abuse to your heart's content."

"I'll make sure to correct the error of my ways."

"I expect nothing less."

I slide a second finger inside her pussy.

Keira huffs hard, grabbing onto my forearms.

She's slippery wet.

I fucking love it.

"How do you want it?" I ask.

"I'm easy."

All movements stop.

"What did I say?" she asks.

"I get that you don't have a lot of experience, but you must know what brings you the most pleasure. Favorite positions?"

"Not really. I know what brings me pleasure when I touch myself, but not with a guy."

I try, I really try, but I fail to keep my dirty mind in check. I can only imagine her with her hands between her legs, chasing her orgasm, as I did the same in the room across from her with my hand fisting my cock.

"You never had an orgasm with your first?"

"I did, but they pale in comparison to when I bring myself to orgasm."

That is so wrong.

Worry veils her eyes. "Is it okay if you help me figure out what I like?" she asks in a small voice.

"It would be an honor."

I resume my mission, pumping my fingers in and out of her pussy.

"Where do you want to come, dimples? On my tongue, my fingers, or around my cock?"

She looks up at me from under her eyelashes. "Decisions, decisions..." her words trail off. She's too busy grinding against my hand to answer.

"My cock is aching. I need an answer."

"Those are hard choices..." She pulls her lower lip between her teeth. "Can I be greedy?" she asks in a smoky voice that makes my cock twitch.

"You want it all?"

Her muscles tighten around my fingers like a vice. My cock swells in response.

Fuck.

"Yes," she says, her eyes hooded.

I pull my fingers from her dripping pussy and lick them clean.

"Good God," she says.

"I knew I'd be addicted to your pussy juices."

"That was so fucking hot."

"There's plenty more where that came from."

Her hair is a little messier, her tits are in full view and her perfectly applied nude lipstick is a distant memory. In other words, she's a beautiful mess. *My* beautiful mess.

"Let's get you out of this dress."

I lower the zipper all the way and let the dress pool at her feet. She steps out of it and I pick it up and walk over to the chaise longue and lay it down with care before returning my attention to the ravishing beauty.

"On the bed," I tell her.

Keira laces her fingers around the elastic band of her panties.

"Did I tell you to remove those?"

She looks confused.

"Let's put them to the test," I say.

"You want to know if you got your money's worth?"

"Exactly!" I wink. "Shoes off."

I don't have to tell her twice.

Keira saunters to the bed, but not before looking over her shoulder and flashing me a sexy-as-all-fuck glance.

Now that we're being honest with each other, I don't feel guilty or tormented for drinking in every tempting inch of her naked body.

My eager cock is threatening to bust the zipper of my pants wide open. Impatience consumes me. I toe off my shoes, remove my socks and strip out of my suit in a flash. I drop everything next to her dress.

I turn to face her, standing there in just my boxer briefs and with an obvious hard-on.

"For the record, I love watching you undress," she says. Her eyes rake over my body. She's sitting on her heels, hands on her knees like a good little girl. Waiting for me. The submissive position ratchets my desire for her. "You're spectacularly built." She tilts her head to the side, as if to catch a better glimpse.

"That's a lot to live up to."

"Stop being coy."

"Thanks, dimples."

"Nice happy trail." Her eyes drop to my waist. "Aren't you going to get naked, so I can see where it leads?"

I don't disappoint.

I push my boxer briefs down and my cock springs free. I kick the briefs away and stand there with my hands on my hips.

Keira's head jerks back, causing her to fall backwards on her ass. She struggles to sit up. When she does, her eyes are glued to my impressive erection. I fist my cock as I stalk to the bed, stroking it in slow, languorous, pumps.

"Good Lord," Keira says. "That— You're— Whoa—" She blinks a few times before lifting her gaze to mine. "You're enormous."

"Thanks for the compliment."

"It was meant more as a cautionary note to myself."

I laugh.

"No, seriously. You're this big guy—all over—and I'm this... little thing."

I squeeze my cock hard. "I'll make sure you're ready for me."

"That could only happen if a lot of booze is involved."

"You said you trusted me."

"I spoke too soon. I had no idea you were packing..."—she waves an animated finger at my cock—"that! I'm not a virgin, but I'm pretty sure after four years, it's like being a born-again virgin."

"We can keep it to my fingers and my tongue."

She sighs. "For the greater good of womankind, I'll take one for the team."

I chuckle.

"So honourable of you."

"I know, right?"

I let go of my cock and sit on the bed next to her.

"Come here!"

She crawls to me on all fours.

"Sit on my face," I tell her.

She wrinkles her nose in confusion.

"I gather you've never tried a sixty-nine before?"

"No."

"Then, I get to be your first after all."

She considers me.

"I really wanted it to be you, Rhys," she says.

I trace her lips with my finger. "It didn't feel right at the time. Now it does."

She nods.

I lie on my back. "Put your knees on either side of my head."

She looks like a deer caught in headlights.

I cock an eyebrow.

Drawing a deep breath, she assumes the position.

Her tempting pussy and ass are hovering right above my face.

Fuck, I've fantasized about this moment so many times.

"I'm not going to suffocate you?" There's no mistaking the worry in her voice.

"That's the point."

"Oh, okay," she says shyly.

My brazen girl is a little unsure of herself.

I trail kisses on her inner thigh. I give the other thigh the same treatment.

She wiggles.

"Ticklish?" I ask.

"A bit."

I brush a finger between her gorgeous pussy lips, scooping up her juices.

She gasps.

These crotchless panties are fucking perfect for this.

I tap her outer legs. "Lower your body!"

She does.

I spread her ass cheeks open and pull her lower until I have her exactly where I want her. I stick out my tongue and tease her slippery lips.

"Oh, Rhys!"

The initial contact of my tongue against her pussy is potent. I lick her, nice and slow, savoring each tongue stroke.

"That's way better than everyone of my fantasies, combined— Oh, shit. My mouth ran away from me. I can't believe I just admitted that out loud."

I push her off me.

She looks over her shoulder.

"Don't ever feel you have to censor yourself around me. As your lover, you can tell me anything."

Her eyes widen.

"I'm barely able to wrap my head around the fact we went out on an actual date. You? My lover? Wow." There's wonder in her words.

Her comment is pretty ironic considering we're both naked, her pussy is hovering over my head, and my mouth was just on her.

"Can your lover go back to pleasuring you?"

"Absolutely!" She flashes me a wide smile before turning her head.

I tease her by skating my tongue around her clit, again, and again, and again, eliciting little mewls from her.

I grab her clit between my lips and suck hard.

"Jesus!" she says, groaning.

I lift my hips close to her mouth, reminding her my cock needs attention.

"Oh, shit, I'm so sorry," she says. "What you're doing to me is so mind-blowing, it's making me lose my bearings. I'm such a bad lover."

I chuckle.

Keira is tentative at first. She licks my cock like she's afraid it will break.

Since my mouth is occupied, I can't guide her.

She gets the hang of it.

Soon she treats my cock to the same long, sensuous licks I grant her pussy.

As her confidence grows, she more than makes up for a slow start. She grabs the base of my cock and squeezes it hard. She catches me off guard when she pokes her tongue inside my hole.

Christ.

I grip her hips tighter in response.

She'll have bruises tomorrow. And fuck if that doesn't do something to me.

Keira goes for it.

Instead of using just the tip, she uses her whole tongue to brush over the engorged head of my cock.

My balls thump at the sensation.

When Keira wraps her lips around my raging erection, my hips jerk off the bed.

She grunts, but with her small hand tightly gripping my base, she keeps sucking me off like her life depends on it. The movement of her other hand matches the bobbing of her head. She gives my shaft as much attention as my tip.

Bless her.

She picks up speed, bobbing her head with more determination. The hedonistic slurping sound she makes is such a turn-on.

I reward her by using my tongue to explore every part of her, relishing in her sweet juices. I ratchet my naughty play by alternating between toying with her hard clit and massaging it with my lips.

She responds by pressing her pussy against my mouth, and the scent of her is divine.

Oh, fuck, yeah.

I use my tongue as I would my cock and dart inside her warmth, pumping in and out to heighten the pleasure. The way she squeezes her legs around my head suggests she's enjoying this as much as I am.

I push her off me.

"Let's make this dirtier!"

She lets go of my cock and looks over her shoulder.

"I'm not sure how this can get any dirtier."

Innocent lamb.

"I want you to bounce off my tongue."

She narrows her gaze.

"You're kidding?"

"I'd never kid about your pussy or pleasure."

She's still incredulous.

"My cock is lonely."

As she resumes her mission, so do I.

I grip her hips and pull her to me until my tongue is back where it belongs.

I wait for her to follow my order, but nothing.

Slap!

Both hands hit her ass at the same time.

That gets her going.

I spread her ass cheeks to tongue fuck her deeper. These sexy-as-fuck crotchless panties are a godsend. I'm calling

French Appliqué first thing tomorrow morning to order a dozen more.

I groan every time she lands on my greedy tongue.

Good girl.

She bounces with more velocity, the globes of her ass jiggling in my hands.

To reward her obedience, I hold her steady, and motorboat between her pussy lips, rocking my head from side to side, spreading her sweet juices all over my face.

This is so fucking hot.

She moans, never slowing down the cadence of her bobbing head.

This is debauchery at its finest.

She surprises me by wrapping her lips around the tip of my cock and sucking hard, as if attempting to suck the cum right out of my balls.

Fuck!

My orgasm is looming, balls tingling like crazy.

But she comes first.

I grab her hips, taking control.

I rub my tongue against her clit with the right pressure to force her to tip over the edge. I slide a finger inside her pussy, coating it real nice before sliding it into her ass. I expect her to object, but she doesn't. Instead, she gasps and clenches around the intrusion.

Goddammit.

My balls are pulsating, threatening to explode. I'm a breath away from christening her hot mouth.

"Keira, I'm going to come, baby," I tell her. "Let go of my cock if you don't want me to come down your throat."

She's dead set on her mission, sucks me harder, squeezes me tight.

"If you keep doing what you're doing, you won't leave me any choice but to shoot my load inside your mouth," I say.

She nods on my cock.

Well, hell.

"You're sure?"

Another vigorous nod and my balls pull up.

I didn't expect this much from her.

"We come together," I tell her.

She responds with a grunt.

She's too busy sucking me off to offer much more.

I'm unprepared when my cock hits the back of her throat, causing her to gag. She's a champion, though. She doesn't let go. She swallows and keeps sucking.

She's my fucking dream come true.

She presses her legs together, trapping my head between her thighs, forcing me to bring her the relief she's seeking.

My lips close over her throbbing clit and I suck greedily.

Her thighs start trembling at the same time as my balls contract in a series of staccato pulses.

She frees her lips from around my cock.

"Oh my God!" The glorious sound of her climax fills the room. "Oh, Rhys!" She bucks almost violently against my mouth like a cowgirl riding a bronco. She's wild. "Oh, Rhys, yes!" She chants over and over again as her sweet-as-fuck juices flood my mouth.

Jesus—

Hearing my name on her lips triggers my climax. *My fucking God!* My balls let go, my cock spasms, and I grunt like an animal as the first spurt erupts.

I gasp in shock when her lips close around my head, sucking my gushing release. Sucking and not letting go as my cock spasms and my hips jerk with each spurt.

Christ, she's perfect.

I'm doomed in the best possible way.

I may have to marry this woman because her mouth on my cock is my new favorite thing.

One final spurt and the tension leaves me. She sucks me dry and collapses onto my legs.

We're sweaty, panting, spent, and if her lifeless body is any indication, fully satiated.

"You okay?" I caress the globes of her ass.

She doesn't answer.

"Was that too intense?" I ask.

Slowly, she lifts off my legs, flips over, and crawls up to me.

I pull her to my chest and wrap my arms around her.

I kiss the top of her head. The chic hairstyle is long gone, replaced by crazy spiky hair.

Her breathing changes, and she hugs my torso, pressing her lips to my chest.

Still no answer.

"Did you lose your voice, dimples?"

Her eyes lift to mine.

"You're always so talkative," I say. "What happened?"

"I've never had an out-of-body experience before, but I'm certain that was close," she says. "Can we do it again?"

"Eager much?"

Her cheeks flush in embarrassment.

I tap the tip of her nose. "I need to catch my breath first. Then, I need to fuck you, because I'm dying to be inside you. *Then*, you can have your wish of another sixty-nine."

She pushes herself up, so she's staring right at me.

The slow smile curling her lips should come as a warning.

"Now, I understand why you kept pushing me to go out with guys my own age," she says. "Older men don't have the stamina to keep going. They need a nap between rounds."

My eyebrows hit my forehead.

Little devil.

I flip her over so she's underneath me.

She squeals.

"Stamina? You're naughty, dimples."

She giggles.

"I'm going to make you regret those words. Don't come crying to me when you can't walk tomorrow."

I crush my lips against hers in a searing kiss.

Chapter 20

Keira

I wake up to the heat of Rhys's naked body pressed against my back.

I moan at the blissful feeling.

If I had to guess, I'd say it's just before dawn. Faint morning twilight seeps through the large panoramic windows, announcing the beginning of a new day.

LA isn't quite up yet, but I am.

So is my lover.

He trails kisses across my shoulders and I relish the touch of his soft lips against my skin. Still sleepy, I'm more than aware of where this is heading.

I approve.

I lift my body, rest my weight on my folded elbows and glance at his handsome face.

"Morning," I say.

"Morning, dimples," he says, his voice so low. *God, I love his morning voice.* "Someone passed out on me."

"I did?" I gasp in horror.

"You did. One minute you were talking a mile a minute, the next you went quiet."

"I'm a terrible lover."

He chuckles.

"You had an eventful weekend, dimples."

"That doesn't justify not staying awake long enough for a second sixty-nine."

My experience might be limited, but that's quickly becoming my favorite position.

He lifts off the bed and positions his body on top of mine, carrying his weight on his knees and the hand that's pressed on the mattress.

His other hand slides underneath me and gropes my breasts. He kneads the flesh in his palm, teasing my nipples into stiff little peaks as he rubs his hard cock between my ass cheeks.

I love his hands on me—all over me.

When he pinches my nipple, I yelp and squeeze my legs together in search of relief.

"You on the pill?" he asks.

"I am."

"I won't fuck you without wrapping up, but my cock is dying to play with your pussy." He whispers the bawdy words in my ear.

A sublime rush of warmth travels through my veins, jolting my tired body to life. My pussy throbs, arousal pulsating.

Permission granted. "Okay," I say.

"I want you on all fours, baby."

I assume the position.

He slides his hard cock between my lips and skates around my slick pussy in slow torturous circles.

He lets out a low groan.

"Dear God," I say. "That feels so good."

"Yeah," he says. "I totally agree."

He presses the tip of his cock against my clit and I swear I see stars. A strange guttural sound I've never heard before leaves my lips.

"Fuck, I love your pussy." His breath is ragged.

Something tightens in my chest.

I so desperately want him to say, *I love you.*

Stop being so sappy. After losing all hope, you're in his bed.

I brush away the silly thought.

For several teasing minutes he works me into a frenzy, running his cock head up and down my lips, pressing it against my clit, over and over. Just when I'm about to come, he stops.

He kisses my ear. "I want to fuck you like this on all fours, so I can go *real* deep."

I can only nod because that sounds so dirty.

"Good," he says. His mouth travels along my shoulders, down my back and around my ass.

When he pulls away from me, I mourn the loss of his warmth. I look over my shoulder and watch as he pulls open the nightstand drawer and retrieves a condom. He sheathes his cock, the thin sheet of latex stretched tight around his impressive length.

He settles behind me.

His hands move in tender circles over my ass. "Part your legs."

I obey.

He grips my hips, fingertips digging into my skin as he nestles his cock between my ass cheeks. The heat emanating from his skin is all-consuming.

He leans in until his lips flirt with the shell of my ear and asks, "You're going to scream out my name when you come?"

The chocolatey tone of his voice is almost enough to make me come right there and then.

"Yes." My heart pulses at the same thumping rhythm as my eager pussy.

He drops a kiss against my back where the lotus flower is located. He kisses each individual letter etched in my skin with such tenderness, it's disarming.

I shiver.

"This might get a bit rough," he says.

"Okay."

"If I go too deep, tell me."

"I will."

"Good girl," he says. "Arch your back and tilt your sweet ass up."

I do as I'm told.

He presses his palm to my lower back to steady me.

"Fuck, you look beautiful like this, so ready for me."

I let out a small laugh.

"You ready for me, baby?"

"I am."

He edges inside my pussy, slow and steady.

I gasp as his massive cock fills me.

He's so thick, so hard, so wide.

So much to handle.

He's huge.

"Good girl," he says. "Can you take it a little rough?"

I nod.

He slides all the way out, and thrusts into me in one swift movement.

I yelp and the breath catches in the back of my throat.

Even with the warning, my body isn't prepared for the assault.

I grab hold of the sheet underneath me, twisting it in my grasp as he starts moving slow and deep inside me, riding me like he means it.

"Fuck, I'm so deep inside you," he says.

I'm no longer certain where he ends and where I begin.

"You like how I use your willing body to get off?" he asks.

"Yes."

"You dirty, dirty girl."

"I am... your dirty girl."

"Damn right you are."

I close my eyes and tilt my head back, pushing against him to meet his next thrust.

He picks up speed, fucking me fast and furious.

It's unmerciful.

Savage, even.

Dear God.

I can't get enough of the hedonistic sound of our bodies slapping together as we move in perfect synch. It's so darn sexy.

I grip the sheets a little harder to withstand the velocity and power of his thrusts.

"You look so fucking perfect under me, baby," he says and slams me so hard I cry out.

"Fuck!" he says and slaps my ass.

I imagine what he must look like—hovering above me and dominating me.

The imagery turns me on even more.

He grips my hips and pumps into me like a piston.

The rhythm is so frantic, his king bed rocks beneath us. He grips his hands around my waist, pulling me closer to his body, and pumps into me as if everything so far was nothing more than a warm-up. His breath changes to a loud heaving sound as he shifts the angle of his hips and drives into me with more determination. In this position, his thrusts are more calculated, more flesh slapping, more mind-blowing, I can barely breathe.

"Goddammit!" His hips grind into me.

He hits a place deep inside I didn't even know existed.

"Holy shit!" I choke on the curse.

"I hit your G-spot."

He does it again.

"Ohhhhhh God." My voice is trembling.

What am I talking about? My whole body is shaking.

"More! More! More, Rhys!"

With a grunt, he gives it to me.

Our heavy breathing overshadows the naughty slapping of our skin. For a few long minutes, nothing matters but taking pleasure from each other.

"You're close?" his voice is so hoarse, it's almost inaudible.

"Hell yes!"

"You're going to come hard for me, dimples?"

"Yes!"

The third vigorous thrust against my sweet spot causes a crescendo of foreign sounds to tear from my throat.

What the hell is he doing to me?

He snakes his arm around my waist until his fingers find my pussy. He parts my lips where he finds my throbbing, swollen clit. He skates his finger hard and fast over it as he keeps thrusting inside me, driving me to a place of blissful desire so intense it frightens the hell out of me.

Little hoarse cries drop from my lips.

I'm unprepared for when he changes his cadence.

He places three fingers flat on my pussy and rubs my clit in dizzying circles, taking me higher and higher.

Yes, yes, yes.

A flush of heat travels at lightspeed throughout my body.

"Come for me!" He traps my clit between his fingers and presses.

I freefall.

Everything inside me shatters as my body ripples around him.

"Oh, Rhys! Oh, Rhys!" I shout over and over again.

"That's it, give me what I want."

I clench hard against his cock, milking everything I can from him.

Good God.

As I'm lost in a heart-stopping orgasm, he thrusts with more force as he chases his own pleasure.

"Christ!" The curse comes out in a harsh breath. The slap of his skin against mine subsides. "I need to mark your heavenly body."

Huh?

"Oh, fuck, Keira," he says.

The next thing I know, Rhys jerks out of me, the condom goes flying past my ear, and a river of warm cum jets onto my back, coating my ass and streaming down my thighs.

I'm speechless.

He marked my heart a long time ago, and now he's marked every part of me.

Chapter 21

Keira

I open my eyes to a shaded room.

Rhys must've pulled the curtain closed.

I flip over to his side of the bed.

I'm alone.

I can't hide my disappointment, but unlike me, he has a company to run.

I pull the sheet over my head, allowing myself one more minute of rest.

His masculine scent lingers.

Breathing in deep, I memorize the smell of him.

I guess I should get up for another day of boredom.

I try to sit up.

My poor pussy is screaming in pain.

Rhys is way bigger than my first and since it's been a while, it feels like I lost my virginity all over again with none of the first-time awkwardness.

My throat is a little sore from screaming out his name so many times from the multiple orgasms.

My God, the man worked me.

I have to go at it slow and steady, but eventually I sit up in bed.

My mind might not welcome boredom, but my body certainly will. I doubt I'll be physically able to do much today other than read and lounge.

I rub the remnants of sleep from my eyes and stretch with a yawn.

God, every part of me hurts.

I hear some clatter coming from downstairs and a sugary scent tickles my nostrils.

Wow. The housekeeper is going above and beyond this morning.

I pull the sheet off my naked body and slide off the bed.

Ouch, ouch, ouch.

This thing is so big, it's like traveling from California to Montana. When my feet land on the floor, I know I'm in big trouble.

My legs feel like lead.

I swear, Rhys's cock should come with a warning.

I look around, but my dress is nowhere to be found. Neither is his suit. The same goes for my strappy heels and sexy underwear.

My eyes land on one of Rhys's t-shirts neatly folded on the chaise longue. I pull it over my head to hide my nakedness before making my way to my bedroom, humming a song from the perpetual jukebox playing in my head. I can't help my smile when I open the door and I'm greeted by my pretty dress neatly laid out on the bed.

He's so sweet.

I grab the t-shirt and boxer briefs I last wore on Friday, still sitting on the chair where I left them, and make my way to the bathroom. After taking care of business, brushing my teeth, and a quick shower to wake me up, I get dressed in Rhys's clothing, and sleek back my new blonde hair.

I go carefully down the stairs and head to the kitchen. Every step is excruciating, my tender pussy a reminder of my boyfriend's formidable cock.

The advantage of a great lover is multiple toe-curling orgasms and discovering new sex positions. The downside is, I'm starved. I once read you can burn between one to three hundred calories in a passionate thirty-minute sex-session. My kind of fitness regime.

When I enter the kitchen, I freeze.

Isn't it Monday today?

Maybe too much fucking makes you lose track of time.

Rhys is standing in front of the waffle iron in nothing but gray boxers, his back to me.

That round ass...

He must feel my presence because he turns around.

"Morning!" he says, grinning from ear to ear.

"Morning!"

He drops the spatula and plate he's holding on the counter and approaches.

"I thought you bought a whole new wardrobe," he says, his eyes sweeping down my body.

"In my defense, the suitcases are still in your trunk, and I kind of love wearing your t-shirts and boxer briefs."

He shakes his head. "I still can't believe you bought so much stuff, you needed suitcases."

When I arrived at the hotel last night, the concierge kindly offered to grab the suitcases. I was a little hesitant after my disastrous Bangkok experience, but given this was a high-end hotel and the owner is a friend of Rhys's, I accepted. You should've seen Rhys's face when I told him.

"It was Phoebe's idea. Not mine." Since I had so many individual bags, she suggested I stuff everything in a few old suitcases she was going to take to the thrift shop. "I never reached the limit you gave me."

"Sure." He shoots me a side gaze.

"I swear."

I even cross my heart.

"I believe you, dimples," he says. "Now, where's my morning kiss?"

"Right here, big guy." I point to my lips.

"C'mere." He grabs me by the waist.

His ravishing kiss is passionate, but out of nowhere, my stomach growls in an unladylike way.

He chuckles against my lips.

I curse my hunger.

"Let me finish breakfast so I can feed you," he says. "I still have to cook the bacon."

He returns to making waffles.

I look around the kitchen, amazed.

"What's up with the feast?" I ask.

"I figured you'd be hungry."

He's been up for a while.

The kitchen island is laden with a glass bowl filled with boiled eggs, a yummy looking fruit platter, a variety of nuts, an assortment of jams, peanut butter and a bottle of maple syrup from Vermont.

This man surely knows how to say good morning in a language I appreciate.

"I'm famished—"

"Three rounds of mind-blowing sex will do that to a girl," he says.

"Indeed."

His grin is epic.

"Nevertheless, it's Monday," I say.

"I know."

"Aren't you going to be late for work?" I ask.

He shakes his head.

"Err... it's nine o'clock. You're usually long gone by this time."

"I called my executive assistant and Beckett to tell them I wouldn't be in today."

"Is everything okay?"

"Everything is perfect."

"So why aren't you going in?"

"I'm the boss and it's my prerogative," he says with a wink.

I roll my eyes.

"All right, Mr. COO. It's good to hold that much power." I laugh.

He doesn't.

He turns off the waffle iron and places the last waffle on a plate, and turns his undivided attention to me, his expression serious.

"I decided not to go in because of you, Keira."

"Because of me?" I point at my chest.

His glacier-blue eyes are intense.

"I want to spend the day with my girlfriend."

Maybe too much fucking inhibits my ability to hear.

"Wh–what?"

"I said, I want to spend the day with my girlfriend."

The second time around doesn't dampen the shock.

My jaw drops and I stand there momentarily dumbstruck.

His eyes bore into mine. "Last week, I was in denial. Last night, we went from wine to sixty-nine. I thought I would be able to take things slow, but I wanted you so damn much–"

"It was mutual."

His lips stretch into a warm smile. "Today, I just want to enjoy you, and spend the whole day kissing you."

I'm grinning like a fool.

"You're just going to keep me trapped in your mansion with your lips on mine?" *And hopefully your lips on my pussy?*

"Pretty much."

"And I don't get a say?"

"Not really. Your mine now and I have access to your lips whenever I want."

"Thanks for the explanation, Mr. Caveman."

I love his possessiveness.

"What can I say? You bring out the alpha in me," he says.

"I thought Dark Compulsion did that—"

Did I really just say that?

Shit, shit, shit.

He narrows his eyes at me.

I avert my gaze.

"Look at me," he says.

Tentatively, I do as I'm told.

"How do you know about Dark Compulsion?"

"Didn't you mention it last night over dinner?" I play dumb.

"No, I didn't."

"You're sure about that?"

"Positive."

"Hmmm..."

The wheels in my head spin faster than a whirligig in a whirlwind as I struggle to find a way out.

"Arianne told you," he says.

"In her defense, she was tipsy."

"What did she tell you about Dark Compulsion?"

I clear my throat, buying some time to find the right words. I don't want to incriminate Arianne more than I already have. "It's a—"

Something takes over me.

I nix the safe answer.

I slide my hand up his chest, to the back of his head, and weave my fingers in his hair.

"I'm waiting," he says.

I bite my lower lip and dive in with both feet. "If you're allowed to bring your girlfriend..." I pause. His blue eyes turn dark indigo. "...she's up for a little—or a lot of—kinky."

His eyes widen and then narrow.

He leans close enough for his breath to skate over my temple.

"You're on."

I swallow hard.

"Now that you have me all worked up, fuck breakfast. I need your pussy swallowing my cock."

Chapter 22

Rhys

I never have a problem reporting for duty, but this morning I just wanted to stay wrapped up in Keira's embrace like I did yesterday. Our day together came and went way too fast for my liking.

Today, is about adulting and not fucking like I have no care in the world. As I ride the elevator from the garage to the executive floor at SCORE, I pull out my phone intending to shoot Keira a quick text. Never mind our filthy morning quickie or our passionate goodbye kiss, I need to hear from her before I jump into what's most likely going to be a hectic day. I'm just about to type a message when one from Beckett flies across my screen.

I ignore it.

Another message from him pops on my screen.

Chill out, man. I just got here.

I'll deal with him in a minute.

Rhys: Hey, dimples, what are you up to?

Keira: Reading by the pool. You at work yet?

Rhys: Just got here.

Keira: I miss you already, big guy.

I shake my head at the nickname.

Rhys: Miss you too.

Keira: Are you going to work late?

Rhys: Nah, I have someone to come home to.

Keira: I'm totally grinning. I'm already counting the hours.

So am I.

Sure, I love women like the next guy, but I'm not a manwhore like Beckett used to be, and I'm certainly not a giant slut like our friend Collin Dennison. I swear that man must secretly take Viagra. He's insatiable.

After being single for most of my adult life, and shying away from monogamous relationships because I never found anyone who kept my interest for long, I can't get enough of Keira.

I don't do things by half and this is no different. I go from being single to living with a woman. I go from not remembering a fraction of the women I've been with to being consumed by one woman.

Rhys: Be good today, dimples.

Keira: Or else?

Rhys: Don't push my buttons.

Keira: FYI, warnings only fuel me.

Rhys: You're impossible.

Keira: But you still like me.

Rhys: I do.

I can't help my smile.

Rhys: All right, I got to go play COO. I'll catch you later, dimples.

Keira: Catch you later, big guy.

I tuck my phone inside the pocket of my suit jacket just as the elevator doors open on the executive floor. I stroll with a decisive step, dropping good mornings, smiling and nodding along the way.

The smell of freshly brewed coffee—and possibilities—permeates the air. SCORE enterprise is in full swing, ready to crush the competition and take even bigger shares of the market.

Even after five monumental years, on some days, I still struggle to wrap my head around the fact I, Rhys Hartford, co-own this goliath company.

After a quick pit stop at the employee kitchen for my second latte of the day, I head to my office.

"Morning!" I say, walking by my executive assistant's desk.

Cecilia shifts her attention from her screen. "Good morning, Rhys." She leans over her desk. Sensing this might be a long conversation, I cradle my mug with both hands and take a long sip of my piping hot coffee. "Is there something I don't know about?" she asks in a hushed voice.

I take another long sip before answering. "You're talking about Beckett?"

"Yes." Her light brown eyes glance furtively around the executive floor. "He's been checking in with me every fifteen minutes to find out if you're in. That's unlike him."

"Yeah, he's been texting me all morning," I say. "Same for Arianne. I was hoping you might know more."

"I'm clueless," Cecilia tells me. "I even checked with Valerie and she has no idea what's going on... and Beckett's executive assistant knows everything."

Interesting.

Valerie always has her ear to the ground. She's also in on Chinese whispers and water cooler gossip.

"I take one day off, and those two stir trouble," I say.

"Speaking of which, how was it playing hooky on a Monday?" Cecilia links her fingers beneath her chin and bats her eyelashes.

It was a fucking great day, but I'm not about to tell you.

"Who says I was playing hooky?"

"You're so dedicated to this company, I usually have to kick you out of the building when you're under the weather because you don't know when to quit. Unless you're traveling for business or away on holiday, you're always here."

"I needed time off."

"Does this have to do with your best friend's little sister?"

"Yes."

"I thought so... I've been thinking—"

"That scares me." Those three dreaded words... she's about to play matchmaker.

"Don't worry, I won't try to hook you up with one of my eight sisters, my army of female cousins, or their legion of girlfriends."

Thank God.

No wonder her parents had to adopt a boy in the end. That's a lot of estrogen in a family.

"Between the recent production issues and the frenzy surrounding SCORE Yours, you have your plate full. If you're looking for someone to hang out with Keira during the day, one of my sons would graciously step in."

Over my dead body.

"I already talked to them. They have time between classes. And they can show her around on days when they don't have classes... like tomorrow."

Show her around their dorm room?

"They can even introduce her to some of their friends—they're all between twenty and twenty-three. It'll be fun for her."

"Thanks for the offer, but I doubt a college crowd is Keira's thing."

Am I taking liberties?

You bet.

"The poor thing must be losing her mind to boredom," Cecilia says.

"Keira has only been in LA for a week. She still needs time to get settled."

I didn't want to spoil our time together by broaching any thorny subject, but my girlfriend will need to find something to occupy her days.

"What about Friday nights and weekends?" Cecilia soldiers on. "The twins are great companions, and I'm sure they'd love to take her out to parties."

Yeah, I don't think so.

"Her Friday nights and weekends are spoken for."

Her cheeks flush.

She sits up straight, visibly uncomfortable.

She brushes her short brown hair behind her ears and

clears her throat. "Perhaps I overstepped my boundaries. It appears Keira is already in good hands."

"She is."

She cocks an eyebrow and tilts her head to the side. "Message received loud and clear."

Cecilia is astute.

She's the one who opened the envelope containing the additional credit card under Keira's name last Friday. My executive assistant's eyes were wide with questions. She has her answer now.

"Let me head to Beckett's office to find out what's going on," I say, changing the subject.

"Sounds like a plan." She returns her focus to her iMac screen.

I don't bother stopping by my office, I head straight to Beckett's.

I knock three times.

"Come in!"

I open the door and step inside.

Beckett and Arianne are sitting at the small round conference table near the large window. Her lips break into a huge smile when she sees me.

"Rhys! You're finally here!"

"It's only eight-thirty in the morning," I say.

"True, but I've been at this since five this morning. I'm so excited by this idea, I couldn't sleep." She claps her hands together like a kid who's allowed to have a second cookie. "I called Beckett and dragged him out of bed and we've been brainstorming since seven. We even had an early morning call with our point person at the advertising agency."

My gaze shifts to Beckett's.

I cock an eyebrow in lieu of a question.

"Trust me, you'll want to hear what she has to say," he tells me. "Take a seat."

I unbutton my suit jacket, sit and drop my mug on the table.

Arianne is giddy.

She does that excited clapping thing again.

"Why are you bouncing off the walls?" I ask her.

"Because of Keira."

"You talked to her this morning?" I ask.

I wonder when that happened because I'm pretty sure I kept my girlfriend's mouth too busy to talk this morning.

"No, I didn't," Arianne says. "Last night, I spoke to Phoebe. We couldn't shut up about our fun weekend with Keira. She's totally adorable."

"She is."

"Phoebe and I wanted to keep her."

"You make her sound like a stray kitten," I say with a laugh.

"In many ways she is. She's just a tiny thing."

"You two are practically the same height."

"Yeah, but she's younger and since I don't have a little sister, I felt a connection. After she opened up about her childhood, I felt so protective of her." I have to man up to Noah. "And that big personality, all that talent and that voice... I'm in awe."

"You're such a fan girl," I say.

"Guilty as charged, but getting to know the real Keira was so vastly different from her public image. I like her even more now I've met her."

"It's showbiz, baby!" Beckett says. "Smoke and mirrors! So much stuff on TV, online, and in the rag magazines is duplicitous and plain false."

Just like me, Beckett has firsthand experience of being in the spotlight. As the former lead singer and guitarist of the rock band Random Misconception, he was considered rock star royalty. Rehab is another thing we have in common.

"He's right," I say. "Publicists master the art of creating a persona to sell albums and concert tickets." I should know.

That's exactly what happened to me when I was trying to make a name for myself as a rapper. The record label fabricated a tough-kid persona that had nothing to do with who I was. I went along with it because I would've killed for fame. My dad had his reservations, but I wasn't willing to listen. In the end, Dad was right. The false tale contributed to my demise when it blew up in my face that it was fake.

"Unless you're in the music business, you're completely oblivious to all the trickery," Arianne says. "It was such a privilege Keira was willing to open up to us."

"She only had praise for you and Phoebe," I tell her.

"That's great to hear. Phoebe suggested we do another all-girl weekend soon."

"I'm sure she'll love it," I say. "She liked hanging out with you two."

"I'm so pleased," Arianne says.

"The perspective of another weekend of shopping and pampering with Keira got you so excited it woke you up before the roosters, and you had to call me into an urgent meeting?" I redirect the conversation.

I take another sip of coffee, but grimace because it's no longer hot. I push the mug away.

"Funny! It's like my conversation with Phoebe sparked something in my brain. I woke up startled when it hit me."

"When what hit you?" I ask.

"We're heading in the wrong direction with the marketing angle for SCORE Yours," she says.

"Why would you say that?" She opens her mouth to answer, but I keep talking. "And if that's how you feel, why am

I involved? I take care of production. Beckett is your point person for marketing and advertising initiatives."

Beckett pats my shoulder. "Hold tight, buddy. She's getting to it."

"Fair enough," I say. "Let's hear it."

"I understand where you're coming from, but this is far more than just marketing," she tells me. "This decision could be the spark that takes SCORE Yours from an amazing idea to a phenomenon."

My eyes shift to Beckett.

He nods.

"You have my full attention," I say.

"This is about the heart and soul of the product," Arianne says. "The image that will sell the consumer on the value proposition."

I draw my eyebrows together.

"I thought we all agreed on the slogan for SCORE Yours yup" I say. "*Unique like you,* is spot on."

"It is," Beckett says. "Nothing's changed on that front. Arianne is talking about the face of the brand."

"I thought you had settled on someone, and the agency was going to send her the contract this week," I say. "Don't you already have photoshoots lined up?"

"The model we selected is the wrong person," Arianne says. "Luckily we have time to get it right."

"The woman is beautiful," I tell her.

"Yeah, but she's *just* another model—a pretty face to look at, but not necessarily someone our audience will connect with," Arianne says.

"And you found that rare unicorn?" I ask.

"We did," Arianne says. "This past weekend."

"That was a hell of a shopping trip," I say.

"Let me explain," Arianne says, "Phoebe being Phoebe was

the first to take note of Keira's striking tattoo. And of course, my best friend had a thousand questions. When Keira told us why she felt so compelled to permanently ink her body, it broke my heart and brought tears to my eye. I wasn't aware of the details surrounding her best friend's and group mate's horrific deaths, or how the record company tried to mould her into a gimmick, or how they figured she'd be willing to keep singing with her other group mate as a duet."

"Yeah, it's heavy shit," I say.

"It's no surprise she's eager to start over and distance herself from her former career. I mean, she went as far as to shave her hair off—"

"Her new hairstyle rocks, by the way," I say.

"It does!" Beckett says. "Arianne showed me photos. Keira stands out more than before... and that says a lot considering the amount of hair she had on her head."

"She's stunning," I agree, doing my best to keep an impartial tone.

"Keira is talented, gorgeous, and courageous enough to take bold steps." Arianne continues to sell my girlfriend's virtues. "Her story tugs at your heart. It's something people can connect with. The fact she has the word *unique* tattooed on her back is something we'd be foolish to ignore." She pauses. "It's a sign. It's meant to be."

My eyes bounce from Arianne's to Beckett's.

They just stare at me with huge grins stretching their lips.

Then, it hits me.

"You want Keira to be the face of SCORE Yours?"

"Bingo!" Beckett says.

"She's more than a face," Arianne says. "Keira is the heart and soul of SCORE Yours!"

Whoa.

Chapter 23

Keira

My phone rings, interrupting me just when my mystery thriller is getting good.

Darn.

I drop my e-reader on the chaise lounge and grab it.

"Hey, you!" I say, answering Michaela's video call.

"Hey, Miss California, how's life in La La Land? Working on your tan?"

"That, and my reading challenge."

"How about the hot roommate? Are you two talking again?"

"We're doing a hell of a lot more than talking," I tell her. That's all it takes for my face to break into a huge grin. "And FYI, he's no longer my hot roommate... he's now my hot *boyfriend*."

"WHAT?!"

"Yup!"

"Wait a minute, the last time we talked, he was avoiding you."

"Not anymore. I have his full attention now, if you know what I mean."

Mikki squeaks out a thrilled noise. "Details! I want details!"

I'm too happy to spill my guts.

"Your big girl crotchless panties did the trick?!" Her laugh bursts through the line.

I join her.

"See what happens when you listen to wisdom," she says and points at herself.

I roll my eyes.

"Seriously, I'm taking full credit for this," she says. "Thanks to me, you finally got your man! If we lived in the same city, we'd totally have to go out for drinks to celebrate."

"You're right!"

"Does Noah know?"

"Not yet."

"Now that you finally have your man, you guys should enjoy each other first. You can tell your brother later."

"Yeah... I finally got him..." I hesitate.

She furrows her eyebrows, her eyes narrowing. "Why do I feel a but coming?"

"Don't get me wrong. I'm elated. And I still have to pinch myself to believe it's true. I've lusted after my brother's best friend for so long I was starting to accept the fact we'd only be together in my dirty fantasies—"

"You guys are dating. Reality trumps fantasy."

"That's part of the problem."

"I can only assume the California sun hit your head hard because that doesn't make any sense whatsoever."

"Rhys doesn't date, but he's been around. A lot."

"Okay..." Michaela nods.

"You know what they say... once a playboy... always a playboy."

"If you two are dating, then Mr. Luva Boy hung up his gloves. End of story."

"My fear is one day soon he'll wake up and realize I'm just Keira—a girl who's inexperienced and drifting with no particular aim. He's a successful billionaire." My eyes lift to the luxurious mansion. "I have nothing to offer, Mikki."

"You make it sound like the guy is settling by being with you."

"It feels like it."

Her jaw drops.

"Where do all these insecurities come from?" Mikki asks. "You're like a bulldozer. Nothing stops you. Nothing frightens you."

I share everything Arianne told me about Dark Compulsion.

"All those insecurities were soft whispers all day yesterday, but when I visited the private club's website this morning, it hit me. He's used to women of a certain *caliber*."

There were no photos on the website, but the description was clear, *where LA's finest comes to play*.

Mikki stares at me, incredulous.

"This is about a bunch of female tycoons, socialites, actresses, models, and singers?"

"Women who are a lot more daring in their sexuality and have a purpose in life."

Mikki considers me for a few beats.

"For the daring sexuality part, you already have a secret weapon."

I frown.

"Crotchless panties!" she says. "They work every single time!"

I laugh.

"I'm partially joking," Mikki keeps talking. "The crotchless panties are a symbol—you took a chance, and it paid off big time. It's clear that episode at French Appliqué was a big turning point for both of you."

"I think so."

"You know so, Keira."

"It was."

"You know his weak spot. Use it. That should keep him interested."

Her response surprises me.

"As for you being aimless, it's bullshit. I heard you singing a cappella. You don't need auto-tune, skirts so short they leave nothing to the imagination, or colorful wigs to get the world to pay attention. I may know nothing about the music industry, but your *real* voice—not the fabricated sound imposed by your former record company—moved me to tears every single time. You were born with a gift, Keira. Don't keep it bottled up!"

I'm speechless.

Chapter 24

Rhys

When I get to my place, I park the car in the garage, jump out of the Aston Martin, and practically sprint to the house.

I'm so fucking excited.

Beckett and I don't always see eye to eye on every decision. But this is a case of a meeting of the minds. I'm one hundred percent behind the direction he and Arianne envision for SCORE Yours.

Even though Keira and I texted back and forth throughout the day, I was careful not to let the cat out of the bag.

I want to make a big deal of it... because it is.

I stride through the house as I head to the backyard. I know where to find her. I approach the lounging area surrounded by the shallow pool—her favorite place in the afternoons.

The sight of her stops me in my tracks.

My girlfriend is stretched out like a fucking goddess.

Keira is soaking up the early evening rays. She's wearing an orange bikini that complements her tanned skin, SCORE headphones covering her ears and designer sunglasses firmly in place, her blonde hair peeking from the top of her e-reader, lost in whatever she's reading.

She notices me standing there.

She lowers the device, removes the headphones, and greets me with a brilliant smile.

"Honey, I'm home!" I say.

"Did you bring home the bacon, baby?" She plays along.

"I sure did, sugar."

She lifts her sunglasses and places them on top of her head. "In that case, I might keep you."

"Yeah?"

"Yeah. You're more fun than the pool boy... and more endowed."

Never mind I have a pool girl.

"Was he walking around in those tight speedo's again?"

"No." She shakes her head. "Today he was wearing a thong. He wanted to showcase his other talents. I told him it was highly inappropriate. After all, I have a boyfriend."

"Yes, you do."

We grin at each other.

"Speaking of which, aren't you going to come over here and give your man a kiss?"

"You're such a demanding boyfriend," she says. "Why don't you come to me?"

"Because I want to watch you walk." That, and I don't want to tempt fate in my five-thousand-dollar suit.

She shoots me a flirtatious smile, drops the e-reader to the side and gets to her feet. She sashays towards me, hips swinging left to right.

My cock vehemently approves.

We stand toe to toe.

She tips her head back and offers her lips.

Even perched on her tippy toes, she's so short without her heels on, I have to lean down to meet her tempting lips.

I cup her beautiful face in my hands and my mouth closes over hers. My tongue strokes between her lips, sending a flourish of lust throughout my entire body. She tastes like mangoes, and I can smell the scent of her sun tanning lotion—coconut, I'm guessing. Our kiss is a passionate dance of tongues. She moans against my lips and I deepen our kiss, her longing as ravenous as mine.

When her hands slide to my belt buckle, I break the kiss.

"No you don't!"

"Why not?" She doesn't hide her discontentment.

"If you put your hand on my cock, I'm doomed. We'll never get out of here in time, and we'll be late for our reservation."

She frowns. "What reservation?"

"We're going out. We have a lot to celebrate."

"We do?"

"Yup!"

She purses her lips together and crosses her arms over her chest, her bare foot tapping against the concrete tile. "Aren't you going to give me more to go by?"

"Nope."

"How am I supposed to know what to wear to this impromptu celebration?"

"Run upstairs and select something hot," I tell her.

"Well, that's not vague at all." She rolls her eyes.

"Fair enough. Run upstairs and when you come back down, I expect you to take my breath away. Clear enough?"

She swats my chest. "Why didn't you say so to begin with?" She laughs. "Ooh! I can totally work with that. Lucky for you I had another day jam packed with nothing to do, so I was able to coordinate my brand new wardrobe." She grins, proud. "Is there a color palette I should gravitate—"

Slap!

"Ouch!" She rubs her ass. "What did I do to deserve that?"

"You're wasting time."

"How was I supposed to know that when you're being all secret agent on me and withholding important information?"

"I had to pull strings to get this reservation." One call to Larkin and I was set. He secured a table at his Santa Monica award-winning restaurant in a flash. "We can't be late. Go on now!" I jerk my head towards the house.

She stares at me.

She's suspicious.

"Can I at least know what I did to be treated to this last-minute celebration on a Tuesday night?"

I trace her lips with the pad of my thumb. "It's not about what you did, dimples." I hold her gaze. "It's about who you are."

Chapter 25

Keira

I'm still not sure what we're celebrating, but judging by my surroundings, I'm guessing it's something monumental. Then again, I could be wrong. Aegean Grill in Santa Monica is a sophisticated, upscale seafood restaurant with an extensive raw-bar option. Raw fish? No Thanks. We both agree on that front. When I saw wild jumbo Mexican shrimp on the menu, I was sold. We'll start with that and share the wild Virginia black sea bass. We just placed our order, and I'm already salivating.

"Here's to tonight!" Rhys lifts his champagne flute.

"Finally, I get to find out what the big deal is about," I say, lifting my glass.

"Oh, no, dimples, not yet." He bursts my bubble. "It's still too early in the evening for that. We'll have that discussion over dessert."

"Are you seriously going to make me wait that long?"

"Yup. I don't want you to get too excited and ruin your appetite. I'm just being a considerate boyfriend. Trust me, it'll be worth the wait."

"You're killing me, you know that?"

"I do." His grin widens. "Here's to tonight!"

I clink my glass with his before taking a long sip of the effervescent liquid.

"Not bad?" he asks.

"You mean, holy shit, this is amazing?"

He chuckles.

Bless the French.

"Have I told you how beautiful you are tonight?"

I blush.

"Not in the last fifteen minutes."

He leans into the table. "Well, my girlfriend is hot, and I can't wait to find out which French Appliqué number she's hiding underneath that sexy dress."

I have to squeeze my thighs together to curtail my throbbing pussy.

Damn him.

When I accepted his challenge, I didn't go at it with half measures. I only had forty-five minutes to get ready. In my spike heels, it was impossible not to hear me coming down the stairs. Rhys's attention was trained on me like a laser beam. When I reached the last step, the intense heat radiating from his blue eyes nearly took the wind out of my lungs. He was speechless for a few long beats before rendering his verdict, *"Mission accomplished, dimples. You took my breath away. Let's get out of here before I change my mind about dinner"*. His sweet and naughty words made me want to beg him to stay home.

"I offered you a peek earlier, but you—"

"Yoo-hoo, oh, Rhys." A female voice interrupts me.

I turn around.

A glamorous blonde glides towards our table. Her wrists are pinned to her narrow hips, exaggerating each step the way a model would sashaying down the runway. In her vertiginous heels, she looks like an Amazonian. The contrast between her long hair and her low cut, formfitting emerald-green dress is arresting. The blonde's large breasts nearly spill out of the top part of the deep décolletage. It isn't a stretch to assume she's a lingerie model. Or an actress. Or socialite. Or a rich and powerful woman. In other words, she's nothing like me.

If I had to put a face—and a body—to my earlier insecurities, this woman is it.

Just like that, the petals of my blooming confidence in regard to being enough for Rhys wilt a little. Okay, a lot.

"Rhys, darling." The blonde stops at our table. She ignores me. "I gave you my number, but you never called," she says before pouting like a child.

Satisfaction courses through me.

Thank you, God. She's not one of his uncomplicated flings.

"Good evening, Addison," Rhys says. His voice is distant. "And for the record, I never made any promises."

"But we had a great night together," the blonde says.

"We talked. Nothing more," he says.

"But I wanted to offer so much more. I wanted to offer you all of this." She sweeps a manicured finger along her tall frame.

Seriously?

"I'm good," Rhys says.

"Oh, darling—"

"I'm not your darling, Addison!" Rhys barks, and I flinch.

"But you could be..." the TV game show model hand gesture ensues.

Cue an eye roll.

"Addison, you're interrupting our dinner," Rhys says.

She does this sound of disgust as her face contorts. For the first time since the beginning of this circus act, Addison's attention shifts to me. She narrows her blue eyes. "Clearly you've *downgraded*."

Oh God.

Rhys's eyebrows hit his forehead. "Excuse me?"

"Please," she says. "You go from this..." She does that ridiculous hand gesture again, "...to that?" She points at me. "It's like downgrading from a top-of-the-line sports car to a mule."

Jesus, she could've gone for the Worst Car Ever award-winner.

A mule?

Sheesh.

"Addison, keep walking," Rhys says.

"Seriously, Rhys..." I guess she didn't hear the warning in his voice. "I'm waaaaayyyy better. *She* gives off the vibe of an inept virgin. And she's wearing white, for God's sake. On a weekday. At a seafood restaurant." I wasn't aware I was committing fashion suicide when I selected my outfit.

I opted for a sexy, but tasteful, white dress that hits me above the knee with a seductive V neckline and an elegant slip. I complemented the look with a pair of Cedrics—aka Cedric de Seignard—skyscraper glitter silver heels. Arianne swears by the French shoe designer. I thought I'd nailed it. Doubt twists my tummy.

"I'm sure she wouldn't know what to do with a guy like you." Addison isn't done crucifying me. "I would."

I'm mortified.

Rhys stands up and throws his napkin on the table.

"I'm not in the habit of making a scene, but you asked for it, Addison."

"I'm just saying—"

"Stop talking." Rhys's tone seethes with anger as his gaze narrows.

Yikes.

"You're interrupting my date. That's rude—"

"But I thought you didn't date?"

"I said, stop talking," Rhys says. "You, Addison, are *not* the type of woman I'd date. Keira, *my girlfriend,* is!" He points at me.

A public declaration?!

Oh my God.

Oh my God.

Oh my freaking God.

Goosebumps explode across my body, running from the top of my head to the tips of my toes.

Just wow.

Rhys just made an official announcement in the middle of a chichi restaurant.

I'm floored.

My chest pumps a little, proud like a peacock.

Take that, bitch!

"But—"

"Men talk amongst buddies, Addison."

"Wh—what do you mean?" There's a distinct tremble of hesitation in her voice.

This is getting good.

"J7."

Huh?

"J7?" Addison asks.

Who's J7?

He leans into her. "Yes, the South Korean boy group consisting of seven members... the guys you allowed to gang-bang you multiple times for bragging rights," he says in a low voice.

Lucky for me, I'm sitting close enough to catch that juicy tidbit.

"A buddy of mine warned me, one man isn't enough for you," Rhys says.

Holy shit!

That's a lot of cocks in one shot! I mean, a lot.

Dirty Addison.

Popcorn would be really good right about now.

Addison takes a step back and straightens her back, her jaw lifted in defiance.

"This is bullshit!" she says. "Men do it all the time! When a woman does it, it's a double standard. How is that even fair?"

I commiserate, my sister, but it just is. You're going to have a hard time selling that one.

"So what if I like it with multiple men at once? It's been my preference forever. It gets boring really fast with one guy. No thanks!"

Go, Addison! Go!

"There's so much discrimination against people who are polyamorous."

This ain't no reverse harem romance book, Goldilocks.

"Think of the extensive experience I bring to the table." Her judgmental gaze slides to mine before returning her focus to Rhys.

I'm okay not having as much experience as you do, Dirty Addison.

"Except for you, I'd keep it one on one," she tells Rhys.

Her generosity knows no bounds.

When they say you can't judge a book by its cover, I wonder if they had Addison in mind.

"Perhaps you didn't hear me." Rhys is pretty pissed off. "Firstly, I'm here on a *date with my girlfriend*. Secondly, I wouldn't touch you even if you promised me twenty billion dollars."

That's a lot of coin.

"Thirdly"—my man pauses, his unimpressed gaze

sweeping down the drama queen's length—"you can take your *extensive experience* and get the hell out of my face."

Addison's back stiffens, which causes her ample bosom to protrude.

The reverse harem addict shoots me one last nasty glare.

I respond with an angelic smile.

She huffs and turns on her heel to an awaiting audience. All eyes are on her as she performs her walk of shame, the confident runway sashay a distant memory.

Buh bye, bitch.

Rhys sits back down. "I'm sorry about that travesty."

"It's not your fault."

He lets out a loud sigh.

His expression is suddenly sullen, as if a war is raging inside him.

"Listen, Keira..."

My stomach drops.

"I'm not going to sit here and insult your intelligence," he says. "My past is bound to crash with the present." He reaches for my hand, interlacing our fingers together. "There isn't anything I can do about it."

"It's okay. I understand."

"You need to believe me when I say, right here, right now, it's about you... only you, dimples."

And just like that, my worries turn to dust.

My heart swells so much, I swear, it's about to explode.

~

After a sincere apology from the restaurant manager and a complimentary bottle of premium rosé champagne, we were able to return to the blissfulness of our date. A few people stared at me a little longer than conformable after the blonde model made her exit. I simply smiled. I don't blame them for pulling out their phones to capture the drama. Since Addison was the main focus, I'm not too worried. Not to mention, my short blonde hair allows me to hide in plain sight.

Dinner was outstanding.

The shrimp was so succulent, I thought I was having a communion with God. The wild sea bass melted in my mouth. The chef is gifted. Everything else was on par with an unforgettable dining experience—from the attentive wait staff, to the irreproachable wine list, to the relaxing atmosphere.

Even though I was stuffed beyond words, I couldn't resist dessert. Neither could Rhys. As we polish off the last bite of the chocolate espresso ganache cake with two scoops of the cherry sorbet we shared, the mental countdown starts in my head.

I drop my fork on my empty plate. "Soooo..."

Rhys mimics me. "Soooo..."

"Don't you think I've suffered enough?" I ask. "I even had to endure Addison."

"She wasn't part of the program."

"She monopolizes people's attention, that's for sure." I tell him.

He grimaces. "Addison Moody is an Instagram model with a massive male following."

I was right about the model part.

"She's an attention whore, and so desperate for relevance she's willing to flash her semi-naked breasts and butt to make sure everyone knows her name. That's how she managed to land a lucrative sponsorship deal with an adult toy company. Other than that, there isn't much to her."

"I see."

"Let's focus on why we're here tonight," he veers the conversation.

"Okay!" I sit straight in my chair.

"I told you about SCORE Yours?"

"Yes! It's your shiny new project."

"Beckett and I feel strongly that this is a game changer for us—"

"I've said it before, but I'm so proud of you and I'm super excited for you!"

"As of this morning, *you're* a big part of SCORE Yours."

My face twists in confusion. "What does that mean?"

"You made quite an impression on Arianne," he says.

"It's mutual, but that still doesn't explain what you just said."

"There's so much you underestimate about yourself, Keira," he says.

"Okay... I thought this was a celebration. Why does it feel like my head is on the chopping board?"

"You have it all wrong, dimples," he says. "Your head is about to become a big commodity."

"Can you translate that in English, please?"

Rhys tells me all about his meeting with Beckett and Arianne.

When he finishes, I stare at him, my eyelashes batting a mile a minute, my heart lurching in my throat.

"Aren't you going to say anything?" he asks.

"Me?" That's all I manage. My hand goes to my hair, playing with the short strands as I worry my lower lip. "Really?"

"Yes. You. Really." If I weren't in so much shock, I'd laugh at his teasing.

"Are you sure?"

"All three of us are on the same page."

"Wow."

"Given what we have planned, your beautiful face is going to be everywhere—here and abroad."

"There was no one else up for the job?" I let out a nervous laugh.

He shoots me a stern look. "There were several other candidates we could've selected, but we want *you*."

"Allow me to repeat my question—"

"Why is it so unbelievable we'd select you?" he asks.

"Come on, you guys can do better than me."

Rhys shakes his head. "I disagree."

"I left LA with big dreams in my pocket and an even bigger attitude, but I return home broken and broke. I have nothing to show for it. How in the world can I represent your product and your company?"

He studies me for a long beat.

My cheeks flush under his inspection.

"You're perfect for this," he says. "You've wanted to make your mark in this world since you were twelve. You stumbled the first dozen times you took a stab at fame, but that's not uncommon. This time, it's about *who* you are. Not a fake persona someone who doesn't truly care dictates. This is about Keira Weatherly—the artist who stood up to her recording company because she wouldn't bend to their creative violation, the faithful friend who despite it all, remained loyal, and proved it by etching it permanently on her skin, the woman who was willing to travel to the other side of the planet to discover who she really was, the fearless rebel willing to shave her head to free herself from her past, and last, but not least, my kickass girlfriend."

A tear rolls down my face.

I don't even bother to wipe it away.

So many emotions swirl inside me... and that's okay.

Chapter 26

Rhys

Once she was over the shock, my little chatterbox couldn't stop talking. She fired a thousand questions at me on the ride back to the house. I answered as many as I could. I'm so grateful Arianne planned ahead. On Thursday, Keira will spend the greater part of the day with the brain behind SCORE Yours, Beckett, and the director of marketing at the advertising agency to kick things off and talk specifics. Then, my girl will spend some time with legal to go over the contract. She'll die when she sees the number associated with being the face of SCORE Yours. I'll front her the money so she can hire her own lawyer to read the fine print. Given Keira's new role in my life and business, I'm fully aware I'll have to come clean with Beckett and Arianne.

Probably after I talk to Noah.

I park the Aston Martin inside the garage, get out, circle the vehicle and help Keira out. With our fingers interlaced together, we trail towards the house. I don't think anything in the world could wipe the grin off her face.

"Where are you going?" I ask her when she lets go of my hand when we reach the top step.

"My room," she says.

My eyebrows furrow. "You're not sleeping in my bed?"

"I'm no longer allowed to sleep in *my* bedroom?"

"Well, no."

"That's a little presumptuous, don't you think?"

"Not at all. You're my girlfriend. You belong in my bed. End of story."

She places a hand against my chest, and taps it a few times. "I must say, as backward thinking as this caveman-possessiveness-alpha-beat-against-my-chest-silverback-gorilla-style-Tarzan-Lord-of-the-Jungle routine is, it's sort of endearing and... hot."

I grin.

"To address your concern, Tarzan, I'll come and join you in a few minutes," she says. A mischievous glee glints from her hazel-green eyes. "There's just something I have to do in my bedroom first."

"What are you up to, dimples?"

"Nothing!" Her voice goes up several levels.

I cock an eyebrow. "You sure about that?"

"Of course I am!" That high-pitched voice again.

"How long before I can expect you?"

"Eager much?"

"I haven't fucked you since this morning, so you could say that."

"Go on!" She shoos me off. "I'll be there shortly."

She strides away from me, my eyes glued to her ass in that formfitting, stunning white dress.

She glances over her shoulder and winks.

My cock wakes up.

It's like I'm one of Pavlov's fucking dogs, conditioned to react when I'm around her.

I shake my head and make my way to my bedroom.

I step inside, turn on the lights, and freeze.

What the fuck?

"Keira, why is there a chair in the middle of my bedroom that wasn't there before?" I shout.

"You'll soon find out." She shouts back.

She must've placed it there while I was waiting for her to get ready.

I'm intrigued enough not to ask more questions.

I slip off my jacket and hang it. I roll my shirt sleeves up to the elbows, walk to the panoramic window and admire the nighttime view. I'm not right on the water, but from this vantage point, I can still see the ocean.

I check my watch.

Several minutes have already gone by.

My impatience mounts.

Where the hell is she?

The door opens, and Keira peeks her head around it.

"Ready?" she asks.

"I'm not sure what to expect, so how would I know if I'm ready or not?"

"Now you know how I felt earlier," she says with a grin.

"Cheeky."

She pushes the door open and walks in wearing a bathrobe and carrying a basket.

"What's going on?"

"It's part of the show," she tells me. "These"—her eyes fall to the basket that's covered with a sheet or something—"are props."

"Show? Props?"

"Yes, there will be entertainment and props are necessary." She drops the basket on the floor. "No peeking."

"Did you drink too much champagne or does this have to do with my announcement?" I ask.

"I didn't overdo it on the bubbly and for your information, this was planned well before you dropped the joyous news in my lap," she tells me. "I know you're getting a little antsy, but it shouldn't be much longer. I just need another five minutes to slip into my costume. Sit. Make yourself comfortable."

"What game are you playing, dimples?" My voice is like gravel.

"Be a good sport. Play along," she says. "Please, sit."

I don't budge.

"Rhys, you're twice my size. It's not like I can move you." She approaches me. "Please, sit."

I make a face.

"I promise, it'll be worth your while." She flashes me a seductive smile.

I oblige.

"I'll be right back," she says.

"This better be good."

"It will be." She singsongs her response as she waltzes out of my bedroom.

I check my watch every five seconds.

Suddenly, I hear a strange clicking sound coming from the ceiling speakers. She must be using the wall mounted iPhone dock in the hallway that controls the multi-room system upstairs.

A weird beeping sound fills the air.

"Oh shit, that's way faster than I expected! False start! Sorry!"

Whatever this is, she's put a lot of thought into it.

She starts the song from the beginning.

I'm no longer a stranger to the beeping sound. Then, the brassy sound of saxophones and trumpets blare into the room.

I can't help my smile.

Little devil.

The hit song is as iconic as the movie.

Some things never get old.

I must've been sixteen years old when a friend from school invited a bunch of us over to his place to show us what he had discovered on his older brother's laptop when he was snooping around. Porn is porn, but *9 1/2 Weeks* will forever more be the ultimate teenage boy wet dream because, holy hell, Kim Basinger was a sex bomb in that movie!

On cue, my girl busts into the room.

"That's what you call a costume?" I ask.

"It is tonight." Her sly smile is dangerous.

She traded the bathrobe for a fitted black suit. The blazer hits her at the waist and the skirt hits her below the knee. She paired the suit with a silky top, heels and fishnet stockings—all in white. She looks classy and vampy.

"Where's your glove?" I ask.

Her grin matches mine. "You've watched the video?"

"You bet."

"This idea came to me this afternoon, so I didn't have time to scour the city for the eighties must-have fashion statement in question. Is that going to be a problem?".

"If you give me a good show, it won't."

"I plan to." Her attention moves to the ceiling. "Oh shit!"

"What is it?"

"Here I am talking and half the song has already played. I haven't even asked you to turn on the flat screen TV."

"I'm supposed to watch TV while watching you do whatever it is you're going to do?" I ask, confused.

"I was going to play the music video while dancing."

"I must've watched Joe Cocker's *'You Can Leave Your Hat On'* video with the striptease scene a million times. I've memorized Kim Basinger's every move. As sexy as she is, I want to see *your* moves," I say. "No TV!"

She seems relieved.

"I was feeling the pressure. Kim is a hard act to follow," she says. "At least now, I can improvise."

"Silly girl," I say. "I'm not dating Kim. I'm dating you."

"Okay, I'll be right back, then."

And, she's gone.

She starts the song again and runs back into the room.

"Okay, we're set!"

She seems a bit frazzled.

I chuckle.

"FYI, you're not supposed to laugh." She frowns in discontentment. "This is supposed to be sexy."

"The song is already halfway through, dimples," I say as she stands there and scolds me.

"Argh!" Her hands go flying in the air before landing on her thighs with a thump.

"Go fetch your phone," I tell her.

She hesitates.

"I'm not putting an end to the entertainment portion of the evening," I say. "Let me be your DJ."

She rewards me with a dazzling smile. "Okay!"

She runs out of the room and she's back in a flash.

She hands me her phone.

I get up and head to my walk-in closet. There's another control station in here. I place her phone on the dock and start the song from the beginning.

"Why didn't you divulge this earlier?" she asks when I emerge from the closet.

"Because I didn't know what you had up your sleeve, woman."

"Fair enough," she says. "Let the show begin. Again!"

I take a seat.

She sashays to the basket, swinging her hips to the rhythm of the music. She bends over, flashing me that perfect ass, and grabs something. She turns around holding a whip in her hands.

This should be good.

With a series of runway strides, she stands in front of me. She lifts her hands and flexes the whip over her head a few times, as if testing it, while doing a little sexy dance with her hips.

My cock approves.

She brings the tip of the whip to my stomach. My eyes drop to where it trails up the pathway of the buttons of my shirt. She then traces it across my chest. Meeting her gaze, I grab hold of it. She's still holding strong to the other end.

"Is it my turn to use it on you?" I ask, my voice rough.

"Let go of the prop," she says, pulling hard.

Too bad for her I'm stronger.

"I asked you a question, dimples."

"Play along, big guy."

I cut her some slack and let go.

"Now I'm out of character," she says with a huff. "I have to take it from the top. Can you start the music from the beginning, please?"

"I will, but I need a kiss first," I say.

"Rhys!" she warns.

"Okay, okay. I'll be patient."

"And this time, no distractions from the audience," she says with a motherly finger wave.

"I like domineering Keira."

She smiles wide.

I run in and out of the closet.

The sexy eighties tune envelopes the room by the time I sit back down on the chair. And from the look of it, she's in full character. She turns her back to me, and to the tempo of the song, she starts unbuttoning the blazer. She slides it off just enough to flash me some skin. She glances over her shoulder to make sure she has my full attention.

Oh, she most certainly does.

She repeats the sexy move, flashing me the other bare shoulder. She wiggles her ass left to right as she slides the blazer off her body. The movement is slow and mesmerizing. She turns around and throws the blazer at me. I catch it with one hand.

"Nice top," I say. "No bra?"

Her protruding nipples are a distraction.

"Not with a silk chemise," she says.

"I've said it before, but it bears repeating, bless the French."

"You have no idea," she says and resumes taunting me.

This isn't the first time I've seen her gyrating her hips like a temptress. I've watched the Lucky Break videos an embarrassing number of times. This is different. This private performance is for my eyes only.

When the bridge hits again, she lets loose.

The shock of pleasure of seeing her in her element burns my veins.

Fucking hot.

"Damn, I don't even have dollar bills to stuff inside your panties. You're wearing panties, right?"

"I'm not going to tell!" She winks. "You'll soon find out."

My cock swells so much, it feels like it's doubled in size. I grip my hair and pull to curtail my arousal, but that's not enough.

She's blissfully unaware of my predicament, lost to the music. She slides the skirt off her body, swinging her hips in perfect synch with the music. When the fabric pools at her feet, she steps out of it and kicks it aside.

Then, she takes it up about twenty notches.

She turns around, parts her feet, and she wiggles her body, her head flipping from left to right.

She's wild, titillating, provocative, and so fucking desirable.

I'm quite partial to the move where she emulates riding a mechanical bull.

"So damn sexy," I tell her.

She runs her hands down the silky chemise, lifting the hem just enough to torment me.

Fuck. Me.

Garter belts.

My jaw, which has gone slack with shock over this blazing peep show, snaps shut. I swallow hard as I fight the urge to close the space between us and put an end to her striptease by burying myself balls deep in her pussy.

Jesus.

I adjust myself... not that it does a damn thing. My cock is still on full alert.

"The garter belt and the heels stay on when I fuck you."

"Whatever you say," she says before slipping a finger into her mouth and sucking on it, her hooded eyes staring right at me.

The dare glittering from her eyes is my demise.

I'm this close to dropping to my knees and begging this woman for mercy.

"Another downside of dating an older man," she says. "The ticker can't always take the heat." She taps her heart for emphasis.

"Oh, you're asking for it."

"I guess I am." She shrugs. "And I hope you'll give it to me real good."

"In spades, baby."

"I better wrap this up, then."

Just when I think the dance can't get any more feverish, she proves me wrong.

Fuck, I'm about to dial 911 as prevention.

The pièce de résistance comes when she bends over and lifts the chemise, exposing a view that nearly makes me lose my shit in my pants.

She's wearing a pair of white crotchless panties and by God her pussy is dripping.

My entire body tenses.

Holy fucking shit.

I'm not old enough for a heart attack, but this feels close.

My entire body vibrates with tension and pent-up lust. I can't take it a second longer.

Enough.

I reach her in one long step, scoop her in my arms, and sling her over my shoulder.

She squeals in surprise.

"Damn you for doing this to me," I say.

"Did I get you all worked up?"

"You'll soon find out." I borrow her words.

"Oh, God. Let go of me, you brute." She feigns outrage. "You can't take me against my will." She kicks her legs.

"Save it, blondie. You deserve the fury I'm about to unleash on your fine ass."

"Are you going to be gentle?" she asks in a sweet voice.

"Fat chance," I tell her. "You knew exactly what you were doing. You provoked me. Now, it's time to pay for the consequences of your actions."

"Have a heart. I beg of you, Tarzan," she says. "There must

be a way I can make it up to you." She even adds a little tremolo to her voice.

Who knew she had acting chops?

I carry her to the bed and sit down at the edge with her in my lap, her ass pressed against my hard-on.

She offers a triumphant smile.

"You hardly sound like someone who wants to repent or atone their sins!" I say.

She frowns. "Maybe I have to try harder?"

"I think you do."

"Would a kiss be a good start?"

"Let's see."

I lower my lips to hers and the contact is like a box of dynamite exploded in the room. I push my tongue between her lips, tasting every inch of her mouth. She cradles my head and moans against my lips as I deepen the kiss.

I could kiss her a thousand times a day, and it still wouldn't be enough.

After a few long passionate breaths, I break the kiss.

I place her on the bed and stand up.

She sits up and scoots a little further up the bed.

"Did I tell you to move?"

She shakes her head.

"I want you right where you were."

She obliges.

I toe off my shoes, remove my socks, and undress in a rush.

"What about your boxer briefs?" she asks.

"I'm keeping them on. It's part of your punishment."

She pouts. "You're cold-hearted, Tarzan."

Chuckling, I sit on the bed, grab her by the ass and pull her onto my lap, forcing her to straddle my legs. And my God, her white crotchless panties leave nothing to the imagination.

She gasps before sinking into me and gyrates her hips against my cock.

"You're so hard and so big," she says, pressing her body against my cock.

"Fuuuuck." The word drawls from my mouth. Her crotchless panties offer no barrier between her dripping wet pussy and my boxer briefs.

Regaining control, I tangle my fingers in her hair and tug. "This is about you repenting, remember?"

She flashes me a mischievous grin, twisting in my lap with more determination. "Sorry."

My cock swells under the pressure.

Slap!

"Stop," I say. "You're gonna make me come."

"Let's get on with my punishment so we can move on to the good stuff." She grins.

I narrow my eyes at her.

Two can play this game.

"You're not going to like what I have in store for you, dimples."

"Lay it on me."

"Let's make it about you first," I say.

"That's my kind of punishment. So, whatcha got for me?"

"You're going to make yourself come. The rule is, you stay on my lap, and I won't help you."

She frowns.

The heat between her legs is burning my cock. I'm no longer sure who I'm punishing.

"Make it good," I say. "Then, if I'm inclined, I'll honor your pussy with my cock."

"Shit." The word just drops from her lips. "You're a hardball."

"And you're a cock teaser," I tell her. "Get to it."

She glares at me.

She's not so eager anymore.

"I'm waiting."

She's hesitant.

"All talk no action?" I ask.

"It's just... I've never touched myself in front of anyone before."

"Then, let me be your first."

I rest the palm of one hand against her inner thigh, opening her legs a little more. With the other hand, I trace the gap in her crotchless panties.

Her head tilts back, and she closes her eyes, a long moan dropping from her lips.

"You get a kick from knowing you have my undivided attention, dimples." Her eyes meet mine. They're veiled with lust. "That was the sole purpose of that performance. This is a bit of the same... just a lot closer and personal."

"You do it. Please, touch me," she says. "Touch me and make me come."

"No. I won't."

"I'll suck your cock if you do," she says to sweeten the pot.

"You'll suck my cock, regardless."

Her eyes widen in surprise before her lips part in a slow grin.

The fact she's still wearing the chemise, garter belt, and heels makes this moment erotic.

"I gave you an order and I expect you to follow it, Keira."

I grab her hand, guide it to the gap in her panties and rub her hand over her pussy lips.

Her breath hitches.

"You're so wet for me, baby."

Even though my fingers aren't in direct contact with her pussy, her slick juices are everywhere.

"God. I like the way you do that."

"I'm not doing anything. You are."

"But you're guiding my hand. It's so fucking hot."

"It is, isn't it?"

She nods.

I pull her hand away from her pussy, and force her to slap her pussy lips.

She yelps.

I grab hold of her middle finger and rub it around her clit in languorous circles.

She lets out a long sigh and her head lolls back, and she starts bucking against her finger. I dig my free hand into her ass, restraining her movements.

I adore the way her breaths are coming faster as we rub her clit together.

Then, I take it all away from her by removing my hand.

Her eyes meet mine, fury and frustration flashing back at me.

"Why did you do that?"

"The warm-up is over," I tell her. "I already explained what I expected. Now give it to me."

She hesitates, but slowly her finger starts moving.

"Good girl. Keep going."

She's bolder now.

"Tell me what you want me to do to that dripping pussy."

"Fuck me."

"You want my cock?"

"Yes, right here." She slips a finger inside her pussy and pumps in and out.

Goddammit.

"You want to swallow my massive cock with your tight pussy?"

She slides another finger inside her desperate pussy and finger-fucks herself.

"I want your cock to do this to me." Her voice comes out shaky.

"Is that how a good girl asks?"

"Fuck me here. Please."

"Not good enough."

"Rhys, please. I need your cock and I'm willing to do whatever it takes."

"Much better!"

I slide my hand to the middle of her back, dip my head, and bite her nipple through the silk.

She cries out.

She gyrates her hips in wild circular motions, rubbing her pussy against my crotch.

The more she bucks against me, the more her juices soak my boxer briefs.

Her breath is getting deeper—more labored.

Fucking perfect.

"Change of plan." I grab her hand and bring it to my lips.

Half lidded hazel-green eyes fix me.

I lick the sweet juices from her fingers.

"God, that's naughty," she says.

"That'll have to do for now until I get my mouth on you."

I grab hold of the hem of the chemise and pull it up her body. She lifts her arms without being told. I pull the silk fabric over her head and fling it aside, exposing her heavenly body.

"Use my cock to get off." My boxer briefs are already soaked. Might as well go the distance. "I'm just going to sit back and enjoy the show."

Her pupils dilate. "I like that."

She places both hands on my shoulders and positions herself.

My firm palm holds her back, giving her more leverage.

"Grind!"

She doesn't disappoint.

The friction is mind-blowing.

A groan slips from my mouth as I watch in awe as my girl chases her pleasure.

The hedonistic sight of her pussy lips peeking from her white crotchless panties while she's still wearing her garter belts will be seared in my memory forever.

And then she starts riding my cock harder.

And harder.

And harder.

She's embarrassingly wet.

She gives herself to whatever hedonistic demon is controlling her. She's completely out of her shell.

She's wild.

Shameless.

Fearless.

I have to mentally coax myself not to come.

I slide a hand down her back until my fingers dig into the flesh of her ass. Her hips gyrate faster as she grinds, and grinds, and grinds, lost to the moment.

"Your... cock," she says. "Take it out, please. Fuck me, Rhys."

"You're starved for it?"

"Yes."

"Not yet. Keep riding my cock and I'll reward you later."

She pulls a fast one on me.

She responds by bouncing off my balls.

The unexpected movement takes my breath away.

Fuck, fuck, fuck.

My cock twitches, desperate to come out and play.

She gasps, and her body shakes, her eyes rolling to the back of her head.

She's close.

"Come hard for me, Keira."

"Oh, God, Rhys!"

"Don't hold back!"

"Oh, Rhys! I'm there! I'm there!"

A sob escapes her lips, and she cries out as she gives in to her orgasm.

It's a thing of beauty.

Her head drops to my chest, and she circles her arms around my neck, pressing her satiated body against my aching cock.

Her breath is as ragged as mine.

"You're so fucking beautiful when you come." I drop a soft kiss on the top of her head.

I feel her smile against my chest.

"You okay?" I ask.

She nods.

"You're sure?"

She nods again.

"Good." I pry her arms loose.

She meets my gaze, her eyes wide with questions.

"On your knees."

Chapter 27

Keira

Holy mind-blowing sex!

My inexperience shines bright because I didn't even know that was possible. I had no idea you could ride a guy's covered cock and come your head off.

That blew dry humping my pillow way out of the water.

I thought I knew him, but Rhys keeps me guessing. He's dirtier than I could've imagined. In the same breath, he's also attentive, sweet and caring. My boyfriend's two opposite sides make him more irresistible and I'm not above admitting I'm falling for him more and more.

Rhys, the protector, is endearing.

Rhys, the domineering seducer, is indomitable. Inexorable, even.

Rhys, the lover, is intoxicating.

The man fucks like a rock star. I guess I should say a rap star.

All these tantalizing thoughts swarm in my head as he pushes me down to my knees.

I slide down the bed to the floor, too eager for my own good.

"Pull me out!" he says.

My eyes land on his crotch and gasp, mortified. "Did I do that?"

"You did," he nods. "Your dripping wet pussy marked me."

"God, that's so embarrassing."

"It's hot as fuck that you respond so beautifully to me. It tells me you want me just as much as I want you." His eyes drop to his crotch. "I gave you a command, dimples."

"Oh, yeah, I finally get to play with your cock."

He chuckles.

He lifts his hips off the bed, making it easy for me to slide his boxer briefs down his legs.

And then, his cock is right there in front of me, massive, impressive, bulging, mouthwatering, the veins throbbing in angry fury, the tip a tantalizing shade of purplish-red.

All mine.

"Take care of your boyfriend, dimples."

I obey.

I lower my head, my lips sliding down his cock.

"Oh fuck," he says, and my heart swells for him.

I bob my head slowly at first.

His thighs go tense and he widens his stance.

"That's it, work your hot little mouth up and down my fat cock, you filthy slut."

Filthy slut?

Fuck, that's hot.

Pleasure courses through me knowing I do that to him.

"Take me deep, baby."

With one hand gripping his base, I swallow a few more inches of his cock.

I'm elated by the sounds of my slobbering mouth gliding up and down his raging erection.

He fists the longer strands of my hair and tightens his grip, forcing a throaty whine out of me.

"You're a vision—your lips wrapped around my cock, your head bobbing up and down, the curve of your waist, your ass—fuck, your ass—the fishnet stockings, and the heels. You're my wet dream come true."

His praise fuels me and boosts my confidence.

I moan and take him in as far as I can.

He thrusts between my lips in controlled movements.

"I never want this to end," he says.

And I can't help but wonder if he's talking about the blowjob or us.

"Jesus, you're gonna pump the cum right out of my balls with your filthy mouth," he says. "I'm not going to let you take me down so easily. You're going to have to work a little harder for it."

And I do.

I suck his cock with urgency, grazing his hard flesh with my teeth.

His groans and grunts and curses ignite my clit.

"Goddamn, your mouth!"

My hand pumps his cock in a rhythmic motion, matching my head bob. I work him harder, determined to break him.

His hands tighten around my shoulders and he pulls his cock out of my mouth.

I look up into fierce blue eyes. "Am I doing it wrong?"

"You're doing it more than right," he says.

"Why did you stop?"

"Because I need to fuck your mouth," he says, lifting his hips off the bed and angling his body with one hand against the mattress and the other hand on top of my head.

I brace myself for the assault, but it's in vain. He uses the leverage to his advantage, forcing himself into my mouth.

Jesus.

I choke and gag over his cock, tears welling in my eyes.

"You need a minute?" he asks.

I shake my head.

"Good girl."

He resumes his mission, slides deeper into my mouth, driving himself with such force, I gag again.

He pulls free, my saliva dripping from his cock end.

"You okay, dimples?"

His length and girth are overwhelming.

When we perform a sixty-nine and I'm on top, I'm in control. On my knees like this, he robs me of the privilege.

I manage a nod and open my mouth wide for him.

"Such a good little slut," he says, and my pussy flutters ins response.

With one hand on top of my head, he eases his cock back between my lips.

"You can do this, baby," he says.

I can. I will do this.

He fucks my mouth, easing deeper with each slow thrust. When his cock touches the back of my throat it brings tears to my eyes but I don't gag this time.

My eyes are fixed on his. So blue. Icy blue.

His gritted jaw.

My God.

I almost gag on a deeper thrust.

My lover doesn't back down.

He dominates the cadence.

He dominates my mouth.

He dominates me.

With his hand holding my head in place, there's nowhere for me to go. I can only submit.

His massive cock throbs in my mouth.

He reaches down and wipes tears from my eyes with his thumb.

"My cock is so fucking hard because, goddammit, dimples, you look so beautiful with it in your mouth."

My pussy flutters again and my clit throbs back to life.

But I just came hard.

"You turn me into a ravenous beast," he says and starts pumping into my mouth, slow and steady. "I've never experienced anything as hot as this before. It's a first for me."

I'm in awe.

With his considerable experience, I'm baffled I could be his first anything.

"I'm not gonna last long," he says.

I nod my understanding.

"You're such a good little girl, I might have to keep you."

Yes, please.

I nod again.

He chuckles.

"You want to stay here with me?" he asks.

I don't have time to answer.

He rams inside my mouth with powerful thrusts, pressing my head down, nearly choking me over his cock.

"You want me to use your mouth like this every single night, slut? Is that why you want to stay?"

I whimper around his cock, the buildup at my core unmistakable.

My clit tingles with need.

I can feel my juices leaking from me.

Holy shit.

I had no idea it was possible to come while giving a guy a blowjob. I'm not even touching myself.

His hips rock back and forth. He's merciless, his cock pumping hard and quick into my mouth.

I'm drooling with every thrust, saliva dripping onto my tits.

Dear God.

"Fuck, I'm struggling here," he says through gritted teeth.

His cock throbs inside my mouth.

He's about to explode.

I'm not sure what takes over me, but I cup his balls and squeeze gently.

He lets out a feral growl that makes my pussy cry.

My body is tight with tension, begging to burst.

"What the fuck are you doing to me, Keira!" There's a tinge of vulnerability in his voice. "This is it. I'm gonna come. I'm gonna come. I'm gonna— Oh, fuck! Oh, baby. Ohhhh God!"

Grunting and gasping with his massive cock throbbing between my lips, Rhys fills my mouth with his cum.

I moan on his cock, drinking every last drop. It's a struggle because there's so much of it.

Dear God. This is so fucking hot.

In a heated rush, my fingers find my clit.

I rub frantically.

It doesn't take long.

The buildup inside me erupts like a bomb just went off. Gasping for air, I dive over the edge, giving in to the sheer force of my blinding climax, blabbing in incoherent words around a mouthful of cock.

Chapter 28

Rhys

My phone rings, jolting me from a peaceful sleep.

My eyes search for the clock on my nightstand.

Fuck.

Keira snuggles a little closer to my body.

I kiss the top of her head.

My phone rings again.

With a curse, I reach for it.

When I see the name flashing on my screen, I close my eyes on a silent groan.

"Hey, Noah," I say, accepting the call. My voice is still groggy with sleep.

"Hey, Rhys. Sounds like I woke you up."

"You did."

He's usually so good with the time zone difference.

"What are you still doing in bed, you lazy bum?" His tone is jovial. It's too early for that kind of cheerfulness.

"You're calling me at six in the morning LA time to barrage me?"

"No, I'm calling you at six in the morning LA time because I'm standing at your door."

I'm fully awake now.

I bolt upright in bed.

Keira frowns at me, upset I've disrupted her beauty sleep.

This fairytale is about to become a horror story, sweetheart.

"Noah?! You're at my door?"

"Well, the guard's staring me down, unblinking, still need the green light from you, but yeah, I'm at the security gate of your Fort Knox-like gated neighborhood."

I hold the phone away from my ear, blinking at it in shock, hoping to God this is a prank.

"Rhys?"

I bring the phone to my ear.

"You're actually at my door right here in LA?" I exaggerate each word. My gaze slides to Keira's. I'm sure the worry I read in her wide eyes matches mine.

"Noah is here?" she mouths.

I nod.

"Holy fuck!" she mouths again.

I nod.

"Man, you can't function without coffee." Noah chuckles on the other end. "Unless you bought another house in another ritzy gated neighborhood you didn't tell me about, yes, I'm here. I'm a short distance from your big ass mansion. Come on, let your brother in. Tell the security guard I'm on your friend's list. I want to see you and my sister."

Fuck! Fuck! Fuck!

"Why didn't you tell me you were coming to LA? I would've arranged for a car to pick you up." I'm grasping at stalling straws here.

"Thanks, Mr. Billionaire, but I can afford a chauffuered car ride from LAX to Manhattan Beach."

"I didn't mean it that way," I say.

"I'm yanking your chain. I know you didn't. Had I told you or my kid sister I was coming, it wouldn't be a surprise."

My eyes move to Noah's little sister in *my* bed.

She's white knuckling the sheets underneath her nose, fear flashing bright in her eyes.

I feel you.

I should've called Noah and manned up. I thought I had time. He lives on the other side of the planet. I didn't account for him dropping by. Who the hell flies nearly thirteen hours for a visit, unannounced?

This is the worst possible scenario. Him finding out like this is like signing my own death sentence. My head is reeling at warp speed as I desperately try to find a spin that'll keep him from knocking my teeth out.

"Shit," Noah says.

"What?" I ask.

"I didn't think of it."

"Think of what?"

"Are you stalling because there's a woman in your bed?" I cringe. "You usually keep your *uncomplicated* fucks away from your home, but things can change."

I pinch the bridge of my nose.

Telling him I'm alone in my bed would not only be a lie, but it would also be a big slap in Keira's face.

"I'm not stalling," I say. "Give me five minutes to put on some clothes and brush my teeth." I need to buy myself some time.

"No rush. The last thing I need is to see your junk," he says. "Once I'm at your door, I'll wait as I enjoy the morning sun."

"All right. Be right there."

I hang up with Noah and call the security desk. Once I'm done, I drop the phone on the nightstand.

"Fuck! I'm knee-deep in shit!"

"Oh my God," Keira says. "Noah is here?!"

I rub my hands over my face. "Yes."

"This is horrible. He's going to freak out."

"Yes, he will, and chances are I'll be on the receiving end of him freaking out."

"We're in this together," she says.

My eyes meet her determined gaze. "You know how protective your brother is of you. This"—I wave a finger between us—"isn't what he meant when he asked me to look after you."

"I'm an adult woman and I can do whatever I want," she says with a firm nod.

Even in this dire situation, she's as spunky as hell.

"Baby, I need you to listen to me and you can't argue."

"But—"

"Keira!"

"Fine. I'm listening." She crosses her arms over her bare chest.

And fuck if my cock doesn't react.

Great. I'm about to walk the green mile and my cock is ready for a morning quickie.

Focus!

"We need to get up. I don't have time for a shower, but you do. You need to wash my scent off your body. While I distract Noah, make sure to clean my bedroom. Hide the prop basket. Hide the whip. Hide the pink fuzzy leather cuffs. Hide the fishnet stockings. Hide the high heels. Hide it all!"

"Okay."

"Don't forget, your phone is still in the iPhone dock in the closet. '*You Can Leave Your Hat On*' sends a definite message."

"Got it!"

"Let's play it safe. Let's find out how long he's in town for.

We'll give him a couple days to settle, and then I'll talk to him. I don't want to drag things on too long. It's too much of a risk."

"I want to be there when you talk to him, Rhys."

"It's best if I do it man to man—"

"Like I'm not involved?"

"Keira, we don't have time for this."

"Fine." She purses her lips.

I fling the sheets off my naked body and rush to the bathroom. I take care of business, brush my teeth, and splash cold water on my face. To hide the smell of sex, I spray a generous amount of expensive cologne all over my body.

Shit.

The scent is overpowering.

I might have overdone it, but at least it might extend my life for a few more days until Noah curls his hands around my neck and chokes me for fucking his kid sister.

Pushing my imminent death aside, I run back to my bedroom.

Keira is frantically picking up damning evidence from last night's naughty peep show.

Good girl.

I race to my walk-in closet, jump into a pair of jeans and pull a t-shirt over my head before sprinting barefoot to the front door.

When I swing it open, the Hulk—I mean, my best friend—greets me with a warm smile.

"Hey, buddy!" He doesn't wait. He steps inside my home and grabs me in a back thumping man hug. "Jesus, Hartford." He breaks our embrace, taking a long step back. "Did you pour the entire bottle of cologne over your body? Those damn New Yorkers can smell you all the way from the east coast." He laughs at his own joke.

"Sorry. I was rushing. I didn't want to make you wait too long."

"You're excited to see me too, right?" His blue eyes sparkle with glee. Finding out Keira and Noah had different fathers explained a lot. They're complete opposites. With his light blue eyes, blond hair, and super pale eyelashes, Noah looks like a Viking. "I knew I did the right thing by surprising you." He grabs me again and squeezes the life out of me. "It's been way too long!"

When he lets go, I can breathe again.

"It's a surprise for sure," I tell him.

"Since I couldn't make it to Vietnam while you were there, I figured I'd make up for it."

"What about the show?" I ask. "You always complain about how hard it is to get away."

"New Zealand was hit by a series of severe storms this past month. It's caused some serious delays in filming to keep everyone safe. There was a small window for me to get away, so I jumped on it." He slaps me on the shoulder. "Where's my kid sister?" he asks, glancing over my head.

I'm six-two.

Noah is six-seven.

I'm quite tall.

He's a tree.

A very large tree.

My eyes land on his wide chest.

Jesus, he's bulkier than before. Has he put on some extra muscle?

Dread washes over me.

The man has always had a mean punch. With more muscle, he becomes a destroyer.

How much plastic surgery will be required to set my jaw once he breaks it?

"Rhys?"

I snap back to the moment.

"Sorry. I'm a little tired. My brain hasn't kicked in yet."

"Did you leave my sis home alone while you got some pussy at Dark Compulsion?" He doesn't give me time to respond. He leans into me. "You and I could drop by tonight..."

"No. I wasn't at the club," I tell him. "I haven't been there in a while."

"Then, my timing back in town is perfect," he says, grinning wide.

I'd argue with that.

"We should go tonight. I love being your guest."

"Don't you want to spend time with your sister?" I ask.

"I will. During the day. But we're talking about *tonight*."

"You're on your own, Noah. I can make arrangements for you, but it's unlikely I'll be your wingman."

"Why the hell not?" He frowns, crossing his bulky arms over his massive chest.

He looks as menacing as fuck.

"Too much on the go," I offer an evasive answer.

"This COO gig is killing your sex life, Hartford," he says with a chuckle.

I beg to differ.

"Like I said, you can go without me."

"Nah. If you're not going, I'm not going. I'll stay here with you and my sister. Speaking of which, where is the little devil?"

"I announced your arrival. She must be in the shower."

"I can't wait to see her."

"Where's your luggage?" I ask, changing the subject.

"It's just one suitcase. I'm only here five days. Let me go grab it."

"Okay."

He returns in a flash.

I close the door and lock it behind him.

"Leave your suitcase at the door. We'll grab it later."

"No problem," he says as he removes his shoes and then his socks.

"Let's go to the kitchen. I'm sure you must be hungry."

"I'm starving," he says. "What time are you leaving for work?"

"Since your visit is unexpected, I'll head to the office later—probably after lunch. I'll text my assistant to warn her."

"It's good to be the boss," he says.

I chuckle. "On most days it is."

He follows behind me.

"Fuck, Hartford, you're living large." His booming voice resonates.

"Wait till you see the rest of the house. I'll give you the grand tour after coffee and breakfast."

"You had barely started the renovations the last time I saw your place."

New Zealand to LA is a long haul, which makes this unexpected visit even more mind-boggling.

"Lots of changes since then," I tell him.

"Speaking of transformations, I still can't get over Keira's. She sent me tons of photos. I love the new hair. It suits her."

"I agree." We enter the kitchen. "Take a seat at the island. I'll get started on breakfast."

"You need help?"

"Nah. You relax. Keira will be down soon. She has a lot to share. Not to mention, my chef has stocked up my fridge."

"Show off."

"I couldn't resist," I say with a grin.

"I just spent God knows how many hours strapped in a confined airplane seat. I need to stretch my legs," he tells me.

"No problem."

I head to the fridge and rummage through it, pulling out the ingredients I'll need for breakfast.

"Eggs, pancakes and bacon, or quiches my chef prepared?" I give him his options.

"I'm up for anything that involves bacon. That'll hit the spot nicely." He nods a few times.

"Excellent."

I get started to keep myself busy and channel the nervous energy running through me.

"I guess I shouldn't be surprised," my best friend says with a slow head nod, "the chef comes with the restaurant style kitchen." He scours the space. "Keira isn't roughing it at your place."

The only rough action she gets is in my bedroom.

"I'm proud of the house and it's great to have Keira around," I tell him.

"I'm sure I sound like a broken record, but thanks so much for everything you've done for her."

"Don't mention it."

"You're taking really good care of all her needs."

In every sense of the word.

"I'm doing my best."

"She keeps going on and on about you, *Rhys this and Rhys that.* In her eyes, you can walk on water."

"The last time she saw me, I was in a different place in my life. I was crawling out of a hole. She's seen the before and after. She hasn't seen the ups and downs in between."

"You know how she is. She can easily be impressed."

His comment rubs me the wrong way.

"We can all have twinkles in our eyes when we don't know the full story," I say.

"I guess you're right," he says. "I hope she isn't breaking your balls."

I wince.

No, but she's doing a great job emptying them.

"Keira is Keira, right?" I say.

He chuckles. "Some things never change. The guy who goes after her is in for a rude awakening. You need balls of steel to be with a woman like my baby sis... either that or no balls at all." He lets out a boisterous laugh and play-punches my arm.

My body vibrates from the impact.

The beating is going to hurt real bad.

He leans in closer. "Seriously, she isn't driving you nuts?"

"Seriously, she isn't."

"Good. If anyone can handle her, it's you. It's a good thing your *cojones* are big enough to handle that fiery temper of hers, huh?"

I really wish he'd stop talking about balls.

"Her personality sure keeps me on my toes," I tell him.

"Don't worry. I'll make sure she doesn't invade your space for too long." He took my words the wrong way. Shit. "While I'm here, I intend on having a serious discussion with her. She needs to get her life back on track so she can afford to move out."

"There's no rush," I say, "No rush at all."

"Rhys, I think I'm already abusing our friendship."

I drop the knife I'm holding on the counter.

"Listen, Noah, I know firsthand what it's like to get back on your feet when you've lost it all. The house is massive. Keira isn't in the way. Things are different now. It's not like before when she lived in LA and she had you, Chelle and me. Do you really want her to live alone in a small apartment in a dubious neighborhood? As for getting her life back on track, you should talk to her. You'll be surprised."

He cocks an eyebrow.

"What?" I ask.

"You sound almost as protective of her as I am."

"It's because I am."

I go back to preparing breakfast.

I'm keenly aware of the moment she enters the kitchen. The floral scent of her new perfume permeates the air.

"Holy hell!" she says, "Rumor has it my big brother is in town!"

I catch a glimpse of her from over my shoulder.

She's wearing a pretty, aqua-blue sundress with spaghetti straps that hits her mid-calf. She's barefoot. Under the morning sun with her short hair slicked back and without a trace of makeup, she's so fucking beautiful.

The urge to kiss her is overwhelming, but I suppress my desire.

The next few days are going to be unbearable.

I shoot Noah a glance.

He looks at his little sister like he always does—with fondness, devotion, and love. As an only child, witnessing their unconditional bond is always a surprise.

"Get over here, Cocoa Puffs, and give me a big hug!"

She runs to Noah.

He lifts her in his arms like she's a tiny puppy. She squeals joyfully. He covers her face with kisses before dropping her back to her feet. The difference of height between them is staggering.

"Good morning, Rhys," Keira says. Her voice is sugary sweet.

"Good morning," I say, keeping my tone even. "Did you sleep okay?"

"The best sleep ever." She offers a bright smile. "And you?"

"Until your brother rudely woke me up, it was a great sleep."

We smile at each other, exchanging a silent complicit conversation.

"Stop pretending you're not happy to see me, Hartford." Noah play-punches me again.

I wince.

"Careful there, you might hurt him," Keira says.

I narrow my eyes at her.

"It's all in good fun. It's not like I'd ever take a real swing at him," Noah says.

"I can't think of a reason why you'd want to do that," Keira says.

Why is she so determined to deliver me to the slaughterhouse?

"Exactly," Noah says. "Rhys is solid. He's irreproachable. A good guy to a fault!" He takes me into another one of his infamous bear hugs.

I close my eyes and thank God for the thirty-one years I've spent on this planet.

My days are numbered and I know it.

~

"Man, you have some hidden talents," Noah says, forking a chunk of sausage.

"So, soooo many hidden talents," Keira says.

I frown at her.

She responds with an angelic smile.

"I hope you'll make this again before I leave. This is fucking delicious," Noah says. "I really miss this dish." He shoves the sausage in his mouth. "Damn. I can't believe I'm saying this, but these are better than your mom's recipe."

"Thanks. It's one of my favorite breakfast dishes, so I perfected it," I tell him.

It was Keira's suggestion I ditch the predictable breakfast idea in favor of one of my specialties—a cheesy sausage and egg bake. She even helped me prepare it. Knowing Noah, I also prepared a plate of bacon. I'm no chef in the kitchen, but I perfected a few recipes, this being one of them.

During the forty-minute bake time, Keira filled in her brother on last night's big news. Understandably, Noah is excited for her. He marvelled at the uncanny timing, considering how determined he was to talk to Keira about her plans to find a new direction for her life. So far, the conversation has been smooth sailing, which is a blessing.

For a long while, we sit in a comfortable silence, enjoying our food. In a blink of an eye, Noah polishes off his second serving, loaded with extra bacon.

I can pack some food, but Noah could eat a restaurant out of business.

"Would you like some more?" I ask him when the coffeemaker bubbles.

"I wouldn't say no," he tells me. "I can get it." He starts to get up.

"Sit!" I tell him. "You're my guest."

He chuckles. "Not really. I kinda imposed myself, but we'll go with your angle."

Keira laughs.

I don't even crack a smile.

"What about you?" I ask Keira.

"I'll have a bit more, and more bacon, please," she says.

With their plates in hand, I walk to the oven, serve them both and return to the kitchen table. I make a second trip to grab my second latte of the day.

"There's more coffee if you guys want some," I say before sitting back down.

Noah eyes my empty plate. "You're done?"

"I'm good," I tell him, forcing a smile. "I just need coffee." I point at my mug.

My stomach is too tied up in knots to eat more. Not to mention, my mind is racing, searching for suitable ways to tell my best friend about my new relationship status. I can only focus on so much at a time.

The Weatherly siblings are chatty people. I'm quieter. Breakfast must be really outstanding because their sole focus is on the food. I'm grateful for the silence because it gives me time to map out how and when and I'm going to drop the bomb on my best friend.

"Rhys and I are seeing each other, Noah."

What the actual fuck?

Noah's forkful of baked eggs freezes halfway to his mouth. His whole body becomes still.

Armageddon strikes.

The apocalypse is now.

Annihilation of the human race is eminent.

It's the end of the world as I know it.

I nearly choke on a gulp of coffee, swallowing down the wrong pipe. I cough so hard, I fear I'll rupture a lung. Keira frantically slaps my back. I take in huge breaths, but it's like I can't get enough oxygen to fill my lungs.

If I die now, Noah won't get a chance to kill me.

"Are you okay?" Keira asks me.

Oh, now you're worried about my well-being?!

"I'm okay," I croak.

No. I'm a dead man.

Noah drops his fork on his plate. His gaze moves slowly to meet his sister's.

"What did you just say?" he asks in a calm voice that sends a shiver of worry down my spine.

The dragon awakes.

"I'm a grown woman and I can see whoever I want." Keira says, holding her brother's furious gaze. "Rhys and I are together, and there isn't a damn thing you can do about it, Noah." She places a possessive hand on my forearm to drive her point home.

I'm surprised she doesn't sit on my lap and start French kissing me to hammer the nail in my coffin.

My best friend growls.

He actually fucking growls!

My mouthy girlfriend lifts her chin in defiance, daring her brother.

Stop poking the bear, dimples.

Keira's impetuous nature characterizes her. Spontaneous and unbridled thinking prompt her to take life by the horns. In bed, it's fucking sexy as hell. But in this instance, it's like sending a condemned man—me—to the guillotine. Being headlong with a pissed-off Noah Weatherly is plain stupid and dangerous.

Sadly, this is my Eddard Stark moment.

There's no glory in dying too soon in a series.

In real life, dying too young is a shame. A crying shame.

"What the fuck is she talking about?" Noah says, and I swear the walls rumble.

Keira soldiers on. "Rhys was going to tell you eventually, but I figured, might as well bite the bullet."

She has no fear.

"I've waited my whole life for him to see me as more than your untouchable little sister. I don't want to not be able to kiss him, or hug him, or touch him, just because you decided to drop by unannounced. I don't want to pretend just because you think I should live in a bubble and remain a virgin until I'm forty. That said, out of respect, I'll sleep in my bedroom while you're here instead of sleeping in Rhys's bed."

For fuck's sake, woman.

It's as if she punched me. A solid blow right to the gut, followed by an uppercut to the chin.

If you look up on Google, *'Best ways to infuriate an enraged grizzly bear'*, that little speech was it.

"First, I'm not talking to you, Keira," Noah says through clenched teeth. "I'm talking to him." He points a finger at me, his eyes flashing with anger. "You're sleeping with my sister, Hartford?"

I stare at him, momentarily struck dumb, struggling to find the words that would appease him.

"I asked you a fucking question," Noah barks.

I clear my throat.

"I'm not sleeping with your sister—"

"Rhys, how could you—"

"That's what she just said—"

"Shut up!" I shout, interrupting them. "Stop talking! Both of you!"

There's a three-way standoff that lasts a few long seconds as we all glare at each other.

Tempers are flared.

Emotions running high.

Nothing between the three of us will ever be the same.

"Noah, your words imply I'm just having a good time in the sack with your sister," I say, willing myself to calm the fuck down. "I'm *dating* Keira. Not just sleeping with her. Big difference."

He growls under his breath again.

"She's convenient because she's living under your roof?" he asks.

"You're an idiot, Noah!" Keira shouts.

I narrow my eyes at him. "What do you take me for?"

"This bombshell makes me reconsider everything I ever knew about you, Hartford."

"How dare you!?"

"You couldn't even man up and tell me. You prefer to hide behind my sister's skirt. She has more balls than you do, coward."

"Newsflash! It's unlikely you'd take a swing at her," I tell him. "I'm sure you're dying to rearrange my face." I rake my fingers through my hair and exhale a long breath. "I was going to tell you—"

"When? When you knocked her up?" he shouts.

I'm dumbfounded.

"I'm not Mom!" Keira shouts. "I'm not her!"

I understand the issues he has with his mother, but I resent the implication.

I don't say a thing.

A retort would require me to reveal too many intimate details. Instead, I glare at him, nostrils flaring. Judging by the twitching of his upper lip, I suspect his erratic heartbeat is as frantic as mine.

That icy stare is usually reserved for assholes.

I never thought he'd put me in that undesirable box one day.

From the dark cloud veiling his blue eyes, I wonder if he isn't plotting my death, and subsequently, how he'll dispose of the body.

"How long has this been going on?" he asks.

"We've been officially dating since Sunday," Keira says.

"It's fairly new," I say.

"Is he your first?" Noah asks.

Whoa.

"You're out of line," I say at the same time Keira spits out, "Fuck off, Noah—"

"No, you fuck off, Keira," he says. "My job is to protect you—"

"You retired from that position when I turned eighteen—"

"This wasn't what I had in mind when I called you and asked if she could stay with you!" His face is so red, it's almost purple. "You betrayed our friendship, Rhys."

"I didn't," I tell him. "I've always kept my feelings in check in regard to Keira—"

"So, you lied to me. This shit has been going on for a while?"

He infuriates me sometimes. "You're not listening, Noah!"

"I understand exactly what's happening here. You took advantage of my sister."

I shake my head. "You're talking shit!"

"Stop it, Noah!" Keira shouts. "He didn't take advantage of me. This is mutual—"

"Mutual my fucking ass," he says.

If I thought I had a shot, I'd punch his lights out for that snide remark.

"You're so obsessed in your crusade to prevent me from ending up like our mother, you smother me!" Keira jumps to her feet. "For years, you've shoved your indoctrination down my throat." She leans over the table and points an agitated finger at Noah. "I heard you loud and clear, big brother. I kept my legs closed. Rhys isn't my first simply because he was too loyal to you and turned me down flat every single time I threw myself at him. And trust me, I tried, and I tried, and I tried. His answer—and loyalty to you—never wavered." She grunts in frustration. "I've always had respect for myself—even in London, your warnings rang in my ears—but I'm allowed to be with someone, Noah." That last part comes out as a plea.

"You want to be together? Knock yourself out." He stands up. "I don't have to stick around to watch this... this... this...

this..." I swear he's about to blow a gasket. "This should never have happened. Fuck this shit!"

Noah storms out of the kitchen, snatching his phone from the kitchen island on his way towards the hallway.

The front door slams.

It's just Keira and me.

I place my elbows on the kitchen table and hide my face in the palm of my hand, exhaling.

I'm glad we were able to talk this through in a calm and collected manner. Not.

Fuck!

"You didn't fight for us, Rhys!" Keira's accusation is like a slug to the chest.

I meet her gaze.

She's still wearing that same choleric expression on her face.

"Are you fucking kidding me right now?" I'm incensed. She's unable to see her part in this. "I told you to give him time."

"I didn't want you to change your mind and back down from telling him," she says.

I groan, rubbing a hand over my face.

"It's like you're afraid of him," she says.

"For good reason! Your brother would walk barefoot on hot coals to save you. He'd take a bullet straight in the heart to protect you. He'd tear a man who's done you wrong from limb to limb and face jail time without batting an eyelash. He'd swim across an ocean if he thought you were in danger. Surely, you're aware of his devotion to you—"

"So I ripped the Band Aid off—"

"I wanted to ease him into it."

"He has to let me grow up—"

"You didn't even give him time to finish breakfast before

you slapped him across the face with news you knew wouldn't go down easy."

"Once I came clean, you were supposed to back me up. Instead, you chickened out."

"I didn't chicken out. We had that conversation a couple hours ago in my bed. We agreed you'd let me lead—"

"I agreed to nothing. I simply decided not to argue with you because my big scary brother was waiting at the door—"

"You're driving me mad right now, Keira—"

"I didn't want to pretend—"

"I asked for a couple of days. You couldn't wait?"

"But—"

"Enough! Your stubbornness may have cost me a long-standing friendship—"

"You choose Noah over me? Over us?"

"For fuck's sake, Keira! You're not listening—"

She lifts a hand up. "Forget it! If we break things off now, you can still salvage your *precious* friendship. It hasn't been that long between us, anyway. I'll get over you. I can find some place else to stay."

She torpedoes out of the kitchen in a whirlwind of anger.

"FUCK!"

~

Keira stomping up the stairs and slamming her door shut after our fight was the straw that broke the camel's back.

I'd reached my quota.

I sprinted upstairs, took a two-minute shower, and adorned a suit. Then, I grabbed my keys and burst out of my house, fury riding my coat tail. I slipped behind the wheel of my Aston Martin, desperate for speed. I didn't head to the office. I went for a long drive to let off some steam. I was still a ball of frustration when I got to SCORE HQ.

If only this morning's blow up was all I had to worry about.

A wall of reporters, bloggers, and paparazzi were awaiting my arrival. As soon as they saw me, questions were volleyed like balls bursting from a tennis ball machine.

"Rhys, are you off the market?" someone shouts.

Huh?

"Did you propose last night?" another shouts.

What are they talking about?

"Rhys, are the rumors true? Did you break things off with Addison for another woman?" another guy shouts.

"Is this the death of #AddRhys?" a man with huge glasses asks.

What the fuck?

It was a mad frenzy at the security gate. Thank God, our security team is highly efficient. I was able to get into the building without being assaulted with more questions.

Between this morning's shit storm and driving around with my phone turned off, I missed the breaking news. Unbeknownst to me, last night's showdown with Addison went viral.

'ADDISON MOODY CRASHES ON BILLIONAIRE RHYS HARTFORD'S DATE WITH MYSTERY WOMAN.'

'ADDISON MOODY FORCED TO DO WALK OF SHAME.'

'RHYS HARTFORD CANOODLING WITH MYSTERY BLONDE WHO LOOKS EERILY FAMILIAR.'

'A BILLION DOLLARS SAYS MYSTERY BLONDE SEEN WITH RHYS HARTFORD IS KEIRA WEATHERLY.'

'BILLIONAIRE RHYS HARTFORD'S MYSTERY WOMAN IDENTIFIED. KEIRA WEATHERLY AIMS HIGH!'

'KEIRA WEATHERLY HIDING IN PLAIN SIGHT IN LA?!'

'KEIRA WEATHERLY. DRAMATIC NEW LOOK. SAME LEVEL OF HOTNESS!'

More fucking drama to add to the list.

Keira was certain she was incognito. She probably was until last night. When the spotlight shines on Addison Moody, no one is spared.

When I got to my office, Cecilia wasn't her usual cool self. Dare I say, she looked frazzled. Calls from the press were pouring in. It was barely ten in the morning and already the day was spinning out of control. As much as I hated being dragged into Addison's circus act, I had to rein things in and protect Keira.

I had no other choice but to open up to Beckett and Arianne. With some quick and ingenuous thinking, Arianne came up with a plan. The three of us had an emergency meeting with our marketing team and our point person at the PR firm. An hour later, we managed to redirect the unwanted attention to an upcoming splashy mystery announcement—SCORE Yours.

Once that was dealt with, I was able to dive into a mountain of pressing work. By mid-afternoon, I decided to check in with Keira and Noah. Neither of the Weatherly siblings was willing to bury the hatchet.

Fuck that.

After work, I considered dropping by the Quintus Hotel—I was this close from getting a room for the night—but decided against it. There's no way I'm going to allow a pint-size impatient, headstrong hellion to lock me out of my own damn home.

As I enter the house from the garage, I pull out my phone and send said hellion a text.

Rhys: I'm here.

Keira: It's your house. You don't need my permission to come and go.

I let out a frustrated grunt.

I can't win with her.

Before stepping into the kitchen, I kick off my shoes and remove my socks. Loosening my tie, I make my way to the bar cart.

Drinking on the job sets an appalling example. Drinking after a shitty day is a requirement to maintain one's sanity.

I'm just about to let an expensive gulp of scotch mellow out the tension when the doorbell rings.

What now?

I drop the tumbler on the bar cart and march to the door, ready to chew up the security guard who dared to show up at my door unannounced.

This better be an emergency.

I don't bother looking through the peephole. I swing the door open. The last person I expected to see after his stormy exit is standing at my door. The tornado I saw earlier in his eyes has tapered down to a mild simmer.

I get to live another day.

"Hey," Noah says.

I don't bother with niceties.

"You must be here to pick up your suitcase," I say with a detached voice. "Let me grab it—"

"No." I expect him to hurl insults, but no. "Nice suit," he says, "Must've cost a lot." His eyes brush the length of my body.

What the fuck? He was raging and now he wants to talk about fashion?

"It's bespoke."

"I guess you went to work."

"I had to get out of here. Your sister is giving me attitude and the cold shoulder."

"Keira!" He shakes his head. "You two are trending on social media," he says.

"You saw the news?"

"It's everywhere. How do you do it? Same for Keira. I couldn't be in the public eye like that."

"A few things—I live in a gated community, I'm used to it, and by four o'clock a bigger celebrity scandal broke. We won't be trending for much longer."

He chuckles and then goes quiet.

"Look, Noah, I'm not sure why you're here, but if it's for round two of our feud, save it."

"Can I come in?" he asks.

"Are you going to hit me?" I'm still not able to read his mood. It's best to proceed with caution.

"No, idiot. I would've decked you when you opened the door... element of surprise and all," he says.

I'm sure that's supposed to make me feel better, but it doesn't.

I consider him.

"I'm not going to hurt you, Rhys."

"I'm just making sure."

"I'd never do that. You're my best friend,"

I cock a brow. "Am I?"

"Friends fight and then they get over it."

"You should've seen the fury in your eyes earlier. I'm man

enough to admit I was scared. I've seen you beat douchebags to a pulp."

"Can you blame me for being angry and a little surprised?" His arms fly open. "You didn't even prepare me. You just dropped a bomb in my lap—"

"Correction. *Your sister* dropped a bomb in your lap. I was going to finesse things in a way that would preserve this handsome face." I point to my head.

"Fucker!" He tries to play-punch me.

I dodge, so he misses.

We both laugh.

"Seriously, can I come in? I'd like to talk. Calmly. No shouting. No cursing. No losing control."

I nod.

I move to the side and let him in, close the door, and lock it.

"Where is she?" he asks.

"Somewhere in the house," I say. "My guess? Her bedroom—or the lounging pool—her favorite spot in the late afternoons. We aren't talking, so you can put your mind at ease. We're not kissing either."

He offers a small smile.

"I was about to have a drink before hitting my home gym," I tell him. "Want to join me?"

"I had three drinks over lunch to calm me down, but that was hours ago. I'd welcome another one. As for the gym, hell yeah."

"Where did you go?"

"When I passed the security gates with fume still billowing from my ears, I grabbed a cab that was driving by, intent on heading to LAX, just to realize on the way there I had left my suitcase at your place. I asked the cabbie to drop me off in Venice instead, where I spent the day."

I chuckle.

Noah follows behind me as I stride to the living room.

"Take a seat," I say. "Scotch neat?"

"Perfect."

I pour his drink and grab mine.

I drop both tumblers on the coffee table before taking a seat on the couch opposite him.

Noah lifts his glass. "Here's to not letting a woman—even if she's my sister—come between a friendship."

"I'll drink to that!"

We take a long swig of our drink.

"This is good stuff." Noah nods.

"It goes down easy... and God knows I needed it."

"I might've been a little abrasive earlier," Noah says.

"You were an asshole," I tell him. "Not only to me, but also to the sister you proclaim to care so much about. True, her delivery sucked, but you implied a lot of awful things about me."

His smile falls away, replaced by a somber expression. "You're right. That's why I'm here. I'm really sorry. I let my emotions do all the talking." He studies me for a long beat. "You're not going to hurt her, right?" He doesn't give me a chance to respond. "I mean, you don't do relationships... not since Dana."

My jaw tenses.

"If you're seriously asking me that question, our friendship is over because that means you know nothing about me, Noah. Will Keira and I disagree? Yes. Am I going to say things that upset her? Yes. Are we going to fight? Yes. I'm only human, and so is she. Would I intentionally hurt her? Never."

He lets out a frustrated sigh.

"You have to let go, Noah," I tell him. "I understand your need to protect her from assholes and douchebags, but to quote your words, I'm neither of those things."

Another loud sigh leaves his lungs.

"I have no idea where this is going because we just made a decision to take the plunge a few days ago," I tell him. "That said, I've had an interest in her for a while—"

"You have?"

"It's a really good thing you don't see her that way, but your sister is incredibly attractive." Telling him she's smoking hot might be pushing it. Still, Noah seems to shrink to half his size at my words. "Her impetuous nature and zest for life make her that much more irresistible. You haven't been around her since she came back from Nepal. She's changed into a more confident and brazen woman. I'm done suppressing my attraction for her. Things lined up perfectly. She's here. Under my roof. Before she left for London, the timing was off—the age difference seemed more jarring than it does now, rehab happened, followed by SCORE, and then she was crossing the pond."

He nods, pensive.

"So, you two are dating."

"We are."

"My best friend and my kid sister... I can't wrap—"

"I shouldn't have to choose between my girl and my brother."

He takes a slow sip of his drink, eyeing me from over the rim of the glass. "You won't have to."

There's acceptance in his statement.

"You're okay with this?" My shock is evident.

"While playing tourist in Venice, I had time to get my head out of my ass," he says. "To answer your question, I'm okay with you dating Keira." He pauses. "At least I'll never have to worry about someone mistreating her or disrespecting her." A slow grin stretches his lips. "My little sis surely knows how to pick 'em."

I chuckle.

"Not to mention, if I'm honest with myself, deep down, I knew she's had a crush on you forever."

My eyebrows rise. "Really?"

"Yes. I figured it was a silly girl thing, but you're right, she's a grown woman and she chose you."

"Hearing you say that means a lot."

He purses his lips and nods.

We nurse our drinks in silence.

He polishes off his drink and drops the tumbler on the table, and the sound of the glass against the wood echoes through the quiet of the living room.

"I need to go apologize to her, but I need to find her first," Noah says, standing up. "It's like I need a map to navigate through your big ass mansion, Hartford. You never gave me a tour earlier. Now's the time. That way I won't get lost."

I laugh.

"You're on."

Chapter 29

Keira

I've lost my concentration for reading a long time ago, awaiting the inevitable.

"Keira, it's me. I'd like to talk." My brother's voice follows the knock on the door.

I heard the doorbell earlier and figured he was back. I tiptoed out of my room to listen in on his conversation with Rhys, but the COO's massive house isn't conducive to spying.

"Might as well get it over with." When I open the door, remorseful blue eyes stare down at me. I step aside and let my brother in.

"Can I sit?" he asks.

I nod.

He lowers himself to the bed. Even seated, Noah's size is impressive.

I sit next to him, but keep a distance.

"I'm going to cut to the chase," he says. "It's been a maddening day. The three of us lost control of our emotions and it turned ugly. I take full responsibility for the way I acted and what I said." He angles his body so he has one leg on the mattress.

That is not how I expected him to start this conversation.

"I can't go back in time and wipe the slate clean, but I can say I'm sorry." He combs his fingers through his thick blond hair. "I already apologized to your boyfriend."

My eyes grow as wide as dinner plates.

"Did you just call Rhys my boyfriend?"

"Yes, I did." Three words stated with unwavering steadfastness. "That's what he is, right?"

"Well, yes, but..." I search for my words. "I was afraid Rhys would be forced to choose between his loyalty to you and what could potentially be us."

"I'm not going to let that happen!" Noah shakes his head. "That would make me the world's biggest jerk. Your boyfriend and me..."—I can't help my huge grin—"...had a long conversation. I was an ass. Plain and simple. Like I said, I can't take back what came out of my mouth, but I hope you'll forgive me."

The sincerity of his words tugs at my heart.

"Apology accepted."

"That's it? You're not going to make me eat humble pie?"

"No. I've been sitting here for most of the day, mulling everything over in my head. I'm the flame who ignited the fire. I broke a promise I made to Rhys when we found out you were at the security gate."

"What promise?"

"I was so much in a rush to announce our relationship status, I ignored his request. He wanted to be the one to tell you."

"I got that much from talking to him," Noah says. "FYI, you really need to work on your delivery, sis."

"I'm sorry. I went off the deep end without considering the repercussions," I say. "We had a big fight after you left. I told him we should break things off. I didn't mean it. I was just upset."

"Did you apologize to him yet?"

"He only just got here." It's a weak excuse to my own ears.

Noah's eyes shift to the nightstand. "Your new iPhone is broken, so you can't text?"

I play-punch him.

With the muscle he's packing, I'm the one who feels the pain.

"No, silly, my phone isn't broken."

"Lucky for you, he's here. You can apologize in person."

I nod. "I will."

"He's in his bedroom changing into his workout clothes. We're going to hit his state-of-the-art home-gym with a view of the ocean for a quick workout. This guy's house is ridiculous."

I giggle. "The first day, I kept getting lost."

Noah chuckles.

"He just gave me the grand tour, so I should be able to find my way. Worst case, you're here, right?" He winks.

"I'm here."

We exchange a warm smile.

"I guess in many ways, I was fooling myself," Noah says.

"What do you mean?" I frown my confusion.

"I didn't want to admit it, but deep down, I knew. It was written all over your face every time Rhys was over at Grandma's house. You've been crushing on my best friend since you were twelve—"

"Ten."

Noah groans.

"It's worse than I thought," he says.

"If we're getting it all out there, I might as well be completely honest," I say with a huge smile.

"The plus side of you dating Rhys is I won't have to waste

money doing a thorough background check on him," he says with a laugh.

"Yeah, that's the kind of thing you'd do." I laugh along.

His face falls.

"You know it's coming from the heart?"

I scoot closer to him on the bed and drop my head on his arm. "I do."

"Granted I can be a little overbearing, and I probably mother you too much—I guess I should say, father you—but I just don't know how to dial it down. I've had this job for so long and I take it seriously." He sighs. "I know I need to learn to let go. I hope you'll be patient with me."

A lump forms in my throat.

"I know you care. A lot. Way more than Mom ever did—"

"You got that right." There's an edge to his tone. It's always there when he talks about our mother.

"The memory of her fades a little more every day," I tell him.

"Nothing worth remembering," Noah says.

A chill runs up my spine.

"I guess you're right."

We sit in silence for a beat.

Our mother died when I was eight. Noah was sixteen. Living with our grandmother was a convenient way for Mom to avoid her responsibilities as a parent by disappearing for weeks... sometimes months on end with some guy without any consideration for her kids.

Most times, she didn't even bother calling to check up on us. She was constantly in and out of our lives. Mostly out. It's like my brother and I were never a good enough reason for her to stay.

Noah kept the painful stuff buried deep, but our strange and somewhat loveless childhood colors how he views the world—hence his over protectiveness and his unwillingness to commit. Not that he'd ever admit it, but I'm certain Noah's long-standing single status is because of our mom. On some subconscious level, he doesn't want to get close to anyone, worried and afraid they might leave.

"It's been the two of us against the world for a while, Cocoa Puffs." He cradles my face with his strong hands, forcing me to meet his blue eyes. "Now, it's the three of us. Rhys is more family now than ever before." Our grandmother died eleven years ago. Noah has been taking care of me ever since. Mr. and Mrs. Hartford guided him along the way in his new role as my guardian.

"You're right. He is," I tell him.

Our childhood and Rhys's are at opposite ends of the spectrum. Grandma took care of us, but it was by obligation. She made that clear. I guess my brother and I were a reflection of our mother's poor decisions when it comes to men. She didn't mistreat us, but she never really loved us, or even seemed to like us.

Rhys's mom is so different from Grandma. Mrs. Hartford is warm, and friendly, and loving, and caring, and she bakes, and she gives kisses, and hugs freely. Mr. Hartford was an incredible dad and a great influence for my brother. The only reason we lived in the same neighborhood as the much wealthier Hartfords is because Rhys's dad inherited a house that had been in his family for three generations. Many renovations later, he refused to leave. Rhys still owns the house. It's being rented.

"I love you so much," I say out of the blue.

"I love you, too." He kisses my forehead. "The press knows you're in LA," he says, changing the subject. "I hate the idea they might hound you in their frantic quest for a scoop about Chelle's tragic death..." he lets his words trail. "Rhys seems to have it under control, so I trust he'll keep you safe."

"Michaela texted me first to warn me. Rhys's and Arianne's texts followed. I knew I wouldn't be able to hide forever. I just didn't expect to be outed this way." Thanks for nothing, Addison Moody.

"Are you going to be able to handle it?"

"I will." I really don't know, but I'm not about to give him another reason to worry about me.

"I'm glad you're not alone."

"Same here."

"Your boyfriend won't let them get in your face."

"He's good like that. Speaking of my amazing boyfriend, I should go and apologize."

"Yeah, you should," he says. "I have one request."

"What's that?"

"I still have my training wheels on, so be gentle. When you go talk to him, please keep it PG rated. I don't need to hear—or see—my sister and my best friend making out. And for the love of God, no make-up sex!" His expression is priceless.

A laugh bubbles in my chest at his unwavering protectiveness.

I place my left hand against my heart and lift my right one. "I promise. No funny business while you're here... just cuddly hugs, chaste kisses, raindrops on roses, rainbows after the rain, and everything nice and sweet."

My brother grins wide. "That, I can deal with!"

I roll my eyes.

~

With a hesitant step, I cross the hallway to Rhys's room.

His door is ajar.

I'm just about to knock, but his echoing voice has me reconsidering. I peek through the opening. His phone is pressed to his ear, and he's pacing his bedroom, wearing nothing more than a pair of gray workout shorts.

Damn.

I have to remind myself why I'm here. Salivating over his sculpted body isn't on the list... not until I'm waving my brother off.

"Okay, Mom," he says. "I'll tell them. Noah will be excited to see you again. No. Don't worry about bringing anything. I have dinner covered. Just get here. See you in ninety-minutes."

He hangs up.

"Knock, knock, knock." I rap on the door.

His gaze meets mine.

"Hey. Come on in."

"Hey," I say.

I swallow, trying to not glance down at his shorts.

"Sorry, I couldn't help but overhear. Your mom is coming over for dinner?"

"She invited herself over when she found out your brother was in town."

I giggle. "Those two have such a great relationship."

"I keep reminding her *I'm* her only son," he says.

I close the gap between us.

I stare up into his gorgeous blue eyes.

"If you're standing here with a smile stretching your lips, I gather Noah and you talked?" he asks.

"We did." I nod.

I keep my eyes on his to pretend I'm immune to the badass ink, the yummy strip of hair that disappears under his shorts, or the divine lines of his V-muscle.

I wonder if I'll ever get used to his godly body.

When I wasn't fuming at him during the day, images from last night's multiple steamy sessions flashed in front of my eyes. I'd love to take credit for the bold striptease and basket of props, but once again, unofficial sex doctor, Michaela Knight, came to the rescue. Apparently, we have one of the employees who works for her hotel to thank because she just discovered the iconic eighties movie, and it revived her marriage. A quick trip to French Appliqué and a few other stores, and I was ready for a sexy night with my boyfriend.

"Keira?"

He breaks my trance.

I blink.

Was he talking to me?

"Where did you go just there?" he asks.

"Long day."

He catches me by the waist, pulling me closer to him. "You can say that again," he says. "But you've ironed things out with Noah, right?"

"Yes, it's all good. Many apologies later and a trip down our sorry ass memory lane, and here I am… standing in front of a guy I'm crazy about, wondering if he's willing to forgive me for acting like a brat." I bite my lower lip.

He tips my chin up with his fingers.

"You're crazy about me, dimples?"

I swat his chest.

"As if you didn't know."

"I don't mind hearing it over and over again."

"I'm crazy about you, Rhys Hartford, and I'm afraid I put my foot in my mouth, yet again—"

"You don't want to break things off between us?"

I shake my head. "I was upset. I should've been more patient and I shouldn't have stormed out on you the way I did. I keep demanding Noah treats me like a woman, but I was acting like a petulant child. I'm sorry. I still want us to be together. I hope you haven't changed your mind about us." *If you have, I'll die.*

"Nothing's changed for me." His voice is deep and sensual. "As far as I'm concerned, my girlfriend and I had a disagreement. End of story."

"Really?"

"Really," he says. "You're going to have to try a lot harder if you want to get rid of me, dimples."

I trace a finger along his muscular arm. "God, no. I don't want that. I want you right by my side."

"You got me, dimples. I'm yours."

My heart swells and my limbs go all liquid.

"Oh, Rhys—"

His mouth is on mine, his hands in my short hair, his bulge pressed against my body, the scent of his masculine cologne flirting with my nostrils. There's nothing about this moment that isn't absolute perfection. No one has ever kissed me this way—with sinful irreverence and abandonment—and I doubt anyone ever will. He wraps a possessive arm around my waist, holding me closer.

God.

Another breath and I'll push him on the bed for a passionate quickie.

It's not just the two of us.

Reluctantly, I pull away from him.

"What is it?" he asks.

"I promised Noah we'd keep it PG while he's here. With you... it's like my lips are connected to my..." I point to my pussy.

"You're right. Now that I'm back in his good books again, let's play it safe."

Chapter 30

Keira

I'm in awe of the woman staring at me in the mirror.

"This dress... I look so grown-up..." *Like someone who has her shit together.* "It's absolutely beautiful." I smooth down the white fabric of the form-fitted dress I'm wearing. "And I love this..." I turn around to admire the deep plunging V back that showcases my tattoo. "It's so dramatic. I was worried, but you're right. It holds in place."

"The magic of clothing tape," Shiloh says, her eyes brushing down the length of my body.

Without it, the dress would slip off my body, exposing my breasts for the world. The seamless panties also keep me prim and proper. "This could pass as a wedding dress," I say. "It's so princess-like. I never thought someone my height could pull off a showstopper like this." I've never dared to wear a maxi dress with a train, worried it would look ridiculous on me.

"You own the dress," Shiloh tells me.

"I do, don't I." I giggle, doing another swirl.

"The dress is va va voom and demure at the same time," Shiloh says. The provocative back is balanced with the long sleeves. "It's pure Hollywood glamour. Local designer Angel Suárez is a master at creating these ethereal styles."

"The guy has talent," I say.

What I'm wearing is almost angelic, while my makeup is dramatic. Vampy, even.

"The deceptive simplicity will play off nicely against the colorful SCORE Yours headphones and highlights the value proposition. Hence, why the dress is backless." She draws a vertical line in the air, tracing the letters of my tattoo.

Shiloh Walden is Flint Guthrie's assistant. From what Arianne tells me, Flint is a big-shot photographer. She assures me it's a miracle of God he could fit me into his jam-packed schedule on such short notice. I'm standing in the dressing room just about to step on the set for a photoshoot—the first of many as the face of SCORE Yours. The shoot was scheduled for next month, but Rhys, Beckett and Arianne decided to have an emergency photo session to appease the press by throwing them a bone. Instead of focusing on my hush-hush return to LA and my relationship with my boyfriend, we're giving them something to talk about.

Noah left in the wee hours this morning. He was bummed he'd miss the photoshoot. I promised him a flurry of selfies to make up for his absence.

This is really happening.

"I'm a bit nervous, Shiloh. I haven't done anything like this in a while... and it's the first time it's only me on the set." I thought Arianne would be here, but she's trapped in an important meeting with Beckett and Rhys. So, I'm flying solo.

Shiloh moves away from the mirror and comes to stand in front of me. Even in heels, the blonde is much taller than I am and I have to tilt my head back to meet her green eyes.

"I promised I'd put a lid on my fan girl fascination..." She was even more excited than Arianne and Phoebe were when they first met me. "...but you can totally do this," Shiloh says. "Flint is a tiny bit flamboyant and a lot eccentric, but he's an amazing photographer. He's going to do a series of warm-up shots to ease you into it. He spent a lot of time prepping for this by scouring the internet, so he already knows your best angles. The fact you're a natural in front of the camera is a bonus. Once you're comfortable, he'll go nuts and snap away like he's possessed. You'll just have to sit there and be your beautiful self."

"Okay," I say, willing my nerves to calm down.

"You got this, Keira," she says.

For a complete stranger, Shiloh is amazing at comforting me.

"Thank you for saying that."

Her phone rings.

She accepts the call and hangs up as quickly.

"That was Flint. He's ready for you."

Oh God.

I take in a deep breath. "All right."

"Let's go show the world what SCORE Yours and the new Keira are all about," Shiloh says.

"Let's do it!" I channel her confidence.

"My girl is representin'!" She singsongs that with a dance move reminiscent of my Lucky Break days. I can't help my laugh.

I follow her, balancing on my high heels. My eyes drop to my feet and can't help but giggle. In Nepal, I lived in flip-flops. That's also been my footwear of choice since landing in LA. The dazzlers strapped to my feet are quite the departure. To my surprise, they're quite comfortable.

"There's our beautiful billion-dollar face!" I hear Flint say. Since I'm trailing right behind Shiloh's tall frame, I can't see him yet. "Holy Jesus!" he says when he catches sight of me sliding out from behind Shiloh. With a hurried step, he approaches. He's not tall for a man. In my five-inch heels, we're nose to nose. That said, his unruly curly dark, almost black hair with streaks of gray give him an extra two inches of height. "Wow. I mean, wow!" Unrushed, his gray eyes take me in. He walks in a circle around me, doing this thing with his fingers like he's trying to capture me in a frame. Then he stops behind me. "The back is spectacular! The tattoo is POW!" He actually shouts the word. "Love it!"

Shiloh wasn't kidding. Flint is over the top.

"I couldn't have said it better," Shiloh says.

"I predict this will be one of the best photoshoots I've done in a long time," Flint says. "I can't wait to have you back next month in my studio so we can try different outfits and moods. Today's session is about capturing *unique*, and you're the definition of the word."

I'm overwhelmed by the weight of his words.

"You, my dear, were born to be in front of the camera," he says before coming to stand in front of me.

"Oh, really?" I ask, my trepidation returning in full force.

I glance around the room. So many eyes are staring right at me. They're giving off positive vibes, but it's just a reminder, this is actually happening.

I said yes.

I agreed to the terms.

I signed on the dotted line.

And now, if I can only keep my nerves in check and smile for the camera, everything will be smooth sailing. Right?

God.

"Are all the mirrors in the dressing room broken?" Flint says, glancing over my shoulder. His expression is as serious as a heart attack.

Crap.

I hope my insecurities won't get Shiloh in trouble.

"No, boss," Shiloh says.

"Why is she not seeing what I'm seeing?" Flint asks.

"Our cover model is fully aware of how dazzling she looks, Flint," Shiloh tells him. "I've already told her a dozen times, and she saw her reflection in the mirror. She's just a little shy."

"We need a third opinion, people!" Flint shouts before doing this grand gesture thing with his hand over his head.

I draw my eyebrows together, as I scour the room, trying to understand what's going on.

"How do you like our model?" Flint asks from over my shoulder.

"I can only assume she looks as stunning from the front as she does from the back!"

My heart jumps out of my chest.

I spin around and gasp before clamping my hands over my face.

"Rhys?" His name comes out sounding muffled.

"Hey, sexy." With a huge smile stretching his lips, he strides towards me.

"I thought you were in an important meeting and you couldn't make it."

"It was a white lie," he says. "Beckett, Arianne, and I all agreed it was best to let you get a head start. They won't be on the set, but I insisted on being here. I wanted to see you in action."

"So, Mr. Client, you approve?" Flint asks with a ta-da hand gesture.

Rhys gives me a onceover.

I return the favor. How can I not?

He adorned another one of his trademark bespoke suits that looks killer on him. Since I had to be on the set early this morning, he hired a chauffeured car for me. The last time I saw him, he was walking around naked in his bedroom.

"I approve!" He flashes me a cocky grin.

"Dress?" Flynn asks.

"Love it!" Rhys says.

"Makeup?" Flynn asks.

"Flawless." Rhys says.

"Lips?" Flynn asks.

"Very kissable." Rhys says.

"Can you do a twirl for us, love?" Flint motions with his finger.

I oblige.

"Back?" Flint asks.

I expect Rhys to answer, but instead, the warmth of his body radiates through mine.

My body celebrates the closeness.

When his finger traces the letters of the tattoo, I shiver.

My eyes shoot down my body, freaked out my nipples might give me away, just to remember nipple covers go a long way.

Thank God.

He leans into me and murmurs in my ear, "You take my breath away, dimples."

I close my eyes so no one witnesses the wave of emotions taking over me.

"We're going to make history today!" Flint says.

Rhys takes a small step forward, just enough for our bodies to touch. "I agree."

If his goal in coming here was to mellow me out, mission accomplished. My stomach is no longer tied up in a knot. On the contrary, it's doing somersaults because he has me all worked up.

"On that note, let's get started, boys and girls!" Flint claps his hands like a teacher.

"From this moment on, everything changes for you," Rhys murmurs in my ear.

I'm still too overwhelmed to talk. I can only nod.

"You got this, dimples."

I nod again.

There's a buzz of activity around me as everyone gets into place.

"Jimmy, help the princess get on the stool!" Flint says.

A tall black guy comes running to me and extends his hand.

Talk about star treatment.

I take it and follow him to the middle of the set.

He holds me steady as I step on the wooden crate before I can sit on the high stool.

I'm the center of attention.

From this vantage point, the full effect of the studio hits me —the lights, the cameras, the tables littered with laptops and other expensive equipment, and all the wires.

There's no turning back now.

Jimmy frets with the lower part of the dress and succeeds in creating a beautiful line, showcasing the trail in such an elegant way.

"Thank you," I say in a low voice.

"You're welcome." He rewards me with a bright white smile. "The boss and the client are right, you look incredible."

I respond with a beaming smile.

"By the way, my twin sister is a huge fan," Jimmy says. "She knows your lyrics and moves by heart. She died when I told her I was probably going to touch your hand."

I can't help laughing.

"Jimmy! Stop distracting the model!" Flint shouts. "We're

going for deep, introspective and soulful. Not comical or laugh out loud!"

"I'm sorry, Flint," Jimmy says. His dark brown eyes meet mine. "Not sorry." He says that in a whisper. "I get to tell my twin I made *the* Keira Weatherly laugh. That'll earn me a medal. At least, her undying respect and admiration."

I bite the inside of my mouth not to laugh again.

Jimmy is funny.

"Who's responsible for the heels?" Flint asks, his eyes lowering to my feet.

Worried he doesn't like them, I do the same.

I think they're kickass.

"I am!" A girl with black hair and bleached blonde bangs raises her hand.

"Pure genius! I fucking love them!"

Flint approves.

She responds with a relieved smile.

When the stylist with the edgy hair and the retro black glasses, told me the price of these babies, I nearly hyperventilated. As gorgeous as they are, Jimmy Choo's Cinderella Edit Avril fully covered in Swarovski crystals with a prominent cluster at the front are a bit rich for my blood.

"Hair and makeup! Touch up! Now!" Flint shouts.

The two men responsible for my sophisticated transformation rush my way.

A little hair flopping here.

A little shine reducing powder there.

Another application of mascara on my lashes, followed by another coat of scarlet red lipstick on my lips.

I'm ready.

"Jimmy! Headphones!" Flint claps.

Jimmy comes running with a pair of colorful SCORE Yours with a colorful graffiti design.

He places them with care over my ears and adjusts them.

"Perfect!" He gives me two thumbs up.

I nod.

I must admit, I'm a little giddy now.

I search the studio and find Rhys standing to the side, arms crossed over his wide chest. His eyes shine with something I can't quite describe. *Admiration?*

I blush.

"Are we ready, people?" Flint asks.

With the headphones on, his voice isn't as piercing.

A collective '*yes and ready*' float around the room.

"I need to see, people!" Flint shouts.

Bright lights spark in front of me.

Blinded, I blink and shield my eyes with my hand.

"Christian! Video?" Flint asks.

"We're rolling," Christian says.

"We're good to go!" Flint approaches me. "Jimmy, I need you to remove the headphones for a minute," Flint says.

The photographer's assistant does as he's told, placing them around my neck.

"Let me set the stage," Flint says. "You're listening to *that* song."

I frown my confusion as I lean forward. "Um... which song are we talking about?"

"Oh, I can't tell you that because it's *your* song." He points at me. "Not *my* song." He points to his chest. "Mine would be very different."

Could he be more cryptic?

"It's the song that touches *your* soul. But because you're listening to it with your brand new SCORE Yours headphones, melodic nuances you've never heard before come pouring through and cut even deeper because the bass is badass."

Was that English?

"I thought I was supposed to sit here, and you were going to take photos," I say. "I'm not trying to be a smart ass. I'm genuinely unsure of what you expect of me," I tell him.

I look to Rhys for support.

He doesn't intervene.

"I don't want another pretty face," Flint tells me. "I want your pretty face to tell a story."

"Okay." I nod, not fully understanding.

"Let me explain what I mean." I guess thoughts carry. "I want feelings! I want big emotions!" he adds in a soft voice. Since stepping into his studio, this is the first time he's not shouting. "When the photos hit the internet, I want people to be so enthralled, so moved, they'll be compelled to drop everything to figure out how to get their hands on a pair of SCORE Yours. This is the spice that was missing from their mundane lives. I want these photos to create a frenzy. Pandemonium, even."

That's a tall order.

"Okay." I nod.

"Dig deep, Keira," he tells me.

"I can do that."

"We're dealing with a professional, people!" There he goes shouting again. "Let's get this puppy on the road." Flint swirls his fingers in a circle above his head. "Jimmy! Headphones!"

The tall black guy with the huge grin stretching his lips places the headphones over my ears, and winks.

I try hard not to giggle.

Flint goes to stand behind the camera and looks through the lens, then back up. He does that a few times.

"And... *emotions*!" he shouts.

For the next several long minutes, Flint snaps shots while I sit there trying to go through the catalogue of songs in my head to find *the one* that touches my soul. It's not like I don't have a million songs stored in my head. I do. After all, I'm a singer, but right now, with everything going on around me, the best I can come up with is a mashup. And not even a good one at that.

Being a model is so much pressure.

"I'm not feeling it," Flint says looking up from the camera. He approaches me. "Did you find *that* song yet?"

Panic sets in.

My eyes move to Rhys.

Oh, no. I'm going to let him down.

Shit.

"It took me a minute, but I did," I lie.

Think faster, Keira.

"Now we're going somewhere," Flint says. "You need to *feel* the song, so you'll *sing it* instead of letting it play in your head."

I pull the headphone away from one ear. "Wh—what? You want me to sing out loud?"

"You have a gorgeous voice—"

"My pop princess days are behind me," I tell him, my tone a bit sharp.

"Nobody's asking you to sing a meaningless bubblegum song," he says. "I asked for a song that moves your soul. Something your heart connects with. I want to read that connection on your face."

Okay, maybe my nerves are affecting my hearing.

I steal another glance at Rhys.

He's leaning against the wall with his hands tucked in the pockets of his pants, one foot crossed over the other at the ankle.

He holds my gaze for a long beat and then nods.

"All right," I tell Flint. "Fair warning. Since it's a cappella, I might be off key."

"You're not giving yourself enough credit." Flint's words surprise me.

"Is it okay if I start with my eyes closed?" I ask.

The audience is a little too intimate.

"You do whatever it takes," Flint says.

"Okay. Thanks."

I scrap the paltry mashup in my head and zero in on an emotional rollercoaster of a song I've not dared to sing in a very long time.

"I'm ready," I tell him with a firm nod.

"Take it away," Flint says.

With the headphone back in place, I hum the opening.

When I belt out the first verse, I choke up.

God, that song gets me every time.

"That's the song!" Flint says.

I try again.

I go at it almost tentative at first. The tremolo in my voice is audible, but I'm quickly swept away by the emotions. The lyrics to '*When We Were Young*' grip my guts. It's more like a desperate plea than a song, really. Maybe that's why the song has been imprinted in my soul since the first time I saw the YouTube video clip. It's exactly the type of heart-wrenching song my former record company would've frowned upon and prevented us from performing because in their eyes, silly and vapid pop songs are an easy sell. I have a good voice, but I'm no Adele, as they loved to remind me.

I open my eyes long enough to watch Flint snap away as he moves in front of me in a half circle. I catch a glimpse of my captive audience and smile. I place my hands over the headphones, bringing them closer to my ears, closing my eyes and returning to the safety of my imaginary bubble by shutting the world out.

I sing louder.

I go deeper.

I go raw.

I don't hold back.

Tears heat my closed eyelids, but I won't allow them to escape.

Not yet.

When I hit the bridge, I'm completely lost in '*When We Were Young*'.

I sing for Chelle.

I sing for Henley.

I sing for the girl in me who's never been loved by her own mother.

I sing for the girl who'll never know her father.

I sing for the girl who thinks she's a failure.

I sing for the girl who thinks she has nothing to offer.

I sing for the girl who tries so hard to pretend everything washes over her.

Tears stream down my face and my voice breaks, but I don't stop singing.

I can't.

This is me—the real Keira—imperfections, fuckups, mistakes, fears, baggage, and all.

I have no desire to hide who I am.

I no longer have to.

When I reach the last note, I have no more tears to cry.

I sit there, absorbing all the thoughts I rarely allow to escape from their glass bottle—realities that would crush me if I allowed it.

I lower the headphones, feeling like I'm suffocated.

My eyes are still closed.

I need to catch my breath.

It's dead silent around me.

Am I alone on the set?

Strong hands cup my cheeks.

My eyes fly open.

Rhys.

The man I've always loved.

I'll never love anyone else like I love him. Never.

But I'm not brave enough to tell him.

He smiles warmly at me.

Myriad emotions veil his glacier-blue eyes.

"That was fucking amazing," he says. Goosebumps blanket my arms. "Where have you been hiding that voice? And more importantly, *why* have you been hiding it?"

I answer with a one-shoulder shrug before bursting into tears.

"Oh, baby, you dug deep," he says in a whisper.

I nod.

He captures my lips in an all-encompassing kiss.

"And... *passion*!" Flint shouts.

Chapter 31

Rhys

I didn't have the luxury of sticking around all day on Flint's set. After an hour watching Keira in all her glory, I had to retreat to the office. The rest of the day was punishing.

SCORE Yours is in full swing.

Around five in the afternoon, while Arianne, Beckett and I were meeting in his office, we received a text message from Shiloh letting us know she emailed photos and video clips from the shoot. For the full effect, she advised a large screen to properly view the photos. Almost in perfect synchronization, all three of us reached for our laptops. The reaction was unanimous. I couldn't believe my eyes. Arianne and Beckett were as amazed. The photos and video clips of my girl singing cement an inescapable truth—the real Keira Weatherly kicks ass.

After an eventful day peppered with milestones, we can finally chill out and decompress in the sanctuary of my home.

"More cake?" Keira asks.

"I'd love another slice."

"I'll have to settle for a sliver of cake instead of a second slice. As the face—and body—of SCORE Yours, I have to watch my waistline." She pats her flat stomach.

I roll my eyes.

"I could easily eat the whole cake in one sitting," she says.

"You can't celebrate without the best cake in town," I say. "Hence, why I had my housekeeper buy it for us."

"The pink champagne cake is too good, but quite apropos for a celebration."

"Speaking of celebration, more champagne?"

"Yes, please!"

While Keira serves more dessert, I top our glasses.

My phone chimes, announcing a text message.

I grab it and grin.

"It's Holt. Again!" I hold my phone up so Keira can see the screen.

He's been texting and calling all day.

She laughs. "The man is relentless in his pursuit."

"Can you blame him? He—along with millions of Angelenos—heard you sing live this afternoon."

"It's wild," she says. "I swear, I was afraid I couldn't pull it off. I guess I was riding high from singing on the set. Thanks to Flint's request, I was able to get over my fear of singing in public again."

"You crushed the challenge."

She pulls her lower lip between her teeth and worries at it.

"Own it, dimples," I tell her.

"Okay, it was a slam dunk!" she says.

I lift my hand, and she gives me a high five.

"That's my girl!"

After the photoshoot, my girl was whisked away to her first interview as the face of SCORE Yours. It's all part of keeping the press's focus on something other than our relationship. She spent ninety minutes in the hot seat with Melissa Hoover and

Parker Flanagan at KLUX 92.9 FM on their *Pull Up To The Bumper* afternoon ride home show. I couldn't tear myself away from the pressing demands of my day, so Josephine (Joey) Boswell—the PR agency's point person—was my girl's chaperone. Since Joey has a reputation for never taking shit from anyone, I knew the interview wouldn't veer into unsavory territory.

Melissa and Parker challenged my girl to their infamous *Switch It Up* challenge where an artist sings lyrics of a song to the music of a different song. Contractually, Keira can no longer sing Lucky Break's songs. The hosts of the show accommodated her by giving her two songs she knew well—the ones that got her to the finals of the talent show that lead to her becoming a star. The end result was fucking incredible. The challenge only lasted a minute and sixteen seconds, but it already has legs. The video clip the radio show posted online is trending big time. The buzz around Keira Weatherly is nearing fever pitch, and that's before the world gets to see the photos and video clips from Flint's photoshoot, which will hit the internet tomorrow.

"After today, your career—and your life—will never be the same," I tell her.

"There's no arguing that," she says. "The best part of this epic day is ending it in paradise with my prince."

We agreed to bypass a five-star restaurant. After filling our bellies with delicious food, we're kicking back in the lounging area underneath the stars.

At night, the setting is dramatically different. Under the dark sky with lights reflecting against the shallow pool's water and the quietude surrounding us, she's right, this is pretty close to paradise. The tall fence, hedgerows, and trees give us enough privacy to pretend there's no one else in the world but us.

This is living.

"Going back to Holt," I veer the conversation. "Are you going to get in touch with him?"

She nods. "Yes, I'll call him tomorrow."

"Promise?"

"Promise."

"I didn't even have to push that hard," I tell her. "You're entering a new era in your career. Your strong and powerful voice brought an entire room to tears… that's what you have to run with." Everyone in Flint's studio was moved after her performance… even the flamboyant photographer. "It's a question of finding the right recording company who's willing to nurture the *real* you."

"You're right. Thanks for being so patient with me," she says in a low voice. "I can be a train wreck sometimes and I don't always think before talking, but you always seem to take it in your stride. Most times, anyway."

"It's because I've known you since you were in diapers," I tell her.

"FYI, that's so not sexy," she says. "It makes you sound like you're robbing the cradle, old man."

"Old man?"

Before she can blink, I'm on her.

She squeals.

Without giving her time to breathe, I claim her mouth, pushing her lips apart and finding her tongue. She melts into the kiss and I deepen our embrace, devouring her mouth with unrestrained passion. With each revolution of our dancing tongues, her nipples grow taut against my bare chest.

Just like that, I'm hard.

I place a hand on her thigh, sliding it higher under her sun dress.

She moans.

"What happened to your bikini bottom?" I ask.

"I removed it earlier when I went inside to grab the cake." She cocks an eyebrow. "I also ditched the top."

"Why would you do that?"

"Why do you think?" she lifts her hips up, brushing against my erection.

I pull my hand away. "That's a little presumptuous, don't you think?"

A mischievous spark lights up her eyes. "No, I don't think so. I'm simply sending a clear message."

"And what would that be?" I play along.

Heavy-lidded eyes slide to my lips. "I want you."

"You're lucky."

"Why's that?"

"Because I want you too."

"Lucky me."

"You have no idea how lucky you're about to be."

"Yes, please!"

"You're excited, little girl."

"Since we had to keep it PG for the last five days, my boyfriend has some catching up to do."

I humor her. "Do you have any suggestions?"

"You're a creative guy. I'll leave it in your very capable hands. Surprise me."

Such effrontery.

She's going to pay for that.

"Strip!"

"Out here?" Her voice goes up several octaves.

"You told me to surprise you."

"I don't want to end up in jail for public indecency."

"You won't," I tell her. "There's a reason I had the lounging pool built on this side of the property. Not to mention, the sheer size of the properties in this area ensures my neighbors can't get too nosey, even if they wanted to. It's unlikely anyone will catch us."

"You're sure?"

"I'm sure."

I wave a finger, silently instructing her.

She's thinking so hard I can see the wheels churning in her head.

"I guess I'm off to bed." I pretend to get up.

"Wait!" she says. "Okay."

She pulls the short yellow summer dress over her head and tosses it aside.

"Lie down on the couch, place your feet flat on it, and spread those gorgeous legs so I can catch a glimpse of your sweet pussy."

She assumes the position.

What a view.

I'm rock hard and desperate to sink into her, but I rein in the urge.

Patience.

I grab the bottle of champagne by the neck.

"You're thirsty?" she asks.

"This is going to be a wet ride, dimples."

"I don't get it." The vulnerability in her eyes stiffens my cock.

I pour a generous amount of champagne from her belly-button to the top of her pussy, allowing the effervescent liquid to trickle between her lips.

She gasps. "It's so cold."

My lips curve into the faintest of smiles. "Not for long."

My eyes lower to the mess I just made. I lean forward, too eager to clean it up. I stick out my tongue and follow the trail of cold champagne to where it pools in her bellybutton. I lap greedily.

"That feels so good," she says.

I glide a finger between her pussy lips before pulling it out and slipping it into my mouth. The combination of her sweet juices and the effervescent nectar hit my tongue with full force.

Goddammit, I missed her taste.

I bring the bottle of champagne over her body again. This time, I'm heavy handed, and I pour a copious amount on her body so the liquid gushes all over her pussy.

With a helpless cry, she sits up.

"Back down!"

"Don't tease me like this," she says.

"I said, back down!"

Her hands curl up in fists at her side.

I cock an eyebrow.

Resignation colors her eyes and like a good little girl she lowers her back to the couch.

"It's been five days since I fucked you, but I doubt that's enough time for you to forget how things work between us, Keira. You take what I give you, when I give it to you."

She lifts her head and glares at me.

I tilt my head to the side.

She gives up and rests her head back down.

"Now I have to start over." I shower her body with more champagne.

Other than a sharp inhale and a slight shiver, she doesn't move.

"It's better when you don't fight me." My eyes drop between her parted legs. "I'm already salivating at the thought of wrapping my lips around your tight little clit."

"Please, please, please, please, Rhys."

"Here's the deal. You keep your eyes on me the whole time. Are we clear?"

"Anything you want."

I bend down and sip the champagne coating her pussy hair. She lifts her hips off the couch at the first contact of my tongue against her pussy.

I take it away from her.

She lets out a frustrated grunt.

"This will be a lot more enjoyable if you follow my rules, dimples," I tell her. "Hips down!"

She obeys.

I resume my mission.

I give her a one long, slow, languorous lick. She rewards the first stroke of my tongue by closing her thighs around my head and pressing hard.

Hell yeah.

Her fingers wind in my hair, her hips thrusting towards my seeking mouth.

That serves as rocket fuel to my arousal.

My balls tighten inside my swim trunks. They're already heavy with cum, too eager to shoot their load.

Nothing supersedes her pleasure.

The next stroke has her yelping as she pulls my hair. The sharp pain isn't enough to prevent a smile of satisfaction.

That's it, baby.

"Rhys..." She lets out a sharp exhale. "God, I've missed your mouth..."

My gaze meets hers. Her heavy-lidded eyes are full of carnal desire. No doubt a mirror of mine.

Fuck, I love it when we lock eyes when I'm eating her out.

Unrushed, I squeeze her thighs as I administer another series of long licks.

She purrs like a kitten.

My tongue finds her engorged clit. I suck it with avarice, making up for the days I had to go without. I alternate between toying with it and massaging it with my lips.

"Dear God," she says, panting, writhing underneath me.

I reach up and cup her breast. The sight of her stiff nipple poking through my fingers sends fire to my balls.

As my mouth works her pussy, I play with her nipples, rolling the peaks between my finger and thumb before squeezing tight. I pinch her nipples with such force, she arches her back, moaning, and gripping the back of my head, nearly suffocating me.

"Please, fuck my pussy," she says.

I grant her wish.

I tongue-fuck her with as much ardor as I would with my cock.

"Yes!" Her closed fist bangs against the couch. "Fuck me good."

I shift my attention away from her long enough to locate the champagne bottle. I grab it, pull away from her and tip more champagne over her trembling body before bringing my lips back to her drenched pussy.

Drunk with desire, I double my efforts.

She wiggles and squirms underneath me.

No, dimples.

I tighten my unyielding grip as my voracious tongue circles her clit.

She hooks a leg over my shoulder, pushing her pussy against my mouth, demanding more.

Good girl.

I show her no mercy.

I flatten my tongue and glide it from her clit to her hole and back, heightening her arousal with each stroke.

I do it again.

And again.

"That's it. Don't stop. I'm close. I'm so fucking close!" she says.

I push her limits.

I use my whole mouth on her pussy.

I lick her clit, making as much noise as possible.

Her entire body trembles.

I place both hands underneath her ass, tilting her hips up. I close my lips over her engorged clit, trapping all the blood there, leaving her no choice but to come.

My eyes are on hers.

"Oh, yes! God, yes!" She thrusts, fucking my face wild and frantic.

She's on the verge of losing it.

Her cries shoot sparks through my bloodstream. I'm holding on by a thread.

After five days of jerking off, I have no idea how I manage to keep it together and not shoot my load.

I press my lips together, putting more pressure against her swollen clit and taking away her last shred of control.

My sweet little slut fucks my face with more determination. With every thrust of her hips, she moans louder and louder until she shudders over my tongue.

Fuck, that's so damn hot.

The orgasm is so strong, she bucks, lifting me up with her. "Rhys! Oh God! Rhys—"

Jesus.

I clamp a hand over her mouth to muffle her climactic cries.

My cock is dripping, the desperate need to sink into her wetness is so overwhelming, it scares the hell out of me.

Chapter 32

Keira

I'm still lost, riding my orgasm when Rhys forces me to sit upright on the couch. Without giving me a moment of respite, he grabs the back of my neck, and crushes his mouth to mine in a fervid kiss. His tongue sweeps through my mouth, dancing around mine, making me hungry for more.

My feet have barely touched the ground, and my pussy is already fluttering with anticipation.

In an urgent rush, he lifts me off the couch and drops me on my feet in front of him.

I'm as naked as the day I was born.

He just sits there, legs wide, eyeing me with a grin, the bulge in his swim trunks so damn inviting.

Oh shit.

My cheeks flush.

Freaked out, I cover my breasts and pussy with my hands.

"No one's going to see you other than me," he says.

That doesn't prevent me from looking left then right for prying eyes. When I feel confident my nakedness won't be splashed on every rag publication in the world, I lower my arms.

He taps his thighs. "Come here."

He closes his legs and I practically leap onto the couch, straddling him.

He traces a slow finger along my jaw and down my throat, pausing on my pounding pulse.

"That was intense for you?"

"Every time you make me come, it's like I'm losing my damn mind," I tell him. "For four years after my first, I really didn't miss sex. My celibacy was never an issue. With you... it's like I can't get enough—"

He slides a hand between us and two fingers slide inside my pussy.

My breath hitches.

"That's why you're still so wet?"

"Yes."

"Tongue-fucking you wasn't enough. Now you want to ride my fingers?"

"No, it wasn't enough," I grind down on his fingers, forcing them deeper.

"You're greedy."

"I'm needy," I say.

He considers me for a beat.

"You want my fingers or my cock inside you?"

"Your cock? Out here?" I almost choke.

"I've already answered that question, dimples."

"Aren't we pushing the envelope?"

"It's going to be a little dirty—"

"A little?" my tone is incredulous.

"Okay, it's going to be downright lewd, but unless my neighbors—who are also my close friends—climb over the high fences with a camera in hand, or a helicopter hovers over our heads with a bunch of piranha paparazzi hanging from it, you don't have to worry. And let's not forget the tall shrubs act as a fortress."

I worry my lower lip, still weighing the pros and cons.

"So, what will it be? My fingers or my cock?"

Fueled by his confidence, I throw caution to the wind.

"Your cock."

"Good answer," he says. "I need to get a condom—"

"It's okay," I tell him, still grinding on his fingers. "There's no need."

"You're sure?"

I comb my fingers through his hair. "I am."

"This will change everything between us. You understand?"

My eyebrows knit together. "Why would it change anything?"

"Letting you go after I come inside you won't be an option, Keira."

I stop grinding and stare at him, my eyelashes fluttering like crazy.

He flashes me a boyish grin.

This is beyond my wildest dreams.

"I'm okay with that," I say.

He pulls his fingers from me and sucks them clean. "Divine!"

I can't help shake my head at him.

"Arms around my neck," he says. "Hold on tight."

I obey.

With me still straddling him, he lifts his hips off the couch, and works his swim trunks down his legs. His cock springs free between us. The sight is mouthwatering. "Up!" I lift off him so he can bring his swim trunks all the way down to his ankles. He kicks them aside. "I'm ready now," he says, a cocky grin tugging his lips.

"Are you ever?"

Unable to contain myself, I reach for his cock and run my fingers up and down his length as I stare into his eyes. Under the dark sky dotted with lights, they're more midnight-blue than glacier.

He clenches his teeth, biting down a growl.

"God, I've missed your cock."

"I missed your hands on my cock," he says through gritted teeth.

When my thumb brushes over the head, his hips twitch.

I can't help my triumphant smile.

"Your cock—"

"Needs to be buried deep inside you, dimples." His voice is gruff.

I'd like to take pity on him, but he's always merciless with me, so I tease him a little more, squeezing his rock-hard cock, just below the head.

He lets out a loud moan that has me drooling, sighing, and leaking juices all at the same time.

I bring my free hand to his lips. "Shhh. You have to remain quiet not to draw attention to our dirty game."

I don't see it coming.

In a snap, he has my finger trapped between his teeth.

He bites gently against it.

The tingling sensation zaps right through me to my clit and it's my turn to moan.

"You were saying?" he says.

"Shut up, Hartford."

He chuckles.

"Seriously, dimples, I love foreplay as much as the next guy, but I'm desperate. You either climb onto the saddle or get off the horse so I can run upstairs and jerk off."

"Hell no, cowboy. I want your cum inside me."

His eyebrows hit his forehead.

Where the hell did that come from?

My frank talk surprises us both.

"Look at you, asking for what you want. I didn't think you had it in you."

"Neither did I."

"I'm rubbing off on you."

"Something like that." I smile.

"Come on, cowgirl, ride this strapping stallion."

"With pleasure."

Grabbing onto his shoulders, I assume the position. I hold his cock in place, and when the tip touches my pussy lips, we both grunt as I lower my body. It's with herculean effort I manage to keep my eyes locked with his. Slowly, my pussy swallows every glorious inch of his thick cock until I'm fully seated.

A hitched breath escapes his lips, echoing my own sound.

We're skin against skin, his cock filling me, stretching me, owning me, possessing me.

His gaze radiates with heat. "This is so good."

"You can stay inside me forever," I tell him.

"I might take you up on that offer."

He smacks my ass cheeks.

"Move" he orders.

I start to rock up and down.

"Fuck!" He leans forwards and slides the tip of his tongue across my lips before dipping it inside. Our tongues are wild, flirting, dancing, teasing.

Arousal flows through me like a drug.

A million kisses from now and it'll still be as passionate between us. At least I hope so.

With our lips still locked in a feverish kiss, he grabs my ass cheeks with both hands and squeezes.

He does it again, this time like he means it.

I let out a helpless sob, his cock so deep.

He uses his feet on the ground as leverage, pushing his body upwards to fuck me deeper. The unexpected movement causes my breath to expel from my mouth and into his. Holding me against him and thrusting hard and fast, he's ramming into me like his life depends on it. Even though I'm on top, he's the one doing all the fucking. Not me. I'm nearly delirious from the combination of his tongue fucking my mouth and his cock fucking my pussy.

Rhys breaks the kiss. I'm surprised I didn't run out of air.

"Fuck, Keira," he says on a breath.

His fingers dig deeper into my ass cheeks and now he's thrusting into me with the same unwavering determination as a rig drilling for oil.

"Jesus!" I cry out.

He drops his head and snags one of my nipples between his lips. I arch my back, encouraging him, one hand tightening around the back of his head.

He doesn't disappoint.

His teeth scrape over the taut tip of my nipple, causing me to jolt in his arms. He teases, flicks and sucks. The sensation is so sublime, it causes my pussy to clench around his cock in staccato pulses, milking everything he has to give. When he bites against my nipple, I fear I'm a breath away from shattering. My nipple is so swollen. To make it better, he blows over the tip, which only arouses me further.

This is so, so good.

"Do it again. Please, Rhys, play with my other nipple." I hold his head in place.

He grants my wish.

He tugs on my other nipple with his lips and sinks his teeth gently around the peak. The sweet punishment causes me to cry out with pleasure. With his gaze burning into mine, it makes this naughty play even more sinful. To ease the assault, the tip of his tongue alternates between flicking and circling my pebbled nipple.

My head lolls back as I moan.

He grabs a handful of my ass cheek, holding me down as he lifts his hips and grinds hard against me.

I let out something that sounds like a cross between a curse and a prayer.

"Fucking you bareback is so damn hot." His free hand slides under my neck and catches me in a chokehold. I gasp in surprise. He squeezes gently, just enough for me to feel the pressure, but not enough to cut off my breathing. The new sensation is both arousing and a bit unsettling. That said, my pussy approves one hundred percent. I clamp so hard around his cock it sends sparks to my throbbing clit.

I'm so freaking close.

I clench hard again. This time in a series of small repetitive pulses.

He responds by driving deeper into the slick clench of my hungry pussy until he hits my sweet spot.

"Oh, yes, Rhys! There! There!"

"Yeah?"

"Yes! Keep doing what you're doing."

I'm not sure what kind of magic power he possesses, but I thank God for it because his cock is doing un-fucking-believable things to me.

He holds my body down and rides me with irreverence.

He's unleashed.

My heart rate spikes, my breath goes short, and the muscles in my thighs are trembling uncontrollably.

Just when I think this can't get anymore hedonistic, he blows my mind.

I gasp when he slips a finger inside my asshole—the spot he hasn't claimed yet. He flexes his finger a few times, and I swear to God I see stars.

"I'm so close," I tell him.

"We come together."

"Together."

The next few heartbeats are blazing hot, both of us desperate to climax.

"I'm— Oh God—"

"That's it, dimples. Don't hold back. Give it to me."

As he surges up one more time, my muscles contract around him, squeezing as hard as I can as I lose myself, totally consumed by my orgasm, his name on my lips.

"Rhys—"

A burst of white light flashes behind my closed eyelids.

"Christ!" he says. "Baby! Keira!"

With one last thrust, he shoots his load deep inside me.

There's so much of him, I feel his cum dripping out as he continues to drive into me.

Holy Jesus.

Long minutes tick away under the dark sky as we both struggle to find our bearings.

My gaze meets his.

For a pounding heartbeat, something in his eyes changes.

"Remember what I told you before we started this mind-blowing ride?" he asks, his breathing still ragged.

"I can barely remember my own name, let alone an actual conversation," I tell him with a laugh.

He doesn't.

An ache fills my chest as I desperately try to remember.

His broad palms smooth down my back.

"I can't let you go now, Keira," his voice is raw.

My heart thuds, stops, then reboots.

"Don't."

One word.

One simple plea.

One simple truth.

I love this man with the same intensity as a thousand burning suns.

Chapter 33

Keira

The buzz of my phone alarm shatters my peaceful sleep.

Noooo.

With my eyes still closed, I tap around the nightstand until I'm gripping the device. I bring it an inch close to my face, open one eye and press the snooze button.

I throw the phone somewhere on the bed and flip over, intent on falling back to sleep.

Not even two minutes go by before my phone rings.

For God's sake.

With a frustrated grunt, I sit up in bed and search around for my phone.

Crap.

It's in the middle of the bed, and I have to crawl to it.

I check the time as I answer the call. "Hello."

God, my voice is groggy.

"You're everywhere! I mean, everywhere!" Michaela's voice comes blaring through the phone.

I pull the device away from my ear before bringing it close again.

"Mikki, it's only seven o'clock in the morning west coast time and you're shouting. My brain is still asleep. You need to take it down by several notches."

"Sorry for being so excited. I just can't help it. I am so happy for you, Keira! Congratulations! You deserve it! You have no clue you're totally famous right now? Are you going to start singing again? Will you go the indie route? Or do you prefer a small label?" Her tone is still too chipper, and she's talking way too fast. Combined with the litany of questions, my mind is spinning.

"Oh, you're talking about the pre-promotional shots for SCORE Yours and the video clip from the radio interview."

"Yes, and yes! I'm also talking about the kiss to end all kisses."

I frown into the phone.

"What are you talking about?"

"Can we do a video call?"

"Hell no! I just woke up. I'm sure I could scare small children."

"Newsflash. We used to be roommates in Nepal. I've seen you at your worst."

"Thanks, friend."

She laughs.

"Come on. We need a face-to-face for this. I want details!"

Reluctantly, I agree.

A second later, her grinning face pops on the screen.

"Oh my God, you and Rhys... so hot. So freaking hot! I can only hope to find a guy who kisses me like that one day. Sigh." She actually bats her eyes at me.

"Wait. There are clips of us kissing on the internet?"

I'm fully awake now.

"Yes! Everyone's talking about it," she says.

"No one warned me the photographer was going to leak them."

"I'm sure it's all part of the promotional machine. Hollywood does it all the time. The same goes for a lot of tech companies," she says. "You give people a taste to whet their appetite."

"I don't see how that's related to the headphones."

"SCORE Yours *is* a tech company," Mikki says. "I'm sure pre-orders spiked today. The press is fanning the frenzy."

"Seriously?"

She nods. "You should see the headlines. My favorites are, '*BILLIONAIRE RHYS HARTFORD CLAIMS SONGBIRD KEIRA WEATHERLY.*' And '*IF THE NEW SCORE YOURS HEADPHONES GUARANTEE THAT KIND OF KISS, I'LL ORDER A DOZEN!*'"

"That last one is hilarious," I say.

"Keira, people are going absolutely nuts. I've already pre-ordered a pair."

"Michaela, you didn't have to do that. I could've asked Rhys."

"Nope!" She lifts her chin up. "I won't hear of it."

She's so sweet. I don't have the heart to argue.

I'll make sure she gets the other colors.

"This is promising to be an epic year for you," she says.

"Yesterday, I expected a photoshoot and nothing more. I never imagined walking on that set would help me find my voice again." I pause. "Rhys has been after me to talk to Holt Christensen—a friend of his who owns a record label. He's a former big time rock star, so it's not only about the money with him—"

"You're going to meet with him?" The excitement shines bright in her green eyes.

"I'm considering it."

"You really should give this another chance," Mikki says.

"If you're dealing with a former artist, surely he won't try to turn you into a commodity like your former record label."

"Rhys assures me Holt won't," I tell her. "Belching out the emotional lyrics to that powerful song on the set, and then a few hours later performing a fun song with a catchy beat... People have never reacted to my voice like that before."

"Because people have never heard your *real* voice before."

I laugh a little.

"What?" she asks.

"That's exactly what Rhys says."

"You owned those songs—"

"Once again, you're in sync with Rhys."

"Clearly, your boyfriend and I are brilliant," she says.

"Har har. Funny."

"On a serious note. Maybe I'm off base here because I don't understand the ins and outs of the music industry," she says. "Your reluctance to step into the limelight again is justified. Your old record company was only interested in fabricated vapid teenybopper bobbleheads. What if the second time around, you work with an ally who will foster the gift God gave you instead of forcing you to be someone you're not? You think you crashed and burned after leaving London. What if it was merely a steppingstone?"

Chapter 34

Rhys

Joey warned me by shooting me a text as I was trailing towards the elevators on my way to my early morning meeting. Flint's crew couldn't stop talking about the candid photos he took of Keira and me lost in a passionate embrace. The famed photographer wanted my permission before releasing a few of those shots along with the ones promoting SCORE Yours on the internet. I never planned on announcing to the whole world my girl and I were dating, but it's bound to come out. I might as well control how it happens.

I gave Joey my blessing, shot my girl a quick text, and headed to my meeting.

By mid-morning, the frenzy was at fever pitch. The photos went viral in a blink of an eye. The pre-orders for SCORE Yours ballooned. Arianne was jumping up and down. Beckett was floored. So was I. He's usually the one who gets tongues to wag.

On the heel of the media frenzy, I was assaulted by a flurry of text messages and emails—the press, friends, colleagues, contacts, family members, my mom and Noah. It was nonstop.

Even a few brave members of the staff came up and congratulated me. My best friend's text message had me in stitches.

> Noah: I don't do the lovey-dovey stuff because I don't go there with women, but I have to admit those photos of you and my sis... Jesus! You two are really into each other.

I never intended on backing away from Keira because I was too far gone, but at the same time, there was no way I was going to lose my long-standing friendship with a guy who's had my back more times than I can count. His acceptance of my relationship with his little sister is a huge weight off my shoulders.

By three o'clock, my brain is mush.

"I need coffee and cheesecake." I stand up from my desk. Since Beckett was in a generous mood when he came back from a meeting with the advertisement agency, he stopped by one of the best shops in town.

Just as I'm about to reach the door, my phone rings.

I shake my head as I accept the call.

"Shane!" I say, walking to the couch before sitting down.

"You're dominating the entertainment news, my friend," he says.

"It's wild. My hashtag is squashing Beckett's and your brother Collin's."

Shane lets out a laugh.

"I never thought I'd see the day," he says.

"You and me both."

"Is pretty boy Beckett able to handle it for a day? After all, he's the media's sweetheart."

"Barely," I tell him. "I guess it's the same for your little brother."

"I'm pretty sure it is. Since we're talking about Collin here,

I'm sure he's plotting a devious way to steal the media's attention away from you."

Be my guest.

"I'm sure he will."

"On a serious note—"

"Oh, because you didn't call just to razz me?"

"Nah. That's Collin's forte. I'm the supportive Dennison brother, remember?"

"True."

"In any case, the last time we talked about Keira, you seemed troubled. Torn, even. The photos of you locking lips on camera flooding the internet suggest you decided to go after the girl."

I nod into the phone even though he can't see me. "Our conversation was a wake-up call. I decided to man up. The only blip was Noah landing in LA unannounced before I had time to tell him I was seeing his sister."

"No shit," Shane says.

I tell him everything.

"I wouldn't want to be on the receiving end of the Hulk's fury. I consider myself fit and invincible, but next to Noah, I'm nothing. The guy could break me in half without even trying."

"That's exactly how I felt. Breaking the bro code has its consequences. I was more than willing to pay the price, but I'm grateful he didn't rearrange my face."

"Another thing to celebrate!" he says. "Let's add it to the list."

"What do you mean?"

"When I bumped into you at LAX on the day Keira arrived, I promised her a Cuban meal. I was going to keep it casual, but there's too much to celebrate. One, the big news of you two dating. Two, her becoming the face of SCORE Yours—great choice, by the way. Three, pretty boy Beckett is off the market—proof God works in mysterious ways. Four, your headphones were dubbed the best thing since Edison's light bulbs—which is a pretty tall order. And five, the announcement of an upcoming red-carpet event to kick off SCORE Yours." He pauses. "There's a hell of a lot happening in your neck of the woods. Low key doesn't cut it anymore."

"You're right, there's a lot to celebrate. A Cuban meal sounds great, Shane."

"I've already placed calls with the boys and everybody can make it. I'd love for you and Keira to come over to my place on Saturday afternoon. We'll stretch out the celebration until the wee hours."

"I'll check with my girl, but I don't see why we shouldn't be there."

"Good! It's settled!"

"Thanks for the invitation. I can't wait," I tell him.

"A heads up. I *have* to invite Collin. He's my baby brother and my neighbor. If I *forget* to invite him, I'll never hear the end of it. It's best if you prep Keira in advance. He's been drilling me to find out if she has a long-lost twin or a sister he doesn't know about."

"He's lost it!"

"Pretty much," Shane says. "And even if she did, I'm sure Noah wouldn't be thrilled about my brother dating his sibling."

"Noah would veto the relationship," I say with a laugh. "Your brother is something else."

"My brother is a pain in the ass and delusional."

"The former is a given, but what brought on the latter?"

"He declared the flag should've been flown half-staff on the day he found out Beckett was no longer interested in manwhoring anymore. He requested the same thing this morning after reading the headlines about your relationship.

He's in mourning. Poor lad. He's losing more and more partners in crime and he doesn't know what to do with himself."

I laugh harder.

"I swear, Collin will be single forever," I say. "There isn't a woman strong enough—or crazy enough—to handle his ass."

"And if she's out there, that encounter will be like two missiles colliding."

"Damn right it will!"

Chapter 35

Keira

When Holt enters the conference room, my nerves propel me to my feet.

"Keira!" He thrusts a hand in my direction as he eats the distance between us. "It's good to see you again."

I drag in a nervous breath and stare up at the tall man adorned in an impeccable navy-blue suit. He towers over me, just like my boyfriend.

For our meeting, I opted for a sleeveless red dress that hits me below the knee, along with a tapered white blazer, which I matched with a pair of expensive red sole heels with an ankle strap—a gift from my boyfriend—and a chic designer handbag also in white. Taking in this elegant man, I mentally pat myself on the back for opting for a more put together look.

"Good morning, Holt." I shake his hand. "It's good to see you, too. It's been a while."

"Since London."

"A lot has happened since then," I say.

His eyes brush the length of my body. "You don't say!" A smile tugs at his lips.

I was unaware of Holt Christensen's success as a rock god until my boyfriend partnered up with his younger brother Beckett. Holt hung up his bass to step into the shoes of music executive. From the sprawling building I'm in, he's crushing his second career.

"I'm sorry I kept you waiting," he says. "It's one of those days."

"I'm sure you must be busy, which is why I'm so surprised you were able to meet me at such short notice. When I called a couple days ago, I didn't expect to be standing in your office so soon."

"Are you kidding me?" His ocean-blue eyes glee with mirth. "Keira Weatherly calls, you better believe I'll make room in my schedule to meet with her."

I blush.

"I'm not sure I can live up to your expectations," I tell him.

"There are two video clips of you singing trending on the internet, gathering hundreds of millions of views as we speak that say otherwise," he says.

"Okay, I officially don't know what to say to that."

"I'm no fool. I'm sure there are others courting you. I want to be the first," he says.

I'm humbled and honored.

"I'm not going to pussyfoot around, Keira. Your raw talent caught everyone in the industry by surprise. It's such a contrast from your days with Lucky Break."

"From the look"—I brush my hand over my short blonde hair—"to the type of music... it's like day and night."

"That's why you're here today. Let's talk about the journey that allowed the world to hear the beautiful voice you've been hiding."

"Okay," I say.

"Please, sit down."

"Thank you," I say, dropping back in my seat.

He sits in the chair next to me and swivels it so he's facing me.

"I see my assistant took good care of you." His eyes drop to the cup and plate in front of me. "Is your latte cold? Do you want a refill?"

"No, thank you. Your assistant brought these..."—I point to the coffee and half-eaten donut— "not long ago."

"Good. How do you like the donut?"

"Oh my God. It's insane! I swear, it's the best donut I've ever tasted!"

"I'm a little partial, but I agree, they're the best," he says.

Holt's ocean-blue eyes are a deeper shade than Rhys's, but equally mesmerizing. That said, they both wear their dark brown hair a little long on top.

"There's a lot about Lucky Break on the internet," Holt says. "There's also quite a lot about Chelle. She seemed to be the one who got the most press... not always for the right reasons."

"It was always a three-way love-hate relationship between my best friend, the fans, and the rags. The months preceding her death, the press, and social media were intent on going after her."

"The tragedy surrounding your two group mates resurfaced because of your surge in popularity," Holt says. "I'm sorry about your best friend." Sincerity shines bright in his eyes.

"Thanks for saying that."

"Since it's sometimes difficult to tell between real and fake news, why don't you fill me in?"

"Okay." I launch into story mode.

The downside of the media buzz is I can't escape my past life. A couple days ago, it came colliding full force with my current life.

First, Joey contacted me to warn me my old record company was hunting me down. I knew I couldn't dodge the bullet forever. I took my courage in both hands and made the difficult call. They're demanding the balance of the money I owe them in one shot. According to my SCORE Yours contract, I won't see a dime for another few months because things weren't supposed to launch this quickly. I could ask Rhys to loan me the money, but I'd hate for him to think I see him as an ATM machine. This is my mess. Not his.

Second, a number of British rags are on a witch hunt to fuel Chelle's haters' insatiable appetites. No thanks. I won't be part of that. Things might've been sour between us in the end, but I won't be a traitor to her memory.

"Without Flint Guthrie, we would all still be oblivious to your incredible voice," Holt says when I finish my story.

I beam with pride.

A compliment like that coming from a guy like Holt means a lot.

"Flint gave me wings to fly," I say.

"I love the way you framed it," Holt says.

"I owe him a lot."

He nods. "You know my background as a bassist?"

"I do. You're one of the best."

"Thank you!" He tilts his head ceremoniously. "I may be wearing a suit these days, but at heart, I'm still a musician and an artist. My mission with Ritual of Rhyme Records is to shine the spotlight on kickass talent and make sure they're treated with respect. I know firsthand what it's like to be screwed over. I never want that for my artists."

"Rhys speaks highly of you."

"I understand your hesitation..." I expect him to continue, but instead, he looks me in the eye. "You have a deep, smoky, soulful voice that begs to be heard. I want to be your ally. Plain and simple. Lucky Break was a great steppingstone, but the poppy tunes didn't showcase you as a vocalist with a mean set of pipes."

His frank talk is refreshing.

The execs at my former record label would never entertain this kind of conversation with an artist, regardless of their success.

"I never had the confidence to believe I could go there," I tell him.

"Your voice *is* there," he says. "You're the poster child for the next big thing in blue-eyed soul music."

"Oh."

"You have a world-class instrument." My eyes widen at his words. "You make people feel. If I close my eyes and listen, I can note every nuance of emotion in your voice. You also possess a gift for tone, something I don't believe can be taught like technique. You either have it or you don't. And you, my friend, have it in spades. I was a few minutes late for our meeting because I was finishing up with a guy who's dying to work with you. He's sitting in another conference room in this building, waiting for the green light."

I frown my surprise. "Who are you talking about?"

"Bridge Peterson agrees with me—"

"Wait. Did you say Bridge Peterson?"

"I did."

My eyes are as wide as dinner plates.

"As in the most coveted vocal coach in the industry?" He must be talking about another Bridge Peterson. This cannot be happening. When I was living in LA, I couldn't even breathe the same air as Bridge Peterson. The idea of working with him is surreal. The man is a hit maker.

"The one and only," Holt says. "Just like the rest of us, he watched the video clips in awe."

"He wants to work with me?" I point at my chest.

"He's been on my case since yesterday. He's relentless. Thanks to him, Vickie Sky's career exploded."

"Oh my God, he's behind Vickie Sky?"

She's just one of the biggest artists on the planet right now.

Holt nods. "By improving your technique, you're set to become one of the defining voices of your generation. I believe it. So does Bridge."

I'm floored.

And incredulous.

And speechless.

And completely freaked out.

"You don't see it—I guess I should say, you don't hear it," Holt says when I'm still staring at him. "You're a phenomenal alto singer with a big voice, Keira. You're characterful, emotional, powerful, and raw."

I'm not used to this much praise, but dear God, I'm lapping it up.

"You signed a bum contract when you became part of Lucky Break because you were desperate for fame. Those reality singing competitions make it look easy and set unrealistic expectations. It's only when you sign on the dotted line that reality slaps you across the face. I'm offering you full transparency. I'm also offering you the world on a silver platter, and the chance to become a legend."

Chapter 36

Rhys

We're sitting in the back of a chauffeured Bentley, trailing behind a long line of chauffeured vehicles, all heading to the same spot. Building 22. The lavish venue is nestled away from prying eyes, and a stone's throw from Rodeo Drive and the Hollywood Walk of Fame.

"Arianne's vision is coming to life," Keira says. Her face is kissing the window in her attempt to catch the action outside.

"Tonight, is the big night," I say. "It seems like only yesterday I was sitting in a meeting with Beckett when she made her presentation. Although punishing and fast-paced, I can't even wrap my head around the fact it's only been three weeks since Flint's photoshoot. Things are moving at lightning speed."

"Michaela and I had the same conversation last night. I'm amazed it's only been six weeks since I landed in LA. It seems like a lifetime ago, yet it went by in the blink of an eye. So much has happened."

"All good stuff, though?"

"Mind-blowing stuff," she says. "The best being... you."

"Of course," I say with a grin.

She rolls her eyes. "Someone has a big ego."

"I was just agreeing with you, dimples." I lean into her and drop a soft kiss against her forehead. I don't want to mess up her beautiful face. "For the record, you're the best thing to happen to me, too."

"I love hearing you say that." Her lips stretch into a warm smile.

My heart flips. It's been doing that a lot lately. Like always, I suppress the feeling. My head needs time to catch up with my heart.

We've been dating for a month. This is the first time I've lived with a woman. I thought I might feel suffocated or trapped, but I don't. I always look forward to seeing her beautiful face at the end of the day when I get back home.

Contrary to when she arrived, my girlfriend no longer has time to sit idle around the pool. Her days are packed with meetings, photo sessions, and a long list of things related to being a spokesmodel. I've had to travel to Dallas and Silicon Valley since we've been together. Being away from her was harder than I expected. Returning to LA usually meant a hot and steamy reunion where I fucked her hard enough to forget my own name.

"I'm excited and nervous at the same time," she says.

"There's nothing for you to be nervous about," I tell her. "The press and the public love you."

"So far, it's been a handful of selected media outlets with Joey as my chaperone-slash-bodyguard. Tonight, the dogs are out."

"Stop worrying. You'll do—"

My phone vibrates.

I fish for it inside the pocket of my suit jacket.

Beckett.

Beckett: Arianne and I are pulling up to Building 22. Joey gave me the heads up. Her team is ready. Security is in place. Where you at?

Rhys: Fifteen minutes away from launching a freaking rocket into orbit.

Beckett: Love the analogy. SCORE will rock LA tonight. Try not to steal all the attention away from me when you step onto the red carpet with a woman who will most certainly outshine me.

I smile at his response.

Rhys: Can't make any promises I already know I'll break. My girl will absolutely be the center of attention. Suck it up, pretty boy. See you soon.

"Is everything okay?" she asks when I tuck my phone into my pocket.

"Beckett is worried the press won't pay him attention since they'll be so focused on me because I'm the lucky bastard who gets to accompany you—the face of SCORE Yours, a soon to be 'Greatest Women in Music', *and* world's bestselling music artist."

A cloud of sadness darkens her hazel-green eyes.

"It'll all be sorted out soon," I tell her.

Once her old record label knew where to find her, they made sure to forward a copy of the contract she signed. Eagerness blinds you when you're a new artist hungry for fame. You'll gladly sign your life away.

"Once again, I royally fucked up," she says. "I finally get what I want, but I can't reach out and grab it, and it's all my fault."

"Enough of the self-loathing!"

"No point in downplaying it!" she says. "I brought this on myself. I screwed up. Again." She crosses her arms over her chest and averts her gaze.

"Look at me."

She ignores my command.

"Keira!"

Her eyes meet mine.

"Holt's lawyers in London are on it," I say.

"I was naïve and arrogant to think I called the shots. This recording contract with Holt might end up being nothing more than a pipe dream at this rate. I haven't even signed on the dotted line and already, I'm trouble."

"You're *not* trouble." I want her to shake this crazy idea out of her head. "There's a reason Holt has badass lawyers in the US and in London. You think you're the first artist to go head-to-head with a recording label? Hardly. It's only been a week. These things take time."

Not surprising, record labels came knocking at her door. The offers were tempting, but she trusts Holt. So do I.

She lets out a heavy sigh. "I'm too impatient, I guess."

"With good reason." I cup her nape and look deep into her eyes. "You finally get to sing the type of songs you were born to sing."

"It would break my heart if this deal with Holt fell through—"

"It won't," I tell her. "Holt will wait."

She nods.

I skim her cheek with my knuckles, brushing my way to her chin. I lift it, forcing her eyes to lock onto mine. Her soft plump lips are tempting, but her nude lipstick is too perfectly applied to smear. I fight the urge to kiss her. "No one is going to take away your dreams. I won't let it happen."

"You're an amazing man, Rhys Hartford. I'm so lucky to call you mine."

"No more than I'm lucky to call *you* mine." I tap the tip of her nose. "To keep things into perspective, SCORE—and tonight—would never have happened if it wasn't for my own collection of screw-ups, and Beckett's."

She offers a small smile.

I'll take it.

Keira never mentioned she owed a substantial amount of money to her former record company. Nor did she mention she never sought legal advice before walking away from her contract. The only reason they didn't come after her sooner is because they had no idea where she was hiding. Until the legal matters are sorted out, she's still *their* artist, therefore she can't sign under Holt's label. I didn't have the heart to scold her for holding back on me, but I was royally pissed off. Open-ended loops can come back to bite you in the ass. I appreciate her unwillingness to take advantage of me, but what's the point of having an obscene amount of money at my disposal if I can't help my girl? Since finding out, I used my power and influence to deal with this shit.

"Mark my words, the face of SCORE Yours will win an American Music Award trophy *and* a Grammy."

"Rhys, that's dreaming big," she says.

"I know it in here!" I tap against my heart. "It'll happen."

For the few remaining miles, we ride in silence, fingers interlaced, eyes focused outside, lost to the scenery.

"Oh gosh, this is it!" Keira says when Building 22 comes into view. "We're here!"

"As we discussed, Mr. Hartford, once we get out of the limo, Officer Dalton and I will flank you and Miss Weatherly," Officer Kaminski says. He's been so quiet since we drove away from the Rodeo Drive high-end jeweler's shop, I almost forgot he was sitting in the passenger seat. Almost. He's one of the two armed police officer-slash-bodyguards assigned to make sure nothing happens to the bling. "We'll stand back just enough for photo ops, but we can't give Miss Weatherly too much leeway," he tells us for the second time. "We need to keep our eyes on the jewelry at all times."

"I understand," I say.

"I wouldn't have it any other way," Kiera says. "I'm walking lunch money."

I chuckle.

Given the press presence tonight, it's no surprise a well-established Beverly Hills jewelry designer wanted to steal a little bit of the limelight. From the stunning necklace to the wide bracelet at her wrist to the dazzling cocktail ring, and the spectacular earrings, Keira is dripping in diamonds. The security detailing isn't optional.

As the car creeps closer to the red carpet, I pull out my phone and text Joey to tell her our limousine is the next in line. When the car comes to a stop, Officer Dalton, who was riding in another car we were tailing, opens Keira's door. He extends a hand and helps her out. Officer Kaminski gets out next and I follow.

As I close the top button to my black suit jacket, I catch sight of Beckett and Arianne working the press line. Collin and Shane Dennison aren't too far behind. As usual, Collin is calling too much attention to himself.

I shake my head.

To make a big splash, you need headliners. Within the next half hour, Building 22 will be bursting at the seams with Hollywood movers and shakers. The illustrious list also includes many of our close friends. Pride washes over me.

Then, I struggle for a second when my throat tightens as an unexpected wave of emotion threatens to overwhelm me.

These big events are a reminder of how far Beckett and I have come—from the lows of rehab to the pinnacle of success. Whenever we step out like this, the realization always hits me full force. Tonight, is no exception.

As I round the vehicle to meet Keira, I search the crowd. Glamour hangs around us like an overripe fruit. I spot Joey. I nod, answering her silent question. I know the drill.

My eyes lower to the beautiful woman standing next to me with a mixture of awe and excitement at the prospect of embarking on a new journey together.

"Ready?" I ask.

"Ready. I think."

"I'm right here, dimples. You lean on me if you need to."

"Okay." She offers a brilliant smile.

We take a step forward.

Earsplitting cheers break into the night.

"Keira, we love you!" A man waves.

"Oh my God, it's Keira Weatherly!" A woman screams, jumping up and down.

"Keira! Keira! Keira!" A group of people chant their devotion.

Some hold signs with hearts and fan messages.

My girl waves and blows kisses.

A cacophony of sound swells from the crowd in response.

With one simple request, Flint changed Keira's life.

A smile tugs at her lips when her gorgeous eyes connect with mine.

"I can't believe this is all for me," she says.

"Get used to it, dimples. It's just the beginning."

From the corner of my eye, something catches my attention. I shift my gaze away from Keira's and catch Joey waving at us.

"Come on, we're holding up the press line," I tell Keira.

"Okay," she says.

Cranking up the charisma, I smile at the men and women who will become disciples in helping us spread the gospel about SCORE Yours. I wrap an arm around my girl's slender waist and pull her into the throng of the media.

"Keira! Over here!" We turn in the direction of a black woman.

Her fashionable bright blue suit, black strappy heels, slicked back straightened hair, bright red lips, and stylish black glasses that frame her dark brown eyes make her stand out.

"You left LA as an unknown artist and you return to the City of Angels like a reigning queen. How does it feel?" she asks.

My girl laughs. "That's a tall order."

"So is he!" The reporter brushes her eyes down the length of my body. "But that also seems to play in your favor. Congratulations on *scoring* Rhys Hartford. What I'd give to be in your *designer* shoes."

"Pretty witty play on words," Keira says. She glances up at me, but the twinkle in her eyes tells me she's flattered and amused by the reporter's remark.

I just laugh it off.

"Well, thank you," the black woman says with a beaming smile. "FYI, Rhys, fan girl over here!"

"I was unaware I still had fans," I say.

"Nonsense," she says. "It's a shame you only had one hit, but I was a huge fan of your flow. And the way you spit those rhymes... kickass."

"I'm humbled," I tell her. "My career lasted a nano second and I'm always surprised when fans remember me."

"You're selling yourself short, Hijinks," the reporter says. I smile at the mention of my stage name. For a beat, I'm transported back. "Your song reached the top 10 on the Billboard

Hot 100 in the US, hit number one in nine countries, and was in the top 100 songs for that year."

I'm impressed she remembers.

"Subsequent songs failed to chart," I say. "It was a fly-by-night success."

"Yet, it had a lasting impression on me," she says.

"I like you," I tell her.

"Don't they all," she says with a wink.

"Seriously, you're great," I say.

"Right back at ya, Hijinks!"

"Keira! Keira! Over here!" A curvy redhead with a cascade of hair and a noticeable British accent calls our attention.

Since tonight isn't about me, I bid goodbye to the reporter-slash-fan and pull my girlfriend along so we keep walking the press line.

"Love, love, love the dress. The color on you... so perfect." The redhead gushes all over my girl. "Who are you wearing?"

"Angel Suárez," Keira says.

"An American?"

"Yes. Angel is an LA based Cuban American designer."

"His style is flawless," the curvy redhead says.

"You stole the words right out of my mouth," Keira says.

Even though Angel's dresses have been featured in a handful of big fashion magazines, it's not until my girl's photo-shoot A-listers and socialites started paying attention to him. Angel considers her responsible for turning him into one of the most coveted designers in the country. Photos of the now famous white dress had such an impact on his career, he's declared her his muse.

Tonight, she's wearing a gorgeous fitted light-purple dress with a strapless neckline that hits her below the knee, accompanied by a killer pair of white python high heels with red soles. My girl is still sporting short blonde hair. It's becoming her trademark. The edgy hairstyle and her bare shoulders accentuate her long neck and showcase her tattoo. She's truly gorgeous. And the best part is she owns it tonight.

She had me waiting downstairs as she was getting ready. When she hit the last step, I was transfixed by the sexy goddess standing before me. As much as I wanted to drag her back up the stairs and ravish her one more time before we hit the road, I knew it would be inconsiderate of me to fuck up her perfect makeup and hair.

"Wow. The jewelry is breathtaking," the redhead asks, her brown eyes shining bright with admiration.

"I've never worn anything this expensive in my life," Keira tells her. "To say I feel like a million dollars would not only be a cliché, but it would be an understatement."

Keira pauses to show off the rocks—all part of the client's expectations. It's unfathomable how much money the jeweller was willing to pay her for this photo op.

A few members of the press oooh and ahh.

"Do you get to keep the diamonds?" the redhead asks.

That question gets old fast.

"Only if I'm willing to fork out the money," Keira says. "And that's unlikely to happen."

The reporter moves her attention to me and gives me a onceover before staring me square in the eyes.

I resent the insinuation I read in them.

"Rhys is my boyfriend, *not* my sugar daddy," Keira answers the redhead's silent question. "The jewelry isn't mine to keep."

That's my girl.

The redhead inhales before shooting off another question. "Rumor has it your former record company is looking to piggyback on all the media attention you're getting. Were those video clips teasers? Are you considering a duet with Trinity after vanishing for so long?"

"SCORE Yours is my focus right now," Keira says,

Great answer.

Good for her for being unperturbed by the redhead's comment.

Her former record label put the duet offer on the table again. Just like the first time, my girl rejected it. Two group mates are dead. The group is defunct.

As a last-ditch effort, the label threw the press a bone—a recording of Keira and Trinity in the studio. The song—and performance—fell flat. Still, the media is turning the old clip into breaking news. It's laughable.

"Don't you think it's a shame to keep your voice bottled up?" The redhead soldiers on.

"I haven't made any decisions yet in regard to my career as a singer. Right now, I'm having fun being a model."

"That, and having *a lot* of fun with..."—the redhead's eyes fix mine with a sharp stare—"one of SCORE Yours's sexy billionaire executives. It's a coveted position to be in. Lucky you."

Holy fuck, she's out of line.

"If by that remark you mean I have a pretty kickass boyfriend who happens to be the COO of the company, then yes, I agree with you, I'm a very lucky woman." Keira's smile is tight. "If you'll excuse me, I see another reporter who's trying to catch my attention."

Bravo.

Keira grabs my hand and pulls me forward, our bodyguards matching our steps.

We're blinded by a thousand flashes, too many mics are shoved in our faces and we're bombarded with a deluge of questions, but it's not like we didn't expect it. Most of the questions are addressed to the dazzling blonde hanging from my arm.

Tonight, I'm not nearly as fascinating as my girlfriend. I'm okay with that.

We keep moving down the press line and soon, we're so close to the entry, I could reach out and grab the door handle.

Finally.

This isn't my first red carpet walk, but it's a lot of pressure to keep your cool. You're under intense scrutiny. You have to keep a stoic face and bite your tongue no matter how stupid or far-fetched the question. If the press gets a reaction out of you, you become easy prey. So far, my girl is doing a bang-up job.

"Keira, one question before you go inside, please," a middle-aged bald guy asks.

"Sure!"

"My name is Jedd Maitland and I'm with the *Hollywood Herald*," he says.

"Hi Jedd," Keira says. "What's your question?"

"In a tell-all interview we're about to publish in our magazine and online, Chelle's mom claims you're partially responsible for her daughter's death. How do you respond to that?"

Keira's body goes rigid on my arm.

My brows crease with concern when my eyes connect with hers.

What the fuck?

She shifts her gaze, returning it to Jedd.

"Chelle's mom refuses to budge from her erroneous assumptions." Her tone is icy.

I search the crowd to see if I can catch Joey's attention. She's standing by Arianne and Beckett's side as they grant WNN—Wire News Network's Enews entertainment program—an interview.

Shit.

I don't want to ring the alarm, but I have a bad feeling about this guy.

"Fair enough." Jedd pretends to accept Keira's answer, then fires off, "Care to elaborate on the jealous feud between you and your best friend over British trust fund baby Paxton Foley? What better time than now to share your side of the story."

What is he talking about?

"There was never a feud between Chelle and me over a guy, so I don't have anything to say about that," Keira says.

All this is news to me.

"Is Chelle's mom lying?" Jedd asks.

Keira's gaze narrows. She's about to answer, but I squeeze her hand to silence her.

She squeezes back.

"She already answered your question, Jedd," I tell him.

"Oh, you're her boyfriend, her publicist, *and* her guard dog?" the asshole says. "You wear too many hats, Mr. Hartford."

I'm about to wrap your tongue around your fucking head if you don't stop hounding and pestering her.

I take a deep breath, my nostrils flaring. "Tonight is about SCORE Yours. If you have questions relating to Keira representing the brand, we're all ears. However, if you're here to cause problems, I have a serious issue with that, so yeah, I'm doubling as her guard dog."

"Something tells me these guys already have the publicity angle for SCORE Yours covered." The bald guy points a thumb over his shoulder in the direction of the mob of reporters.

I stare him down, willing myself to keep my composure.

"No doubt they're all dying to report on the designer Keira is wearing, or take photos of the diamonds on loan, or request you two lock lips on the red carpet for the perfect photo op old Hollywood style. I'm more interested in digging into the past. *Her* murky past, to be precise!" His head jerks to my girl.

"That's *real* news." The corner of his lip lifts into a smirk, a precursor he has no intention of playing nice. "She decamped London pretty quickly. There's *a lot* of unfinished business—"

I let go of Keira's hand and take a step forward so I'm standing toe-to-toe with him on the other side of the red velvet rope. I tower over him by easily ten inches. "Let it go."

"Or what?"

The defiance in his eyes suggests he won't back down easily.

I glance to my left then my right.

I can't chew his head off without having a hundred cameras pointed in my direction.

This could turn ugly—and viral—real fast.

I suck it up and step back, my eyes still shooting daggers at him.

Asshole.

"You want to know who killed Chelle?" Keira's question breaks the tense standoff.

"Finally, you're willing to talk," Jedd says, moving his attention away from me.

What I'd give to punch the smirk off his face.

"Piranhas like you," she says, lifting her chin, her voice coated with anger. "You pretend to be a reporter, but in reality, you're nothing more than an ambulance chaser who gets his kicks from fishing for lies, ready to twist anything in your favor for more website views or to sell more magazines filled with half-truths. It's all about the money. Never about the people you hurt..." She shoots him a contemptuous glare. "Or worse, the people you kill. You want to believe Chelle's mom's story, knock yourself out."

With that, Keira heads for the door, the two officers in tow.

What the hell just happened?

Chapter 37

Keira

Rhys's strong hand holds mine as he eats up the floor beneath him. He's walking so fast, I struggle to keep up in my five-inch heels. Officer Dalton and Officer Kaminski's long strides match his. People stare at us, but I'm still too shocked by that idiot reporter's questions to care. He doesn't stop until we find a quiet spot inside Building 22.

"I'm just going to have a word with my girlfriend," he tells the officers.

"We'll give you a little privacy, but we can't go too far," Officer Kaminski tells me.

"I understand," Rhys says.

He flips me around so my back hits a wall. "What the fuck was that about?"

I'm about to answer, but he fires off another question.

"Is that why every time I asked if you were going to visit Chelle's mom, you were always evasive?"

"Yes. Chelle's mom has this crazy idea in her head."

"Why?"

"Because of all the lies Chelle fed her."

"Mrs. Camden has known you since you were a kid. You'd never be capable of something so abominable," he says.

"Chelle's insecurities not only broke our friendship, but they also served as the springboard for all the lies she kept telling herself. Since she's so close to her mom, it's no surprise Mrs. Camden would come to the wrong conclusions."

"Explain!"

"Without Superstardom, Lucky Break would cease to exist—"

"You're not telling me anything new, Keira." I'm testing his patience.

"We were walking on sunshine on the night of the launch party for the announcement of our first album. The ballroom at the venue the record company secured was packed with big names—celebrities, musicians, legends. Paxton Foley was also present."

"According to Jedd, Paxton is a trust fund baby. What was he doing at your party?" Rhys asks.

"If you can't be Paxton Foley, you can live vicariously through him via social media."

"Oh, he's one of those," he says, rolling his eyes.

He lets go of my shoulders and takes a step back.

"Yes, he is," I tell him, "and he's a master at it. Paxton turned his mommy-and-daddy-funded-multi-million-dollar-lifestyle into a lucrative brand. He has a ridiculous number of followers and he gets invited to the best parties in London. An acknowledgment from Paxton, and your brand is sitting pretty. Even after leaving the UK as a child, Chelle's mom was still connected to all things British. That's why Chelle knew who Paxton was. I didn't."

"Back to the launch party," he says.

"When Chelle spotted Paxton, she nearly lost her mind. After recovering from the shock, she declared she was going to do something about her long-standing infatuation. I cautioned her, reminding her guys like Paxton tend to go for socialites, actresses, models and singers. Chelle took offense to my warning, reminding me we were singers, and about to become the biggest girl group on the planet. She accused me of thinking too small and being stuck in a loser mentality for not upping my game when it comes to men—it was a jab at you. Back then, SCORE wasn't what it is today. I washed my hands of it because I couldn't handle her when her bitch dial was on high. I didn't stick around to watch her put the moves on Paxton. When I caught up with her later, her mood was off. I asked her what happened with Paxton. She simply said he wasn't nearly as interesting as she thought. I was floored. All that pent-up lust for a fleeting moment of utter disappointment? I mean, she couldn't shut up about the guy. I didn't understand, but I didn't push. Later in the evening, Paxton cornered me, stating he'd been eyeing me all night, and he wanted to take me out on a date. It threw me for a loop."

"What did you tell him?" he asks.

"I was flattered, but I didn't think it was a good idea. He demanded to know why—".

"Prick."

"Although handsome, I wasn't attracted to him. Obviously, I didn't tell him that. I turned it into a joke and told him if he was interested in one of the Lucky Break girls, he should ask Chelle out instead of me. That's when he showed his true colors. He told me Trinity and Henley hit on him, but they're not his type. As for Chelle, he made a disparaging remark about his high standards and her weight, stating he'd never be seen with a girl who has no control over what she puts into her mouth. I was dumbfounded. When I picked up my jaw from the floor, I was done with the asshole. I excused myself and left his sorry ass standing there."

"How did that encounter turn into a feud over a douchebag?" he asks.

"Chelle had lied to me about Paxton—she didn't lose interest, he turned her down. In public—but I wasn't going to bring it up. I figured it was best to let it go. The next day she started acting strangely. It started with her only having a *cuppa* for breakfast. By lunch, she was doing the whole carrot-and-celery-sticks-with-hummus routine. I called her out on it, but she assured me she wasn't hungry. She skipped dinner that night. During the following weeks, she spiraled down this crazy yo-yo diet path. Because Chelle was so desperate for attention—and yes, coming from me it might sound hypocritical considering I wanted fame as much as she did, but I drew the line when it came to what I was willing to share on social media—she shared everything. Not surprising, it opened the door to criticism and haters. Since no one can live on these restricted diets forever, Chelle would go on these massive food binges. She was completely obsessed with her weight. As a result, her mood was all over the place. She was angry, and bitter, and bitchy. As time passed, the unhealthy obsession moved to her looks. She turned to plastic surgery with a vengeance. It was all documented online. I tried to step in as a friend numerous times, but she just kept pushing me away. She was nasty about it, too—"

"I still struggle to understand how she could just shut the door in your face like that. She was your best friend. God knows I've had my disagreements with Noah, but we always work things out. We even managed to navigate through the biggest point of contention that could've caused a permanent rift between us—you."

We exchange a small smile.

"The pursuit of fame fucked Chelle in the head," I say. "That's the best way I can explain it."

"Unbelievable."

"Soon, Chelle bonded with Henley, who preached the virtues of cosmetic enhancements. She took extreme measures to change her appearance a year into our fame because she hated everything about herself."

"What a pair," he says. "There's nothing wrong with wanting a little enhancement if you're unhappy with what God gave you, but in their case, it was an addiction."

"Exactly! In any case, I didn't know you could suffer from heartbreak over the loss of your best friend, but every time I saw Chelle cozying up to Henley, it was like a stab in the heart. The finality of our friendship was unsettling, but in time, I grew cold and threw in the towel."

"Wow!" Rhys shakes his head.

"Through it all, Chelle never stopped pining over Paxton. She wouldn't admit it, but she was doing all this shit to her body for him. Flash forward eighteen months after we got our big break, and Lucky Break is topping music charts around the world. At the release party for our second album, Paxton was there. Again."

"Don't tell me," he says. "He still wouldn't give Chelle the time of day."

"Pretty much. And at that point, she was a walking stick-figure."

"It's a shame she gave him that much importance and power," he says.

"It really was."

"Did he hit on you again?"

"He did. In fact, he never stopped. He constantly reached out to me on social media, asking me to reconsider. I always turned him down. Even though I wanted to chew his head off, I was always polite because once it's out there, you can't take it back. I didn't want screenshots of our conversations to go viral, showcasing me as a raving bitch."

"Why the hell did he keep pushing?"

"I doubt it had anything to do with me. It had everything to do with the fact I dared to turn him down. Very few women refuse *to be seen* with Paxton Foley," I say the last part with air quotes.

"None of that gives the foundation to support the outrageous accusations Jedd made."

"They don't. Like I said, Chelle blew things out of proportion and lamented to her mother."

"You're going to have to give me a little more to go by," Rhys says. "Your best friend's mother thinks you're responsible for her death."

I take in a deep breath. "A week after the launch party, Paxton contacted our publicist out of the blue to arrange a date with Chelle."

His eyebrows knit together. "That's quite the turnabout."

"I wasn't buying it. Even though Chelle and I had grown apart, I couldn't let her walk into the dragon's den without a warning. I told her Paxton had been hitting on me since the first launch party, even though I turned him down several times. I knew it was a big risk, but I wanted her to wake up to who this guy really was. I even took it one step further and revealed some of the mean things he said about her."

"How did she react?"

"She accused me of being a jealous and envious bitch. She told me I was lying about Paxton asking me out. I wasn't his type. *She was.* I insisted she read the thread of our conversation on social media, but she refused. Then she became verbally abusive. It didn't take long for her to grate on my last nerve. Instead of spiting more truths in her face, I hightailed it out of the house the four of us shared and stayed in a hotel for a few days."

"I'm really sorry you had to endure that. Chelle had so much baggage, it could qualify as cargo."

He hits the nail on the head.

"She went on a date with Paxton in the end."

"Not surprising given what you just shared," he says.

"Paxton never wanted to date her," I say. "He wanted to humiliate her."

"What do you mean?"

"Italian food was Chelle's favorite. Because her life was an open book, the world knew she missed pasta so much, she joked she would be willing to give up a vital organ if it meant she could eat it without gaining weight—"

"I don't like where this is going."

"In many ways Chelle and Paxton were a perfect pair—they both documented every aspect of their lives on social media." I let out a loud sigh. "The asshole took her to an Italian restaurant and proceeded to order practically every dish on the menu. I'm willing to bet he paid the waitstaff to stack the heaping dishes of food in front of Chelle. It was too well staged for it to be a fluke. The creep used the perfect devastating photo op to his advantage—"

"You've got to be kidding me."

"It's classic Paxton," I tell him. "From my understanding, he cajoled Chelle into having a forkful of fettuccine alfredo. One forkful led to another. And pretty soon, Chelle was eating to her heart's content. Paxton not-so-candidly snapped photos, alternating with shooting a few video clips."

"Jesus Christ," Rhys says.

"The next day, the internet was littered with unflattering images of Chelle eating with gusto. The mocking memes ensued. It was horrible. Stupid me, I swallowed my pride and returned to the house to comfort her. Bad move. Her wrath was unbearable. I promised myself it was the last time I gave two shits about her. Later that day, news leaked, exposing the date as a big fat joke. Paxton lost an ultimate dare challenge to a friend who happens to be a big YouTube personality with over forty-four million subscribers—"

"It was a prank?"

"Sadly, it was."

"Motherfucker!"

"Chelle quickly became the laughingstock of the internet. It took her three days to muster up the courage to set foot outside again. Trinity told me Henley and her were heading out for a day of shopping therapy. The paparazzi ambushed them." I let out a loud breath. "They never came back."

"Paxton Foley has a black heart." Disdain colors his words.

"He's a snake with a god complex who's still grinning for the camera, blissfully unaware of his role in Chelle's and Henley's demise."

"Chelle's mom is pointing the finger at the wrong person," Rhys says.

I let out a loud sigh. "I've made peace with the fact I may never get through to Mrs. Camden."

Chapter 38

Keira

The last two days have been so hectic, I'm surprised I didn't forget to breathe. It's coming at me from all directions. It's all good, though. The reaction from the press and the public after Flint's photoshoot caught us off guard. That pales in comparison to the frenzy that followed the red-carpet gala. Orders for SCORE Yours are coming in monster waves. Mind-blowing doesn't even start to describe it.

As a result, I'm the new 'It' girl.

Considering my non-model height, I'm taken aback by the number of fashion related sponsorship opportunities pouring in from big brands. I suppose when I'm sitting down, I could pass for an Amazonian. If those companies are willing to pay me handsomely, I'll gladly sign on the dotted line.

This deluge of goodness is a lot to take in. I'm still trying to wrap my head around seeing my face everywhere. Noah is beside himself and can't get over my shooting star. Michaela is as thrilled. She's just upset she's on the other side of the country and not in LA, soaking in all the excitement by my side. Arianne and Phoebe have made it their mission to text me anytime my name pops up in the media. At this rate, it'll soon be their full-time job.

After another frantic day as SCORE Yours' face, I'm back at Rhys's place. Since it's late afternoon, and I don't expect him back until much later because he's having drinks with a friend, I gear up, hop on one of his bikes, and hit the road. There's nothing like the adrenaline rush of riding a motorcycle to wash the day away. Cue *'Born To Be Wild', 'Bad To The Bone',* followed by *'Wanted Dead Or Alive',* baby!

On the heel of our first ride to Malibu—that included our freaky ride back to Manhattan Beach—I decided to take a refresher motorcycle course. Then, I took a more advanced defensive riding training taught by a former motorcycle stunt rider. The second I can afford it, I'll buy myself a new bike—something expensive—in the meantime, my boyfriend has offered me carte blanche on his collection.

Gridlock traffic and LA are synonymous, but there's a small window where the roads aren't obstructed by a million vehicles. I venture up Sunset Strip, past the iconic Beverly Hills Hotel, and up to Pacific Coast Highway. After a thrilling ride and stopping on the way for homemade ice cream, I retreat to Manhattan Beach. Since I'm running low on gas, I stop in Santa Monica because I don't want to chance it.

As I fill the tank, I hum a Top 40 catchy song in my head. Once done, I put the gas nozzle back in place. I pull out my wallet and grab Rhys's credit card and swipe it through the payment machine.

As I collect the receipt, someone calls out my name. "Keira!"

I turn my head.

A bald man I recognize approaches me.

Oh, no. Not him.

"Jedd Maitland from the *Hollywood Herald.* What a coincidence!" He flashes an insincere smile and sticks out his hand.

I ignore it and proceed to stuff the receipt into my wallet.

"No guard dogs today?" he says, scouring the gas station.

I curse under my breath.

"It seems you're the girl of the hour."

I keep pretending he's not standing next to me.

"Rumor has it, renowned designers and brands are throwing themselves at you."

I really wish he'd stop talking, but no, like a little Chihuahua, he yaps along.

"Lots of sponsorship deals to choose from. That's a windfall of bucks coming your way. Nice work if you can get it."

I glare at him and fight the urge to inflict pain by striking him with my helmet.

One.

Two.

Three.

I count in my head, forcing myself to calm down.

"Not that you need money, because you're dating a billionaire. Must be cushy," he says, smirking. "Does your boyfriend have a brother? Joke. I'm not gay... but for a billionaire I might be..."

Idiot.

"Leave me alone, Jedd."

"Come on, Keira. Don't you want to get your side of the story out there?"

"I already told you, I have nothing to say."

"By keeping quiet, you're admitting to being guilty."

Asshole.

My eyes dart to his.

The words are burning my tongue, but as long as I'm under

contract, anything I say has an impact on Rhys's company. I bite my tongue.

"I really wish you'd get your facts straight."

"Are you going to share some of the money you'll earn from your new found fame with Chelle's mom? It's the right thing to do considering your role in her daughter's—"

"Why are you so intent on assassinating my character by weaving a web of lies?" I ask him.

"I'm simply digging for the truth," he says.

"You have a warped understanding of the word, truth. You're pushing so hard, I have to wonder what's your payoff? Did Margaret Camden promise to *thank you* by sleeping with you for dragging my name through the mud and elevating her daughter to sainthood?"

It wouldn't be the first time.

"Guilt weighs heavy on your conscience?" he says. "Is that why you want me to shut up?"

Asshole.

He rolls his eyes like a teenage girl.

"No, I want you to shut up because your voice irritates the hell out of me."

Since nothing seems to faze him, he opens his mouth and vomits more words. "It's a struggle for Margaret now that she can no longer count on Chelle's big fat transfers." He shakes his head with a disapproving tsk on his lips. "So, so sad. It's tough in LA for a single mom."

Patronizing prick.

"And you'd know how?" I can't resist.

"Margaret has confided in me," he says. "Rumor has it a UK publisher approached her for tell-all book."

That should line her bank account.

Given how my friendship with Chelle dissolved, I'm not surprised her mom has no allegiance to me.

Mrs. Camden has a lot in common with my mom—they constantly pick the wrong men.

Chelle had little recollection of her dad. He walked out when she was four years old and returned to his native Australia, never to be heard from again.

Like most of the men Margaret has been with, her last boyfriend wasn't a prize. That didn't stop her from claiming she was madly in love two months into their extended bootycall. The bastard hightailed it back across the border to his native Vancouver when he found out she was pregnant with triplets. That was two years ago and another motivation for Chelle to make it big.

"Just get away from me. You're harassing me with your stupid questions!" I tell him, my anger blooming anew.

"We're simply having a conversation—"

"I can't stand another minute of this bullshit!"

I snatch the helmet from the handle, secure it on my head, lower my visor, slip my gloves on, jump on the bike, rev up the engine, and get the hell out of there. I gun down the road, hoping to put as much distance between Jedd and me as I can.

I stop at a red light at an intersection. I'm in the middle lane. Jedd fucking Maitland pulls up to my right.

He waves.

Great.

With a smirk twisting his lips, he launches into question mode, leaning against the door, shouting loud enough for people living in Kentucky to hear him. The creep is grating on my last nerve. I want to scream *Leave me alone,* but instead, I turn my head to the left, intent on ignoring him.

He shouts louder.

Jesus.

Fuck off!

I rev the engine, ready to bolt when the light changes to

green. When it does, I'm gone. On the highway, I'll hit the gas and speed away. Within the city limits, I have to be more careful, which is why, at the next red light, we meet again. And again, he pesters me.

Dammit.

My attention is on the traffic lights, praying for them to change.

Come on. Come on.

I peek to my right, Jedd has both hands on the steering wheel, ready to keep up with me.

We leave the intersection at the same time when the light turns green, but we don't go far.

A deafening crash and the screeching sound of tires have me jumping out of my skin. My head whips to the side just in time to watch in horror as a vehicle—that must've run the red light—slams into the back passenger side of Jedd's car, causing it to swerve in my direction.

Holy fuck!

In an attempt to change lanes to save myself, a vehicle rear-ends me, causing me to lose control of the bike.

Shit, shit, shit.

Everything happens ridiculously fast, at the same time it's like everything is in slow motion.

Right before the bike—seven-hundred-plus pounds of metal—hits the asphalt with me still straddling it, I leap off it, using my advanced training as my guide. There's no time to worry about oncoming traffic. I can only pray. I hit the ground hard, and my body rolls a few times until I land on my back.

I'm still alive.

I try to move, but everything hurts.

I try again.

Same result.

Dear God.

Panic sets in.

As I lie there motionless, I'm aware of the frantic commotion surrounding me. People are shouting and horns are blaring.

"Call 911!" A man shouts near me. "Now!"

The man kneels by my side, his leg brushing my arm. "I have CPR training, but you landed pretty hard," he tells me. "I don't want to shake you in case of a spinal injury. Can you hear me?"

My mind must be playing tricks on me, because the voice sounds familiar.

"Can you hear me?" He yells when I don't respond.

I shift my eyes so I can catch a glance of the man hovering over me through the smoky dark tint of my visor. I burst into tears when I recognize him.

"Shane." My throat is scratchy and my voice comes out too faint for him to hear me.

"Squeeze your hand into a fist if you can hear me," he says.

I do as I'm told.

"Good." I hear the relief in his voice. "Help is on the way."

I move my fingers, calling him to me.

He leans closer.

"You're going to be okay," he says.

"Shane," I say as loud as I can.

His head jerks back. "How do you know my name?"

"It's Keira."

"Keira?"

"Yes."

"Rhys's Keira?"

"Yes."

"Jesus Christ," he says. "I'm not leaving your side, Keira."

I can't hold back the tears.

"Everything hurts, Shane."

"Fuck," he says. "Collin, get over here!"

His brother is here?

"I called 911," Collin says. "I'm sure a bunch of people did."

"It's Keira," Shane tells him.

"Rhys's Keira?"

"Yes."

"Holy shit! Why aren't you removing her helmet?"

"I don't know what condition she's in," Shane tells his brother. "She could have a spinal injury. Removing her helmet could be dangerous."

This is the second time Shane's mentioned a spinal injury. The thought sends chills down my back.

"Got it," Collin says. "Can I touch her hand?"

"Be careful," Shane says.

"Shane and I are here for you, Keira," he says, wrapping his large hand around mine.

"Collin, my leg. It's wet and cold. And it hurts like hell," I tell him.

The searing pain makes me see stars. It's so sharp and intense, I pray for numbness.

"You're bleeding and you probably landed on it," Shane says.

My heart sinks.

"Collin, go find out if amongst those drivers there's a doctor or a nurse," Shane says. "Usually, they step up to the plate, but it doesn't hurt to check."

"On it!" Colin says.

"Hang in there, sweetheart," Shane tells me. Then his hand is squeezing mine. "There are quite a few hospitals around. The response time should be quick."

"Okay."

The movie of my life flashes in front of my eyes. I try to rein in the cyclone of thoughts and the weight pressing against my bleeding heart, but it only deepens my sorrow.

My mind races into a dangerous territory—finality.

I open my mouth to ask Shane for a favor, but hesitate.

For once, everything in my life is perfect. I'm happy and content. Blissful, even. God even granted me *the* man. *My* man... the one my heart can no longer live without. And now it seems being in the wrong place at the wrong time might steal everything away from me.

This might be my last chance.

The thought shatters me.

A deluge of emotion lodges in my throat. In what might be my last-ditch effort, I pluck up the courage to speak.

"Shane."

"Yes?" He hovers right over me again.

"If I don't make it, tell Rhys I love him." My voice is trembling, and a river of tears tracks down my cheeks.

"No, sweetheart, you're going to tell him yourself because you *are* going to make it," he says.

"Please, Shane. In case I don't. Promise me."

His answer doesn't come immediately.

"I promise to tell him."

"Thank you. Tell him I love him with all my heart. Tell him I've loved him forever, and I'll keep loving him in the afterlife."

Blaring sirens tell me help is near... right before everything goes black.

Chapter 39

Rhys

Late afternoons bring a different crowd to the Quintus Hotel. Some patrons linger after a late lunch. Others pass time at one of the award-winning bars before seeking an early evening hookup at the private adult club hidden right behind the hotel. Others, like myself, are here to connect with a good friend who's also a Dark Compulsion member.

"Here's to a second career that eclipses the first!" Piers, the blond man sitting across from me, lifts his martini glass.

I laugh.

"Hear, hear!" I clink my tumbler with his.

He takes a long swig of his straight martini, while I gulp down my Grey Goose on the rocks. Although we're sitting in the Golden Finger Whiskey Bar, it pays to be part of the owner's small group of friends. It allows us to order drinks that aren't on the menu. Neither Piers nor I are in the mood for whiskey.

"Even though I couldn't make it to the red-carpet event that took place a couple days ago, I already placed my order for my SCORE Yours headphones in every design," Piers says. He was at the International Beer Strategies Conference in London. He got back in town yesterday. "I also asked my executive assistant to coordinate things with our top performers so they can get their pick,"

"You're a good friend. Thanks for the support," I tell him.

His eyes crinkle with amusement. "Please. My order is a drop in the bucket," he says. "The product isn't even out yet, and you guys are already breaking records."

"Beckett and I are thrilled," I tell him. "This is well beyond our expectations."

"So, the consultant was a great investment?"

"Arianne was a phenomenal investment for our company and a hell of an *investment* for pretty boy Beckett!"

We laugh.

"I still can't believe Christensen pressed the pause button on his manwhoring," Piers says. "Now that he's no longer sowing his oats, we can only rely on Collin Dennison to carry the torch."

"You should talk," I say. "Last time I checked, you were still single."

"Oh, that hasn't changed, but unlike Beckett, my dick never makes the first page of the entertainment publications or websites."

"Good point!" I chuckle.

Forty-year-old Piers Somerville is my sponsor. Over the years, our relationship has transformed into a real friendship.

His journey resembles Beckett's.

Where I rocked the audience with my flow, rhymes and smooth hip-hop moves, Piers charmed his devoted fans on the big screen. He was a child actor on top of the world who made a successful transition until he came tumbling down.

He believed he was invincible, therefore, untouchable. He coped with the highs and lows of life with drugs. Like me, he rose from the gutter of addiction—he now owns a successful craft beer company. Once his life was in order, he started mentoring other addicts. Neither of us takes our second wind of success for granted.

"Seriously, man, congratulations." His amber eyes hold mine. "I'm really proud of you. You've come a long way. Not only with SCORE Yours, but in every aspect of your life and now... you're dating the most coveted face in Los Angeles."

"I can't keep up with all the changes in my own life," I say. "Why don't you come over this weekend? I'd love for you to meet Keira."

"I'd love that," he says.

"Sunday afternoon work?"

"Absolutely!"

My phone rings.

"Shit. Let me turn that off," I tell him. I pull out my phone from the inside pocket of my suit jacket. I'm just about to put it in silent mode when a text message flies across my screen.

The call is from Shane while the text comes from Collin.

I shake my head.

"What is it?" my sponsor asks.

I chuckle. "The Dennison brothers must be up to no good because they're both trying to reach me at the same time."

"Don't hold back on my account," he says.

"Let me see what they want," I tell him.

"Shane—"

"Rhys, it's about Keira," Shane says. He's out of breath.

"What about Keira?" I ask.

Piers cocks an eyebrow.

I shrug.

"She was in an accident—"

"What?" I sit up straight in my chair.

"The paramedics just drove off with her to the hospital," Shane says in one breath.

My heart stops dead as my world comes to a careening halt.

"Hospital? Accident? Keira?" I fire at him. "Shane, what the fuck are you talking about?"

He lets out a loud breath.

He does it again.

And again.

"Shane, you're scaring the shit out of me. Talk to me, man!"

"Sorry. I'm still running on adrenaline. It's all coming out jumbled and a little incoherent," he says in a calmer voice. "Keira was on her motorcycle—"

"She went for a ride?" I ask.

"Apparently."

"Where are you now?"

"Santa Monica." *She's a long way from home.* "Long story short, an asshole, too much in a rush to wait the freaking one hundred twenty seconds for the light to change caused a horrific accident when he ran the light—"

"Is she dead?" I shout into the phone.

"No, no, no," Shane says. "She's in bad shape. I just pray she didn't suffer from a spinal injury. Goddammit, she landed pretty hard. By the time the paramedics arrived, she was unconscious, but she's alive. She was spared."

My heart thuds. I'm stunned, and it takes me a moment to process everything that just came flying out of Shane's mouth.

"Rhys? You still there?" he asks.

"Spinal injury? Unconscious?" I ask when I can speak again.

"I'm not one hundred percent certain, but after what I witnessed, it's my assessment. I was afraid to touch her, just in case. And yes, she was unconscious." I was hoping I misheard him. "There's a lot more to share."

"Jesus Christ." I rub my face with my hand.

"Collin and I would've contacted you earlier, but we didn't want to leave her side. Not to mention, we didn't know which hospital she was going to end up in. Once we knew, we wanted to warn you. That's why he was texting you, just in case your phone was on mute."

"I understand. Which hospital?" I ask.

"UCLA Medical Center."

"I'll be right there."

"Okay. Collin and I are taking the McLaren he was test driving back to the dealership and then we'll make our way there," Shane says. "You might want to call Noah before the press is all over it."

His chilling words turn my blood into ice.

"See you there," Shane says.

I hang up the phone, still in disbelief.

Jesus Christ.

The shocking news paralyzes me.

"Let me drive you," Piers says.

My gaze lifts to his, but it's like I can't see him.

"Let's go. I'll drive you."

I swallow before I can open my mouth.

"I drove here." My voice is monotone.

"You're in no condition to drive, Rhys," he tells me.

I clear my throat. "You're right. I can't." *...because I'm obliterated.*

~

The half-hour bumper-to-bumper ride is excruciating.

My stomach is tied up in a ball of nerves. I can't even talk.

Piers doesn't attempt to fill the silence.

He leaves me be with my thoughts.

Bless him.

Noah was on set when I called. It went straight to voicemail, so I texted him. He got back to me. He's frantically making arrangements to return to Los Angeles. I also called my mom, Arianne, and Beckett. They're all meeting me at the hospital.

I let my mind wander.

Shane said she's alive, but will she be okay?

Spinal injury?

Fuck.

It's not like Shane has a medical degree. What if he's way off base? What if things were to take a turn for the worse?

Noah wouldn't survive this.

I let out a heavy sigh.

"She's alive, Rhys. That's all that counts." Piers says as if he can read my thoughts. While we were making our way to his car, I filled him in on what Shane shared with me. "If you're not happy with UCLA Medical Center, you have the means and influence to get her the best care in the country."

He keeps driving.

My mind keeps going to dark places.

When we finally arrive at the hospital, a wall of reporters awaits. The minute they see us approaching, they rush towards us, and chaos reigns supreme in the parking lot.

I blink and shield my eyes as the night sky lights up like Christmas when the camera flashes burst to life. The reporters shout questions all at once, waving recording devices in my face.

Fucking vultures.

"Back off!" I yell.

They come at me with more determination.

"Back the fuck off!" Piers's voice booms so loud, a few reporters jerk back. "I understand you have a job to do, but give the man a chance to breathe. He hasn't even set foot inside the hospital. How the hell can he answer your fucking stupid questions?"

That does it.

Standing five feet ten, Piers might not be nearly as menacing as Noah, but when he adds that *don't fuck with me* grit to his voice, you better get the hell out of his way.

I nod my appreciation.

He nods back.

Inside, we make short work of navigating the hallways to where Shane and Collin are waiting for us.

I fucking hate hospitals.

Painful memories wash over me as a pang of panic hits me. The feeling spikes, engulfing me at an alarming rate. The floor feels like it's about to cave in. My step falters and I brace myself against a wall, gripping it for dear life, as everything seems to disappear around me.

Goddammit.

"Rhys?" Piers asks.

Incapable of answering him, I clamp a hand against my chest as I struggle to breathe.

Shit.

"Memories of your dad?" Piers says.

I nod.

I can't form words.

Piers comes and stands in front of me, and places a comforting hand on my shoulder. "You're not the same man. You're not going to go down that path again. You're more equipped to handle difficult situations. You're not going to slide. I won't let you. Neither will your mother or your friends."

I nod again.

I'm too choked up to talk.

"I'd worry more about Noah than a relapse. Your best

friend won't hesitate to carry your ass—fireman style over his shoulder—right back to rehab."

I laugh a little.

I stand up straight.

"Your girl needs you," Piers says.

"I'm good," I tell him. "Thanks for being here."

"Don't mention it."

The last time I set foot in a hospital was after my dad had suffered from a heart attack. He spent many days in a coma. As he was fighting for his life, I was getting high. I refused to believe my superhero of a dad might not be invincible. If I got fucked up, I wouldn't be able to feel.

Then, one morning, Dad flatlined. The doctors tried to resuscitate him, but it was in vain. I was at an overnight binge party—one that involved copious amounts of booze, drugs, fucking, and watching others fuck—somewhere in Bel Air, when he passed away. I'm still sick to my stomach at the way I dealt with that traumatic episode in my life.

I'm entirely ill-prepared to be here, but Piers is right. I have to suck it up for my girl.

Shane and Collin jump to their feet when we enter the waiting room. The somber expression on their faces eats a hole in my chest.

"What is it?" I ask, not even bothering with greetings.

"They just took her to the operating room," Shane tells me.

Collin pats my shoulder. "She's getting the care she needs."

"Thanks for being there for her. I owe you guys."

"That's what friends do," Collin says. "If you can't be there for your girl, it's our duty to step in."

I nod.

The Dennison brothers are known for their unwavering loyalty. This is another example.

"Hey, Piers," Shane says.

The three guys greet each other.

"Shane and I weren't able to find out which room Keira is in," Collin says. "That information is reserved for family members only. We told the nurse she's an orphan, and her brother lives abroad. It didn't help. Finally, we explained her boyfriend would be showing up soon. She said you need to go to the nurses' station when you get here."

"I'll head there now." I give him a small smile and rush off.

After a few keystrokes, the black woman sitting behind the computer informs me someone will come for me when Keira is out of surgery. That's all she had for me. At least, I have my girl's room number. Resigned, I return to the waiting area.

Standing at the threshold, I call Shane over.

"So?" he asks.

"I'm on standby."

"Figures."

"Can you walk me through what happened again?" I ask him, desperate to put the pieces of the puzzle together.

"Everything happened so fast, it was almost a blur," he says. "Collin and I were test driving a new McLaren he's considering buying when we stopped at a red light. As were debating about the car, a kickass Softail Breakout bike—clearly custom—catches our eye—"

"The Softail is my bike," I tell him. "I added Keira to the insurance."

"The bike is in pieces," Shane says.

"The bike isn't important. It's replaceable. Keira isn't."

"Thank God for her quick thinking. It saved her life." Shane gives me the play-by-play. "Once the police arrived, the area was taped off, so it's not like I could get close, but based on the wreckage and the magnitude of the impact, I'm guessing the asshole responsible for the nightmare was drunk."

Anger causes my lip to twitch. "Motherfucker."

"The motherfucker didn't make it," Shane tells me. "He was propelled through the windshield of his car and crashed against the asphalt, face down. By the time the EMTs got to him, he was swimming in a pool of his own blood. Seems he wasn't even wearing a seatbelt."

"What about the other car?" I ask. "The one that was hit."

"Not sure. The EMTs took the person to a hospital."

"Okay, thanks." The tale is as unbelievable as it was when he offered fragments of the story when he first called me.

Once Shane is done recounting the tragic facts, we join Piers and Collin in the waiting area. As we do, my mom, Arianne, and Beckett arrive. They're full of questions. Since the Dennison brothers witnessed it all, I let them tell the story. Hearing what Keira went through again, twists my gut. If the motherfucker weren't already dead, I would've tracked him down. When everyone is all caught up, we start the nail-biting procession of waiting, and waiting, and waiting. After what seems like a lifetime, someone calls my name.

"Mr. Rhys Hartford."

"Yes!" I jump to my feet. Pure adrenaline carries my legs as close the gap between me and the woman scouring the room.

"You're Keira Weatherly's boyfriend?" the black woman asks.

"Yes, I am. We live together."

"I'm Dr. Cuthbert," she says.

"Can I see her now?"

"Does Miss Weatherly have parents? Siblings?"

Is her evasiveness the precursor to bad news?

"No. I mean, yes!" I shake my head. *Breathe.* "Her mom passed. Same for her grandmother. Her father isn't in the picture. Her older brother lives in New Zealand. He's doing his best to return to LA as quickly as he can. So, right now, I'm all she's got. Is she out of surgery?"

Dr. Cuthbert nods. “She is.”

“Can I see her?”

“We need to talk first.” Her expression is unreadable.

I’ve never before felt such dread, the ache in my heart unbearable.

Chapter 40

Keira

One month later

As I stroll across the executive floor at SCORE, I smile, wave and return thumbs-ups. I'm soaking up the love from the staff members.

During my convalescence, so many of them reached out via Rhys's executive assistant with heart-warming messages of support. The last time most of these people saw me, I was on crutches. Thank God, I can finally walk unassisted.

"Look who's here," Cecilia says when I park myself in front of her desk.

"Hey Cecilia!" I return her smile.

We've grown close over the last few months. She was kind enough to come by Rhys's place every night to drop off the flowers and stuffed animals fans left at SCORE's security gate. She's an absolute sweetheart. I've also grown much closer to Rhys's mom.

When she wasn't working, Dawn spent nearly all her free time mothering me. She didn't care that her son had hired topnotch help to assist me, she forced herself into the mother role and I was more than happy to let her.

Mikki flew in as well. In fact, she came back not long ago. Having her around is super fun. We might be new friends, but we have a great bond.

The second time around, she just showed up at Rhys's door, unannounced. She planned on staying a couple of weeks, but she's still in LA. My life may be drama-filled, but it pales in comparison to what she's been dealing with. Jaw-dropping stuff.

"You're finally one hundred percent!" Cecilia says.

"I'd say I'm ninety percent," I tell her. "My left leg isn't quite there yet." My eyes lower to my ballet flats. "I won't be able to wear heels for a while."

"You're still standing strong—pun very much intended—that's all that matters," she says.

Amen to that.

The advanced motorcycle training saved my life. The helmet, heavy motorcycle riding pants, and armored leather jacket are close seconds. Since I had lost weight since leaving LA, my boyfriend bought me new gear that fits properly. I balked at the eye-popping price tag at the time, but he wouldn't hear of it. Thank God he ignored my protests. Although, I'll end up having to replace all my riding gear, they were instrumental in keeping me alive.

I had to wear a neck brace for a while, but I didn't sustain a spinal injury or trauma. I can't thank my lucky stars enough. That said, I was badly bruised, suffered from severe road rash, and I broke a bone in my lower left leg. It took the doctor an hour to reposition it. I was in a cast for weeks. The recovery was difficult and frustrating. It was also agonizing at times. I promised myself I wouldn't rely on painkillers, but I had to cave in. Rhys was watching over me like a hawk. He wouldn't say it, but we both knew he was worried. People get hooked on painkillers all the time.

Noah was by my side, doting all over me for two weeks. When he went back to New Zealand, he took a little piece of my heart with him. The accident opened my eyes. I begged my brother to come back to LA. There are six months of production left for the series he's working on. This is the last season. After that, he's coming back home for good. There's no shortage of work in Tinsel Town for his skill set.

"You look like you mean business today." Cecilia gives me a onceover. "Anything I should know about?"

"Maybe," I say, brushing my fingers through my hair. My whole life, I've had a curtain of hair, extending down to my waist. After shaving it off in Nepal, I knew it would grow back. After the accident, cut and color were the last things on my mind. Once I was back on my feet, I couldn't wait to get it cut short and colored blonde again.

"Come on, spill the beans," Cecilia says.

I shake my head. "I can't yet. I haven't even told my boyfriend yet."

She smiles wide. "You're in luck. He just got in twenty minutes ago. Fair warning, he's a little grouchy."

"Yeah, even when you get some shuteye, a red eye flight is always brutal," I say. Rhys was at a conference in Chicago and another in Detroit.

"It's more than that." She leans into her desk. "If I could figure out how to get Margaret Camden to shut her mouth, I'm sure Rhys would give me a big fat raise. I fear only a miracle of God would make that happen." The bitterness in Cecilia's voice doesn't go unnoticed. "This morning's interview was laughable. The things that came flying out of her mouth were farfetched." She rolls her eyes hard.

I sigh. "She's exhausting."

"I understand she needs to feed her children, but that isn't the way to do it," Cecilia says.

"As my publicist says, I'm a low hanging fruit and Margaret is determined to milk it."

Cecilia crosses her arms and leans back against her chair, her lips curled up in disdain. "Whatever happened to common decency?"

"Apparently, it can be sold to the highest bidder."

Based on what I was able to read online, Jedd Maitland is lucky to be alive. He narrowly escaped with his life, unlike the man who caused the accident in the first place. According to the reports, the careless drunk had enough alcohol in his system to down an elephant.

Without her partner in crime, aka Jedd, Margaret Camden cranked up her defamation campaign and took her one-woman show on the road. The tell-all article Jedd threatened me with was never published. I can only assume he never wrote it since it's been mum's the word from the *Hollywood Herald* camp. Chelle's mom on the other hand can't seem to shut the fuck up. She's willing to tell her story, knitted with lies, to anyone willing to listen.

My new publicist advised me to ignore her, which I've done. I only made one statement—right after the accident when I was still in the hospital—to rebut Margaret's ludicrous comments. She dared to compare me to the angel of death, blaming me for Jedd's accident. There are cameras in every corner in LA. The video footage tells the story like it really happened, disproving Margaret's grotesque lies.

I'm woeful things turned out the way they did with Chelle and her mom, but it's no fault of mine. They changed.

"Oh, well." I shrug. I refuse to let Margaret ruin my day. "Let me go poke my head inside my boyfriend's office before he's too busy to remember about me."

"Like that's ever likely to happen," Cecilia says.

"A girl can never be too cautious," I say.

She laughs.

With a spring in my step, I close the short distance to my man's office.

"Knock, knock, knock." I rap my knuckles against the door.

The door swings open.

A tall, delicious man flashes me a sexy smile before he circles an arm around my waist, pulling me to him.

"Get in here," he says.

He closes the door shut behind us.

"Well, hello to you, too—"

Rhys's lips crash against mine.

He slides his tongue inside my eager mouth, flirting with mine, ratcheting my desire and devouring my mouth in a domineering display of possessiveness I've come to crave.

A soft moan escapes my throat.

My neglected nipples harden beneath my blouse, begging for his touch, his mouth, and his cock. I love when he teases the peaks of my nipples with the engorged head of his cock.

Oh, God.

My lady bits pulse.

I tell myself the light-headedness hitting me is because I'm walking on sunshine after my epic morning, and not because of the man I can't live without. I know better. Kissing Rhys is an experience so intense, I feel it all the way down to my toes.

"Fuck, I missed you, dimples," he says, pulling away from me. His voice is rough.

"I've missed you, too, Rhys."

"Let me take you in," he says, taking a step back. "Give me a twirl."

I drop my designer handbag on the console near the door and grant his wish.

"You look so sexy." He grazes my chin with his fingertips.

"Thank you."

"Did the outfit seal the deal?" he asks.

For my big day, I selected a black blouse with an oversized, feminine bow at the neck which I paired with a hot pink fashionable A-line raw silk skirt that hits me right below the knee. My scar is still visible, but that wasn't enough to stop me from exposing my legs. The dermatologist says the scar should fade in time, but there will always be a trace of it. I can walk again. I can live with a scar.

"It did!" My smile is epic. "Your girlfriend is officially a new artist at Ritual of Rhyme Records! I no longer have any financial or contractual ties to my old record company."

Rhys picks me up in his arms and kisses me all over before dropping me to my feet.

"Congratulations, baby."

"I'm so excited to start this new chapter in my life."

"I am so happy for you," he says.

"Can you handle it?"

He draws his eyebrows together.

"You're going to be dating a model *and* a chart-topping singer. That's a lot to handle, big guy."

"I can handle your sexy ass just fine," he says. "I reckon someone needs a refresher."

With one swift motion, he has my back pressed against the door, one hand holding mine over my head and the other up my skirt.

How the hell does he move that fast?

"We have *plans* for later, Rhys."

"You're going to make me wait?"

"Yes."

"Are you fucking kidding me?"

I lift my chin up. "I'm dead serious, Rhys Hartford."

"Are you saying you don't want me to make you come?"

Bastard.

He had to go there.

Toys and fingers don't measure up to his masterful touch. After ten days on opposite sides of the country, I'm dying for his fingers and his big fat cock. Add to that, the fact I was in so much pain after the accident, and later the cast was in the way. It's been a while since we've been intimate. I'm as desperate as he is. I'm this close from begging him to make me come or better yet, a quickie in his private bathroom, but I mentally chastise my pussy to behave.

His nostrils flare and his gaze burns into me.

I sweeten the pot.

"If you're patient, I'll make it worth your while." My voice is light, but the rest of me is combustive.

"Fuck, woman, it's been a week and a half. You have to give me something to tide me over. One more minute of this..." He grabs his crotch and squeezes his cock hard, "and I'll be suffering from blue balls permanently."

"What if I lick your balls later to make it better?" I emphasize my lewd offer by sliding a finger between my teeth and give him a helpless poor little me look.

"Devious little flirt." He shakes his head.

"Well... it is tonight's theme."

"I can't wait," he says.

Neither can I.

He lowers his head closer to mine. I expect another heated kiss. Instead, he buries his face in my neck, nuzzling me, inhaling my scent before sucking the sensitive flesh there. He takes me right back to where I was when he kissed me—on the edge of frenzied delirium.

I grab his waist and slip my fingers through the loop of his pants, pulling him closer to me.

His cock is impossibly hard.

I tilt my hips forward, grinding against his hard-on. My desire builds with every rotation of my hips.

He responds by pressing hard against me.

Damn him.

My body trembles, as does his.

"Fuck," he says.

Our teasing ways will be my demise.

If this little steamy interlude is any indication, tonight should be explosive.

Just when I'm about to change my mind about us fooling around, I remember what I have in store for him and force myself to rein in my raging libido.

"We need to put a stop to this right now," I say.

Rhys ignores me

"Please, be good, baby," I tell him.

He sighs in frustration.

He pulls away from me, lust veiling his glacier-blue eyes.

"I'll meet you at Dark Compulsion," I say. "Once I'm done with the meeting at the advertising agency, I'll head to Phoebe's. I dropped off my things there this morning. Arianne and I will change at her place for tonight's party."

He stares at me in disbelief.

"What are you talking about, Keira? I'm not going to see you back at my place?"

"Nope. I want to remove any temptations on both sides. It's clear we can't keep our hands off each other."

"Jesus Christ, woman, you might as well chop off my balls." He's suffering. "I can coax myself to wait until we get to the club to fuck you, but I can't even get a blowjob beforehand?"

I feel for him, I really do.

"You catch on quick, big guy."

"You're going to pay for this," he says.

"I surely hope so. God knows I spent enough money at French Appliqué."

He growls.

I swear, he shows teeth like a wolf.

Poor baby.

Chapter 41

Keira

From the moment we step out of the chauffeured Rolls-Royce Beckett and Rhys hired for us girls, it's an experience that tantalizes all the senses. Linked arm in arm, Arianne, Phoebe, and I traverse the long pathway towards the club that's been transformed into a Vegas-worthy show. We're in awe. Fire performers light up the night with their spectacular flames. A badass female knife juggler takes my breath away with her harrowing prowess.

Respect to her.

Acrobats dazzle with their awe-inspiring stunts. The beautiful white tiger is both frightening and alluring. Thank God the animal is kept in a cage, and its trainer gives off a strong ringleader vibe. There's also a series of mystical characters greeting us as we trail along the red carpet towards the entrance.

Little did we know the magical setting outside the club was just the beginning.

"Holy hell," I say.

"Wow. I mean, wow," Arianne says.

"Ladies, we've arrived!" Phoebe says.

We're rooted in place when we enter the main room at the club. Our gaze bounces to every corner. We're surrounded by LA's crème de la crème. Everything about our surroundings screams influence and prestige. I even recognize a few heavy hitters.

What a way to kick off the weekend!

"Beckett told me the room would be decorated to match the theme, but I didn't expect this," Arianne says.

"Rhys said the same thing," I say. "This is spectacular!"

"Look at those!" Arianne points.

"Wow!" I marvel at the eye-catching and exquisite chandeliers hanging from the ceiling.

"It's like a movie—or video music—set," Phoebe says.

She nailed it on the head.

Rhys didn't downplay it when he said the owner of Dark Compulsion made it his mission to dazzle members—and guests—by creating an enchanted setting.

"Even the music is on point," I say.

On cue, we lift our hands over our heads and do a sexy dance move before dissolving in laughter.

Tonight's theme is slumber party. We had this oldies theme-appropriate song playing on repeat as we danced, sang, and shook our thing while getting ready at Phoebe's place. Dark Compulsion's slumber party has nothing to do with what we used to have when we were kids or teenagers. We're talking about at a decadent get-together amongst beautiful people where men wear silk pyjamas and women wear sexy-as-fuck sleepwear.

Arianne, Phoebe, and I are dressed for the occasion. Our silk chemises and robes offer just enough of a peek to entice, without giving away too much. Scouring the room, it's clear some women decided to be a lot bolder in their approach. Others are putting it all out there, strutting around in see-through lace chemises or mesh ones. They went as far as nixing the robe. Talk about dare to bare. We opted for something a lot less risqué.

I selected a bright-pink silk-satin combo with embroidered white flowers. It's a bit of a splurge, but when the sales clerk told me it was hand-sewn by skilled artisans in Belgium, I couldn't resist.

Arianne is channeling the femme fatale in her with a red and black combo.

Phoebe's emerald-green combo looks striking on her.

My friends went the distance with faux-feather high-heel mules. I had to keep it to flat ones, which makes me feel short. At least I look good.

The shopping trip to French Appliqué is one we're unlikely to forget anytime soon. To avoid mayhem due to my presence, I arranged for us to shop before the boutique opened on a Saturday morning. The selfies of the three of us were pretty hilarious. If I control what's published on the internet, I have the upper hand.

"The vibe is so sexy," I say, soaking it all in.

"So, so sexy," Phoebe says.

"Good God, people are already making out." Arianne tilts her head and moves her eyes to the left.

Phoebe and I pick up on her cue.

Holy hell!

A man with silver streaks running across his temples is hanging from a woman's enormous boobs, sucking at them with avarice as if no one is watching. I can't tell what the woman is enjoying most, the attention from others or what her partner is doing to her.

My eyes move to a couple getting it on behind them and I nearly choke.

"Those two over there need to get a room," I say, blushing. I fan myself, hoping to cool down my burning cheeks.

"Where?" Arianne and Phoebe ask, scanning the room.

"The seating area behind the couple going at it," I whisper shout.

My friends turn around and flip right back to face me.

"Jesus!" Phoebe says.

"I didn't even know that was a thing," I say.

"Neither did I," Phoebe says. "I'm so begging Oscar to try that out tonight."

Hmmm... she's onto something.

Arianne leans into our circle and says, "They're exhibitionists. Same goes for the other couple."

"I guess that makes us voyeurs," Phoebe says.

I'm not sure what to make of her statement. I knew exactly what I was walking into tonight. I didn't expect to be turned on by watching strangers going at it in public. And to think, the night is still young.

"Cotton Candy." A tall man approaches us. Two large men follow close behind him.

It takes me a beat to register.

Oh, yeah, he's talking to me.

How does he know my club name?

I smile, but I don't recognize the incredibly attractive man.

"It's an honor and a pleasure to have you at one of my parties," the man says. He's dressed in appropriate-theme-wear, but his shadows are in black suits.

Then it hits me.

Larkin.

"The pleasure is mine," I say.

He reaches out a hand and I place mine into his palm.

"My name is Zeus," he says, his cognac-colored eyes boring into mine. Rhys gave me the kinky club etiquette 101 crash course, so I'm well versed on the basics. Calling the owner Larkin or Mr. Gallagher at the club is the kiss of death. "I asked my staff to announce your arrival. I'm glad to see you're back on your feet." He gives me an appreciative onceover.

"So am I." I smile.

His amber eyes moves to Arianne and Phoebe.

"Where are my manners?" I say.

This experience is a little overwhelming.

"This is Jazzberry Jam"—I point to Arianne—"and this is Outer Space." I point to Phoebe.

After signing the disclosure agreement—which all three of us read carefully—we were fitted with purple cuffs and then given a club name for the evening.

When I inquired about the origin of the names, the stunning blonde who was part of the welcoming committee explained guests' names are a random pick from the Crayola rainbow of colors. Arianne and I nearly lost our mind laughing when Phoebe got her name. How fitting?

"Ladies, thank you for gracing me with your presence tonight," Larkin says. "Paragon, Dagger, and Mahogany are lucky men."

Unlike our playful names, Dark Compulsion members get computer generated names. The club names for Rhys and Beckett are so manly, badass, and edgy. Oscar got a sexy Crayola color.

"I congratulated them on their impeccable taste. You ladies are a vision for sore eyes." Larkin's gaze moves from mine, to Arianne's, to Phoebe's.

"Thank you," we say, one after the other.

"And may I say, for the record, I never thought the day would come when Paragon and Dagger would change their playboy ways. From notorious bachelors to relationship bliss?!" Larkin shakes his head. "I guess anything is possible."

Since Phoebe kicked out Oscar so we could get ready at their place, Beckett reached out to him and took him under his wing. Our men spent the evening together—drinks at Beckett's, followed by dinner at the Quintus Hotel. Then, they made their way to the hotel's whiskey bar to pass time until we showed up.

"We're honored to be here," Arianne says.

Phoebe places a hand against her chest and says, "This was on my bucket list, Zeus. I can die content."

"You can't die just yet, Outer Space, there are so many more naughty parties on the calendar. You'd be missing out on a lot," Zeus tells her.

"In that case, I'll definitely stay alive," Phoebe says.

Arianne and I laugh.

"Zeus!" A man approaching our circle calls out.

My jaw drops.

That man is a big Hollywood star. Same for the famous female star by his side.

Wow.

Privacy at the club must be guarded with as much ferocious zeal as the White House because the power couple didn't even bother with a mask. Mind you, no one else did, but still, these are really big celebrities.

"Ladies, it was a pleasure. If you'll excuse me," Larkin says.

"Of course," I say.

"Have a great evening," Arianne says.

"It was a pleasure meeting you," Phoebe says.

With that, Larkin joins the celebrity couple.

We look at each other and just shake our heads.

Freaking amazing.

"Now, I'm really excited," Arianne says.

"I can't wait to get this party started!" Phoebe rubs her hands together, a gleeful glint shining bright in her mischievous eyes.

"The party has already started," I say.

"Oh no, honey." Phoebe shakes her head. "I'm not talking about this party..." She points to the floor. "I'm talking about the party that's about to start when I meet my man upstairs in our designated room."

Along with our club name and cuffs, we were handed an envelope containing a colourful card with a bar code. Once we scan it against one of the iPads near the elevator, it will show our room number and the location of said room.

Very classy.

"You're too eager for your own good," Arianne tells her.

"Are you kidding me?" Phoebe says. "I'm about to get down and dirty with my man under the same roof as Hollywood royalty. I love you guys, but I don't want to hang out here and talk when I could be doing something a lot more interesting with my mouth."

I'm shocked by her candor.

"Please, Phoebe, tell us how you really feel," Arianne says.

"Horny as hell." Phoebe doesn't miss a beat. She has no filters. "Catch you later, *amigas*." She waves and struts off with a confident swing in her step.

Arianne stares at her receding form, stunned.

"I'm sorry. I have no explanation for her," she says.

"Although that was a lot more information than I needed to know, she does have a good point. I'm dying to see my man," I say.

"Far from it for me to keep you away from your man for one more second than necessary." Arianne offers a complicit smile. "I'm going to run up and enjoy mine."

"Let the party begin!" I borrow Phoebe's words. "Have a sexy night!"

"Right back at ya!" Arianne winks.

I weave my way through the crowd.

The trepidation of excitement skyrockets every time my eyes land on a couple interlaced in a naughty embrace.

Chapter 42

Rhys

I'm way too impatient to suffer through the opening party. I'm desperate for alone time with my girl. I agreed to not see her until we arrive at the club, as long as we bypass the warm-up session downstairs and jump right into action behind closed doors. If she really wants to soak in the vibe, we can always go downstairs when I'm finished ravishing her body. Once people satiate their carnal desires, the mood changes dramatically. It goes from feral to mellow.

Since we're not allowed to use our phones inside the club, my girl sent me a text right before getting out of the Rolls-Royce. She should be here soon.

I pace the luxuriously decorated room, a tumbler of scotch in hand. When the distinctive sound of the door opening echoes, I rush to it. Keira pushes it open, steps into the room, and closes it behind her.

My heart fucking stops.

"Holy shit, you're hot." The words spill from my lips.

She smiles wide.

Hazel-green eyes brush over my body. "You look handsome."

"Please," I say. "My navy-blue silk pyjamas don't hold a candle to the cock-hardening combo you're wearing. First thing Monday morning, I need to find out if I can buy stocks for French Appliqué. If I can't, I may have to consider buying the business."

"You like?" she asks, giving me a twirl.

I drink up every delicious inch of her little body.

The bright-pink silk chemise is quite short, but the robe that hits her right below the knee balances things nicely.

"I want to see you. Take off the robe."

She does as she's told and throws it to the nearby armchair.

She gives me another twirl.

The chemise is a loose fit, and the barely-there straps harden my cock.

"Come here," I say, reaching out for her.

I crush my lips to hers.

I kiss her with urgency, passion, and hunger. I've dreamt of locking lips so many times over the past ten days, it's embarrassing. My tongue strokes along all the curves and hollows of her beautiful mouth. My hands roam over the body I've missed and longed to touch. With each caress and with each tongue stroke, my cock grows harder and thicker, aching with the unreasonable need to be inside her.

I break our embrace and run my hands down her arms. "How do you want it?"

"No appetizers, champagne, or desserts first?" she asks.

"Beckett and I made sure you ladies had plenty of champagne and desserts on the way here." We're not stupid. We nixed any possible objections. "So, to answer your question, I know for a fact you're ready to go."

Each room has a wine fridge and a fully stocked bar. I can

also order food and dessert with just one phone call. For the sake of my hungry cock, it's best not to mention it.

She responds with a wicked smile.

"I get to choose?"

"You get a say," I tell her. "I'll let you know if I'm in the mood or not. What'll it be, dimples?"

She hesitates.

"I'm waiting!"

She averts her gaze. "I saw something downstairs..."

"Eyes on me."

She obeys.

"What did you see?"

She pulls her lower lip between her teeth and peers up at me from under her lashes, which look like they're ten inches long right now.

"A couple..." She lets out a nervous laugh.

I place two fingers under her chin and force her gaze to mine.

"You understand what this club is about?"

"Yes, I do, but... it was pretty out there..."

Whatever her heart desires, I'll give it to her—no matter how lewd. Though I put my foot down at sharing her with another man or woman.

"You want to try whatever you saw?" I ask.

She stares at me, debating.

As she does, a new song kicks in.

I can't help but chuckle at the bridge, *'Tonight I'm Fucking You'*.

"That's exactly what I'm trying to do to you." I point to the speakers encased in the ceiling. "Help a guy out."

She laughs.

"Come on, woman, tell me what you saw."

"Your fingers."

I knit my eyebrows together. "All this drama and angst because you want me to finger-fuck you? I don't get it, dimples. That's hardly a novelty."

"It's a lot more than that."

"Then tell me."

"It would be easier if I showed you."

"Now you're talking," I say with a grin.

"Sit down," she says.

I cock an eyebrow.

"Please, Rhys."

I'm usually the one giving the orders, but I'll allow it.

I move to take a seat on the couch, but she stops me.

"The couple downstairs were on a chair. You should do the same."

I have no idea where this is heading, but I'll play along.

I drag one of the two chairs situated behind the small round table in the corner of the room to where she's standing.

I take a seat and wait.

I know my girl well enough to tell when she's nervous. A rarity for her.

"You've come this far, go all the way," I tell her.

"Well..." Her cheeks flush, competing with her bright pink chemise.

"Yes?" I nod a few times, hoping she'll give me more to go on. "Keira, you're never shy asking for what you want."

"Nothing like this," she says.

"Try me," I say.

"I think the idea is for me to fuck your fingers," she says.

"We've already been down that road."

"It's not what you think," she says. "The woman was wearing a short baby doll top, and from the way she was riding the guy's hand, I'm guessing she either went commando or she was wearing crotchless panties—"

"Are you wearing crotchless panties?"

She shakes her head. "I'm not."

I'm disappointed.

"Keep talking," I tell her.

"The guy's hand was on his lap and the woman was bouncing up and down on his fingers as if she was bouncing on his cock." She blurts that out in one breath.

A burst of adrenaline shoots through my bloodstream. The salacious visual assaults my senses in the best possible way.

"Too much?" she asks, watching me with uncertainty.

"Come sit on Daddy's lap." I reach out a hand to her.

She takes it. "I gather you're up for it?"

"I'm definitely up for it, little girl."

Giggling, she straddles my lap.

I run my hands over her skin and her chemise. Her bare thighs are warm under my touch as I skim the silk fabric upward, bunching it around her waist.

When my eyes land between her legs, my cock stirs.

"No underwear?" I ask.

"No. You kept reminding me all day long you couldn't wait to have access to my pussy. I figured, why bother with a barrier?"

I nod my appreciation. "How many fingers do you want?" I ask.

"How many fingers do usually give me?" she says.

"Depends on my mood," I tell her.

"I'll let you decide." Her voice is deep and chocolatey. The reverberation travels to my balls.

"You asked for it," I say.

"I certainly did," she says with a grin.

I drop a soft kiss against her lips.

"Get up!"

She does as she's told.

I place the back of my hand on my thigh and hold up three fingers.

She looks down, a cocky smile pulling at her lips. When our eyes meet, the hunger and lust shining bright in them is mouthwatering.

I tap a couple times on the side of my other thigh. "Hop on."

She slowly lowers herself over my fingers.

Fuck.

My body is so tightly coiled with need, I could come without her touching my cock.

"Remove the damn chemise. I need to see my fingers fucking your pussy."

I don't have to ask twice.

"You're dripping wet." My eyes are fixed to the spot she left on the dark silky fabric of my silk pyjama pants.

"This is so hot," she says.

"You're so hot," I tell her.

She responds with a lazy smile.

"Ride my fingers, baby."

She places her arms over my shoulders and starts to move slowly, up and down.

"Oh God," she says.

Her movements are restrained, as if she's testing the water.

"Don't make me waste my time," I tell her.

Her eyes shoot to mine.

"Either you fuck yourself with my fingers, or get off."

A flash of anger sparks in her eyes.

She moves with more determination, grinding her hips in circles and coming down in a precise angle so her clit rubs against my hand.

"That's more like it," I say.

She narrows her eyes at me.

"This is my fantasy, but for some reason you're taking ownership of it."

"Like I take ownership of every delicious part of you," I tell her. "We both know you like it that way."

I'm rewarded with a wide smile.

She picks up the pace, gyrates her hips and bounces off my hand over and over again. Her gorgeous tits bounce in sync as she gives herself to pleasure.

My God, she's beautiful.

Nothing brings me more pleasure than to watch her take hers.

I place my free hand over my cock, moaning as I squeeze hard. I can't decide if it's to prevent me from coming or push me to spill my cum.

She laces her fingers behind my neck and loses her fucking mind.

I try to ignore the impatient demands coursing through my veins because this is about her.

Each time she lands on my hand, she lets out a helpless cry. The sight of her unleashed calls out the most feral and savage part of me.

"I can smell how much you're enjoying our dirty little play," I tell her.

She whimpers.

"Your hedonistic scent is doing things to me."

"Dear God!" She grinds harder over my fingers.

This woman is making me lose my goddamn mind.

Right on cue, the song changes.

The lyrics of *'I Put a Spell On You'* explain my predicament better than I ever could.

I'm under Keira's spell and I wouldn't want it any other way.

"I'm so close," she says, circling her hips in wild bucks. She slams hard against my hand and clenches her pussy tight around my fingers.

Jesus Christ!

Her cadence is feverish.

I catch her lips with mine and devour them in a punishing kiss.

"You want more?" I ask against her panting mouth.

"I'm not sure I can take more," she says. Her hazel-green eyes darken with desire, contradicting her words.

"You can. I want you to come so hard, they hear you on the first floor."

A long sighing moan escapes her lips.

So fucking beautiful.

So fucking perfect.

So fucking mine.

I heighten her pleasure by curling my fingers, searching for her sweet spot.

"Yes! There!"

To ensure she gives me what I want, I press my thumb against her clit.

"I'm close! So, so close." Her head lolls back.

"Eyes on me."

She obeys.

Her heavy-lidded eyes are veiled with so much lust, you'd think she was drunk.

"Now give me what I want and no holding back. Understand?"

She bobs her head a few times.

If I thought she was wild before, I was wrong.

"That's it, baby," I say.

All movement stops, her breath hitches, and her mouth drops open. Her pussy leaks with sticky juices running down my hand and staining my pyjama pants.

"Good girl."

"Oh God!" Her hand travels to my nape, her fingers pulling at my hair.

Fuck, yeah.

"Oh God. Oh God. Oh God." She's staring right at me, but I wonder if she can see me or if she's too lost to her pending orgasm.

She rocks her dripping pussy over my palm, angling her hips, pressing her clit against my thumb, taking what's hers. Her breaths are ragged and a moan escapes me as I admire her in awe.

My cock gives a sharp, tense throb where it's trapped inside my pyjama pants and begging to be freed. I squeeze my cock hard, telling myself not to come.

"I—I'm gonna come."

She arches her back.

"That's it, chase after your climax, slut."

She's frantic.

On the heel of her next thrust, her body tenses, trapping my fingers deep inside her.

"Oh, yes! Oh, yes! Oh, yes! Oh, fuck, yes!"

She's loud.

"I'm coming! I'm coming!" Her hoarse cries cause my cock to swell.

Fucking beautiful.

Her sated and boneless body slumps against mine. We're fused together and I'm certain she can feel my heart thumping in my chest.

I kiss the top of her head.

"Wow..." she says. "That was so incredible and so powerful. I feel the need to track down that couple and thank them."

I chuckle. "You came hard for me, baby."

"I thought I was going to faint."

"That was a good warm-up, but we're not done yet."

"Don't I get a break?"

"You will. Once I'm done fucking you," I tell her. "Feel how hard I am after watching you come so beautifully."

She presses a hand on my cock, stroking me. "Someone needs relief."

"Someone's about to get it."

I stand up with her in my arms.

She wraps her legs around my waist. I step over to the bed and drop her on it.

With impatient fingers, I unbutton my pyjama top and shrug out of it. The bottoms come off in a flash, and my angry cock points north. It throbs so hard, the pulse hammers in my temples.

I fist my cock, hard and hot in my palm. I move my hand up and down my erection, enjoying the way her heated gaze is glued to me. I groan as a bead of cum leaks.

"Fuck, I missed your big cock," she says.

Her words flame my desire.

The first month after the accident, sex was off the table. As days rolled into weeks, we fooled around, but she had a limited range of movement because of her cast. I'm also responsible for our forced celibacy. I was so paranoid we would make things worse and delay her recovery, I reined in my appetite. My fist became my best friend for a while. It was a sacrifice I was willing to make for her. But now, I need to be inside her so fucking bad.

I lower myself to the bed next to her.

The missionary position is usually last on the list, however, tonight, I want her eyes boring into mine when I fill her up with my cum.

"On your back, dimples."

She does as she's told, spreading her legs open.

Soon, my cock will be balls deep into all this goodness.

I position myself on top of her and angle my cock between her pussy lips, rubbing her clit with the tip. My lover moans so beautifully, I have to squeeze my cock to stop from coming.

Christ Almighty.

I part those puffy pussy lips with my engorged cock head and slam into her in one swift thrust.

"Dear God!" Her hands grab my ass. "Fuck me, Rhys. Fuck me!"

A few frantic thrusts, and my balls tighten, announcing the end of the ride before it even begins.

Shit.

I fuck my girl like a hormone-raging teenager with zero control and zero game. I try to slow down my pace, but a stronger force takes over.

"Don't stop, Rhys. Please. Don't stop." Her throaty moans are my undoing.

"Your clit." It's a struggle to say those two words. "Touch it."

With her eyes fixed on mine, she licks her finger and then works her clit.

I fuck her harder because this is so damn hot.

"Fill me with your cum. I need it all," she says.

Well, hell.

I'm sure it's a combination of the illicit setting, my desperate yearning, the many lonely nights of solo sex and the straight up horniness, but goddammit, I love her dirty mouth.

"I can't get enough of this sweet little pussy."

"Then fuck my sweet little pussy harder, big guy! Harder!"

Jesus!

I grant her wish.

Her inner muscles clench in response.

Fuck!

She does it again.

And again.

I can barely breathe.

I'm going to die. I'm going to fucking die.

"I'm— Oh, Rhys— I'm—"

Hearing my name on her horny lips is more than I can bear.

"Oh Rhys—" she jumps off the edge of the cliff with me, giving in to her orgasm at the same time as I succumb to mine.

I fuck my baby like a man possessed, grunting and gasping as my cock erupts inside her, and for one long moment it feels like we're lost in each other, crying out, bucking as one until the final slam.

Slowly, I slide out of her and fall to the bed next to her. I wrap my arms around her, pulling her close to me.

"I missed this. I missed us," she says, panting for breath.

"Same here, dimples." I wipe the sweat from her brow with my thumb. "These past ten days nearly killed me. I hated being away from you for that long."

"It was the same for me."

"I want you every second— No, I *need* you every second of every day," I tell her.

"Oh, Rhys."

"I love you." The words slip from my lips, but I don't want to take them back because I realize now that's how I feel about this gorgeous woman.

Her eyes widen. "You—you didn't just say that?"

"I did."

A tear trickles down her beautiful face and she shakes her head, as if she's unwilling to believe me.

"Keira Weatherly. I. Love. You." I leave no room for misinterpretation.

"You do?"

"My love for you is crazy, dimples. You're my everything. If

I wasn't sure about it before leaving LA, being away from you affirmed what I already knew in my heart."

"You have no idea what hearing you say that does to me," she says with a sob.

I kiss away her tears.

She nuzzles her face into the crook of my neck.

"I love you so much, Rhys." Her confession comes out muffled.

"You can't say something like that and not look me in the eye."

She laughs a little.

She lifts her gaze to mine. "I love you, Rhys Hartford," she says. "I never thought—" she hiccups. "I never thought we'd get to this point." She pauses. "When the accident happened, I begged Shane to tell you how much I loved you just in case I didn't make it. He refused my request at first, but I wouldn't shut up until he promised. I didn't want to die without you knowing I'd loved you for most of my life."

"Shhh..." I press my lips to her forehead. "I'm glad Shane never told me. He didn't have to. *You* get to tell me."

"I love you," she says. "I no longer have to hide my feelings for you. You're the one. It's always been you, Rhys."

"What a declaration, dimples."

"It's been trapped inside me for years, percolating. That's why it came out with as much gushing force as a geyser." She laughs and cries, all the while dropping kisses all over my face. "You own my heart, Rhys."

"Oh, Keira, I fucking love you."

Epilogue
Keira

Sixteen months later

I have a front row seat to history in the making, and from the looks of it, World War III might erupt anytime soon.

"You faulted on the *bariolage*," Tomas his music partner.

"I did not," Anders says.

This competitive banter has been going on for a while.

Even from down here, it's clear Anders seems pissed off. At least, I think he is. You never know with these two. Tomas Lazović and Anders Benković love to razz each other. The Cello2Cello guys play so well together because they have insane synergy... unless they're arguing, like they are now.

"Anders, you totally did," Tomas says. "This is rock, not baroque. Pick up the pace, mate. Maybe a little more head-banging as well."

"Fuck off, Tomas," Anders says.

"Just sayin'." Tomas flashes his music partner a devilish grin. "We're playing tomorrow night to a sold-out crowd and we have some of the best musicians on stage with us. You don't want to come across like an amateur newbie."

I lean into Levi, who's sitting next to me.

"See what I have to endure when I work with these two?"

"I feel your pain," Levi says. "Anders and Tomas have perfected the good cop, bad cop routine with a twist. In their case, it's more like the uptight cellist, pompous cellist routine."

I crack up.

"It's not difficult to figure out who's who," I say.

Levi grins from ear to ear. "Tomas Lazović is definitely the cocky *and* pompous cellist."

I chuckle.

Levi Aldridge and I are sitting in the audience while some illustrious musicians warm up for Cello2Cello's big concert for two thousand adoring fans taking place tomorrow night. It's happening right here at the Walt Disney Concert Hall.

Contrary to the musicians on stage, Levi is more of a behind-the-scenes kind of guy. The tall man with brown hair and mesmerizing aqua-blue eyes is part of Rhys's entourage. He and his brother Linc are the genius magicians responsible for the set design for tomorrow's concert.

Along with their talented drummer extraordinaire, Anders and Tomas, aka Cello2Cello, invited rock gods to perform with them: Beckett and his band—Random Misconception—which includes Holt, their cousin Jace Halsey, and drummer Hall of Famer Rod Wolfe. Badass female guitarist Stasia van Gameren will also join the cellists and the rockers on stage in an unprecedented musical collaboration. Judging from the rehearsal, tomorrow night will be wild.

Like Levi, Rhys is hanging out amongst friends. I'm here because Tomas and Anders asked me to sing the closing song tomorrow night. I'm honored beyond words. We've been practicing a lot and I'm totally ready, but it never hurts to fine tune our performance. Not to mention, the concert marks the release of my new single, so we want to nail it.

"Keep talking shit, Tomas, and I'll shove my bow right up your ass!" Anders's repartee elicits a round of laughter.

"Tsk, tsk, tsk, Anders," Tomas says. "So testy."

Anders ignores Tomas and rolls his eyes.

"Isn't it ironic that amongst us, you two are still single, yet, you sound like an old married couple," Rhys says. He's on stage with them. "You guys should learn from Beckett and me. We have a great working relationship. You'll never catch us bickering like five-year-olds."

"Fuck off!" Anders and Tomas shout in unison.

We all laugh.

"Let's take it from the top so I can make you eat your words," Anders tells Tomas.

"Challenge accepted!" Tomas says.

They take Nirvana's *'Smells Like Teen Spirit'* from the top and crush it.

Anders and Tomas are classically trained cellists. It was a struggle for them to get noticed. The cello doesn't scream cool... that's until they came onto the scene. They single-handedly brought back to life an instrument that was almost a relic. Once they meshed the deep tenor of their classical instrument with edgy rock music, there was no stopping them. Their electric cellos add to the whole dazzle effect. Today, they're on top of the world.

When the musicians on stage reach the last note, I jump to my feet and clap like a crazy woman.

"That was amazing!" I yell. "Bravo!"

Anders and Tomas stand up and take a bow.

"Let's take a break and then we'll rehearse *'Thunderstruck'*," Anders says, dropping his cello on his seat.

Everyone agrees.

"Hey, Rhys, why don't you earn your dinner and sing us something," Tomas says. "Oh yeah, you can't sing. You can *only* rap."

"Fuck off, Tomas!" Rhys says.

"For once, I agree with Tomas," Anders says. "But since I have more manners and tact, I would've phrased it differently. Rhys, it's been a while. It would be great to hear you work the mic."

"Really?" Rhys asks.

"Yeah, really!" Anders says, walking up to my boyfriend and handing him a microphone. "I'm sure I'm not the only one. Let's ask the audience. Anyone else want to hear him rap?"

There's a collective *yeah* and head nods.

"Hijinks! Hijinks! Hijinks!" I chant his stage name.

"Calm the hell down, woman," Rhys shouts into the mic. "You're too excited for your own good."

I ignore him.

"Hijinks! Hijinks! Hijinks!" I chant again.

"Okay!" Rhys rolls his eyes, "The hottie wins!"

"What you're willing to do for a nice pair of legs," Beckett says, shaking his head.

"Watch your mouth, pretty boy," Rhys says. "That's my girl you're talking about. And for your information, she doesn't have a nice pair of legs, they're *stunning*!" He winks at me.

I blow him a thousand kisses.

"I stand corrected, and you're right, I should show her a lot more respect," Beckett says. "After all, it's not every day you're in the presence of a multi-award winner. Your girl wiped the floor at the StreamTunes Music Awards, American Music Awards, *and* Grammy Awards."

I blush from ear to ear.

I should be used to it by now, but I still have to pinch myself for my deluge of good fortune.

This past award season was ridiculous. I was so humbled by the public's acceptance of the musical direction I took with my career. Holt and his team gave me wings. Ditto for my amazing boyfriend, my brother and my friends. Without them, I doubt I would've had the courage to go all the way.

Other than the encounter with Jedd Maitland in his tunnel vision pursuit of a lie, my life since I landed at LAX has been a dream.

I was floored when Jedd reached out through my publicist to apologize after the accident that left him in pretty bad shape. He felt responsible for what happened. In his view, had it not been for him, I wouldn't have been at the wrong place, at the wrong time.

Margaret's fifteen minutes of fame fizzled faster than a votive candle burning out. She went under the radar after her publishing company dropped her. Her tell-all book was never published. The string of interviews where she spewed venom at me quickly became a liability and put a brutal end to her aspirations as an author. I never heard from her again. I'm okay with that.

"You forgot something *very* important on the list," Holt says to his brother.

"Oh, yeah, what's that?" Beckett asks with a cocky grin.

"She's one of Ritual of Rhyme's rising stars," Holt says with a tinge of pride.

I beam.

I'm so happy I went with my gut.

Holt is an artist first and foremost, and that has a huge impact on his business decisions. He's not a soulless corporate type who only cares about numbers, willing to produce unoriginal overused auto-tune pop trash just for the sake of downloads or sales. His artists are real singers. And it's not only about his ideas. He's receptive to yours. He transformed me from a bubblegum singer to a real one.

"I lucked out," Rhys says.

My boyfriend and I stare at each other, huge grins stretching our lips. We've been together for a year and a half, and sparks still fly. Another blessing to add to a very long list.

"Start rapping, Hartford, or get a fucking room!" Tomas says.

"Don't get your boxer briefs tied up in a bunch, Lazović," Rhys says before turning his attention to the audience of two. "I need another voice for the song I have in mind," he says. "Levi, wanna do a duet?"

"I'm no Tupac Shakur, but I'm game," Levi says. "What song were you thinking of?"

Although Levi only raps for fun, Rhys says he has some impressive skills.

"'*Shake That*'," Rhys says.

"Old school?" Levi asks.

"It's the only way to go," Rhys says.

"I can manage some old school Eminem." Levi's confidence is audible.

"Good stuff," Rhys says. "I need the music score without the lyrics."

"I'm sure I can find it online and buy it with one click," Beckett says. They share a complicit look. "When I do, I'll plug my iPhone into the sound system."

"Excellent!" Rhys says. "Looks like everything is coming into place. Now, if I could only find a sexy backup dancer at the last minute..."

"Pick me! Pick me!" I wave a frantic hand over my head as I jump up and down.

Rhys shields his eyes with one hand and pretends to look around the concert hall, searching for the eager beaver.

His gaze lands on me. "You want to come up here and show me your dance moves?"

I shout back a resounding and enthusiastic, "Yes!"

He sighs into the microphone.

"Since it's slim pickings tonight, come on up, shorty!"

I cross my arms over my chest and shoot him an *are you fucking kidding me* look.

"Don't be like that, shorty," Rhys says. "Come up and impress me."

"That, I can do." I offer a coquettish smile.

"Make sure to follow her up here, Levi," Rhys says.

"I will," Levi says.

I balance on my high heels and run to the side door with Levi in tow. Holt is holding the door leading up to the stage and waves us over.

"I got the music!" Beckett says as I step onto the stage. "We're all set on my end."

"You're ready?" Rhys asks Levi who's scrolling through his phone while he's walking.

"Found the lyrics! I'm ready!" he says.

"Drop the beat, Christensen!" Rhys says.

"You got it!" Beckett says.

The old school rap song blasts through the speakers.

Oh, yeah!

Rhys may be impeccably dressed head to toe in expensive all black designer wear he wouldn't have been able to afford back then, but his rhyme is as smooth as it was when his career exploded into the stratosphere.

His flow is tight.

His hip-hop dance moves are badass.

And he owns the stage like he did in his old music videos.

God, he's so freaking hot.

"Hold up! Hold up!" Rhys lifts a hand.

Beckett stops the music.

"What's going on?" I ask.

Rhys approaches me, places two fingers under my chin, and tips my head back so our eyes meet.

"I didn't invite you on stage for you to stare at me, shorty," he says. "You promised to impress me. I'm waiting."

"Did you just call me out in front of your friends?" I ask him.

"I did," he says. "What are you going to do about it?"

He did not just challenge me.

"Oooohhhh! Game on, Hartford!"

"Finally, you're going to do justice to the sexy ass shorts you're wearing," he says with a grin.

We're done talking here, buddy.

"DJ, drop the beat!" I tell Beckett.

"Yes, ma'am!" he says and takes it from the top.

The beat blares out and everyone starts swaying to the music's thumping beat.

Rhys and Levi bring it on.

I step into the role and start dancing like my life depends on it. This is so crazy-good it doesn't take me long to lose myself in the song. When the bridge hits, I do as I'm told and I shake my ass, dropping low.

The guys whistle and holler.

I pull my best Lucky Break moves to my audience's delight.

The lyrics aren't the most empowering for women, but the beat is incredible.

I glance at Rhys from over my shoulder.

He holds the mic real close to his mouth, his eyes eating me alive.

Oh, yeah, baby.

I congratulate myself on my wardrobe choice. It's a cross between runway couture chic and rocker girl badassness. I selected a pair of sexy shorts and a sheer blouse to complement a stylish sequin tuxedo blazer. All black. The super high designer heels with a strap at the ankle add a vampy element to the sex kitten look. My makeup is subdued because it's all about the outfit. I'm still sporting short blonde hair. The overall look is super feminine and the outfit transitions perfectly for later.

We're all going for dinner at the Quintus Hotel after the rehearsal. We have a private dining room to celebrate tomorrow's concert and my single with Cello2Cello, which drops at midnight.

When the lyrics allude to me being *his* slut for the night, I mouth, "Hell, yeah."

He grins, his glacier-blue eyes flashing with malice.

The guys on stage are bobbing their heads to the beat, mouthing the lyrics. Beckett takes it one step further by performing some killer dance moves.

I call Stasia over so she can be my dance partner. She shakes her head—and a finger—in protest. The girl can dance, I guess she's not in the mood.

I laugh.

Levi is effortlessly keeping up with Rhys's rhymes. It's been years since my man stepped on stage as a performer, but Hijinks can still bring down the house. Once a rapper, always a rapper.

The bridge hits.

Oooohhh!

It's time for me to shake my *thang* again.

I do.

Rhys comes and stands behind me, and we dance together, feeding off each other's electrifying energy. We're so in sync, you'd think we practiced this routine.

I turn to face him, and we really go for it.

God, the man can dance.

As the song fades, I take it down several notches, expecting it to end, but another song loops in.

It's a slow R&B vibe.

To my absolute amazement Rhys begins to sing.

He can sing?!

Just because you can rap doesn't mean you can sing. Rhys always says that.

I'm stunned.

He has a great singing voice.

Why has he been hiding this from me?

The lyrics are poignant.

And then to my utter disbelief, Rhys drops to one knee.

My hands fly to my mouth, shock coursing through me. Four words from the bridge of the song cause my heart to stop, *Will you marry me?*

Oh my God, oh my God, oh my God.

As if I'm not already completely dumbstruck, my brother Noah—who still lives in New Zealand—steps on stage.

Epilogue

Rhys

This rehearsal is a ruse.

Anders, Tomas, Random Misconception, and Stasia already spent hours rehearsing earlier today. At its core, the inclusion of Beckett's band as part of the opening act for Cello2Cello's concert might be his idea—and a little self-serving—but that didn't prevent me from piggybacking on the perfect opportunity.

Everyone here is my partner in crime. Tomas didn't ask me to rap because he wanted to hear my voice. It was a sneaky way to lure my unsuspecting girlfriend onto the stage.

Other than Stasia, there's a reason none of the girls are here. Keira thinks we're going for dinner at the Quintus Hotel after this. She's wrong. We're celebrating our engagement party in style amongst friends at a private room of one of the most luxurious hotels in the city. Michaela is manning things there.

All the fiancées, wives, and kids are already at the hotel. My mom, Phoebe, and Oscar are also there. Michaela texted me to confirm.

The diehard New Yorker lives in LA now. Her first year

living in La La Land rivaled the craziest rollercoaster rides, but now she's an influential force. Keira and her are as tight as sisters.

Along with a number of close friends, the Dennison brothers are on the invite list. Larkin is also part of the celebrations. For tonight, he'll step out of his role as omnipresent lord of the castle and he'll just be another one of our esteemed guests. He won't be a regular Joe—not that that's possible for a man in his position—as I had to concede to having two of his bodyguards posted at the private room's door.

When I reach the last note of *'Marry Me',* Keira's beautiful face is covered in tears.

I'm not about to cut a single anytime soon, but thanks to Beckett who helped train my voice over the last three months, I'm able to carry a tune. Levi and I also practiced for hours to get it just right. He was the perfect wingman.

Stasia, who approached my girl while I was singing my heart out, has an arm wrapped around her in a hug. That doesn't prevent Keira from trembling like a leaf.

Beckett and Holt are on video duty.

Cello2Cello are my appointed photographers.

Noah approaches her.

Stasia takes a step aside.

Noah and Keira interlace fingers.

I'm still on one knee.

My best friend doesn't say anything. He just stares at his little sister.

"He loves you," Noah says, jerking his head in my direction.

"Not as much as I love him," Keira says.

"You two belong together," my best friend tell her.

"We do," Keira says. "You're here, Noah. You're finally here."

"Rhys wanted to surprise you. I'm back in town for good, sis. It took a little longer than expected, but Los Angeles is my home now."

"Really?" Keira asks.

Noah nods. "I figured I should be close by just in case I become an uncle soon," he says with a wink.

"I didn't even pop the question yet and you're talking about babies!" I roll my eyes.

His apologetic gaze meets mine. "Sorry," he says.

"I'm still so shellshocked to process anything, anyway," Keira says.

"Get out of the way before you do any more damage," I tell my best friend.

He chuckles.

It's not that I was looking for his approval, but I wanted Noah to be aware of my intentions in regard to his sister. He was a hundred percent behind me. Giving who he is and what he means to me, I wanted him to be right by my side—like he always has been. Not to mention, he's Keira's only living relative.

Noah has been back for three days. He's been hiding at Shane's place. After the accident, he promised Keira he'd be back in LA once the production for the show wrapped up. There was a kink in his plan. Hardcore fans refused to accept the end of an era. To appease the hungry audience, the producers extended the show by one more season. Noah told Keira he'd travel a bit before returning to LA. That was also a ruse. Nothing would've prevented him from being here tonight.

I take Keira's hand into mine.

"I want you to be by my side for the rest of my life," I tell the woman I love with all my heart. "Without you, Keira, this life is meaningless."

"Oh, God, Rhys," she says on the heel of a sob.

"I've had a thing for you for a long time, but I didn't want to lose my balls by going after the Hulk's baby sister."

Everyone laughs.

"You're making me sound like a monster. I'm not that scary," Noah says.

"Yes, you are," resonates across the concert hall.

Another round of laughs ensues.

I shoot Noah a pointed look. "Quit butting into my proposal," I tell him. "I'll be an old man by the time I ask her the question."

Keira giggles.

"Shit, I'm doing it again," Noah says. "Sorry, man. I'm more excited than you are."

Not quite as excited, but close.

"As I was saying." I move my attention back to my girl. "A year and a half ago when you landed at LAX, you knocked me off my feet and took my breath away. You were a different woman, but you were still Keira. It didn't take long for you to become my world. I can't believe we've been going strong for a year and a half. It feels like just yesterday I was taking you out on our first date. And look at us now..." My voice cracks.

"Rhys, I've tried a million times to figure out how to break free from the incessant stranglehold you've had on my heart—"

"Did you ever figure it out?" I ask.

She laughs. "No, I never did. For once, I'm glad I failed. My heart will always belong to you."

"And mine to you," I tell her. "My feelings for you consume me, dimples."

"Oh, God, Rhys."

"Keira Eve Weatherly, will you do me the honor of becoming my wife?"

"Yes, Rhys! I want to be your wife!" she shrieks before throwing herself into my arms, almost knocking me over. I catch her and straighten up. She cradles my head and bursts into tears, clinging onto me like I just rescued her from drowning.

I hold her tight.

My friends cheer, clap, stomp and holler.

After a moment, I drop her to her feet.

She sniffles and wipes away the tears streaming down her face.

"It's about time you sealed the deal, Hartford, or else I was going after her!" Tomas says.

I shake my head at him.

Anders punches his arm.

I swear to God, he could be Collin Dennison's twin brother.

I nod at Noah.

He steps forwards and hands me a small, black and gold box.

"I'm a little tall to be a ring bearer, but here I am carrying the ring," he says.

I open the box and present Keira with the ring.

She gasps, her hands flying to her mouth.

When she lowers her hands, her jaw hangs open.

"Dear God, that is gorgeous!" she says.

"Yeah? You like it?" I ask.

"I freaking love it! It's perfect. It's beautiful. It's stunning. It's so me. How did you figure it out?"

"I have my ways," I tell her.

Stasia winks at me.

I needed a task force to figure out a style that best suited Keira's taste and aesthetics. While Arianne was helping Oscar figure out which style of ring to buy to pop the question, Michaela and Stasia were instrumental in helping me pin down the perfect ring for my girl. It's an six-carat pink oval cut diamond ring set in rose gold with pavé diamonds around the band.

I take it from the box and slide it onto her trembling finger.

More cheers, claps, stomps and hollers from my friends.

"Oh. My. God!" Keira says. "We're getting married. We're actually getting married."

I tip her head back, forcing her eyes to lock with mine. "This is it, dimples, you're stuck with me."

"I want to be stuck with you, Rhys," she says.

I take her lips in a tender kiss.

My Keira.

My forever.

Bonus Scene

Michaela

This scene takes place two months after Keira's accident.

Turns out, all those snarky remarks the rest of the country makes about LA's horrendous traffic are true. My bladder knows firsthand what it's like to be trapped in a vehicle, on the highway, moving at snail's pace in a sea of cars. I was in the back of a taxi for so long, it feels like I should've crossed a border to justify the never-ending trip.

Taking the red eye from New York to LA would've meant I landed at LAX in the middle of the night. I would've been able to skip the bottleneck traffic on my way to Rhys's place, but that would also mean I would've ended up waking up my friend and her boyfriend. I'm pretty sure they wouldn't appreciate it... especially, since they aren't expecting me. I figured if I landed at nine o'clock, I'd bypass the morning rush hour by the time I collected my luggage. Boy, was I ever wrong.

Between the heavy traffic and an accident, it took two excruciating hours for me to get to the gated community located in Manhattan Beach where Keira lives.

Since I was here last month, my name was on the list of approved people. One less roadblock. I just needed to flash my driver's license, and the security guard let the taxi through.

Now, I'm standing in front of Rhys's big ass mansion, ready to beg and grovel.

Thank God the taxi driver took pity on me and helped me with my very large suitcase sitting at my feet.

I ring the bell and wait.

I fan myself before wiping off a the sweat forming above my upper lip.

Welcome to the Golden State.

It's not even midday, and it's scorching hot. Although I chose appropriate LA fashion—a cute yellow summer maxi dress and wedge sandals—I'm already sweating.

I let out a few calming breaths, praying everything will go my way.

"Mikki?!" Keira's voice comes through the speakers.

There's a peephole, but since Keira is as short as I am, I bet she's using the video feed to confirm who's at the door. There are a lot of spectacular things about Rhys's home, his sophisticated security system being one of them.

I slap on a dazzling smile. "Do you know another fabulous Mikki from New York?" I make light of the situation that might very well explode in my face in the next five minutes.

"What are you doing here?" she asks.

"Aren't you going to invite me in?"

"Why didn't you tell me you were coming?"

She's right to chastise me, but this was a last-minute trip.

"Surprise!" I do a theatrical hand gesture, extending my pageant smile so wide, my cheeks hurt.

She laughs. "Hold on tight, I'll hobble to the front door."

"Holding!"

My friend swings open the door, her hazel-green eyes already wide in surprise.

She looks me up and down before her gaze lands on my suitcase.

"That's a much bigger suitcase than the last time you were here," she says, using her cane to point to it.

She's getting stronger with each passing day, but after relying on crutches for weeks on end, she still requires a walking aid. Her camo-print tank top and ripped black jeans shorts reveal unhealed scars on her arms and legs. They're still as visible as they were when I was here a month ago, but hopefully in time, they'll fade. After that scary accident, she was badly battered and bruised. Road rash is no joke. Thank God she was wearing appropriate riding gear. It's been a rough road, but she's recovering nicely.

"An extended trip requires an extended wardrobe," I tell her.

"Oh yeah? Where are you heading to?" she asks.

I bounce on the balls of my feet, clapping my hands together. "Lucky me! I've arrived at my *final* destination!"

She eyes me with suspicion. "What's going on, Michaela?"

Worry twists my stomach in a knot. "Aren't you going to invite me in?" I sound desperate. "We can talk about it over a late breakfast and coffee, maybe?"

"You're my friend, so obviously, I'll invite you in, feed you and caffeinate you properly, but only *after* you tell me what's going on," she says.

Okay, time to change tactics.

"I'm just being a good friend and checking up on you." I play-punch her arm.

"Well, *friend*, you never mentioned you were coming back so soon."

I drop the charade and give a big sigh.

"I had to get out of New York, and frankly, I have nowhere else to go," I tell her.

Concern colors her eyes. "Does your father know you're here?"

I nod. "He does." I hesitate. "I sort of convinced him you were extremely lonely, and you needed me to keep you company. To my surprise, he thought it was a great idea. In fact, he insisted I use our air miles to book a ticket. So, I did." I let out another long sigh. "His blessing caused a war."

"What do you mean?" Keira asks.

"His stupid wife threw another one of her legendary temper tantrums. She accused Daddy of spoiling me rotten and turning me into an ungrateful brat who thinks she can run away whenever a situation ruffles her feathers or bruises her overly sensitive nature. Bullshit."

"Oh, Mikki. I'm sorry." The genuine concern in Keira's face sets me off.

"My stepmonster is driving me mad and Daddy seems apathetic about it all. It's almost as if he's checked out. I don't get it. Instead of telling her to shut the hell up or reminding her it's none of her business, he just retreats. He doesn't fight. He doesn't tell her off. He doesn't stand up to her. Why did he marry that woman? I hate her. I just hate her."

A tsunami of the emotions I've been bottling up since I returned from Nepal comes pouring out of me with the same rushed fury as a raging river breaking through a damn.

Leaving all pretence behind, I burst into tears.

Keira circles an arm around me. "Mikki, don't cry." She rocks me side to side. "It's going to be okay."

"No, it's not," I say between sobs.

I appreciate what she's trying to do, but comforting words won't do me any good. My sorrow is so deep and I'm so rooted in despair, only an intervention from God or my father divorcing a woman he should've never married in the first place would allow me to breathe again. Until then, I'm trapped in a nightmare. If my father is determined to stay married to that awful woman, I'm determined to stay the hell away from New York. Going back would kill my soul. Running away is the only way...

Bonus Secret Chapter

For a bonus secret chapter about Rhys and Keira (Keira's POV during the striptease scene), subscribe to my newsletter!
www.MyRomanceAddiction.com

Who's The Next Filthy Rich Book Boyfriend in This Scorching Hot Series?

Keira's friend, Michaela, wakes up to a big fat surprise when the announcement of her impending wedding is splattered across the first page of a popular gossip site. The only problem is, she didn't know she was getting married. Heck, she doesn't even know her supposed-to-be future husband.

Michaela Knight escapes to Los Angeles to distance herself

from her detestable stepmother. Little did she know, her time away from New York City allowed her father to turn her into a pawn.

She has a difficult choice to make. A marriage of convenience to a complete stranger to save the family legacy her deceased mother left her, or refuse and lose it all...

Binge-read now: Billionaire Mogul—Phoenix

Psst... you can read a sneak peek of Billionaire Mogul—Phoenix at the end of this book.

Reviews are sweet as pie!

It only takes a few minutes to leave a review, which makes a huge difference for an indie author like myself.

Here's the link to leave a review for: Billionaire Mogul—Rhys

Scarlett's Book Banter!

Dear Sexy Reader,

What's there not to love about Rhys Hartford?

Along with Roderick Wolfe (**Billionaire Hotshot—Roderick**), Rhys is another alpha who spent years dealing with his demons.

He's so different from his business partner, Beckett. In many ways, they're polar opposites. In my humble opinion, that's what makes their business partnership so strong. That, and the fact he's willing to call out Beckett on his bullshit.

When it comes to going after his best friend's little sister, no wonder he's a bit apprehensive. Noah is a menacing giant.

Rhys and Keira belong together. It took a while, but they finally got their happy ever after... with Noah's blessing!

Now let's talk about Michaela.

There's a lot of over-the-top drama in Michaela's story.

The whole premise of contemporary marriage of convenience is over-the-top, added to that some pretty wicked twists you didn't see coming, and you have yourself a page-turner.

Phoenix is delicious in so many ways. He's yet another one of my billionaires you'll fall head over heels for.

If your electricity bill goes way up because you have to turn on the A/C to the max, that means I'll have done my job.

If you love the marriage of convenience romance trope, you'll devour this steamy romance.

Binge-read now: Billionaire Mogul—Phoenix

(Psst... make sure to read the sneak peek of Billionaire Mogul—Phoenix at the end of this book.)

That's it for me.

Back to writing!

Much love,

Scarlett Avery

P.S. Reviews are always appreciated and let me know I wrote a swoon-worthy story! Thanks a *billion* in advance.

P.P.S. I keep writing because of your hunger for my stories. Thank you for your fervor, love, and loyalty. I'm humbled and incredibly grateful. Without you, there's very little reason to keep coming up with new stories.

P.P.P.S. For access to an EXCLUSIVE Secret Chapter, go to the next page!

Get the Secret Chapter for Billionaire Mogul—Rhys!

Thank you for purchasing this romance!

I have an EXCLUSIVE Secret Chapter to share with you!

For the Secret Chapter, you get Keira's POV during the striptease scene.

Trust me, you're going to love the extra tidbits.

When you sign up on my list, you'll receive an email with further instructions!

Sign up TODAY!

www.MyRomanceAddiction.com

***If you've already signed up to my list from previous books, you can visit the same page to download the Secret Chapters and/or Storyboard for this romance. ***

Sneak Peek of Billionaire Mogul —Phoenix

Chapter 1 | Michaela

I'm in blissful communion with my first steaming hot latte of the day when my friend breaks the silence with an ear-shattering screech.

"You're getting married?!"

I lower my cup. "What?"

Keira's eyes lift up to mine. "You're getting married."

My eyes drop to her cup. "Did you spike your latte with a copious amount of cognac? And if so, how come I didn't get any?"

"I can't believe you've been in LA for two days and you haven't even told me." She ignores my dig and keeps talking, still not making a shred of sense. "Sheesh, I thought we were friends, Mikki." She rolls her eyes. "I was wrong. I guess I can kiss my dreams of being your maid of honor goodbye since I didn't even get an invitation."

I'm hanging out with Keira Weatherly during the tail end of her convalescence. After a morning swim—I swam while she played referee on the side of the pool—we're sitting in her boyfriend's kitchen, enjoying a leisurely breakfast. Well, it was leisurely until she started talking crazy.

I knit my eyebrows in confusion. "Is this a joke?"

"It says so right here!" She points a frantic finger at her iPad.

"Where?"

"On JustSpotted.com's website," she says. "According to them— Wait a minute." She grips the device with both hands, brings it really close to her face, widens her eyes, and then pulls it away. She does that a few times before speaking again. "Holy deliciousness, Mikki. You're getting married to a really, really hot guy!"

I drop my cup on the saucer. "Keira, how can I be getting married when I'm not even dating?" I let out a sarcastic laugh. "Celebrity sightings in La La Land must be at an all-time low if a leading gossip site like JustSpotted.com is making up stories about me." I shake my head at the absurdity of it all.

I'm no stranger to being featured on celebrity sites or magazines. The press has dubbed me, *the goody-two-shoes hotel heiress*, because until recently, my life was devoid of drama. In the past, when the spotlight was on me, it was usually because of my social outings in New York or to dissect my fashion selections. I haven't crossed over to the dark side or anything like that, but thanks to my emancipation trip to Nepal, I've kicked the goody-two-shoes and Pollyanna image to the curb. These days, the press doesn't know what to make of me. Good.

"I must have a celebrity-doppelganger running around LA, fooling everybody." I run my hand over my super short hair. "That's the only logical explanation."

"Speaking of hair, JustSpotted.com posted old photos of you—"

"See! They got it wrong! They have photos of my identical-twin-from-another-mother, her long, dark locks flowing in the wind, passing as me."

Keira's lips turn up in an unimpressed frown.

Okay, so I'm not a poet.

"Mikki, even if you had a celebrity-doppelganger, the chance of the two of you having the same name is practically impossible," Keira says. "This article is about you and your husband-to-be—"

"For crying out loud, Keira, I'm not getting married!"

"Here"—she drops the iPad on the kitchen table—"you tell me you're not getting married."

I snatch it, ready to laugh my ass off, except I don't.

My jaw drops.

My mouth is agape and I'm certain my eyes are bulging out of their sockets.

What in God's name?

'MICHAELA KNIGHT SOON TO BECOME MRS. KÖNIG!'

I read the headline in shock.

Because I'm certain this is a joke at my expense, I click open another tab and type my name in the search bar.

I'm unprepared for the deluge.

'MICHAELA KNIGHT SPOTTED IN LA GETTING READY FOR UPCOMING WEDDING.'

'PHOENIX KÖNIG + MICHAELA KNIGHT. LONG LIVE THE KING AND THE QUEEN!'

'WHO'S WHO FROM COAST-TO-COAST EXPECTED

AT PHOENIX KÖNIG AND MICHAELA KNIGHT'S WEDDING.'

'PHOENIX KÖNIG + MICHAELA KNIGHT TOPPING THE CHART OF THE MOST GORGEOUS COUPLE EVER!'

'PHOENIX + MICHAELA. IS THIS FOREVER?!'

'KING KÖNIG TO TAKE A QUEEN.'

King König?

Phoenix König?

Who the hell is that?

I read page after page of results, utterly stunned.

As my eyes scan the headlines, my rage boils.

My stepmonster did it again.

"What a manipulative bitch," I say.

"So, you're not getting married?" Keira asks.

My eyes shoot up to hers.

"No, I'm not! I don't even know this Phoenix König guy!"

"Well, if you're going to get hitched to a stranger, he's a great one to pick. Holy hotness! He's totally fitness-model material. And did you see his eyes? Rhys has—"

"Oh my God, Keira! Stop it! I don't care about his eyes. I'm not getting married to a person I've never met before." I'm too perturbed to pay attention to the hotness level of a stranger I'll never meet. I have bigger fish to fry. My life is front and center of the gossip rags and someone is responsible for this travesty. "Obviously, my stepmother decided to use fake news to drum up business. Again," I mutter through gritted teeth.

"You think she's behind this?" Keira asks.

"Of course, she is!" I say, handing over the iPad. "Who else loves to meddle in my love life and can't resist the urge of pawning me as bait? Remember how well things turned out with pervy Freddy III?"

Keira grimaces. "Gross."

"Yup, the man is disgusting."

Halfway into our first coffee date, Frederick William Pliskin III asked me if I was okay being blindfolded with my arms tied behind my back and gagged with his jizz-filled underwear while he fucked me from behind. He also wanted to watch as his three cousins took turns fucking me—another of his kinks. Let me think... Hell no, fucking pervert!

My stepmother is incapable of picking a decent man. Given her taste in the men she selects for me, I have no clue how she ended up with my father. No matter how many times I ask her to mind her own business, telling her to back off is like waving a T-bone steak in front of a famished dog and expecting it to behave. Pointless.

"At least she's stepping up her game." Keira's words drip with sarcasm. "Unlike her multiple previous laughable attempts, this time your stepmonster picked a winner. Maybe marrying Phoenix König isn't a bad idea." She keeps scrolling through the iPad. "He's a local businessman— Scratch that!"

"What?"

"He's a tycoon!" Her hazel-green eyes are huge when they meet mine. "According to this article, he owns a shit load of real estate and—"

"Good for him." I dismiss her commentary with a shrug.

"No, seriously, Mikki, think about it. You'd get to move to the west coast, and we'd hang out more often. Who knows? Your future husband lives in Manhattan Beach and we'd end up being neighbors."

I roll my eyes.

"I love New York way too much to ever leave."

I can't see myself trading the fast pace of the concrete jungle for the mellow vibe of the City of Angels. I'm a New Yorker through and through.

"If we lived in the same city, it would be reminiscent of our time in Nepal—two badass rebels against the world!" she says.

"Nepal..." The memory washes over me like a caress and I offer my partner in crime a warm smile.

Keira and I met not long ago, but you'd never tell by how well we get along. Even if we live on opposite sides of the country, we're constantly in touch. We're the same age, and we both ran away from our lives when everything around us came crashing down.

That's how we ended up on the other side of the planet at the same time. For six months Nepal was her refuge. I was there for two. We left the monastery we were staying at with a greater sense of self-awareness, self-actualization and a lot less hair. Leaving that safe cocoon was bitter sweet. I returned to a city I love, a father I worship, and to a stepmother I loathe. Keira moved back to her hometown.

I pluck my phone from the table, my fingers already typing the gossip site's URL.

"I need to put an end to this madness. The celebrity blogger needs to retract this ridiculous wedding announcement before people start believing the lies. Then, I have to deal with my stepmonster."

"Oooohhh, the shit's about to hit the fan!" Keira says.

"Damn right. Someone needs to butt out and shut up!"

"Where are you going?" Keira asks when I reenter the kitchen to the main house an hour later.

Since she returned to LA, she's been living with her older

brother's best friend who's now her boyfriend. Rhys Hartford's guesthouse is quite posh, but pales in comparison to his magnificent, modern mansion, aka the main house.

"You're not dressed to hang out at the pool," she says.

After breakfast, I swapped the jeans shorts and yellow tank top I was wearing for a more fashionable getup.

"No pool time today, *chica*. I'm going to battle, so I had to dress the part."

Her eyes travel the length of my body.

"What does that mean?" she asks.

"There's no phone number to reach the gossip site. I sent numerous emails, but given their influence, I'm sure they're bombarded with messages. No doubt, mine is lost somewhere in their inbox. I tried to call my stepmother, but it goes straight to voicemail. Ditto for my father. Exasperated, I called my father's executive assistant. At least I was able to reach her."

"And?"

"Apparently, everyone is walking on eggshells on the executive floor."

"What happened?"

"My father and stepmother are locked in his office and they're engaged in a yelling match. From what I hear, it's ugly."

"Your stepmother is a piece of work," Keira says.

"Daddy has to be really pissed off to lose his composure in front of the staff. I can only hope he's finally tired of getting stepped all over. I love him to pieces, but marrying that woman was his biggest mistake."

Keira gives me another onceover. "Okay, there's a war raging in New York, but that still doesn't tell me where you're going."

"I'm not holding my breath when it comes to getting a response from the gossip site and since my dad is duking it out with his wife, I have to rely on Plan B."

"Which is?"

"I want to know why Phoenix König and my stepmother concocted this little scheme. What's in it for him?"

With a careful step and balancing on her cane, Keira comes to stand in front of me. The top of her blonde head reaches just below my chin. Barefoot, I'm an inch shorter than her, but since she's wearing flip-flops and I'm wearing high heels, I'm really tall right now.

"You called and made an appointment with the tycoon?" she asks. "He had time in his busy calendar to fit you in at the last minute?!" Her tone is laced with skepticism.

"I tried, but his guard dog—whoever is manning the switchboard is giving me the runaround. Even though I kept giving the person my name, she refused to believe me. I have a sneaky suspicion she thinks I'm a whack job."

"If your text and social media messages exploded, I can just imagine how it must be for someone like Phoenix König," Keira says.

At least she stopped calling him my husband-to-be.

I roll my eyes. "Puh-lease. This is part of a well-oiled publicity machine. Phoenix König must be enjoying every minute of this."

It's official.

The fake news of my pending wedding has gone viral.

Lucky me. *Not!*

It's a little freaky how fast fake news can travel. Suddenly, my phone was lighting up like the giant Rockefeller Center Christmas tree. I let it all go to voicemail. Until I have answers, I'm ignoring everyone. Too bad for me, the two people I'm dying to hear from haven't called me back.

"Innocent until proven guilty, remember?" Keira says. "It's the legal principle our great country was founded upon."

"Yeah, well, I'm about to administer my own legal principle."

"What do you have up your sleeve, Miss Knight?"

I adopt her formal tone. "I'm glad you asked, Miss Weatherly. I pinned down King König's HQ—"

"Oh, this sounds very James Bondish." Keira's eyes sparkle with excitement.

"Trust me, it feels like a covert operation," I say. "All that to say, I know where to find him. Thank you, Google! Now, I'm going to pay the king a little visit."

Keira shrieks. "You're going to drop in unannounced?"

"I am!"

She squints at me. "Is that a good idea, Mikki?"

"What other choice do I have?" I ask. "Sure, I could open a bottle of wine at nine o'clock in the morning and get drunk, but that won't do much to help me understand how I got entangled with this stranger."

"What if he can't meet with you?"

"If he's in connivance with my stepmother and willing to spread lies, he'll make time to meet with me," I say, lifting my chin up.

"You should wait it out," she says. "I'm sure you'll be able to get through to your stepmother eventually."

"She's barely interested in talking to me when she's in a chipper mood, unless it's to shove a 'suitable lifemate' down my throat," I say with quotation marks. "Given the drama in New York, I doubt she'll want to talk to me. It's not like Daddy knows anything about this farce. I want answers and I want them now. If not from her, then from this King Kong Tycoon."

Keira laughs.

~

While my cabbie weaves his way through traffic, I frantically research as much as I can on King Kong Tycoon. It wouldn't be wise to walk into battle without an ounce of preparation.

Keira was right.

My never-to-be-husband is a serious tycoon.

Given my family is also in the hotel industry, you'd think I would've heard of Phoenix König before. His name probably came up in conversation, but I forgot it as quickly.

The Königs play in a whole different league from us. In essence, it's like comparing a goldfish to a blue whale. Phoenix's family owns a plethora of commercial real estate and luxury residential complex buildings across the country, on top of owning the biggest flagship of luxury hotels in California, the second biggest in the nation. They also own many luxury hotels around the world. King Kong Tycoon's dad, Soren, is the CEO, but he runs the corporation along with his four sons—Phoenix, the oldest. Slate, the middle child. Wilder, the other middle child. Roman, the youngest.

I was dead set on finding as much dirt as I could on Phoenix, but I got sidetracked by the numerous articles about the patriarch's recent heart attack. As I was reading about the heart-wrenching ordeal, I tried, but failed to push aside traumatic memories of Daddy's close call three years ago. I don't think I could've survived losing a second parent.

A taxi ride later and I arrive at my destination. I pay the cabbie and get out of the car. Even if I'm wearing shades, I shield my eyes from the blinding sun as I crane my neck upwards to take in the grandeur of the Pompadour Hotel & Residences. Impressive skyscrapers rise above me. They're not nearly as tall as the average building in New York, but they still touch the sky. The Pompadour is an uber modern luxury complex composed of three sleek glass towers. It isn't only a pied-à-terre to the extremely rich and wealthy, it's also where the beast presides over his empire.

Let's see what you have to say King Kong Tycoon.

I stride across an ocean of asphalt to the Beverly Hills premier HQ, each step of my Christian Louboutin shoes stomping with the determination of a take-no-prisoner warrior.

Good God, it's hot.

I pinch the front of my dress with two fingers and fan myself, hoping to avoid walking into my meeting with the beast looking like a hot mess. Unsightly underarm sweat stains would make for a poor first impression.

It's like a freaking sauna.

I'm no stranger to New York's 90/90 summers—ninety-degree and ninety-percent-humidity—but LA is much hotter. I swear it feels like it's two hundred degrees. I can't fathom what it will be like by midday.

As I trek to the entrance, I take note of the hustle and bustle—the revolving door of new faces. That's one of the constants about life as a hotelier.

Everything about these buildings screams corporation. It's the antithesis of the Villiers Grand Hotel. Our family boutique hotel in New York brims with rich history and welcoming old-world charm. Even from the outside, the Pompadour seems a little too sleek, cold, and impersonal. I doubt it will be any different once I pass the threshold.

Pompadour. Hmph. Pretty pompous, if you ask me.

When I enter the hotel, the cool air hits me like a speeding freight train.

Thank you, God.

I pause long enough to scan my surroundings. My eyes bounce to every corner. A swarm of newly arrived guests take residence in the opulent lobby, and the hotel staff is busy attending to them.

How do I get to you, King Kong Tycoon?

I either have to ask a concierge for help or figure it out myself. The scale of this hotel is far more eye-popping than the Villiers Grand, but I'm willing to bet everything to my name, there's a dedicated set of elevators leading to the executive floor. As I debate, a group of four men talking, coffee cups in hand, pass right by me.

My bionic ears catch a snippet of their conversation.

"Yeah, we should be locking down the purchase on three old office buildings we'll convert into high-end hotels-slash-residencies in Dallas by end of day," one man says. He's wearing a purple shirt, black pants and tortoiseshell glasses.

"We should secure two soaring towers in Cleveland by end of the week," a tall blond wearing a flower print shirt says.

Bingo!

With the agility of a spy, I trail behind the foursome, balancing on my four-inch heels, as they lead me to the Promised Land.

Operation King Kong Tycoon commences.

I step into the elevator right before the doors close.

"Good morning," I say with a bright smile.

Four pair of eyes rake up and down the length of my body.

"Good morning," they say, practically all at once.

The lack of subtlety in their tone is as heavy as a brick. I'm surprised they didn't punctuate with, *And how you doin'?* a la Joey from *Friends*.

I'm not one to play damsel in distress, but it's the only card I have right now in my deck.

"I'm here to see Mr. Phoenix König. Silly me, I forgot which floor he's on."

"He's expecting you?" purple shirt guy asks. The tinge of suspicion in his voice doesn't go unnoticed.

Think.

Think.

Think.

"I'm here about..." *Dammit. Think faster.* "A family run boutique hotel on Park Place," I say. I cock my head to the side and knit my eyebrows together for effect. "It's one of those very hush-hush deals Mr. König wants to snag before anyone else."

Giving them the name of our family hotel would be like sounding the alarm. I want to catch Phoenix König with his bespoke pants down.

"Oh, yeah." The tall floral shirt guy nods. "Great address."

He fell for it?!

This covert operation is turning me into a real spy—one who thinks on her feet.

Go Mikki!

When I'm under pressure, I use Monopoly as my get out of jail card. Along with being the least landed-on spots in the game, Park Place is also the name of a park that's long gone. I Googled this useless piece of information one day for no good reason. I can't believe it's my lifeline.

Board game to the rescue!

It's with herculean effort I don't roll my eyes hard.

"Isn't it?"

The men nod.

"All five Mr. Königs are on the top floor," purple shirt guy says. "I guess I should say, all four Königs since Roman is still bedridden on the other side of the planet after the freaky accident." He presses the button before sliding a key card into a slot.

I read about that. Thank God he's still alive.

I smile. "Thank you."

"No problem." He winks. "Take a right when you get off the elevators. Lydia Gillanders is Phoenix König's executive assistant. She'll take good care of you."

"Got it! Thanks again!" I smile wide.

I didn't expect things to go this smoothly. This must be my lucky day.

I lean against the wall, eyes cast to my designer heels, pretending I'm unaware the men are eating me up with their eyes.

The ride to the top floor of this fourteen-story hotel is super short. These elevators seem to be powered by jet fuel. Nothing compared to the slower speed of our elevators at the Villiers Grand.

The foursome gets off on the twelfth floor, taking with them the awkward tension that was lingering over my head. I'm thankful they didn't drill me with questions about my fictitious hotel.

A nanosecond later, I reach the top floor. When the elevator doors open, I step out. Thank God there aren't any CIA-type security codes required. It would be a shame to get busted this early in the game.

I lean forward as I take in the lay of the land. I peek to my left, then my right.

So far, so good.

Only a set of glass doors separates me from my target—that and the gatekeeper.

You're close, girl.

I summon my lady balls and take a confident step forward. I stride down the hallway, praying all the angels in Heaven to watch over me.

Here goes nothing.

I pull open the glass door and step inside King Kong Tycoon's sovereign world.

No one.

The desk is empty.

I catch the name on a plate on the desk. Lydia Gillanders.

I'm at the right place.

My heart beats a little faster.

I just want answers.

I get on my toes to peek at the computer screen. It's as black as night.

Is Lydia on a break?

My eyes move to the heavy-looking wood door behind the desk where I'm certain my target is hiding.

What to do? What to do?

My inner wisdom speaks out, *"Patience, Mikki."*

As I pace the space, waiting for someone to show up, I run the possible scenarios of how things are about to go down in my head, and choose to eliminate the one where I get escorted out of the building by the police like a common criminal.

I got this.

Well, I hope I do.

We'll soon find out.

Another minute goes by.

Then another.

And another.

And another.

Dammit!

Where is Lydia?

Just when I'm about to run out of patience, the wooden door behind her desk opens.

Finally!

A tall man emerges.

"I want answers and I want them today, Slate," a deep, commanding voice from inside the office says.

"I'm on it, Phoenix," the man standing at the door says.

King Kong Tycoon is in his office.

I was worried my timing might've been off. After all,

Phoenix could've been trapped in an endless meeting or worse, absent from the office.

Score!

The man I now know as Slate senses my presence and shifts his attention to me. His arresting, piercing eyes meet mine. They're the clearest arctic blue eyes I've ever seen.

Wow.

The man is stunning.

His stylish dark-brown hair, his pristine, perfectly cut dark-gray suit, and his gorgeous shoes, scream power.

He's far more handsome than I remember from the photos I perused through on the way here. Then again, my focus wasn't on the König men's hotness meter, but rather, their profiles.

I should've paid more attention.

When I meet his eyes again, I snap back to the moment.

This isn't the time to get sidetracked by good looks. You're on a mission!

I offer the man still checking me out a coquettish smile.

He responds by flashing me a flirtatious, wide grin, flashing a set of gleaming white teeth.

He gives me a quick onceover and cocks an eyebrow, nodding.

I wink.

The megawattage of his smile grows to blinding levels.

Men are so easy.

I take this as my omen.

I don't think twice.

I charge forward like a linebacker running with the ball towards the end zone. The man stares at me, stunned, as I zoom right past him.

"Wait! You can't go in there!"

I ignore him.

Too late, buddy. I'm in!

Sneak Peek of Billionaire Mogul —Phoenix

Chapter 2 | Phoenix

I'm startled when a whirlwind gusts into my office like a torpedo. Confused, my eyes bounce to my brother. He's as surprised as I am.

I shove out of my chair and shuffle to my feet, ready for the worst.

"May I help you?" I ask the woman who just barged in.

"My name is Michaela Knight. We need to talk," she says.

I study her for a beat, certain my eyes are deceiving me.

"You look nothing like Michaela Knight," I tell her.

"Interesting, you know who I am." She lets out a sarcastic laugh. "Until a couple of hours ago, I didn't know who you were," she says. "As for the way I look, the hair is a bit of a dramatic transformation."

No shit.

She moves her attention away from me, fumbling through her designer bag.

I lift my hands in surrender. "Whoa. No need to get violent."

She rolls her eyes at me. "I'm not looking for a gun. I'm

pulling out my driver's license to prove my identity. It's still my old photo, but at least you can verify my name."

The woman standing in front of me is unquestionably gorgeous, but her hair is a vast departure from the photos I've seen of her. She chopped off the curtain of dark brown, almost black hair. Without the long mane, her remarkable features stand out. She's now sporting a short, edgy haircut that makes her look much younger. If I didn't know better, I might be tempted to think she's barely legal.

"You're demanding for an intruder," I tell her.

"Hear me out before kicking me out," she says.

I consider her.

"Okay," I say with a nod.

She pulls out her wallet.

I doubt this tiny tornado is much of a threat. Given this morning's freak media show, I can't wait to hear what Miss Knight has to say in her defense.

This should be interesting.

I tear my gaze away from the feisty woman and shift my attention to my brother. He's just staring. I know that look. His lopsided grin is also a dead giveaway.

Yes, I have eyes. She's smoking hot.

"I'll catch you later, Slate," I tell him.

"Why don't I hang around? You might need a referee," he says.

"I got this," I tell him.

"You're sure?" he asks.

"Positive."

"You never know—"

"Slate."

"Okay, okay. I'm gone."

He closes the door behind him in slow motion, his eyes

taking in every inch of the woman dressed in a stunning hot pink dress.

I shake my head.

He grins.

"Here you go!" She flings her driver's license on my desk.

I pick it up, study it, verifying both her age and her identity.

"You *are* Michaela Knight." *Thank fuck she's legal.*

"Told you! Care to explain why you're dead set on fucking up my life?"

Her surly tone is borderline rude.

I drop the driver's license on my desk and inhale a calming breath. I close my fists and anchor them against my desk. From this vantage point, I get an eyeful of the swell of her tempting breasts. The neckline of her dress is sexy and classy. It commands attention without ever being trashy. The hot pink shade isn't as defining as red, but it still means business.

She looks up, fixing me with a pair of big, green eyes in a breathtaking shade I've never seen before in my entire life. Her barely there makeup is flawless and those damn black lashes are a mile long. Her perfect pale skin suggests she hasn't been in LA for long.

She clears her throat and takes a step back.

She squares her shoulders. "I asked you a question and I expect an answer."

I glance down.

My desk is an annoyance, a barrier I could do without.

I circle it and come to stand right in front of her. My eyes trail down the length of the pint-sized spitfire glaring up at me.

I approve of how beautiful she looks in this form-fitted dress that hits her just above the knee. I'm also quite partial to those sexy-as-fuck white high heels with a strap circling her delicate ankles. The immaculate white offers a flawless finish.

She crosses her arms over her chest, revealing more than a hint of cleavage. It's an effort not to stare.

"Well?" She has the audacity to tap an impatient foot on the floor.

My eyebrows rise to my forehead.

"You have some nerve," I say. "You trespass—"

"Newsflash! It's a hotel! I'm not trespassing."

Her voice doesn't match the rest of her. It's all expensive, smoky whiskey, while her look is all diamonds and champagne. If she wasn't snapping at me like she is right now, I'm sure I'd enjoy listening to her talk for hours.

Focus.

"You have no business on the executive floor," I say. "You're lucky I haven't called security to haul your fine ass out of here."

"Please leave my ass out of this conversation," she says.

"I said your *fine* ass."

"Too bad you'll never know."

Feisty.

The long list of things I'd do to her ass is one hundred percent X-rated, but this is neither the time nor the place.

"Ask nicely," I say.

"What?" She blinks in confusion.

"You're in my domain, Miss Knight. You want answers, ask nicely."

She shoots a *fuck you* glare at me.

"You're spreading lies about me. About us!" Her finger moves frantically between us. "Make it stop. Now!"

The muscles in my jaw flex.

This tiny woman has a fierce fighting spirit, the likes of which I've rarely seen in the women I date. She isn't accommodating. Nor is she a pushover. She stands on her own two feet. She's a real study in contrast. Miss Knight is nothing like what I expected.

"I'm not the one behind this grotesque PR grab," I say. "You are!" I point an accusatory finger at her.

She points one back. "No, you are! You're the manipulative asshole who's using me for God knows what reason. What did my stepmother promise you in exchange for being willing to destroy my life like this?" she asks through gritted teeth.

Her nostrils flare, her eyes shoot daggers at me, and her chest heaves.

Stop staring at her breasts.

"Did she trick you into believing you were getting a virgin bride?"

"What the hell kind of statement is that?" I ask, because it's so preposterous, I doubt I heard her correctly.

"Rich men seeking young, dumb virgins so they can shape them to their will—and manhood—and be the first to plant their seed into their womb," she says.

"You think I bought your virginity via your stepmom?" I barely manage to keep my voice calm and professional.

"Yes!" Michaela nods. "She keeps reminding me I have a precious commodity worth preserving for a dirty old man with pockets lined with money"—she rolls her eyes—"and, most likely a tiny, limp, shriveled dick."

The crude word coming from her mouth is an insult to my ears.

"She insists it's all part of a new woman's empowering movement. And, apparently, it's a lucrative market. I guess you must be her newest prospect."

For the love of fuck. What does she take me for?

"Well, I'm not a virgin," she says.

Good to know.

"I just don't bother correcting my stepmom because it's none of her business." She shrugs. "The joke's on you, dirty old man."

"Tread carefully, kitty cat," I say.

"Kitty cat?"

"You barge in here, ready to claw my eyes out like a kitten perched on a tree I'm trying to rescue—"

"I don't need to be rescued." She huffs. "I need answers!"

"First, I've never met your stepmother. Second, I don't buy women for sex or for any other reason. Third, I steer away from virgins. And fourth, I'm not an old man." *Dirty, yes, but old, no.* "I'm only thirty-one. Enough answers for you, kitty cat?"

Hesitant green eyes scan my face. But just as quick as a whip, suspicion flashes back at me.

"What's in it for you?" she asks. "Why are you lying to protect my stepmother?"

"I'm not! I've never met the woman."

"Well, this stunt has her signature all over it—" Michaela brushes a dismissive hand in front of her face. "It doesn't matter. How are *you* going to get JustSpotted.com to retract the fake announcement?"

I release a breath, my temper ebbing. "We can't."

"Hence why I didn't include myself in the statement," she says. "I don't have that kind of power, but obviously"—she extends her arms out, as if encompassing my luxurious office—"you do."

Even her mocking smile is charming.

"You must have a pricey PR firm at your beck and call. Get them to work their magic! We're not getting married!"

My brother Slate caught wind of the JustSpotted.com article before I did. He immediately called to warn me. I thought he was pulling my leg, but he wasn't. As I scrolled through the screaming headlines, I was certain Michaela Knight had played a part in this farce. Her outburst suggests she was caught off guard by the sneaky PR stunt as much as I was. The thing is, she doesn't have the full story. I do. And I'm about to burst her bubble.

"There's more to this than meets the eye," I tell her.

"No, there isn't! There's been a mistake. *You* just need to fix it."

"It's not entirely a mistake, Michaela."

Her long eyelashes flutter at the mention of her name.

Then, it hits me. This is the first time her name has passed my lips since she busted into my office.

"You're missing parts of the puzzle," I say.

She stares for a long beat, flabbergasted. And then she bursts out laughing. Full on belly laughs.

"You're cute and all, but either you're missing a screw or you're deaf. We. Are. Not. Getting. Married," she says, enunciating every word.

"Even though I don't approve of how things were done, I'm not one to renege on a deal, especially not this one," I say.

"I swear on everything that's holy, you're being a stubborn prick just to irritate the hell out of me," she says. "We don't know each other. We're not getting married. End of story." She jabs a finger at me, a harsh edge breaking through each word.

My eyes rattle back and forth like a ping pong ball from her manicured finger, to her sultry mouth, to her gem-like eyes. She really thinks she has leverage here. I'm on the bitter cusp of pulling her onto my lap to teach her who's in control.

"You have a mouth on you," I tell her.

"Congratulations on your power of observation! That still doesn't change the fact, we're not getting married!"

Exasperated, I ask, "Have you talked to your father?"

Her disdainful smirk falls.

She doesn't answer.

"Had you talked to your father before barging in here, trespassing on private property, flying off the handle, wailing about foul play, shrieking and keening like a goddamn banshee, you'd know what's at stake here."

She purses her lips together, conceding I've one upped her. "I tried to call him, but he's dealing with a situation."

"I'm willing to bet my fortune your father is behind this—"

"My—my father is behind this?" She stutters.

Ah. A tiny crack in her armor.

"I'm certain of it," I say. "He has the most to gain from this publicity stunt."

"You're not making any sense," she says. "My father would never do such a thing."

"He would if he was looking for extra leverage."

"Leverage on what?"

"Your father and I have a deal."

"A deal?"

"Yes. An ironclad deal, which is why I don't know why he felt the need to force my hand."

"What kind of deal are you talking about?" she asks.

"Like I said, you should've talked to your father before coming to me."

"Well, I'm here now and I'm asking you. Instead of answering my question, you're being elusive, which is characteristic of a manipulative liar."

"I'm not the one using undermining tactics, sweetheart. Your father masters the art of deception."

A thunderous storm rages in her eyes.

She leaps towards me like a bull in a ring charging at full speed towards the matador's red cape.

I'm quick.

I reach out to snatch her wrist before her palm hits my cheek and force her hand to rest against my chest.

She flinches at the contact.

So do I.

For a brief moment we both seem startled by the proximity.

It's a good thing I'm too fucking wound up right now to enjoy the warmth of her body against mine.

She breathes in and out, seemingly preparing for a second attack.

"I wouldn't do that if I were you," I say, my steady voice betraying the frantic palpitation of my heart.

"Stop it with your lies," she says. She tries but fails to break from my grip.

Even when she's immobilized, she's willing to fight with all her might.

"The ink is already dried on the contract," I tell her. "As of two days ago, my company owns the Villiers Grand Hotel."

The revelation takes the wind out of her.

"My father sold the hotel?" She's incredulous.

"Yes."

She studies me for a long beat.

I hold her murderous gaze.

Suddenly, a hysterical laugh leaves her lips.

"You're such a bullshitter!" Okay, I have no idea how to read this woman.

"And you're blind," I say.

"You're a pretentious asshole!"

Time to remove the kid gloves. "If you deigned to get off your high horse and open your fucking eyes, you would've noticed your father is drowning in debt. He owes a ton of money he can't repay," I tell her. "But no, you're here pretending to know what you're talking about, but in reality, you know shit, and you're only shooting your mouth off."

Her shoulders stiffen at the insult.

"That's right, sweetheart, you're not the only one who can throw the punches," I say.

For several long seconds we enter a Mexican standoff,

nostrils flaring, eyes trained on each other, breaths meshing together.

"I don't believe you," she says.

Niels Knight was supposed to step up to the plate and explain his precarious situation to his daughter. The onus wasn't supposed to fall on me.

Michaela is still staring at me like she wants to stab my eyeballs with a fork.

"Everyone has a price, Miss Knight." My words are cold. "Niels made a promise to your mother. A lot has happened recently, making it harder and harder for him to keep that promise. I'm unwilling to go into details—that's your father's job, not mine—suffice to say, his back was up against a wall. He needed a quick exit strategy. I just so happened to be in the market for a new hotel in Manhattan."

Her lips form into an O.

I didn't expect our first encounter to be sugary sweet, but this hostility is amped up by the fact she has no clue how much shit her father is dealing with.

"As far as merger-marriages go," I say, "it's part and parcel of everything else I've agreed to. Your father had a very long list of demands I was willing to meet."

"A merger-marriage?"

"Yes."

"What does that even mean?" she asks.

"The merger part is where I bail out your family hotel and fold it under our umbrella of hotels to prevent it from going into bankruptcy."

"Bankruptcy?" Her question comes out on a stunned breath.

I nod.

"The hotel is no longer ours?!" she asks.

"Not until the debt is paid off."

"But that'll take forever," she says.

"There are ways of shaving off a considerable number of years from the repayment plan."

"What kind of ways?" she asks.

"That's where the marriage part kicks in." I allow for a pregnant pause. "You and me... in holy matrimony." A little sarcasm never hurts.

She hitches a breath. Her green eyes are so huge right now.

"I'm tied to you by my father's debt?"

I tilt my head left to right. "Something like that."

She stares at me in shock.

"No. No way!" She shakes her head. "Nope. Not happening. We are never ever entering into holy matrimony. Not in this lifetime. Not in the next."

Let me break it down for you, sweetheart. "I'll be sinking in two hundred million dollars in exchange for your agreement to become my wife for three-hundred-sixty-five days."

Her jaw drops.

"Daddy sold me?!"

"He did what he had to do."

Silence surrounds us.

Myriad emotions flash in her green eyes.

I don't know her well enough to decipher them all, but what I see reflecting from her gaze indicates I'm her least favorite person on the planet right now.

I don't rush her.

I give her time to process everything.

Once she accepts her new reality, we can figure out the next steps.

"Let go of my arm," she says.

Not the reaction I expected.

"I said, let go of my arm." Her tone is slicing.

I do.

Her green eyes snap up at me in rebellion. "This meeting is adjourned!"

My eyebrows shoot to my forehead. "Are you kidding me?"

She doesn't respond.

She pulls the strap of her designer bag over her shoulder and squares her shoulders.

"Do I look like I'm fucking kidding?" Without waiting for an answer, she turns on her heel.

"Where are you going?" I call after her.

Michaela throws her parting words over her shoulder, still striding towards the door, "I'm sure you're pulling a fast one on me. My father would never sell the Villiers Grand. Never. He'd die before he ever let that happen. And, if he were in any kind of financial trouble, he would've told me about it. I wouldn't have to hear it from you—a complete stranger." She pauses and turns around to face me. "I'm sure you make it a sport to step all over the little guy, Mr. King Kong Tycoon."

Huh? King Kong Tycoon?

"But we're not going down without a fight. I don't know what kind of fucked up, twisted, and pathetic mind game you're playing, you cruel corporate sadist, but I'm out of here."

I'm so dumbfounded, words escape me.

Jesus.

Her tongue is sharper than an obsidian blade, her attitude as abrasive as sandpaper.

"I pray to God I never see your face again, Phoenix König." She flips me the bird, and she flies out of here like the flames of hell are licking her designer high heels. She slams the door behind her so hard, I'm surprised the windows don't shatter.

Who the hell does she think she is?

She storms in and out of here like she owns the goddamn building.

I should be pissed off. Livid, even.

That little cyclone did a number on me.

Every cell in my body is buzzing.

I'm pulsing with adrenaline. Arousal?!

My mind fights it, but my cock stiffens at visions of her stripped naked, bent over my desk, my tongue trailing all over her sinful body before I fuck her like it's my new mission in life. That would teach her a lesson. One I'm sure she would enjoy just as much as I would.

Binge-read now: Billionaire Mogul—Phoenix

Billionaire Moguls Series

Billionaire Mogul—Beckett

Billionaire Mogul—Rhys

Billionaire Mogul—Phoenix

Billionaire Mogul—Gage

The Billionaire Moguls is part of the **Billionaire Hotshots'** world.

Billionaire Hotshots Series

Billionaire Hotshot—Levi

Billionaire Hotshot—Roderick

Billionaire Hotshot—Lochlan

Billionaire Hotshot—Holt

Billionaire Hotshot—Jace

Billionaire Hotshot—Jagger

These sexy as sin Billionaire Hotshots are notorious bachelors forever... that's until they cross paths with the women who bring them down to their knees.

You'll find **all my books** and **reading order** on my site:
www.ScarlettAvery.com

I hope you enjoyed ***Billionaire Mogul—Rhys***! Can't get enough of Rhys and Keira? Subscribe to my mailing list and you'll get instant access to an exclusive ***Billionaire Mogul—Rhys*** secret chapter and/or storyboard. Just use the QR code below.

Already subscribed? You would've received the link in the first email I sent you. If you can't find it, you can email us. If you've changed your email address, simply resubscribe.

About the Author

USA TODAY Bestselling Author Scarlett Avery unapologetically pens all-consuming love stories featuring sexy as sin billionaires who have the determination of a thousand warriors. Her kickass heroines are smart and sassy. And you should always expect edge-of-your-seat twists.

Scarlett's stories are intense and passionate, emotional and steamy, and always leave you begging for more. In other words, they're the perfect blend of swoony and sinful.

Fair warning...

Once you start reading Scarlett's novels, there's no going back!

Printed in Great Britain
by Amazon

38706383R00280